BELMONTE

A TALE OF THE OLD WORLD

JOHN HARRIS BRADLEY

ISBN 979-8-9895522-0-7 Paperback
ISBN 979-8-9895522-1-4 Ebook

Published 2024

BELMONTE

"Habit, routine, our daily humdrum apathy and indifference, this is the shield we put between us and reality, the shield with which we protect ourselves from life while we are engaged in the business on living. It is the function of the arts to pierce that shield, to re-awaken in us a forgotten knowledge."

John Hall Wheelock, American poet, 1886-1978

Introduction

I envisioned the book *Belmonte* as the first in a series of books telling stories of the transition from an Old World paradigm to a New World paradigm. As a tale of the Old World, *Belmonte* portrays a particular and peculiar Templar world view characterized by the first four centuries on the *intentional* nation of Portugal, begun in 1128.

I use the term "intentional" because Portugal was conceived and established in the early twelfth century by the returning victorious Templar Knights of the first Crusade to re-capture Jerusalem. Portugal was instituted by its Templar fathers and spiritual patron, Saint Bernard. The founders endowed the polity with certain virtues and values promoted, in greater or lesser degree, for 450 years by an unbroken sequence of thirteen kings, between 1128 and 1578.

These early Portuguese virtues and values found useful expression when the Portuguese began sailing into unknown waters. They discovered new opportunities for commerce, contributing to the Templar international banking system. Wherever the Portuguese went, they intermarried, not seeing foreign cultures and their people as either inferior or superior but simply part of the human family.

Spiritually, the Templar virtues and values focused on the Holy Spirit, which, in some form is common to all religions.

Mentally and aesthetically, the Templar mind-set would embrace the virtues of truth, beauty and fresh creativity wherever these qualities existed, instead of stale habit, dogmatism and bigotry.

Pre-dating this Templar overlay upon the land of Lusitania, and pre-dating the Islamic culture of southern Iberia, was the Roman domination. And within this period, and perhaps pre-dating it also, was an ancient Judaic culture. How this came to be is a mystery yet to be solved. However, one of the epicenters of this old Jewish culture was the hilltop town of Belmonte, located in central Portugal, between the Serra da Estrela range and the Spanish border.

As the reign of 450 years, which I loosely call the reign of the Templar Vision, was coming to an inglorious end, three defining events occurred in Portugal:

In 1496, King Manuel I ordered the deportation of all the Jews in Portugal who refused to be baptized.

In 1500, Brazil was discovered by Pedro Álvares Cabral of Belmonte, and Portugal began the creation of a maritime empire stretching from East Asia to Brazil.

In 1506, over 2000 Jews were massacred in Lisbon over Easter weekend.

The Templar vision and aspiration of Portugal's founding fathers finally died of exhaustion and corruption at the turn of the sixteenth century. This is the ambient of the book *Belmonte*.

Two of the four main characters of the book begin as best friends, teenagers from the Belmonte area: Davide, son of the local Rabbi, and Ruy, son of an enterprising doctor and grandson of the physician, friend and financial advisor to Pedro Álvares Cabral, the discovered of Brazil.

A third character is also Portuguese Jewish on his mother's side and Berber-Muslin on his father's. Daniel has been raised in the family business as a maritime trader, and carries the qualities of adventure, fair trade and justice.

The forth character, Juancinto, is an older Gypsy, a soul from a completely different culture, but one very much at home in Iberia. Like his three younger associates, Juancinto has become an outcast and joins the brotherhood, now tasked with the karmic challenge of resolving an injustice in the Old World before crossing the ocean sea to the New World.

Narrative Perspective of Endovélico

I have an obsession with imaginative history; *not* fake history, but imagining real history. I like to walk in the shoes of imaginary characters through obscure but genuine historical times. My Old World and New World tales are grounded in history, with an imaginative twist toward dramatization, hopefully invoking a personal walk-through. Aspiring to this approach, I felt my stories needed a unique storytelling narrator, a voice out of the Lusitanian past of Portugal, maneuvering through history yet transcending it.

An image from the Anthropological Museum at the Jerónimos Monastery in Lisbon came to mind; a Roman-era bust of an Iron Age shaman called Endovélico. One of Endovélico's specialties was *incubation,* an ancient practice whereby the believer seeking help would sleep in, or near, the temple of a god or goddess, with the expectation that the deity would visit the aspirant in dreamtime, giving guidance or inspiration. The cult of Endovélico was so popular among the ancient Lusitanians that, when the Romans occupied the land, rather than suppress the cult, they promoted it and participated in it.

I used the character of Endovélico as a *deus ex machina,* I gave him a personality, part angelic and part human, living in the Imaginal Realm, defying space and time on a whim.

Two of my four protagonists are seventeen-year-old men from Belmonte, Portugal. Before leaving for the University of Coimbra, they enjoy their last boyhood summer as shepherds on the side of a mountain, tending sheep belonging to one of the boys' fathers. There, they discover an enormous sculpted boulder. They make it their campsite, sleeping in the smooth flat top of the rock in ancient sepulcher-like shallow tubs carved in the massive outcrop. They learn that the place is called the "Rock of Endovélico." Soon after, the Lord of Dreams visits them.

Endovélico challenges each boy with a gift. The gift is that each chooses, from history, an event he is most curious about. After falling asleep, Endovélico will appear and take him back in time to witness that curious event. To better understand what they are about to see, Endovélico offers each a history lesson in the timeless dream state.

Endovélico sets the stage and melts into the background letting the two boys witness history first-hand. In this character, Endovélico, I found the perfect storytelling voice I was looking for, always lurking, eavesdropping, taking notes behind the scenes of history. I liked him so much that he also became the voice behind the scenes of *Joara,* the subsequent New World story of the four characters developed in *Belmonte.*

Contents

Chapter 1

Ahmad and Bela Almeyda

Alexandria, Egypt
Autumn 1565

It was a Thursday, the fourteenth day of November in the year 1565. The *Rainha de Alcântara,* a sleek Portuguese caravel, entered the arms of Alexandria harbor under a light starboard breeze with Captain Ahmad Almeyda at the wheel. Bela, his wife, came up from the galley after evening scullery tasks to help moor the vessel. Calls to Maghrib prayers erupted from the countless minarets that rose above the clamor of the city. The setting sun dappled the harbor's waters with orange, red, and violet shades as the ship sliced noiselessly toward its berth.

Not bad timing, Ahmad thought. Another night on the vessel whose name meant the Queen of Alcântara, then into the city with the crew in the morning.

Ahmad planned to join the brothers at the mosque for Friday *Jummah* prayers. At the same time, Bela would accompany the crew's Christians to the cathedral to give thanks for a safe voyage. He and Bela would later rendezvous at the market and discharge the crewmen until Sunday night. Once free of the crew, they would hire a horsecar to the lake. Like last time, they'd take the night air in a quaint Jewish neighborhood on the roof of Bela's uncle's boathouse on a sizeable round bedtick with silk mosquito netting. After all, Rumi teaches that Friday is the night for love.

And so it was they found themselves on the boathouse roof just as Ahmad had imagined. A soothing serenade of crickets, frogs, lake birds, and humanity enveloped their bed without piercing the privacy of their gossamer cocoon. The gentle breeze from the lake required only a single cotton sheet between the star-filled night and Ahmad's body. "Your fragrance is enticing, Belinha," he whispered, using the diminutive Portuguese form of her name. "Put out the lamp and lay beside me."

"Baba," she breathed. "I cannot see without the lamp. I'm afraid I'll fall over the edge into the water. Were the moon full—"

"No, love." Her husband spoke in hushed tones. "Put out the lamp and take my hand. Come inside my web of silk. A fingernail of a moon is enough. In its light, I can see you're even more beautiful now than our honeymoon night."

"This is not Fez, twenty-two years ago, love. Look at me—my hair is well-streaked with silver, my curves are no longer firm."

"We all grow old, Belinha, but you're graced with wisdom, confidence, and serenity—qualities radiating a beauty that words can't describe."

Bela extinguished the lamp. She disrobed, lifted the net, slipped beneath the sheet, and rested her arm on his.

"Remember reading to me? We held hands in the garden."

"Rumi's little poem?" Ahmad smiled. "I remember it."

"You had almost memorized that poem, *meu amor*. Can you still recite it after all these years?"

"I can paraphrase it. *Bilarabiati? Ou português?* Which do you prefer?"

"Portuguese. You know how Rumi's Arabic—even his Persian—leaves me in the dust."

"Give me a minute," he said.

Minutes passed, but not in silence. The drone of crickets was broken only by the bark of distant dogs and the water lapping on the boathouse walls as the high tide flooded the canals on its way to the lakes. Ahmad began.

At this moment,
when we are lying here,
two figures,
with one soul,
we're a garden,
with the sounds of the lake

and the city
moving through us.
The stars appear.
We are out of ourselves
but still in ourselves.

Baba grasped Bela's hand and raised it toward the moon.

We point to the new crescent moon,
its discipline and slender joy.
We don't listen to stories full of anger.
We feed on laughter and a tenderness
we hear around us,
when we are together.
And even more incredible, sitting here in Konya,
we're at this same moment in Khorasan and Iraq.
We have these forms in time,
and another form in the elsewhere
that's made of this closeness. 1

That night's only equal was in Fez twenty-two years before, when the couple conceived Daniel.

The call to the *Fajr* prayer awakened them, and they thought of Daniel, the incarnation of their love. His circumcision, according to Jewish tradition, came eight days after his birth over Ahmad's protestations. According to *halacha*—the traditional way of the Jews—the faith passes through the mother. Bela thus claimed Daniel with the backing of his maternal grandparents, Simão and Isabel.

Ahmad Almeyda was born the oldest of three brothers in Ceuta. After a superb education in Fez, he trained as a pharmacist like his father. But Ahmad disappointed his parents when he became an apprentice sailor and merchant in the land and marine mercantile business of a well-known Jew, Simão Sampaio..

Under the tutelage of Sampaio, Ahmad soon led camel caravans to the interior cities of Morocco, then quickly progressed to the rank of first mate on maritime expeditions to ports east and west of Gibraltar. Ahmad had a natural gift for language and moved beyond his native Portuguese and Arabic to Farsi, Berber, Spanish, Catalan, Gallego, and Italian trading lingo. He became indispensable to the business operations of Simão Sampaio. At the same time, Ahmad was irresistibly attracted to Sr. Sampaio's only daughter, Bela. And the attraction was mutual. Bela and Ahmad soon married, but not with the approval of Ahmad's parents, who refused to attend. While Masoud Almeyda did not formally disown his son, he kept a safe distance. For him, being a Muslim in the small, fanatically Catholic city-state of Ceuta was hard enough. But for Jews, the suffering was worse. They endured the antipathy of Catholics, Sunnis, and Shiites alike.

With Dominican priests descending on Ceuta like vultures on dead meat, Masoud knew the cruel ceremonies of the *auto-da-fé* could be conducted any day as they had in Portugal and Spain. Masoud could not endure the thought that the Inquisition might round up his son and future grandchildren and burn them at the stake for adhering to the religion of his daughter-in-law.

Daniel was born in the first year of the marriage of Ahmad and Bela. Coming from his mother's line, Daniel was regarded as a full-fledged Jew, an irrevocable status in the eyes of God and the Rabbinical Council. To counterbalance the weight of Hebrew tradition, Ahmad enrolled Daniel in the best madrasa at an early age. There he developed his skills in Arabic and studied the Quran and the *hadith*, a record of the Prophet Muhammad's sayings and traditions. In addition to learning Hebrew and studying with the rabbis, Bela and Ahmad thought it wise to educate their child in the Portuguese Catholic school system of Ceuta. At sixteen, they sent Daniel to Fez to study classic Islamic and Sufi literature along with alchemy, algebra, and geography. When Daniel returned after three years, he could manipulate an abacus and an astrolabe and possessed the education and financial backing to be anything he desired. For Daniel, the choice was simple. He had been brought up to be a man of the world, so he would *be* a man of the world, walking in the footsteps of his father and Jewish grandfather as a maritime merchant.

Like his father, Daniel led caravans of camels before graduating to merchant vessels. By the age of twenty, he had earned the right to be his father's first mate on the *Rainha de Alcântara*.

Daniel arranged with his mother to accompany Ahmad on the short spring voyages to Sardinia, Sicily, and Italy. Bela would sail with her husband on the long voyage from July to December, trading at all the major ports along the coast of North Africa between Ceuta and Alexandria. Life promised to be good.

CHAPTER 2

DANIEL ALMEYDA

**Portuguese Ceuta, on Morocco's Punta Almina promontory
December 1565 to January 1566**

With the arrival of December Daniel's pulse quickened in anticipation of his parents' return. The *Rainha* was due in port around the twentieth, Christmas Day at the latest. If the economies were down, trading would have been quick, and they might return early with a full cargo bay. They might extend their voyage to a new port or two if things were bad. Daniel saw little use in speculating, and there was no reason to bother his grandfather. The old man had enough on his mind.

Two weeks before, four men in black burgled the central warehouse on Rúa de Alfau, knocking one guard unconscious and chasing away the second. The man later reported that the two most violent thugs had Berber accents. At the same time, the other two spoke the Portuguese of Lisbon. They did not take much—only carpets and wall hangings—but Avô Simão was most distressed by the ransacking of the office. They even rifled through the desks. Were they looking for information? Why?

Chanukah passed uneventfully, and Christmas was approaching. Daniel carried his parents' *sumo,* their itinerary of ports, in his vest pocket. Gaza to Alexandria, then to Benghazi, Tripoli, Tunis, Palermo, Alger, Oran, Saïdia, Melilla, then home to Ceuta. Daniel lingered on the pier and quizzed every captain and mate coming from the east. He learned the *Rainha de Alcântara* was last seen sailing from Tunis on or about December 1. His parents were on schedule, but Daniel still worried.

He convinced Avô Simão to outfit him with two of the best camels and took Idir, a trusted Berber caravan guide, along the Moroccan coast in search of news of his parents. They set out on January 5. They rode five days along the coastal track to the port city of Melilla, now a Spanish enclave.

Upon arrival, they sought out the harbormaster. As expected, the man's record-keeping was meticulous—typical of a Spanish civil servant. Daniel discovered alarming news. The *Rainha de Alcântara* had indeed made port in Melilla on December 20 with her cargo bays full. She did not trade in Melilla and departed the next day. After two days of tailwinds, she would have reached Ceuta. But sixteen days had passed. The Melilla harbormaster's log indicated that two Spanish-flagged vessels bound for Cádiz had pulled away from the pier an hour before the *Rainha.*

Daniel asked the harbormaster for information about the two Spanish boats. How long had they been in port? What was their mission? Who owned them? The vessels were out of Cádiz, hired by the Archdiocese of Sevilla. They had spent two weeks in Melilla. The harbormaster speculated that the two captains came to confer with the Bishop of Melilla about newly fortified trading missions along the coast, or they'd come on Inquisition business. Two priests of a prominent order traveled on the *Ronda,* the larger of the crafts. The harbormaster furnished the names of the two captains—Alejandro Sánchez and Raúl Estigarriba. They had not been seen in Melilla before, and their crews were rough and well-armed, as if—as Daniel conjectured—they were pirates! A grim picture formed in Daniel's mind.

There was no time to waste. Daniel and Idir needed to backtrack along the coast and search for signs of the crew or a shipwreck.

They reached the small harbor town of Al Hoceima, a third of the way back to Ceuta, two days later. Daniel learned that three vessels had made port two weeks ago—the *Ronda,* the *Santa Teresa,* and the *Rainha de Alcântara.* The crews spent the night ashore at Al Hoceima and sailed the following morning. Daniel found the inn where they lodged; a transfer of *dinares* procured information he did not want to hear. There were no more than fifteen crewmen between the three vessels. None were Berbers, no one spoke Portuguese, and there were no women.

Confounded by the news, Daniel mounted his camel without speaking to Idir. He returned to the beach and coastal pathway. When Idir overtook him, he implored Daniel to return to Ceuta to tell his grandfather and report the crime. Daniel would neither answer nor stop.

"We covered every league of beach between here and Melilla," Idir said. "We asked every person we encountered. If something had washed up . . . if there'd been a survivor, we would've learned about it. Let's get back home as fast as we can." With tears in his eyes, Daniel consented.

Daniel and Idir stopped only to water and feed the camels on the return journey to Ceuta. In less than three days, they entered the city walls and made their way to the house of Simão Sampaio. As they approached the gate of his grandfather's residence, a guard barred their passage.

"Is my grandfather inside?" Daniel demanded. The guard shook his head. "What have they done with him?"

"Last week, they took Sr. Sampaio to the basement of the barracks in the bishop's compound—the Inquisition's dungeon.

"*Who* took him?"

"Dominicans," the guard said. "They made the Governor act against his will. A new band of blackbirds arrived from Lisbon last week with a list of names to reignite the Inquisition here. Your grandfather was high on that list. This place is now off-limits. No one can enter while the Dominicans collect evidence."

Daniel and Idir walked to the warehouse by the pier. They learned that all the cargo boats had sailed to Algeciras in Spain and that the camels were on route to be sold in Tangiers.

Daniel's home was not under guard, but the servants were disturbed. The sight of Daniel and Idir brought them a brief instant of hope. Daniel informed them that the *Rainha* had been lost at sea or captured by pirates. They found no trace of his parents and the crew. Daniel pressed Manuel, the estate's *mordomo*. "Tell me everything you know about my Avô. What have they accused him of?"

"You wouldn't believe it, Sr. Daniel—they've accused Sr. Simão of kidnapping Christian and Muslim babies and selling them to Jerusalem rabbis for sacrifice. They have accused him of cheating on his taxes and working as a spy for Spain, even though the Dominicans themselves are Spanish."

Nothing surprised Daniel. The churchmen had seized his grandfather's wealth. The murders were committed, the evidence was destroyed. The bodies were likely in the sea, bloated beyond recognition. The Inquisitional Tribunal paid, frightened, or blackmailed the witnesses into giving false testimony. Only one thing remained—go to the Governor and see what it would take for him to reduce Avô's sentence.

The next morning, Daniel arrived at the Governor's Palace to report the disappearance of the *Rainha de Alcântara*. Governor Miguel Andrade, a long-time friend of Daniel's grandfather, had followed the budding career of Sampaio's grandson. Andrade expected Daniel. He described his trip on the Moroccan coast and how he learned the *Rainha* had been hijacked, the crew murdered by thugs in the church's service. Daniel told Andrade he was sure the evidence was still moored to the pier in Cádiz.

"These are terrible times, *filho*—times that shame me, but we must deal with life the best we can. I will tell you this: your grandfather is doomed, your family erased . . . except for you. You bear a noble history. You are the culmination of generations of extraordinary men and women. Escape, Daniel. Don't allow yourself to be sucked into the whirlpool of evil. Ride at once before the Inquisition summons you. Gather what you can, dismiss the household, go to Tangier to catch a westward ship. Get yourself away from this iniquity—it clouds the minds and hearts of all these people. Go! Go to the New World."

"But what about my grandfather? I can't turn and run away, leaving him to burn at the stake. Surely they're scheming to convict him. Why would they accuse him of such a preposterous thing if they did not intend to use it to murder him?"

"You're right. They're going to burn him unless we can develop some creative defense."

"He lent the city a lot of money to repair the western wall and the aqueduct. He still holds those notes. Perhaps I can arrange to have those debts forgiven."

"What good are the notes when your grandfather is a pile of ashes? Do you expect to inherit those notes and call the city on them? I don't believe so."

Daniel hummed. "Suppose I leave the municipality or the diocese with the deed to my parents' estate. Is it valid only upon the declaration of their deaths and only with the willing endorsement of my grandfather to make sure they keep him alive?"

"That might work. I'll talk to the prosecutor this afternoon if you want to make that offer. I may have an answer by tomorrow."

"*Obrigado, Governador.* I will come back at first light."

Daniel returned to the house and charged Idir with equitably dividing all its contents among the household staff according to responsibility and years of service. The camels and horses were to go to Idir, except for the fleetest Arabian stallion that would carry Daniel to Tangier. Ahmad and Bela had no slaves to emancipate. Daniel collected some gold coins and the most valuable jewelry his father had given his mother. He asked Idir's wife, a seamstress, to sew them into the linings of his two jackets. He then sought out his Christian schoolmate, Diogo, now a lawyer and notary. He bade him draw up papers to transfer ownership of the house and estate, with the proviso that the authorities officially declare his parents dead. The transaction also required his grandfather's endorsement.

Once done, Daniel retired early and slept for an hour. He passed the night and early morning hours in the courtyard on a bench by the fountain under the orange tree and a full moon. His attention was initially anchored in prayer but then drifted into thoughts of revenge and ways he might kill the men who murdered his parents and the crew. After exhausting his ideas of vengeance, Daniel's thoughts wandered into his new life and into an adventure—unplanned and unrelated to his last twenty years. The only continuity would be the spear of revenge he wanted to plunge into the hearts of the evildoers. Only then could the gods determine his future. And speaking of the gods, he returned to a prayer for his parents, followed by thoughts of his grandfather and how he could not leave until Avô was safe from the flames of the *auto-da-fé*.

As dawn broke, Daniel saddled his muscular steed, loaded the two saddlebags with his possessions, and rode in the direction of the governor's palace. The steady clop of hooves against cobblestone and the rhythm of breaking waves helped him focus his resolve as he approached the wrought iron gate decorated with the escutcheon of Ceuta.

The governor received him at eight o'clock. He had spoken with the head of the Tribunal—the verdict was favorable. The Archdiocese of Lisbon would drop the kidnapping charges and all mention of the *Rainha de Alcântara*. The governor read from a letter he had received from the bishop: "the Tribunal will find Simão Sampaio guilty of tax evasion, spying for Spain, and selling secret information about Ceuta to the Spanish. As a punishment for these treasonous acts, and because

Sampaio lost his entire fortune at sea, Sr. Simão Sampaio will be required to wear a yellow *sambenitado* 2 with the word *Judeo* sewn onto it whenever in public for the rest of his life."

Daniel paused to digest the turn of events, then pulled out the papers that Diogo had prepared. He signed them with the governor signing as a witness. Daniel knew his Avô would never leave his house again, but he would remain alive.

By mid-morning, Daniel was on his way to Tangier. That night he spread his bedroll behind a sand dune with his horse tied to a nearby palm. Melancholy and loneliness mixed with gratitude as Daniel arranged his bedroll to pray toward Jerusalem first. Then he arranged it toward Mecca to pray. The prayers invigorated him. Gazing into starry infinity, he could make out the constellation Sagittarius, the archer centaur who traveled across the heavens. Daniel fell asleep in anticipation of the first day of the rest of his new life.

By noon the following day, he was at the camel market on the outskirts of Tangier. He sold his Arabian stallion and hired a horsecar into the city and down to the port. As luck would have it, Daniel soon found the fifty-ton Portuguese merchant caravel, *Graça de Tavira*, captained by Diogo Santellano, bound for Cádiz. He booked passage at the last minute and sailed off.

Once underway, two crewmen younger than Daniel approached. They were Portuguese, wearing the tattered clothes of sailors but speaking with the tongue of nobility. The larger of the men approached Daniel and said, "You're going to Cadíz. Will you join the armada to Florida?"

"I don't know about any armada to Florida," Daniel replied. "I'm on personal business." Daniel did not wish to discuss his affairs with strangers. He distracted them by observing they were not tending to their duties, trimming sails, and adjusting the rigging.

The boys approached Daniel again later. "You speak like a sailor," the small one said. "Are you from Ceuta?"

"Yes," Daniel replied. He stretched the truth by adding, "I've captained a bigger ship than this to Egypt and back."

"Really?" The larger youth squinted with disbelief.

"Really." Daniel retorted with irritation. He spun and walked off in the direction of the galley. Before reaching it he turned back to get another look at the out-of-place Portuguese boys, and to his surprise they seemed to be talking to a large squawking seagull which had just landed on the gunwale near them. Daniel dismissed them as crazy.

CHAPTER 3

RABBI ELIAS
TAKES A NAP AT CENTUM CELLAS

**The ruins of Centum Cellas, Belmonte, Portugal
August 1565**

Shafts of sunlight shone through the window openings of the ruined temple of Belmonte. Although difficult to imagine, locals called it Centum Cellas—"a hundred cells" in the two-story structure, which measured fifty feet by thirty. A roof no longer sheltered the ornate, thick granite walls, and there was something of a courtyard in a state of shambles. The rabbi had been taught that the structure had been a synagogue from the time of the Lusitanian culture before the Romans conquered their land. He found this strange—he had never heard another rabbi speak with certainty about the Jews who were alleged to have built the ancient tower. The Hundred Cells, Rabbi Elias speculated, might have been either a prison or a place for Christian monks. The legend that made the most sense was that the structure had been part of a Roman tin merchant's villa, built around the time of Jesus Christ. After all, the strait Roman road running three hundred miles from Portuguese Braga to Spanish Mérida crossed Belmonte. Perhaps Centum Cellas was simply a Roman tollbooth, trading post, and waystation situated in a level place between rugged mountain ranges.

Of all the mysteries that could be conjured about this place—its origin, the strange lights and sounds—there was only one fact Elias knew for sure. Years ago, he and his father buried a treasure in a lead-lined copper box under a cluster of stones in the tower wall. He now considered himself a custodian of this sacred place and regularly filled it with morning prayers and evening meditations. This early August afternoon, feeling the sun's warmth on his face after a bellyful of soup and bread, Elias took a siesta in the shade of the ruins, enjoying the pleasant summer breeze blowing through the valley.

Elias prepared a place on the ground next to the outside wall of the ruins facing the mountains. Stealing an armful of hay from the pile he had set aside for his donkey, he made himself a resting place. With his back against the ancient sunbaked stone, he bathed in the golden orb's glory. Unconsciously, his body tapped all the energies this hallowed place could bestow.

He thought about his son, Davide, finishing his first year at the university in Coimbra. He had not seen Davide for the better part of a year and hoped he was in good health, not expending his funds too quickly. Although the rabbi was not worried about his son, he cranked his head around to where he thought Jerusalem lay and slowly began to chant a prayer, *Ana BeKo'ach*:

> Please with the power, the greatness of your right hand, untie
> what is bound up. . . . Our appeals accept and hear our cries,
> O You who know all of the world of our secret hope.

Why am I praying this? I am making an appeal . . . but for what? Am I reciting out of habit? Or is it something else?

He pushed up straw for a pillow, laid down, and gazed at the sky. Before long, a solitary white cloud lazily lumbered across the radiant blue.. The cloud drifted west from the Spanish border while Dom Elias mused. If the cloud maintained its integrity, it would be over the high ridge of the Serra da Estrela in half an hour. An hour later, it would hover over Coimbra. Elias imagined that once there, if the cloud desired, it might linger over the university and, in exchange for some brief shade and a few precious drops of moisture, the cloud would acquire the cosmological knowledge to steer itself across the ocean sea to the land of Brazil and undiscovered territories. He imagined he might hitch a ride on that cloud and drop in on Davide and his friends, Ruy and Toninho. What a surprise that would be!

Elias slowly closed his eyes and imagined himself floating up to the cloud. In pleasure, he opened his eyelids ever so slightly to see the countryside below. To his astonishment, he saw he was being gently carried in the beak of a corvine bird. Looking down, he could see ravens emerging from Centum Cellas. Elias saw the black birds ahead of him flying in a formation that took the form of *aleph*, the first letter of the Hebrew alphabet, Another group of birds flying behind those that carried him flew in the formation of the last letter of the alphabet, **tav.**

Reaching the cloud, it was no longer white and fluffy but grey and ominous. Soon the cloud passed over the barren summit of Serra da Estrela, then down the expansive western slope, dotted with tiny white villages with orange tiled roofs. Beyond the mountain, the rolling hills were green, even lush, with nascent streams from Star Mountain joining to form rivers full of boat traffic. A walled city perched on a hill came into view. Elias thought it must be Coimbra on the Mondego River.

The cloud picked up moisture, and Dom Elias began sweating. The cloud drifted over the white city with the university on the hill. The sky darkened and began to rumble. The cloud, now with a mind of its own, progressed across the Mondego over the narrow, low bridge spanning the river that divided the city. Elias no longer saw or felt the birds. The carpet upon which he had rested was gone. Losing his balance, he felt a rush of cold fear. A dazzling blue-white light enveloped him, followed by a jolt that Elias felt in all his bones. The electric atmosphere reverberated but soon calmed to a soft, trembling silence. A gentle rain began to fall. The droplets of life quenched the arid lands of the forest below. The tall trees welcomed the cloud as if it were an old friend. The cloud tenderly deposited Elias's dream body beside a fountain. When his body contacted Mother Earth, Elias woke with a start to find himself again resting by the ruined walls of Centum Cellas. He thanked God it was only a dream. He heard the bleating of his sheep in the field beside the tower where his sheepdog, Gaspar, kept them under control. Secure, he slipped back into quiet reverie.

CHAPTER 4

THE STORY OF RABBI ELIAS

Belmonte, Portugal
Toledo, Spain
1496-1565

The year 1496—twenty-seven years before Rabbi Elias was born—was the year soldiers found Elias's grandfather, Rav Jaco, hiding in the ruins of Centum Cellas. The Dominicans took him to the Inquisitorial Court in Castelo Branco. Rav Jaco had been the principal rabbi for the community centered around the ruined synagogue in tiny Covilhã, located about ten miles south of Belmonte. Until recently, the substantial Jewish population of this region had been tucked under the eastern shadow of Serra da Estrela. Legends said this area had been a haven for Jews for over sixty generations. The year was now 1565, and Rabbi Elias was forty-two.

In 1496, young King Manuel, previously a protector of the Jews, displayed moral weakness and ambition by accepting the outrageous demands of his prospective in-laws, Isabella and Ferdinand of Spain, the "Catholic Monarchs." As a condition for marrying their daughter, Manuel had to force Jews to convert on penalty of death.

Rav Jaco, the patriarch of the Mendes de Oliveira family, successfully convinced most of his family to convert. He did not do so himself but continued to observe the old laws.

Elias heard the story as a child—when the Dominicans came to Covilhã and forced all the Jews to sign, all were there except Rav Jaco. The next day, the authorities found him in Belmonte at Centum Cellas. With his back against a wall, he gazed at the clouds crossing the mountains toward Coimbra. They judged him in Castelo Branco and burned him alive in the central plaza. Rav Jaco was thus one of the first souls to suffer the ritual of public penance called the *auto-da-fé*. Elias never understood the ceremony's name, "act of faith."

Elias's earliest memories were the lush warmth of his mother's presence and the echo of her lullabies accented by his father's gentle yet commanding voice. In the home of his father, Rav Salomão, Hebrew was the mother tongue. Elias's training did not end with bar mitzvah but continued until Rav Salomão's death when Elias was twenty-two. By that time, Elias had come to the troubling realization that the Jews of the Covilhã and Belmonte regions had bestowed on him the mantle of rabbi. Having been born into a line of rabbis, he accepted his fated duty.

To his community, Elias was the Rabbi of Covilhã. But for the non-Jewish population—the vast majority—Elias assumed the identity and profession of farmer and shepherd. Being a shepherd with a farm allowed him to be alone in the countryside with his flock, where he could study his treasured books at leisure. When his people called upon him to be their rabbi, he answered.

With the help of his clandestine community of *cristãos-novos*—New Christians—Elias purchased Centum Cellas and the fields around it. He kept his flocks in these fields, occasionally driving them into the hills on the flanks of Serra da Estrela. The ruined tower became, in a sense, Elias's unofficial synagogue. People in need could usually find him there.

Elias would concede that the tower of Centum Cellas was an enigma because of its mysterious lights, sounds, and origins. But for Elias, it was his grandfather's last refuge. Deeper still, buried in the rubble, was a fabulous treasure known to only two people—Elias and his father. And now only himself.

On Elias's twentieth birthday, when Rav Salomão was still alive, his father invited to the house a famous sage from Toledo named Rabbi Aryeh ben Gavriel. At Centum Cellas, Rabbi Aryeh gave Elias a present—a leather-bound book written in the Hebrew fire script. The extravagantly illuminated first page bore the title *Zohar, Book One*. Rabbi Aryeh described the book as a continuing revelation given to Rabbi ben Akiva and his associates in Jerusalem at the time of the destruction of the Second Temple, about a generation after Jesus Christ.

Book One was but the first of twelve books revealed to Rabbi Akiva and his followers as they wandered the landscape of Israel after the Romans destroyed their Temple. They roamed throughout the Holy Land, questioning the true and hidden meaning of Creation, the Patriarchs, the Torah, the Alphabet, the Tree of Life, and the evolution of souls.

Rabbi Aryeh explained that the books had been lost or concealed for a thousand years. Two hundred years ago, the books were revealed again to Rabbi Moshe de León, then a resident of Toledo. The rabbi cautioned that being caught with one of the books would bring a death sentence in Spain and Portugal. "Have no fear," the rabbi said. The *Zohar* is the key to the Gates of the World to Come if you but digest its contents. He placed the book in Elias's hands. "Guard it. Treasure it. *Become* it." Then he was gone.

Soon after this event, Salomão commissioned a New Christian tinsmith to make a large lead-lined wooden box to contain a smaller copper box but big enough to accommodate twelve large books. It was created to resist water, rust, and mold. No lock was fashioned for the box because it might indicate valuable contents. Beyond that, copper and lead would never stop a thief, regardless of the lock.

Salomão and Elias dug a hole in the corner of Centum Cellas large enough to accept the new box. Elias placed the book's container into the hole, covered the lid with a few inches of dirt, and dragged large stones over it. Father and son built a shack near the tower, ostensibly for Elias to occupy during inclement weather while tending the sheep.

For two years before he died, Salomão came to study the *Zohar* with Elias every Thursday afternoon. When Salomão passed, Elias had the first volume of the *Zohar* practically memorized. Elias shared his knowledge with a few wise elders in the community, but not the hiding place in Centum Cellas. Those who learned from Elias's teaching from the *Zohar* soon understood that Elias had only the first of twelve volumes. One of these ardent followers was Covilhã's renowned physician, Dr. Lourenço Gonçalves. Dom Lourenço spearheaded a campaign to match the money the late Rav Salomão had paid for *Book One*. Once done, Doctor Gonçalves commissioned young Rabbi Elias to travel to Toledo, find Rabbi Aryeh ben Gavriel, and obtain a copy of *Book Two* of the *Zohar*.

Elias had never traveled beyond the Spanish border. By horse, the journey would take two days to reach the border by way of Castelo Branco. Another three days east would put him in Toledo. Elias's ear was no stranger to the language of Castile—Spanish merchants frequented Covilhã to buy wool. He could understand their tongue, but on crossing the border at Termas de Monfortinho, he found they could not understand his. On the fifth day, he approached the massive walls of Toledo, the formidable old capital of Castile. He crossed the Tagus on the Roman bridge with a group of peasants, peddlers, and priests. Elias knew these were the headwaters of the mighty Río Tejo, which flowed into the Atlantic at the place where Ulysses founded the city of Lisbon, according to legend.

Dom Elias asked the whereabouts of the Priory of St. Benedict. He was directed to the quarter of the city where it was located. He knew the old synagogue had been converted into the new priory in recent years, and he assumed that the many Jews who had lived in the neighborhood had not moved away after the 1492 Edict of Expulsion. Like Portuguese Jews, they simply became "New Christians."

After quartering his horse, Elias stationed himself by a butcher's stall where he could observe customer transactions while reading a broadside paper he picked up in the street. Occasionally, he saw a customer pay extra for a piece of meat fetched from a nearby storeroom. He assumed the meat was kosher. Elias approached one such customer, a portly matron with dark, luxuriant hair that contrasted the lines on her face.

"Excuse me, *señora*, I am looking for Dr. Aryeh ben Gavriel. I am his relative from Portugal. I have news for him and reason to believe he resides in this area." She did not answer but studied Elias from head to toe, as if wary of his foreign dress, accent, and the lack of a crucifix around his neck.

"*Shalom*," the woman finally whispered. Elias returned the greeting, and she gave him directions to Dr. Aryeh's house, only five blocks away. It was a small compound of whitewashed structures against the city wall.

A servant met Elias and asked his purpose. Elias complied, and the servant directed him to the *consultorio* in the rear of the complex, where he joined a group of patients sitting under a shade tree waiting to see the doctor.

The rabbi appeared in the doorway. He surveyed the souls waiting, turned, and ordered his assistant to serve the guests some cool water from the well. He walked up to Elias, looked him up and down at an arm's length, then embraced him. "*Shalom, meu filho*," he whispered. "We've been expecting you. I hope your journey was uneventful."

"Yes, Rav . . . Dr. Aryeh. No problems to speak of. I've come with a request from my community." Aryeh put his finger to his lips to indicate silence. He escorted Elias to the operating room in the *consultorio*.

"I've come for a copy of *Book Two*." The rabbi nodded. "My study group has collected funds for the book, assuming it would be comparable in size to *Book One*. If it has more pages, then we will pay more, and for delivery—"

Rabbi Aryeh stopped him with his hands up. "Save your money." Aryeh's reply was stern, making Elias slump his shoulders. "I mean the delivery. We were expecting you. *Book Two* is ready for you to take now, and I'm sure the sum of money you've brought will be sufficient to cover our costs."

"Rabbi," Elias asked incredulously. "How did you know we were in the market for *Book Two?* Our study group is secret . . . for us, it's a matter of life and death."

"Yes," the Rabbi replied. "In the physical world, there are impenetrable secrets, but in the spirit world, there are no secrets from those who truly seek or from those who are attentive. Besides, your study group is not so secret. Dr. Lourenço Gonçalves is a member, is he not? He has business with a close friend and member of my congregation. He reports Gonçalves is a man at peace with himself, with relaxed anticipation and awareness that exudes confidence in what he does and the people he deals with. He talks endlessly of how you memorized a secret book and shared it with him. And if that's not enough to answer your question, I'll make it simple. Three years ago, when I delivered *Book One* of the *Zohar* to you on your birthday, it was no accident your father chose you for this boon. Your father, Salomão, told you there were eleven books to follow and helped you with your studies until the end of his days. May God bless him. We knew you had memorized the first book. But is a starving man who is invited to a banquet satisfied with a mere appetizer?" The rabbi smiled. "And besides, do you think printing another copy of *Book Two* on our

Hebrew press would be a wasted effort? Leave your bag of money. Take your horse to the livery stable down the street. Next to it is a Marrano [3] cobbler who can provide you a bed in his shop. His name is Ricardo Riviera. Trust him—he is a member of our study group. His wife will feed you, and I advise you to retire early. Don Ricardo will wake you before midnight and bring you here. Your arrival is timely because, by luck, our group meets tonight. Go now. Feed your body. Get some rest."

Don Ricardo was a curious fellow with spindly, quick-moving legs that contrasted a powerful upper body. His smile was tranquilizing. The cobbler shop contained a blacksmith's forge—which explained Ricardo's strong hands—he made footwear for both man and beast. He welcomed Elias as an old friend to his kitchen table, where his wife Hannah had spread a hearty meal with soup, lamb, greens, fruit, and wine. Elias retired after sunset. Within minutes, his spirit fled his weary body for a wordless adventure, only to return when a strong hand shook his shoulder. "Rabbi Elias, it's time," Ricardo whispered.

By the light of the crescent moon, the two men made their way to the house of Rabbi Aryeh and his operating room, where they met Rabbi Aryeh and Rabbi Jose Vispula and his son, Juan. The four descended into a secret chamber below. They donned kippahs and robes and sat with others in chairs against the walls under the glow of candlelight. The chamber walls were tiled with scenes from the Torah—the lives of Abraham, Joseph, Moses, and David. The sweet aroma of incense filled the space. A young robed man strummed a guitar, accompanying another man singing a verse from the Song of Solomon.

Those assembled welcomed the young Elias to their study group and expressed regret that other members of the Toledo group could not attend.

A large marble box supported a menorah candelabra in the middle of the room. Rabbi Aryeh removed the candelabra and slid the box's lid ajar to reveal twelve leather-bound tomes. He turned to Elias. "These are the original books of the *Zohar*, penned by the hand of Moses de León here in Toledo 180 years ago." Aryeh removed a volume, replaced the lid, and placed the book on the marble box. He turned to Elias and announced: "I want to welcome our young brother from the Star Mountain of Portugal, Rabbi Elias Mendes de Oliveira. He is the son of our dear friend Rabbi Salomão, who left us three years ago. He is also the grandson of the great teacher, Rav

Jaco of Belmonte—who, some years ago, sacrificed himself after securing his community from the Inquisition. May the spirits of Jaco and Salomão be with us tonight." You may recall that Rabbi Salomão commissioned a copy of *Book One* of our sacred transmission expressly for his son. You might ask why Rabbi Elias has come to us. It's because his curiosity is not satisfied. He wants us to copy *Book Two.* Can you imagine! His study group has sent him for more of this magical medicine! Not happy with what they have, they think there is more. They think they are stuck in the first chapters of Genesis, and they are ready to travel on. They say they are tired of Rabbi Elias's endless recitations about the contest between the twenty-two sacred Letters to create the universe, with the prize going to *Aleph* and *Bet.* They want to hear what comes next!" The rabbi turned to Elias. "Are you ready for questions to demonstrate your knowledge level?"

"I am ready."

"What is happening in the *Zohar?* What is going on here?" Rabbi Aryeh asked.

"From what I gather, Rabbi Shimon is wandering the countryside of Galilee conversing with his fellow rabbis. As they travel, they discover the Torah's secrets, share their discoveries, and discuss them."

"And who is this Shimon?"

"I am told Shimon was the son of Rabbi Yochai, who was taught by the great teacher, Rabbi Akiva."

"And why was Akiva so great?" Rabbi Aryeh inquired.

"Rabbi Akiva lived when the Romans destroyed Jerusalem, after the time of Jesus Christ. I don't know what made him pure and wise, but he was the one who led an expedition with three other rabbis up to the Highest Heaven. The Merkabah Chariot came down and carried them up. Only Rabbi Akiva was prepared for the trip—the other three died or went insane. Only Rabbi Akiva was ready for the ordeal, and he returned to tell us what he saw."

"Good enough," Rabbi Aryeh affirmed. "Now tell us how Shimon makes these discoveries with his companions in Galilee?"

"They have their eyes open and their hearts pure, and they make an effort and . . . oh, yes, they have help from the Assembly."

"The Assembly? What is this Assembly?" Aryeh asked.

Elias was ready. He felt the words he had memorized fall into place. He asserted that Elijah came down from his cave on Mount Carmel to the beach below and confronted Rabbi Shimon. Elijah told Shimon that the Lord, the blessed Holy One, reveals the Word to the Assembly on High. "I believe the Assembly is a gathering—a supreme concourse—of saints, prophets, and angelic entities."

"So, Rabbi Elias Mendes de Oliveira, you've memorized the portion of the *Zohar* allotted to you. What an extraordinary feat. Can you tell us more about this Academy on High?" Rabbi Aryeh challenged.

"I believe it is an Inner School where the souls of the righteous study the Torah with the Elohim," Elias replied.

"And who are these Elohim?"

"They are the gods or forces that unify all things in moving inter-relationship, from seraphim to angels to men and women."

"Very good. If the Academy on High is only for righteous Jews to study the laws governing creation, can others gain admission to the Inner School?"

"I am not qualified to answer, Rabbi Aryeh. I feel that all the righteous souls of the world attend the Assembly. They posthumously continue to seek the eternal mysteries. They retain the will to impart their knowledge and wisdom to rescue souls here who are in danger of disintegrating into the wretched chaos of the world that surrounds us on this plane."

"Wretched chaos of the world surrounding us? Is that what you said?" Rabbi Aryeh challenged. "Did not Elijah say to Shimon on the beach at Mount Carmel, 'When I behold Your heavens, the work of Your fingers, the moon and stars that you set in place . . . YHVH our Lord, how majestic is your name throughout the earth?!' I ask you—is YHVH's work really so wretched and chaotic?"

"Rabbi," Elias groaned. "All the synagogues in Spain and Portugal have been destroyed. We are underground to escape attention. If the world around us discovers the books in that box, they will roast us alive like my grandfather. This is *indeed* what I call wretched!"

"Oh—this is where I want you, Elias. Things have never been worse. Is that what you're telling me? Did you know that the Romans tortured the illustrious Rabbi Akiva, who ascended to the Highest Heaven, to death? Rabbi Shimon ben Yochai, the mouthpiece of the *Zohar*, whom you just quoted, fought the Romans and hid in a cave for thirteen years with his son, Eleazar. After the destruction of the Temple in the Roman year 70, their world was broken. But certainly, *they* were not broken. They were glorious human beings. And we can be the same. The setting is the same. Now is the time for new Akivas and Shimons. . . . But enough. Let's get on with our study. Rabbi Aryeh looked at the son of Rabbi Jose Vispula and said, "Juan, pick up from last week's session. From *Book Two*, read the story of Abram's family in Ur of the Chaldees with his father Terah and brother Haran and the story of the idols and the furnace."

Juan began reading. "Tradition says that Terah, Abram's father, made and sold idols. That was his business. One day, Terah traveled to another town, so he left his shop for his son Abram to tend to. A customer appeared to want to buy an idol. Abram asked, 'How old are you?' And the man replied, 'Fifty years old.' Abram looked at him incredulously and said, 'Woe to such a man! You are fifty years old and would bow down to an object one day old!' The man left in shame. Then a woman came to the shop carrying a plate of fine flour as a gift to the idols. She said, 'Offer this flour to them.' When the woman left, Abram took up a stick and broke all the idols, except for the largest. Then he put the stick in the hand of the unbroken idol. When Terah returned, he demanded, 'Who did this?' Abram replied, 'How can I hide it? A woman came with a plate of fine flour and told me to offer it to them. The idol on the floor said, 'I will eat first!' Then the other one on the floor said, 'no, *I* will eat first!' Then the big one arose with the stick and broke them both.' Terah was enraged. He said, 'Why are you mocking me? Do they know anything?' Abram replied to his father, 'Don't your ears hear what your mouth is saying?' Terah seized his son and delivered him to Nimrod.

"Nimrod said to Abram, 'Let us worship fire!' Abram retorted, 'Let us worship water, which extinguishes fire.' Nimrod responded, 'Then let us worship water!' Abram elaborated, 'Let us worship the clouds which carry the water!' Nimrod replied, 'Let us worship the clouds!' Abram added, 'Let us worship the wind, which carries the clouds!' Nimrod complied. 'Let us worship the wind!' Abram pushed further, 'Let us worship human beings who withstand the wind.' Nimrod replied, 'You are playing with words. We will worship only Fire. I will cast you into it, and let your God whom you worship come and save you!'

"Haran, Abram's brother, was standing by undecided. He told himself, 'If Abram is victorious, I will say that I side with him. If Nimrod is victorious, I will say that I side with him.' Abram descended into the fiery furnace and was saved. Nimrod turned to Haran and asked, 'With whom do you side?' He responded, 'With Abram.' Thus Haran was cast into the fire and died in the presence of his father. And therefore, it is written in Genesis, 'Haran died in the presence of Terah, his father.'"4

"Well done, Juan," Rabbi Aryeh boomed. "Now, let us see what is written in the *Zohar* about what transpired next." He took the book in hand, opened it to a page, and pointed. "For as soon as Terah saw his son saved from the fire, he came around to fulfilling Abram's desire." 5 "What was Abram's desire?"

Don Ricardo responded to the question: "To go to the land of Canaan."

"Yes," Aryeh said, pointing again to the book and reading. "YHVH said to Abram, '*Parashat Lekh Lekha!*' These words rang in Rabbi Elias's ears like an echo from a deep well. '*Lekh-lekha, Lekh-lekha . . . Lekh-lekha, Lekh-lekha.*' 'Go you forth, go you forth . . . go you forth, go forth. . . .' 'Go you forth from your land, from your birthplace, from your father's house to a land that I will show you.' 6

"Notice, my friends," the rabbi asserted, "miracles did not attend to Abram until he had aroused himself. Abram became aroused in his father's idol shop, perhaps by the falsity of the idols. But he was aroused in any case—enough that his father took him before Nimrod. He argued and stepped into the flames without being burned. Thus we learn Abram was so aroused about YHVH—the Truth and the Way—that YHVH became aroused by Abram and preserved him, paving the way for the accomplishment of his desire to go to the land of Canaan."

"Come and see: An entity above is not aroused until there is first aroused below that upon which it can abide". 7 " Come and see: Once it is written: They set out with them from Ur of the Chaldeans . . . immediately, YHVH said to Abram, "Lekh Lekha, Go for yourself, to refine yourself, perfect your rung. Lekh Lekha— you are not to stay here among the wicked. Mystery of the matter: Lekh Lekha, for the blessed Holy One granted Abram a spirit of wisdom, so he discovered and tested the conduits of the inhabited world, contemplated them, balancing them with the balance, till he knew the powers appointed throughout the world.

Once the blessed Holy One saw his arousal and desire, He immediately revealed Himself to him, saying: Lekh Lekha, Go to Yourself, to know yourself, to refine yourself. 8

From your land— from that habitation to which you cling. From your birthplace—from that wisdom through which you envision and gauge your birth, the precise moment you were born, under which star and constellation. From your father's house to succeed in the world. So, Lekh Lekha. Go you forth!— from this wisdom, this speculation.

To the land that I will show you— I will show you what you could not comprehend and could not know: the power of that land, deep and concealed.

I will make of you a great nation because it is written: Go you forth!

I will bless you because it is written: from your land.

I will enhance your name because it is written: from your birthplace.

You will be a blessing because it is written: from your father's house.

From here on, blessings to others, nourished from here, as it is written: I will bless those who bless you, and whosoever curses you I will curse. Through you, all families of the earth will be blessed. 9

Rabbi Aryeh put the book down. Silence ensued. After a few moments, he motioned at Rabbi Jose Vispula. The latter removed a guitar from a leather case and began to play a soft, enchanting melody. All present fell into a quiet revelry. Elias was unsure whether he slept, dreamed, or became the music. Eventually, the melody stopped, and the dream left him feeling like he was standing on a rung of a ladder he couldn't remember climbing.

Rabbi Aryeh sparked all eyes to open back to the present time and space with a loud clap of his hands. He stood up with book in hand and began again: "Come and see." This cycle continued throughout the early morning hours until the sound of distant roosters broke the dark silence of their sanctuary. Doña Maria, Rabbi Aryeh's wife, knocked three times on the floorboards. All knew it was time to return to their dwellings under the cover of darkness.

Rabbi Aryeh presented Elias with the breadbox containing the second volume of the *Zohar* in the secret compartment with two fresh loaves of bread on top. The rabbi withdrew the book and opened the leather cover. The book was rich with gold-leaf illumination and was dedicated to the communities of Belmonte, Covilhã, and Fundão.

Rabbi Aryeh assured Elias the third volume would be waiting for him and his community when they were ready.

Seven days later, Elias was back at his shack at Centum Cellas. Under cover of darkness, he removed the copper box from its underground hiding place and inserted the companion volume.

Over the next two years, Elias committed the second volume to memory, and his study group enjoyed a new level of comprehension. This pattern repeated itself over two decades until he buried all twelve books under the earthen floor of Centum Cellas.

Dr. Lourenço Gonçalves, a physician from Covilhã, sponsored the acquisition of *Book Two* twenty years ago. He did well for himself in the subsequent years. Although his first wife died soon after their marriage, she left him with a daughter. He remarried. His second wife bore him a son, Ruy, whose birth preceded Rabbi Elias's son, Davide, by a few months. Ruy and Davide were best friends from the time they learned to walk.

For two decades, Lourenço Gonçalves continued as a faithful member of Rabbi Elias's Thursday night study group. His *vila* on the mountainside above Covilhã was peaceful; his clinic in the middle of the city's old Judiaria neighborhood was all hustle and bustle. Dr. Gonçalves had well-trained assistants to cover for him on his extended business trips, often outside the country.

At eleven, Ruy and Davide began their religious studies under Rabbi Elias at Centum Cellas. Two years later, both participated in a secret bar mitzvah ceremony conducted by Rabbi Elias in the ruins of Bet Eliahu Synagogue, just below the castle in Belmonte. The buried *Zohar* had remained a complete secret until the boys attained the age of fifteen.

The revelation came when they visited their contemporary and best friend, Antonio "Toninho" Cabral, who lived in the old Cabral Castle in Belmonte. He was a grandson of the discoverer of Brazil, Pedro Álvares Cabral. Ruy's grandfather, Dr. Emanuel Gonçalves, was the Great Navigator's private physician. Ruy's father and Rabbi Elias were close friends with Toninho's father, Fernão Cabral, a nominal Christian. but not an undercover Jew.

Ruy, Davide, and Toninho spent their childhood together between the castle in Belmonte and the houses in Covilhã. Their fathers continued their own friendship and shared particular financial interests and investments.

One day in the spring, after taking their *almoço* meal at the castle, the three teenagers spent the afternoon roving the countryside below Belmonte Castle. They left the old fortress and proceeded north, down the hill where the town was perched. After crossing many fields, Centum Cellas came into sight. As they approached the ruins, they spotted Rabbi Elias inside. They crept up silently, thinking to surprise him, but stopped when they saw him remove a heavy copper box from the ground. He took out a book, returned the copper box to the secret chamber, and covered it. The rabbi opened the book in his shack and began reciting words in Hebrew with a musical cadence. At length, Elias sensed the presence of the three boys. He turned and faced them through the window of his structure.

They froze for an instant, and all but Toninho realized the import of what had just transpired. Elias smiled, reaching around to close the book without dropping his gaze. "What a surprise, *rapazes*, what brings you?"

Davide answered, "Nothing, Father. We thought we'd go to the creek and cut some twigs for kites. We just stopped to say 'hello.'"

"I'm in the middle of something, and I need to finish."

Davide and Ruy needed no further explanation. The boys continued their journey to the creek, but Toninho wanted to know the contents of the box Davide's father kept buried in the ground. Davide and Ruy had not seen the *Zohar* books, but they had heard tell of them and suspected the rabbi had a hidden source of knowledge. They could not reveal what they knew to Toninho, nor could they speculate that the rabbi kept a treasure map or treasure book in the ground, lest word get out.

Toninho tenaciously nagged Davide, who finally said, "I have no idea what was in the book or the box, but on your behalf, I will ask my father and tell you what he says. The words pacified Toninho, but Davide knew he would have to follow through with his pledge. When he finally did, his father admired his son's wise decision not to invent something. Elias wanted his son to tell Toninho that he kept old family records of methods and formulas for improving the quality and fertility of sheep. "Tell him the knowledge is old but effective—I want to keep it secret and safe from the elements . . . but in a place where I can use it to assess and divide the sheep. Can you trust Toninho to keep silent?"

He secured the pledge of secrecy, and the explanation satisfied Toninho.

The three lads soon forgot the event. The event's more immediate portent was as a sign to Rabbi Elias: the time had come for Davide and

Ruy to step into the *Zohar's* shallows. Soon after the unexpected encounter, Elias introduced the boys to the copper box's contents, and they began a systematic study of the *Zohar*.

The two boys met once a week, either at the shack at Centum Cellas or at the rabbi's home in Covilhã. They devoted the first hour to the formal study of the Torah; in the second, they explored the mystic commentary from Elias's memory of the tomes in the copper box.

After the first year of studying the *Zohar*, Rabbi Elias and Dr. Lourenço took their sons on a memorable trip to Toledo to secure the last and twelfth volume. Davide and Ruy passed a magical night in congregation in the secret chamber under Dr. Aryeh's operating room. They were transported into indescribable realms and would never forget the experience. It promised to alter the course of their lives.

Returning to Portugal, they began the second year of study of the *Zohar* under Elias. Having completed *Book One*, they grasped an understanding of the forces of creation and the qualities of the living letters of the alphabet. They covered the story of Noah and the destruction of the world by water. They were now entering the world of *Book Two*, where they would dwell upon Abraham.

View of Centum Cellas

Distant view of Centium Cellas

Remains of Belmonte Castle

View of the Serra da Estrela mountain range

From the hilltop village of Belmonte

CHAPTER 5

FERDINAND MAGELLAN, FRANCISCO SERRÃO, AND THE SPICE ISLANDS

Portugal
Spain
Goa
Malacca (Singapore)
The Spice Islands
1504-1515

One afternoon in the late fall of 1504, two strapping young men on horseback looking for Pedro Álvares Cabral found their way to Covilhã and up to the mountainside gate of Dr. Emanuel Gonçalves's villa. They had come by riverboat up the Tejo River and rode north to Castelo Branco for a day. From there, another day's ride put them at the villa.

The riders dismounted gingerly and introduced themselves as cousins bound for the Far East, seeking advice from the great Dom Pedro Álvares Cabral. The doctor was called to the gate. The talkative visitor was Fernaõ de Magalhães— otherwise, Ferdinand Magellan. Magellan's silent, smiling cousin was Francisco Serrão. They had recently signed up as officers on the armada of twenty-two ships sailing from Lisbon in the spring of the coming year, bound for the Malabar coast of India. Magellan's idea was to use these idle months before the voyage to gather useful information about their destination—hence the audacious idea to seek an audience with the now out-of-favor, thirty-seven-year-old legendary navigator, Pedro Álvares Cabral.

"Would the good Doctor be so kind as to introduce us to the Great Navigator?"

Emanuel Gonçalves replied that luck was with them—he was about to leave for Belmonte and invited them to accompany him to the castle. The doctor could not guarantee Cabral would see them because he was suffering an attack of the fevers, and he'd just been summoned to treat him. The ride to Belmonte at a slow trot would require about an hour and a half.

On the road, Magellan told the doctor his father had been mayor of Aveiro, but when the plague claimed both parents, he was orphaned at the age of ten.

"By the grace of God," Magellan asserted, "Our beloved Queen Leonora took me into her court as a pageboy. Once there, they gave me the same teachers as King John II's own son, Prince Afonso. He was five years older but took a liking to me. He called me "a spunky orphan." In my first year at court, Afonso taught me to ride. He was sixteen and already a great horseman. He died on the river road after his horse threw him, and no one believed it. Afonso's Spanish valet was supposed to have been with him, but he disappeared after the accident. King John had the valet tracked down in Spain, but it was too late. The Spanish had already cut his throat, so no words could pass through it. Some reward for a dirty deed, eh? The queen educated me with the other pages. I love nautical science and have always studied the latest maps. I wanted to attend the special school in Sagres that old Prince Henry started years ago, but they said I wasn't noble enough as an orphan for that level. It was reserved for future navigators. Francisco and I educated ourselves in the school of the world. Queen Leonora gave me a good start, and with lucky Francisco here, we can't go wrong."

Francisco nodded in agreement as Magellan continued speaking. "I'm the talker with brains; he is the brawn with good looks, a fetching smile, and all the luck in the world. I'm in it to make a name for myself and to get rich—he's in it purely for the adventure."

When they arrived at the village of Belmonte, the doctor bade the boys wait at a tavern across from the castle. He would send word if and when Cabral would see them. Some hours later, a messenger came.

The young men were led into the Cabral's living quarters, where the Great Navigator was sprawled on a couch before a roaring fire. Wet towels to reduce the fever covered his bare body, and bowls of cold water stood around him on the floor. Emanuel Gonçalves had already given the man quinine and laudanum for the pain.

Cabral was a large man with dark, penetrating eyes. A manicured beard framed his sharp features, and silver streaked his head of wild black hair. The doctor had briefed him about his visitors.

"With whom are you sailing?"

"Sir, I believe the *capitán-maior* is to be Fernaõ Soares. They are preparing twenty-two ships—seven caravels and fifteen carracks," Magellan replied.

"Twenty-two?" He hummed. "I know Soares is a good navigator, but he will not command an operation with twenty-two ships."

"No, sir. I understand that aboard the flotilla will be Dom Francisco de Almeida, the famous commander from campaigns in Africa and Granada. He is to become the first governor and viceroy of Portuguese India."

"I know him," said Cabral. "But I know his son Lourenço better. Almeida is a good choice—he will be strong. Don't get in his way. Don't defy him, and you will be all right. You may have to work with his son, who is not much older than you, but be careful with Lourenço. He is courageous but foolhardy. He thinks he is invincible. Don't volunteer to sail with him unless the stakes are high." Magellan and Serrão shook their heads as if they comprehended the advice.

"How much do you know about the mission, Ferdinand?"

"I have heard that before Almeida can claim the viceroy's commission, he has to build four coastal trading forts, two in Africa and two in India." Reflecting to himself, Magellan considered that the new King Manuel must have learned something from his brother-in-law, John II, who mysteriously died."

"Nothing is free—make them earn it," Cabral muttered. He looked up at Magellan and Serrão and announced, "I can tell you this: India is where the action is. Go for it. I'd like to go there too, but you see I'm sick now. Stuck at home, pushed aside and forgotten by King Manuel in favor of the da Gamas."

Silence followed Cabral's words. Magellan broke it: "Will you give us some advice, Dom Pedro? If I may call you Dom Pedro. We are indebted to you for receiving us—we two foolish youths knocking at your door." Then Francisco's calm voice asserted itself for the first time, "We've got time on our hands and energy to burn, sir. What should we be doing to prepare for this great life adventure? What can we do to give us an edge?"

"When—?"

"March."

"Nothing in life is free, as you know. You must pay for any further advice."

Magellan replied, "Sir, we have but few resources. That's why we want to sail—to get rich, to gain the resources we don't have. But what do you require?"

"Your resources are yourselves alone, my two adventurous *amigos*. I will lend you advice and perhaps a letter or two of recommendation. In return, I expect the information you acquire on your journey. I will give you the name and Lisbon address of my *advogado*, who handles my affairs. I want to know who among your commanders are making the decisions and how they fare. Who are the rulers—the men in power—in the cities where we have factories? What are their strengths and weaknesses? Who are our friends, our enemies? Follow the money— determine, as best you can, how much cargo space in how many ships they devote to which commodities. Who owns the space? What price are these commodities trading for in the ports along the way? Ask questions and keep your eyes open. Most important, discover where the Spice Islands are and how to get there. In return for this information, I will give you letters of introduction to the rulers of Cochim and Canonor, both of whom I know well. But you must keep these letters secret. Guard them with your lives—who knows what the consequences would be if the wrong people found them? I will also give you some practical advice on using your time wisely in the months before you leave."

"We will certainly do this for you, Dom Pedro," said Magellan, excitedly leaping from his seat.

"And we will guard your letters with our lives," Serráo said with calm determination.

"Put your heads together and write me a report at least once a year. Give it to the quartermaster of one of the ships in the armada before the January departure for Portugal. Address the letter to one of your sweethearts but use the address of my lawyer." Cabral motioned for

Emanuel Gonçalves to bring him his quill, ink, and paper. He wrote the address of his lawyer and gave it to Magellan.

Looking up, Cabral grinned and said, "Now for the advice. What languages can you speak?"

Ferdinand and Francisco looked up in bewilderment.

"Uh. . . ." Magellan sputtered. "Portuguese, Spanish, a little French, and the Galego I learned spending summers with my uncle in Santiago de Compostela." Cabral laughed and said Galego would only serve him if his shipmates were from Galicia.

"I assume neither of you speaks Arabic," said Cabral. "So, tell me, do you have any friends who speak Arabic?"

This question was delicate because the year was 1505—and tension was building. At Easter the following year, Dominican priests would incite a Lisbon mob to round up and kill over three thousand Jews and Muslims. Magellan and Serrão were to witness the tragedy firsthand.

Serrão burst forth with an answer: "Yes! I have a girlfriend . . . well, not exactly a 'girlfriend,' who can speak Arabic. Her name is Zulmira. Her father was a teacher—an imam—at the old mosque in Alfama. They stayed in Portugal and became New Christians like the Jews."

"Could you convince Zulmira and her family to teach you Arabic?" Cabral asked.

"I think so," replied Francisco. "Particularly if we paid them. Zulmira trusts me—she will believe me if I tell her I want to learn Arabic because it will help me in the Indies."

"You know, *amigos*," Cabral affirmed, "here in Europe, if you speak Italian, French, or Spanish—even if you know Latin—you can communicate everywhere you go. The same goes for Arabic in the Indies. Once you round the terrible Cape of Good Hope, as King John called it, Arabic is common. You don't have to bother with a thousand and one languages and dialects. Anyone with status speaks Arabic. More importantly, our most significant enemies speak it. The more you learn, the better off you will be. Arabic may even help keep you alive." Cabral drew a deep breath and continued, "The trade winds across the Indian Ocean reverse themselves over the year. On the way east, if you fail to reach Malindi on the east coast of Africa by mid-summer, forget it. If you put in at Malindi in time—during June—the trade winds will speed you to India in weeks. But if you miss that opportunity, you may have to wait in Africa for a year before prevailing winds return. Study the winds and currents—learn to anticipate them. Many important decisions can be made accordingly. And whenever you board a ship for a lengthy voyage, take plenty of oranges and lemons, even if you must stow them until they rot. The Arabs say it's a remedy against scurvy, and I believe them. Everything revolves around money. *We*, the Portuguese, understand that. King Manuel understands, and the people with whom we trade in the Indies also understand. Keep this straight—don't get mixed up with religion, and don't tangle with women unless they are whores. Two things will get you killed in the Indies faster than money—disrespecting their religion and women. Don't fall in love. If you do, be prepared to die there."

With his quill in hand, Pedro Álvares Cabral wrote two short letters of introduction to the rulers of Cochim and Canonor. Emanuel Gonçalves brought him wax and a candle. Cabral applied the seal with his ring. He gave one letter to each young man, embraced them, and bid them be on their way.

Magellan and Serrão studied Arabic assiduously with Zulmira and her family six months before the expedition. Zulmira's father was hesitant, but Ferdinand delivered a sample of Haji Ishmael's ceramics to his patroness, Queen Leonora, who commissioned a tea set with other projects to follow. The haji's house became a school of Arabic and Muslim culture with the haji as the master, his wife and children as teachers, and Francisco and Ferdinand as students.

On Easter Sunday, trouble began at the Church of St. Dominic with assaults on the New Christians, scapegoated for a prolonged period of drought and plague. Violence soon spread to the Jewish quarter and into the Muslim neighborhood of Alfama. Ferdinand hurried to the palace to seek the queen's protection for Zulmira's family. She was at a country estate, but Magellan prevailed upon the royal chamberlain to post a guard in front of Haji Ishmael's house. The family was thus spared provocation and destruction.

A curious love had developed between Zulmira and Francisco. It grew with the change of season from winter to summer and was punctuated by the Easter catastrophe. The winter seed of casual attraction blossomed into a summer lotus flower on a tranquil pond. The lovers wisely restrained themselves from stirring the waters of passion and demurely gazed upon the other from opposite sides of the pond. The restraint gave Francisco the energy to be the better student, but Ferdinand's desire for a sharp career advantage put him in close pursuit of his cousin in acquiring the strange vocabulary.

The armada weighed anchor at the Lisbon wharves in mid-summer. Upon reaching the east coast of Africa, they spent time in forts and factories until the trade winds of 1507 carried them to the Malabar coast of India.

Viceroy Almeida began constructing forts at Cochim, Angediva Island, Quilon, and Canonor.

Magellan and Serrão, to their discomfort, were dispatched to the squadron under the command of the viceroy's son, Lourenço de Almeida. A battle was imminent. The Zamorin of Calicut, one of Cabral's old enemies, had assembled a fleet of two hundred vessels and was sailing toward Canonor to stop Portuguese fort building. The young Captain Lourenço Almeida's six carracks—strongly built, heavily armed, and highly maneuverable—intercepted the Zamorin's fleet in the deep waters outside Canonor harbor. For the Portuguese, it was target practice. The Zamorin's hodgepodge fleet was like ducks in a pond, unable to fly. They were devastated, and Ferdinand and Francisco had their first taste of battle at sea.

Ferdinand and Francisco also remembered Cabral's advice. At the first opportunity, they managed to be transferred from the son's command to that of the father.

This was a fortuitous move—Captain Lourenço, feeling invincible, began ravaging Arab and Hindu ports and shipping lanes along the Malabar coast as far as Ceylon. The Zamorin, undaunted by the humiliating battle of Canonor, unified his angry allies and, with one of them, Mir Hussain, an Egyptian Mamluk, managed to trap Captain Lourenço's death squadron of six carracks at sea. They isolated Lourenço's ship and captured him and his crew for later execution.

The grief of the viceroy over the loss of his son was indescribable. He poured his sorrow and grief into furious fort building. He won another battle against a hundred ships but did not pause to celebrate. His quest for revenge was so overpowering that, with the surprise arrival of Afonso Albuquerque, his replacement as viceroy, Almeida refused to step down, jailing Albuquerque instead.

Eventually relieved of his command and forced to step down, Francisco de Almeida began the return voyage to Lisbon. However, natives killed the great soldier on a beach at the southern tip of Africa, a fate not unlike that which would befall Magellan eleven years later in the Philippines.

At this point in Magellan's life, however, things were improving. Now battle-hardened, eager, intelligent, and conversant in Arabic, Ferdinand and his cousin attracted the attention of the new viceroy, Albuquerque. In 1509, the viceroy chose Magellan and Serrão to accompany Diogo Lopes de Sequeira, his ambassador, to the prosperous state of Malacca. Later, Malacca would be known as Singapore, situated in the vital strait separating Malaysia and Indonesia.

Sultan Muhammad Shah initially welcomed the four ships of the Portuguese mission to Malacca. However, coincidental with their arrival, Viceroy Albuquerque conquered India's major port of Goa. In the sultan's court in Malacca, Goan Muslims persuaded the sultan to turn against the Portuguese delegation, arguing that he would suffer the same fate as Goa. A plot to murder the Portuguese embassy was hatched. The sultan summoned Sequeira and Serrão to a meeting while Magellan stayed in port aboard the ship.

With his broken Arabic and power of persuasion, Magellan contacted a few new friends among the sultan's court. A One friend informed Magellan of the plot. Magellan made his way to the Palace in time to warn his companions. They escaped with the four ships, but not before losing several sailors—some killed, some held hostage.

When the mission landed in Goa to deliver the bad news to Albuquerque, who was now in Goa, the viceroy surprisingly welcomed the news. He declared Goa the new Portuguese capital of the Indies, according to instructions from King Manuel and the Academy of the Order of Christ, a relic of the Templar movement. The king had instructed Albuquerque to first employ diplomatic and commercial tools to achieve his objectives. If the natives rejected their initiative, then conquest was the order. Albuquerque regarded the plot to murder the

Portuguese ambassador as a perfect excuse to attack and subdue the strategically located sultanate of Malacca.

In April 1511, Albuquerque set sail from Goa with twelve hundred men on seventeen ships, including Ferdinand Magellan and Francisco Serrão. After forty days of negotiating and then fighting, Malacca fell. Albuquerque divided the inhabitants into three groups: Hindus, Christians, and Muslims. He executed all the Muslims.

For participation in the battle and events leading to the conquest of Malacca, Magellan and Serrão received considerable plunder. Magellan was also given a promotion. However, Magellan retired from military service with his newfound wealth and returned to Portugal, parting ways with his cousin Francisco, who remained in the Indies.

Advancing in the viceroy's good graces, Serrão was commissioned as captain of one of three ships appointed to find the legendary Spice Islands in the unexplored seas east of Malacca. Albuquerque had already learned that the epicenter of the Spice Islands was a small group called the Bandu Islands. Francisco Serrão's assignment was to find Bandu—the source of valuable nutmeg, cinnamon, and cloves.

Sailing through the Straits of Malacca, Serrão was among the first Europeans to enter the South China Sea. Sailing along the north coast of Sumatra and Java, they made port at Gresik, a regency that one Portuguese trader called the "jewel of Java." There, Serrão disregarded Pedro Cabral's advice—he fell in love and married a Javanese woman who accompanied him on the rest of his journeys.

Arabic was no longer sufficient. Francisco began learning Javanese from his wife and the Malaysian pilots he employed. The three Portuguese ships sailed east along the coast of Bali and the lesser Sundras chain, then north toward the Moluccan Archipelago and Bandu. Serrão's vessel was wrecked, but all hands survived to arrive in Bandu, where the Portuguese ships were loaded with spices and dispatched back to Malacca, Goa, and other western destinations.

This was another turning point in the curious life of Francisco Serrão. In Bandu, he bought a sizeable Chinese junk and filled the cargo hold with spices. Although near, he had not yet found the legendary Spice Islands. Serrão explored the rest of the Moluccan Islands with his new vessel, accompanied by his wife, nine Portuguese sailors, and nine Indonesian sailors. However, the junk broke up in a storm on a reef off a small island. The inhabitants of the island were renowned as scavengers who lived off shipwrecks. As the scroungers approached, Serrão and the crew pretended to be desperate and unarmed. At the opportune moment, they turned on the pirates, seized their boat, and forced them to sail to the main island of Amboim. Serrão had finally made it to the Spice Islands.

Serrão's weapons and armor instantly attracted the attention of the sultan of Ternate. This sultan saw the chance to employ Serrão and his band as mercenaries to fight his rival on a neighboring island. The sultan made Serrão his chief military advisor. He and Francisco Serrão became close friends, and the sultan gave the Portuguese a palace and a permanent salary. Serrão stayed—his life had become too good to do anything else.

The Spice Islands were added to the trading routes, and the Portuguese enjoyed a monopoly on commodities. With trade secured between his new home and Portugal, Serrão communicated by mail with his cousin, Ferdinand. He sent a letter to Magellan in which he mapped all the islands from which the valued spices came. Francisco opined that because the Spice Islands were so far from the Straits of Malacca—requiring weeks of sailing—it was highly probable that the Spice Islands lay in the Spanish half of the world rather than in the Portuguese half, as designated by the Treaty of Tordesillas.

Upon receiving news from his cousin, Magellan schemed to persuade the Portuguese king or, if not him, the monarchs of Spain to finance a voyage to discover a westward trade route from Europe across the Atlantic and Pacific Oceans to the Spice Islands. For the thirty-three-year-old Magellan, in his prime in 1513, scheming came naturally, but he also had to attend to making a living. When his search for employment as a navigator brought no offers, he settled for joining a Portuguese military campaign in Morocco. He sustained an injury in battle that left him with a permanent limp. The regimental commander denied Magellan compensation for his injury, alleging that Ferdinand had illegally traded with the Moors.

Enraged, Magellan deserted. He was charged with the crime of leaving his post without permission.

When Ferdinand Magellan eventually gained an audience with King Manuel I, hoping to exonerate himself and present his plan to the king, he experienced the king's displeasure and subsequent dismissal. Not only had Magellan failed to persuade Manuel to fund the search for the Spice Islands by sailing west, but the king made it clear Magellan could not expect future employment as a navigator from Portugal.

Magellan thus made plans to move to Spain.

CHAPTER 6

MAGELLAN IN SEVILLA AND ACROSS THE PACIFIC

1516-1522

Arriving in Sevilla in 1516, Ferdinand Magellan soon found himself in the company of the Barbosa family, with whom he shared a common language and disdain for King Manuel of Portugal. Duarte Barbosa, Ferdinand's contemporary, had gone to India with his father, Diogo, in de Gama's second armada to the Indies in 1502. Duarte stayed. Like Magellan and Serrão, Duarte was good with languages. He made a name for himself as an interpreter for the viceroy, Afonso Albuquerque.

Duarte Barbosa served the viceroy for thirteen years. However, when the viceroy passed him over for a promotion Duarte thought he deserved, he returned to the household of his father, who had migrated from Portugal to Sevilla.

Duarte's father, Diogo Barbosa, was raised in the service of the powerful Duke of Alvado of the Portuguese House of Bragança, the same house from which King Manuel claimed descent. Manuel had appointed the duke as a special emissary to Castile to arrange his marriage to the daughter of the Spanish king and queen. After completing his mission and ingratiating himself with the Spanish royal family, the duke elected to stay in Spain. He settled in Sevilla and was eventually appointed mayor.

The Barbosa family opened their arms to Magellan, who soon married Diogo's daughter, María. Ferdinand's brother-in-law, Duarte, was to accompany Magellan to realize his grand plan.

In Sevilla, Magellan encountered another expatriate in the person of Rui Faleiro, a well-known Portuguese cartographer and one of the most accurate mapmakers of the day. However, because of an irascible personality and disagreeable nature, Faleiro accumulated enough personal enemies in Lisbon to mandate a move to Spain to preserve his career.

Faleiro confirmed that, in his opinion, the Spice Islands would fall within Spanish territory according to the Treaty of Tordesillas. Magellan made Faleiro his partner to give geographical authenticity to the presentation of his plan.

The major geographical impetus and urgency behind the plan arose because the Spaniard, Vasco Balboa had, only three years previously, crossed the Isthmus of Panama on foot to discover the Pacific Ocean.. No one had yet found a maritime passageway to the Pacific. Still, Magellan and Faleiro were convinced it was there to be discovered. They persuaded others of their convictions, and with the Grace of God and the backing of the Spanish Crown, they would find it.

The arguments were enough to convince Diogo Barbosa's patron, Duke Alvado, mayor of Sevilla. He, in turn, brought Magellan's proposal to the receptive attention of Bishop Juan Rodriguez de Fonseca. At the Casa de Contratación de las Indias in Sevilla, the bishop had controlled all Spain's expeditions, colonization, and trade for years. Bishop Fonseca, a cleric with enormous power, was intrigued by the proposal. He urged the mayor to have Magellan contact Juan de Aranda, the factor, or chief financial intermediary, at the Casa de Contratación. The meeting occurred in October 1517. Discussions continued between Aranda, Magellan, and Faleiro for the next six months. The two Portuguese finally won the support of Juan de Aranda, who granted them an audience with Charles I, the Spanish king and prospective Holy Roman Emperor.

The proposal was timely. It had been twenty-six years since Columbus discovered the New World in his attempt to find a western route to the Spice Islands. Four years had passed since Balboa discovered the Pacific Ocean. The previous year, 1516, while looking for a navigable passage to the Pacific, Captain Juan Díaz de Solís had sailed as far south as the Río de la Plata before his death at sea. The argument was that if the Portuguese and da Gama could find a way around Africa, there must also be a way through or around the New World Continent to the Pacific.

Without revealing the contents of Francisco Serrão's letter, Magellan managed to convince the Spanish monarch that he possessed the necessary experience, ability, and command to execute the mission. The king agreed but had reservations about the cartographer, Rui Faleiro. After five months of negotiating, the king provided 270 men and five ships, provisioned for a two-year voyage. He made Magellan and Faleiro captains and, if successful, would appoint them governors of the discovered islands, with twenty percent of the voyage's profits.

Preparations for the expedition, which was named the "Armada de Molucca," would take about a year. After the initial jubilation, things became problematic for Magellan, Faleiro, and friends. Rui Faleiro was upset by the king's requirement that two additional cartographers be included on the voyage. Unfortunately, Faleiro's disagreeable nature turned the Casa de Contratación against him.

Over forty percent of the crew Magellan enlisted were of Portuguese nationality. In addition to his occasional recruitment forays across the border into Portugal, Magellan's actions gave rise to accusations of spying and whispers that the whole scheme was a devious Portuguese conspiracy.

Preparations for the armada had come to a standstill—the chief reason was not one of personality or allegiance but insufficient funds. The young King Charles I of Spain was about to become Charles V, the Holy Roman Emperor. To achieve this, he incurred enormous expenses to support an army in Italy to capture Milan. Navarre and the Netherlands were in revolt against him. He had taxed the population of Castile to the maximum, and the discontent eroded his power base. King Charles I was on the verge of bankruptcy, and the funding of the whimsical armada to the Spice Islands was not high on his priority list.

In the fall of 1518, with his dream so close to fruition, Magellan became desperate to prevent it from slipping through his fingers. He journeyed to Portugal with his Malayan indentured servant, Enrique. Magellan heard that the Great Navigator Cabral had moved, perhaps for health reasons, from the backwoods castle at Belmonte to a comfortable villa in the old city of Santarém on the Tejo. Magellan and Enrique found their way to the gate of Cabral's villa, where guards summoned the help of a young man who presented himself with a calm but welcoming air of authority. Lourenço Gonçalves remembered Magellan from his visit to Belmonte fourteen years before.

"You appear to have traveled many leagues, sir. I assume you are here to see Dom Pedro. He is sick—and my father, his physician, is tending to him. May I relay the purpose of your visit?"

"Please inform Dom Pedro that Ferdinand Magellan has traveled from Sevilla across mountain, plain, and downriver for three weeks to apologize for not communicating from Goa. I have come to redeem myself if the navigator would be so generous as to give me an hour of his time. And, please tell me, is his personal physician the same Emanuel Gonçalves from Covilhã? If so, he may also remember my cousin who came to Belmonte fourteen years ago and me."

"The man is my father. My name is Lourenço—please come and refresh your horses. I will convey your request to my father and Dom Pedro, who himself may not be able to see you."

Enrique took the horses to a small fountain by the stables while Magellan waited with apprehension. How would he be received? Within minutes, Dr. Emanuel Gonçalves appeared, followed by his son.

The elderly doctor confronted Magellan, "You have a lot of nerve showing up here again. You didn't fulfill your agreement with Dom Pedro. He put his faith in you and your cousin. If the captain does not cast you out, you have five minutes to apologize . . . then you must leave. I don't want you to shorten his life further. His urine is already dark with kidney failure. He cannot rid himself of the poison that anger creates."

"I have come to make amends, Dr. Gonçalves. After the first years in Goa, Francisco and I did not write. But I have a document that will more than redeem those fourteen years of silence if Dom Pedro will but hear me with patience."

"Follow me," Dr. Gonçalves said with a brusque tone. He and his son escorted Magellan through the palace to a courtyard where Cabral rested in a hammock between two palms.

"Unless you have come here with something good, you are more shameless than I expected, even after fourteen years."

"You are right, Dom Pedro." Magellan bowed his head. "I am not that shameless. I have not come to ask for your pardon with nothing to offer or account for my actions. I came alone, with only my servant. My cousin Francisco is not with me—but not because he is dead . . . although, God knows, we had many opportunities to lose our lives. Francisco is now the personal advisor to the sultan of the very Spice Islands on which you wanted information. Don't believe what I say, but have faith in what you read in Francisco's letter."

Magellan slipped the letter from his breast pocket and presented it to Cabral. The old captain's eyes widened as he studied the map Serrão had drawn of dozens of islands, each describing the spices found there, the capacity to provide a market, the prevailing prices, the ruling powers, and the market alliances.

"Is this for me, Magellan?"

"It's addressed to me, sir. I'm sure it's engraved in your memory, Dom Pedro, and I am willing to let you make a copy of it, including the map, if you are still a gambling man. Now that you have seen the letter, I want to tell you about my arrangements with the Crown of Spain. After you hear what I want to say, if you want to gamble on a sure thing that will make you as rich as King Manuel, I will let you copy the letter and the map."

"Keep talking. We are listening." Cabral motioned for Dr. Gonçalves and Lourenço to assemble three chairs beside the hammock. Cabral handed the letter to the doctor and his son to read. At the same time, Magellan recounted everything that had transpired since the meeting in Belmonte in 1504.

Magellan concluded his discourse by explaining that young Charles I, in addition to outfitting and provisioning five ships, had agreed that Magellan and Faleiro would each be appointed governors of the lands found, each wielding ownership of an island and a healthy percentage of the commercial profits.

The reward structure could not be better, except that it bore no fruit. The young king spent his time and the Spanish treasury on his Italian military campaign. With his success, he was to be named Holy Roman Emperor, but he exhausted his funds achieving it, and the Casa de Contratación put a stop to all expeditions until revenues caught up with expenses.

"That explains why I am here, Dom Pedro," Magellan said.

Cabral looked at Dr. Gonçalves and Lourenço to gauge their reaction. Seemingly satisfied with what he read on their faces, Cabral asked Magellan to leave the room.

"Wait in the kitchen, Ferdinand." He pointed to a door. "It should only take a few minutes. We will send for you."

Within half an hour, Lourenço appeared in the doorway and signaled Magellan to re-enter the courtyard. The old doctor stood over the Navigator in the hammock. Cabral turned his head toward Magellan and, in a slow, soft tone, said, "We believe in you, Ferdinand Magellan. Your letter from Francisco is worth more than the dozens of reports you did not write me. On the condition that I can make a copy of that letter, we are willing to support your venture at participation of ten percent or the equivalent of fifty thousand ducats in return for ten percent of all your earnings from the venture for the next ten years.

If you are amenable to this, Dom Emanuel will draw up the papers tomorrow for you to sign. We will place the money directly in your hands with an armed guard disguised as merchants to accompany you and your servant to Sevilla.

After you have the funds in your saddlebags, you will give Lourenço the letter from Serrão and the map. He will copy the documents in your presence and return them with a copy of our agreement for you to sign. As far as you are concerned, this agreement is solely between you and me. There are no other parties to it, and I advise you not to let it be known that your newfound money came from Portugal. If they press you at the Casa de Contratación, tell them the money came from Duke Alvado, the mayor of Sevilla. If these funds are not sufficient to reinvigorate the venture, return to me, and we will find another way to realize your dream. I will also arrange with him to vouch for this dream. And Magellan—one last thing—if you fail to honor our agreement, I have ways, of which you cannot conceive, to redress the injury and extract justice."

The unexpected threat left Magellan at a momentary loss of words. His heart swelled into his throat. "Once again, Dom Pedro, you have saved my life. I am your eternal servant. I agree to all your terms. You are generous beyond expectation."

"When did I save your life the first time, Ferdinand? My memory fails me," whispered the Great Navigator. His black eyes peered from their frame of unruly silver hair.

"When you told me to learn Arabic, sir. That's when you saved my life the first time."

The navigator's face broke into a smile of satisfaction as Dr. Gonçalves clapped his hands.

"Good," the doctor said, bringing the conversation to a close. "Dom Ferdinand, you and Enrique must stay for the next few days while I write the agreement, ready the funds, and enlist the bodyguards. Rest—make yourself at home. And please, I ask you, spend as much time as possible with Lourenço. Tell him what you know about the Indies. Make up for the absent reports. Tell him about yourself and your health. He is a physician like myself, ten years younger than you, but he has my experience, and he was first in his class in Salamanca and in Lisbon. Tomorrow, when we have the funds, you will allow Lourenço to copy the letter and the map."

"Yes, I will do it. I welcome the advice and friendship of your son."

The trip from Santarém to Sevilla proceeded without incident. Magellan, Enrique, and the bodyguards entered the city through the Barrio de Triana with its Gypsies and seamen and rode right to the gate of the Casa de Contratación. Magellan bid farewell to his traveling companions and entered the building with his saddlebags of gold ducats in hand. Seeking his friend, Juan de Aranda, he was guided to the factor's office. He entered unannounced. With the surprised Aranda sitting at his desk, he let the sacks fall to the ground with a loud thud.

"There! That's fifty thousand ducats on my account. Let's finish up our business and get those boats downriver and on their way to the Spice Islands."

Juan de Aranda jumped up, startled and confused. "Where have you been? We have been frantically searching for you. Did de Haro send you with this money?"

"No, this is *my* money! And I know of only one de Haro— Christopher— a Lisbon financier. This is not *his* money."

"Then you don't know." De Aranda shifted his weight. "Many things have happened while you were in Portugal this past month. There is an important meeting tomorrow morning at the Casa. Both Bishop Fonseca and Christopher de Haro will attend. You, too, must attend with your partner, Rui Faleiro. They will be discussing the expedition. De Haro's company, the Fudder Group, is prepared to fund it. He is no longer in Lisbon—he had a falling out with King Manuel. The Fudder Group will no longer finance Portuguese overseas missions. De Haro claims to know you from Lisbon . . . I hope that's not a bad thing. Bishop Fonseca told him about your letter from Francisco Serrão, and he is intrigued. De Haro is a cash cow—he has come to Sevilla to have his teats pulled."

The news caught Magellan off guard. Was it good or bad? He would need time to sort it out. But he understood his immediate priority was to safeguard his gold.

"Yes, I know de Haro. That is wonderful news. There will be no excuse for not getting those boats on the water. But look what's at my feet. I won't feel safe until we get these bags into the Torre del Oro, a receipt in my hand . . . signed in blood!"

De Aranda called for a carriage with an armed guard. When it arrived, he, Magellan, Enrique, and the gold jumbled down the street toward the bridge over the Grand Canal. Magellan recalled his encounter with Christopher de Haro six years ago and what the factor had said about de Haro's cash reserves. The carriage clattered over the bridge to the old Torre del Oro, a dodecagonal watchtower built by the Moors. As the coach jostled to the rhythm of hoofbeats on cobblestone, Magellan gazed southward—down the wide canal to where it joined the Guadalquivir River. In the distance, beyond the clamor of vessels and voices, he could see the shipyard where workmen were outfitting his five ships. Squinting, he made out the masts of the *Trinidad*, his requested flagship, a slender caravel of Portuguese design. Nearby, four sturdy carracks bobbed gently in the incoming tide. One would be captained by Francisco Serrão's brother, João. Magellan's gut shot a surge of adrenaline into his chest, filling him with gratitude and delight. This is going to happen, he thought. God's will—my dream, or *my* will and God's dream—but they're one and the same. He strained himself; the excitement turned his bowels to liquid. He hoped there was a private place at the Torre del Oro to relieve himself without embarrassment.

The carriage halted in front of the Torre, which resembled a windmill stripped of its blades. Enrique held the gold while Juan de Aranda guided Magellan into a private room where he could address nature's requirements. When Magellan returned, the factor exchanged the bags of gold ducats for an official receipt. Aranda assured Magellan that he would have the documents prepared to show Magellan's adjusted share by the next day's meeting.

As an afterthought, Magellan asked de Aranda if he knew where Christopher de Haro was lodging. He was informed de Haro was at a residence near the Alcázar wall in the old Judiaria Quarter off Plaza Doña Elvira.

"Seek the residence of Don Aaron Pérez."

Magellan and Enrique wandered through ancient streets and alleyways in the direction of the Cathedral. Behind it, they found the Alcázar, the great Moorish castle that once controlled all of Andalucía. Following the wall, they entered the Jewish quarter. After a few inquiries about Pérez's house, they were directed to a nondescript black iron door. A servant opened, and after some interrogation, confirmed de Haro resided there.

De Haro soon appeared, a massively-built man with friendly blue eyes and curly silver-blond hair and beard, dressed in a silk robe.

He embraced Magellan as an old friend.

"Ferdinand! Look what fate has done! A few years ago, we were two strangers overindulging in green wine at the Taverna de Naufrago in Lisbon. Now we are in Sevilla for a common purpose, *inshallah*."

"You can't be more surprised than me when I heard you were in Sevilla. I can't tell you how delighted I am to see you."

"We have much to discuss," said de Haro, pulling on Magellan's elbow and motioning toward the passageway leading to a courtyard. "What is this? You are limping. What happened?"

"I was looking for a commission at sea when we last met. But it never happened. I was running out of funds—I had to join the Morocco campaign. Worst decision ever. I was adjusting a cannon's elevation when some *bobo* with a torch ignited the firing block fuse. He lost his life, and I almost lost my leg. I am lucky, I guess."

Magellan entered the passageway with de Haro and felt the mosaic tiles surrounding him. He had a touch of nostalgia for Lisbon, but these were not the ubiquitous Portuguese blue-and-white scenes of classical myths. Instead, they displayed a full spectrum of colors—red-yellow-green—woven into elaborate geometrical designs. He was not in Portugal, but the large courtyard reminded him of Cabral's courtyard in Santarém with its palms and orange trees. Magellan had the same feeling that that previous encounter engendered. The residence was three stories high, with a balcony surrounding each floor and a sizeable, teardrop-shaped pool in the courtyard's center. The air hung pungent with the scent of jasmine, and for an instant, Magellan imagined he was in heaven. De Haro guided him to a bench by the pool.

"Let's sit and enjoy the last rays of the sun." He motioned to his valet, who stood in the shadow under an arch. "Bring us a good bottle of Portuguese wine and a couple of glasses." De Haro turned to Magellan and said, "We're in the house of Bartolomeu Pinto. He is a countryman of yours, although Jewish. He has lived in Sevilla since John II. As you see, he does well for himself in the ivory and precious stones trade. My brother-in-law, Jakob Fudder, has done business with him for years."

"Christopher," Magellan interrupted. "If you don't mind, I must ask what brings you here? What happened between you and King Manuel?"

De Haro sighed. "Thanks to your cousin, Francisco Serrão, my business with the king dried up. When Captain Antonio de Abreu returned to Goa with two ships laden with spices from Bandu and the Clove Islands, it was a great day for the Portuguese but not so good for me. King Manuel decided he would not need our help financing trade armadas to the newly found Clove Islands. Financing for Brazil, Africa, India—yes—but not the Spice Islands. He tried everything to keep the whereabouts of the islands secret. Even from me. *Especially* from me!

"As you know, there is a whole new world on the other side of the Atlantic. Portugal does its best, but maybe Portugal's best days are past. Your country is barely interested in Brazil, and the little rooster of Lusitania—fuck the natives as it may—doesn't have the population to fill the New World. But Spain does have the interest and people to colonize the New World. Spain's greed and religious fanaticism are ruthless— fueled, guided, and legitimized by Bishop Fonseca and the Church of Rome. You probably know that King Charles is soon to be named Holy Roman Emperor."

"Yes, I know, and it has been a problem," interjected Magellan.

"That may resolve itself to our advantage," de Haro replied." But to answer your question, when Manuel told me the Fudder Group would never finance a Portuguese trade mission beyond the Straits of Malacca, that was it! I left. But tell me *your* story."

"Not much different from yours, but on a smaller scale. On more than one occasion, I presented Manuel with my plan to find the western route to the Spice Islands. He finally told me he wasn't interested. Then he said even if he *were* interested, he would never permit me to command a Portuguese ship."

"What about the letter?" de Haro asked.

"What letter?" Magellan played dumb.

"The letter and maps from your cousin, Serrão! Did you tell King Manuel about the letters?"

"Of course not. Do you think me a fool? He would have killed me. The king and his council already have first-hand knowledge of all the information in Francisco's letters. But they don't know that he wrote me. If they did, they would kill me."

There was silence.

"How do you know about the letter and the map?" Magellan whispered.

"Bishop Fonseca. That's the reason I'm here. We've been waiting for you to return from wherever you have been so we can get this mission going again and put those ships on the seas. Where *have* you been? I hope it's not going to be a problem.

"Portugal—to secure investment money. Charles's exploits in Italy drained the funds for the expedition. I'm sure you know more than me. I was desperate, Christopher. This is my life. It all leads to this: I went to Portugal to seek money from a friend."

"You were successful?"

Magellan nodded.

"Who is your friend? You had better tell me because this complicates things."

"You won't believe it when I tell you. And I am sure you know my friend, or at least know *about* him—it is Dom Pedro Álvares Cabral."

"Really? Ferdinand—I can hardly believe it. I don't know Cabral personally, but I do know he was royally mistreated by Manuel in the same way you and I were. Your story makes some sense. But how is the Great Navigator, Pedro Cabral, your friend?"

"In 1504, before we left for Goa, Francisco and I visited him at his castle in Belmonte. We had time to kill. I wanted to get some advice and maybe even his blessing. Cabral gave us good advice, and some of it saved our lives. In return, we promised to send him yearly reports from the Portuguese Indies."

"Did you?"

"At first. Then we were too caught up in events to take the time."

"Why did you go back to Cabral if you failed to deliver on your end of the bargain?"

"Because I knew Cabral and his friends were investors, and the prospect of gain would prick their interest."

"And did it—?"

"I showed them the letter." Magellan shrugged. "So, they agreed to contribute fifty thousand ducats for twenty percent of my earnings for the first ten years of revenue from the expedition."

"And if you don't return? You left collateral?"

"A copy of the letter and the map—the only things of value I have."

"And they handed you fifty thousand gold ducats? Where is it now?"

"Juan de Aranda and I delivered it to the Torre del Oro."

"I need to ask a question, the answer to which will determine the fate of your plan to find a western route to the Spice Islands. Whose name is on the receipt? In *whose* name is the investment?"

"I deposited the gold in my name only and told the factor it was an inheritance from a Portuguese relative."

"Good."

"My next question: who are these people? Who are *they?* Who are your 'friends?' Who am I potentially in partnership with?"

"Doctor Emanuel Gonçalves, who had been the personal physician of Pedro Cabral for twenty years, and his son Lourenço Gonçalves, who is also a physician. The elder Gonçalves invested with Cabral in the second armada in 1502—the one that discovered Brazil and came back from India with three ships loaded with spices. Everybody made a fortune. Cabral and the Gonçalves family have been investing ever since. I call them 'the Cabral Group,' not to compare them with 'the Fudder Group,' of course, because they are minuscule by comparison, but just to keep it straight. They moved to Santarém from Belmonte and Covilhã to escape the cold winters. Cabral came back from the Indies sick with frequent attacks of malaria. From his look, I don't think he has too many more years to live."

"In your opinion, are the two Doctors Gonçalves Jews?"

"I guess so. Most doctors are, or at least they used to be. I'm sure they are *cristãos-novos.*

"From my knowledge of Portugal," de Haro said, "the area of Beira Baixa, from Castelo Branco north behind Serra da Estrela, including Belmonte to Trás-os-Montes, has always been the Jews' traditional home. As you say, we can assume the Gonçalves are *conversos,* and the Cabral Group has Jewish ties. When the owner of this house, Bartolomeu Pinto, arrives tonight, I will ask if he has heard of the Gonçalves family. In the meantime, the facts are these: fifty thousand gold ducats of the Cabral Group's money sit in your name in the Torre del Oro. We cannot take it out. Never mention the Cabral Group. If I come to an agreement tomorrow with Bishop Fonseca and the Casa, all the funding for this operation will be directly or indirectly from the Fudder Group. Your fifty thousand ducats will be funneled into the Fudder Group funds, probably with no questions asked. More than likely, Cabral and friends have a good reputation, and this I will ascertain from Pinto and his associates. We must deal with respect and delicacy in any case because, as you have revealed, they have a copy of the letter and the map. To compound matters, they are Portuguese, and we already have enough problems. You and Faleiro recruited a forty-percent Portuguese crew, and there is already suspicion of espionage. The only publicly-known investor in this venture outside of the Spanish Crown must be the Fudder Group. If all goes well tomorrow, I will draw up papers to include your fifty thousand ducats as your personal stake in the proceeds to be distributed from the Fudder Group revenue should the mission be successful. Heaven forbid you should perish on the voyage—but I will honor your commitment to your Portuguese backers. You have my personal guarantee, although I will not put it in writing. Cabral and the Gonçalves have a copy of Serrão's letter. Revealing this to the wrong people could make life difficult for all of us, whether you survive the trip or not. With this plan, we can all be victorious. Without it, God help us."

"I trust you with my life, Christopher," said Magellan. "I'm sure Providence has fated great things for us. Look how we've come together! I feel it in every pore of my body. It's a miracle."

"We'll meet at ten o'clock tomorrow at the Casa de Contratación. Where are you staying?"

"Across the canal in Triana, near the wharves."

"Go now, Ferdinand. The sun has set. Get some rest after your journey. Tomorrow will be a big day."

The following day's meeting went well. Christopher de Haro made Bishop Fonseca, who spoke for the Spanish Crown, an offer he couldn't refuse. The Fudder Group would contribute one-quarter of the funds for one-quarter of the profits. In addition, it would lend the Crown three-quarters of the necessary funds at a high interest rate. Magellan transferred and secretly incorporated his contribution from the Cabral Group into the Fudder Group funds without notice or contention.

On August 19, 1519, the Armada de Molucca left Sevilla, sailing down the Guadalquivir River to the Mediterranean harbor of Sanlúcar de Barrameda. Magellan felt in good company in the presence of his brother-in-law, Duarte Barbosa, and João Serrão, his cousin, Francisco's brother. A month later, in Sanlúcar, the *Trinidad*, a caravel commanded by Magellan, set sail westward for points unknown along with four carracks—the *San Antonio*, the *Concepción*, the *Santiago,* and the *Victoria.*

Soon after departure, the flotilla was spotted and chased by a Portuguese squadron sent by King Manuel. Magellan's fleet eluded them.

The trade winds pushed Magellan's small fleet to the South American continent. They avoided Portuguese settlements in Bahia, the continent's northwestern protrusion, and made landfall at what is now Río de Janeiro. They proceeded down the east coast of South America to the southern tip. On March 30, 1520, Magellan found a suitable natural harbor at a place named Puerto San Julián and wintered there. The decision was controversial, and, on the following day, three of the five captains of the fleet conspired to mutiny.

With the help of Duarte Barbosa, Magellan took quick, decisive action. He defeated the mutiny and punished those who had instigated it. The conspirators were beheaded, their bodies quartered, impaled, and gibbeted on the coast. The gibbets were discovered by Sir Francis Drake fifty-eight years later when he wintered at Puerto San Julián before attempting the Strait of Magellan.

Most of the men who had followed the three mutinous captains were essential; they were forgiven. This included Juan Sebastian Elcano, the captain of a merchant vessel out of Sevilla. Elcano had transgressed Spanish law by surrendering a ship to bankers from Genoa in payment for a personal debt. He was pardoned for this act in return for service as a subordinate officer on the Magellan expedition.

For his participation in the mutiny, Magellan sentenced Elcano to five months of hard labor in chains during the harsh winter in Puerto San Julián.

In October 1520, after five months of bitter cold at Puerto San Julián, Magellan sent the *Santiago* down the coast to explore a possible passageway. Short on captains, he pardoned Juan Elcano and put him in charge of the *Santiago*. The carrack was wrecked in a storm along the coast. Elcano and his crew made it back to Puerto San Julián by land.

Soon after that, the four remaining vessels set sail down the coast and eventually found a salty inlet that promised passage to the ocean beyond. Magellan directed two ships to explore the waterway, the *Concepción* and the *San Antonio*. They became separated within the labyrinth of islands in the strait, and Captain Esteban Gomez of the *San Antonio* deserted the expedition. He found his way back to the Atlantic and sailed the *San Antonio* to Spain, where he was promptly imprisoned.

The two remaining ships sailed on through the icy maze of channels. They rejoined the *Concepción,* and the three carracks entered a vast ocean on November 28, 1520. After enduring the tumultuous waters of the strait, Magellan named these relatively calm waters *Mar Pacífico.*

After resupplying and exploring the coast of what is now Chile, they sailed out westward and found a current following the sun. At sea for two months, they finally reached the Mariana Islands on March 6. Two weeks later, they dropped anchor on the Philippine island of Homonhon.

With Enrique, his indentured servant, at his side as a translator, Magellan found his way to the local ruler, Rajah Humabon, on Cebu Island. Following the instructions of Bishop Fonseca, Magellan informed the ruler of the advent of Jesus Christ and of the obligation of the Rajah and his neighboring rulers to become Christian. They would thereby receive salvation and the rewards of trade. If they refused, the pain of destruction would be their fate.

Rajah Humabon gladly consented to be baptized along with the rulers of most of the nearby islands. There was one exception: a ruler known as Datu Lapu-Lapu. Magellan attempted to convert Lapu-Lapu but was rejected. He then led a small, well-armed force of forty-nine men to attack Lapu-Lapu's island. They had planned to use artillery against the houses on the hills above the beach, but because of rocks and a coral reef, Magellan could not bring his cannons to bear on the warriors or their village.

Magellan and his men boarded rowboats, then waded in waist-deep surf for a few hundred yards before reaching the beach. Once on the beach, Magellan ordered some soldiers to ascend a hill and start burning the houses to terrorize the villagers. But this only infuriated them, bringing as many as fifteen hundred people upon the Europeans.

Their armor, muskets, and crossbows were ineffective against the native throng. Some islanders recognized Magellan as the leader and targeted him with their bamboo spears. One native wounded Magellan in the face and was immediately impaled on the captain's spear, but he could not withdraw it from the body. Leaving the weapon in the man's body, Magellan unsheathed his sword, but another bamboo spear wounded him in the arm. Sensing the captain's vulnerability, the aroused mob closed in with cutlasses. Little of Ferdinand Magellan's body remained intact. What did remain was kept as a trophy by Datu Lapu-Lapu. Lapu-Lapu was offered a generous ransom of copper and iron for Magellan's parts, but he refused.

With their leader gone, the expedition fell into disarray. The surviving members could not decide who should succeed Magellan. They finally elected a joint command—Duarte Barbosa and João Serrão. Magellan had held both in high esteem, and they were intensely loyal to him. However, four days later, both Barbosa and Serrão were murdered in a massacre at a feast hosted by Rajah Humabon, the Christianized chief they believed was their ally.

After this treachery, the expedition was listless and virtually leaderless for the next six months. The casualties suffered in the Philippines left too few seamen to sail three ships. They abandoned and burned the *Concepción*, leaving the *Trinidad* and the *Victoria*. Distracted and disoriented, the remaining two vessels drifted due south toward the armada's official destination—the Moluccan Islands, otherwise known as the Spice Islands.

Juan Sebastian Elcano emerged as the most qualified to lead the mission. He was eventually recognized as the expedition's captain. On November 6, 1521, almost a year after traversing the Strait of Magellan, the two ships anchored in the Spice Islands with a remaining crew of 115.

Aware of the Portuguese trade monopoly with the Sultan of Ternate, they found their way to the port of his rival, the Sultan of Tidore. They learned that Francisco Serrão, of whom Magellan had much to say, had mysteriously died on the neighboring island of Ternate about the same time that Magellan was slain. Rumors said Serrão's own patron, the Sultan of Ternate, had poisoned him.

In Tidore, Elcano reprovisioned the two vessels and filled their holds with cinnamon and clove. On departing Tidore, the *Trinidad* developed an irreparable leak. João Carvalho, captain of the *Trinidad*, remained aboard with fifty-two seamen, hoping to find a port to repair the vessel before sailing back across the Pacific to Spain. The Portuguese eventually captured them and destroyed the *Trinidad*.

Elcano and the carrack *Victoria* continued eastward through the Strait of Malacca, past Ceylon and the tip of India, then crossed the Indian Ocean and rounded the Cape of Good Hope. Proceeding up the west coast of Africa, the *Victoria* reached the Portuguese Island of Cabo Verde in July 1522. On the voyage from the Spice Islands, twenty men died of starvation. The vessel was overweight with twenty-six tons of cinnamon and clove, and Elcano chose to leave thirteen crewmen in Cabo Verde to lighten the weight.

The *Victoria* arrived in Sanlúcar de Barrameda, Spain, on September 6, 1522, almost exactly three years from the expedition's departure. Juan Sebastian Elcano had become the first man known to circumnavigate the globe. Ferdinand Magellan had accomplished his dream of finding the westward route to the Spice Islands.

It is not known whether the Great Navigator and the Cabral Group were ever made whole from the venture.

Chapter 7

Upon the Rock of Endovélico

On the eastern slope of Serra da Estrela, near Belmonte, Portugal Summer 1563 and 1564

For Ruy and Davide, who grew up in the shadow of Serra da Estrela, the highlight of the summer was accompanying Dom Elias to the high pastures of Star Mountain to tend sheep. In the summers when the boys were sixteen and seventeen—before they went off to the university—the two tended the sheep alone.

During their first summer as shepherds, the two migrated with the flock to various pastures up and down the mountainside. On the last week of summer, bored with their routine, the two found new pasture on the slopes beyond Valhelhas, dominated by an extraordinary boulder. From their perch atop the monolith, they could look south, down upon lush green fields, where they nourished the sheep. From the rock's other side, they looked down upon a spring bubbling out from the base of the massive stone. Lower, the spring became a creek. The boys often rested at a pond a few hundred feet below the rock, where they bathed and caught trout.

From atop the prominence, one could trace the outline of the long hill upon which Belmonte sat on a clear day. At night, they could make out the flickering hearth lights of the town. They were as familiar with Belmonte as they were with their hometown of Covilhã. Seeing Belmonte and Centum Cellas in the distance gave the boys a connected feeling, which countered the eeriness of the place they had discovered.

The boys knew they were not the first to appreciate the magnificent sarsen, which was the size of a two-story house. A spiral staircase carved in granite circled to the top, which was flat and smooth. The top took an oval shape, six paces long and four paces wide. In the oval's center, two graves had been carved into the rock, each the size of a man. However, on closer inspection, they were more like sunken beds less than a foot deep. The boys treated the trenches as beds rather than tombs and lined them with straw. They found that the rock radiated warmth on cool mountainside nights, and their cradles shielded them from strong winds.

After the first week of sleeping on the rock, the boys noticed their dreams were more vivid than usual. When they awoke with the rising sun at their feet, they found themselves comparing dreams as if competing to see whose was the most interesting.

After returning with the flocks to Belmonte one late summer day, Davide told his father they had camped at a great rock with a staircase to the top. On the smooth surface, they'd slept in two coffin-shaped depressions chiseled out of the granite.

Rabbi Elias said they'd found the place some people on the mountain called the "Sanctuary of Endovélico."

Davide questioned him further.

"Endovélico was the chief god of the Lusitanians, the people who occupied the land before the coming of the Romans. Most of us have Lusitanian blood running through our veins. Endovélico's sanctuaries were where pilgrims came to be healed and have their dreams interpreted."

"Were the first Lusitanians giants?" Davide inquired. "Those who built the stone circles and dolmens—who balanced those huge stones on top?"

"No, Davide. When the Romans came, they found the Lusitanians to be the size of you and me. The only difference between the Lusitanians and the other tribes in Iberia was that the Lusitanians were impossible to tame. But they weren't any bigger."

"Then who built the sanctuaries of Endovélico? The circles of standing stones and the stone walls that fit so perfectly?"

"That is a great mystery."

"Do you think the same people who built the Sanctuary of Endovélico also built the Centum Cellas?"

"Good question. I believe that Centum Cellas was a like Roman hotel on the road halfway between Portuguese Braga and Spanish Mérida. I know it has also been a synagogue. The Sanctuary of Endovélico, on the mountainside, was there before the Romans, so yes, the Lusitanians could have built it.

"Pai, do you think harm will come to us if we make our camp on the Rock of Endovélico?"

Elias replied, "If you treat the sanctuary with the respect it once enjoyed and keep Yahweh in your prayers and hearts, you will not be harmed. You may even benefit from the spirit that resides there."

At the beginning of the following summer, Davide and Ruy used the Sanctuary of Endovélico as a base for transhumance. Their imagination and storytelling skills improved over the winter months, and, for young fellows still in their late teens, their abilities were impressive. But they still felt no presence of a supernatural being until the night of the summer solstice, when something strange happened.

In the early evening, the boys sensed a thundershower approaching. They gathered up dry organic matter for fresh mattresses for their coffin beds. Then they secured a large, oiled tarpaulin to poles they had erected over their beds, creating a tent with open sides. A light rain soon fell, followed by thunder and lightning from the south along the ridge of the mountains. Lightning suddenly struck with a jolt that seemed to hit the rock itself. White light lit the entire landscape as the boys lay wide-eyed. They sat up momentarily, relieved to be alive, before lying back down in their beds.

"The earth smells alive," Ruy said.

Davide agreed, but instead of checking on the sheep, as it was his turn, he rolled over in the straw and slipped into a sleep from which he did not awaken until sunrise. When he did, he sat up, rubbed his eyes, and shook Ruy. "I saw him!" Davide exclaimed.

"Who?" Ruy asked.

"Endovélico! He came to me and called me by name, just like he did with Abraham. I said, 'Here am I,' and he appeared. He was muscular, bronzed like a Greek or Roman god, but older and—"

Ruy interrupted. "Had curly white hair and a short white beard and a kindly face and—?"

"Don't mock me," Davide protested.

"I'm not," Ruy said in wonderment. "I saw him myself."

"What did he tell you?"

"He said he enjoyed listening to the stories we cooked up in this holy place, and he had a special gift for each of us—traveling in time. I told Endovélico that was great because we were both about to leave for the university . . . the future would be good to know as we set out toward our destinies."

"Yes," Davide said.

"The Angel called me by name. He said, "Ruy, I can see the most probable future for you and Davide. But it is one of many futures, and each destiny can be changed depending on how strong or weak, how noble or ignoble you are at any one point in time." Ruy continued. "Endovélico said, 'If I gave you too many clues, you might be frightened into a premature death or become too complacent to fulfill your destiny. On the other hand, as you lead your life, forge ahead into the unknown. You will not be alone. We will give you signs. If you make efforts for us, we will guide you in our ways.'"

Davide asked, "What about the gift that involves time travel?"

"Endovélico said the future is insecure, but the past is done. For each of us, the gift will be to choose a mystery in the past. Then he will come when we are asleep and take us back in time, so we can learn a truth that will help us through life."

Davide pondered what Ruy said. "I know what I'm going to ask. I've been thinking about it for years—not even my father can shed light on it."

"What?" Ruy asked.

"I won't tell you until Endovélico agrees to take me there," Davide replied.

Fragas de Panois (Sanctuary of Panoias) near Vila Real, Portugal.
Pre-Roman to the 3rd Century, attributed to the Lapiteas people.

CHAPTER 8

DAVIDE'S DREAM; FIELDS OF PLENTY

Nile Valley, Egypt
1665 BCE

As the summer sun passed over the mountain and darkness settled in, Ruy left Davide alone to fall asleep in his rock-bed without their normal end-of-day chat.

Entering the dream world, Davide found himself surrounded by chirping birds celebrating the dawn of a new day. He rubbed his eyes and realized he was atop a mountain, but it wasn't Star Mountain. To the east, in the glare of the rising sun, the ruins of a Moorish castle stood high upon a rugged plateau. He could hear and see the great ocean to the west for the first time. He heard a rustling from below. The birds flew off, and there was silence.

Endovélico made his presence known as he pulled himself onto the slab of rock where Davide sat. He was hardly recognizable from Davide's dream. Endovélico was now clean-shaven and barely dressed, wearing a starched white pleated cotton tunic. Covering his white hair was a headdress in the style of a Pharoah's nemes, descending behind his ears and over his shoulders. He strutted on the rock with a devilish smile, examining Davide from head to foot with the same penetrating, sparkling eyes he'd seen in the dream.

"Where am I?" Davide asked.

"On the roof of a dolmen on top of Sintra Mountain. Look west; you can make out the Atlantic. Look north, where you can see the village of Sintra waking up. Look south, and you can see smoke from the cookeries of Cascais and Lisbon beyond that, reaching up to greet the morning sun."

"But *why* are we here?" asked Davide.

"I like this place. And it is a good place for you to learn to fly."

"I can't fly, Dom Endovélico. I'm human. I have no wings."

"How did you get on this mountain in the first place?"

"I don't know."

"It's because you are in the dream world, Davide, where anything is possible with the correct knowledge. Considering where we are going, you are overdressed in your woolens."

"How is that, Lord Endovélico? I haven't yet told you where I want to go."

"True, but I know what is on your mind. I, too, want to see the beauty of Joseph again."

"My father told me about it—that Shekinah made him beautiful . . . or was Shekinah attached to him *because* of his beauty?"

"What did your father teach you about the Shekinah?" Endovélico asked.

"He said it was the fertile moon energy of the Holy Land—it acts like a female."

"Not bad," Endovélico said. "What else did he teach you?"

"He said when the Shekinah mated with the sun, or a man like the sun, everything flourishes. He said that the Shekinah was a presence. She dwelt with Rachel, who was in love with Jacob. Jacob was the sun for Rachel's moon." My father told me that when Rachel died, the Shekinah, abhorring sadness, began to move away from the family of Jacob and his sons. But the Shekinah was particularly attracted to Joseph, Rachel's oldest son. When Joseph's brothers sold him into slavery, he was taken into Egypt, and the Shekinah followed him. She dwelt in Egypt, and the beautiful Joseph became her sun. Eventually, everything flourished. That's what I want to see—everything Joseph did to make Egypt flourish."

"Very well. That is a noble request. You shall have your wish." Endovélico asked Davide if he had ever flown like a bird in his dreams. Davide shook his head.

In a soft, penetrating voice, Endovélico urged Davide to breathe deeply and imagine himself a crow. Davide knew he was already dreaming—the Earth Spirit was now asking him to dream within a dream. Davide tried to visualize himself as a bird instead of a human, and something deep inside urged him to comply. Davide continued breathing and imagining himself as a crow as Endovélico put his arm over Davide's shoulders. Davide realized that his arm was now a wing; its soft, black feathers bore the smell of pine and eucalyptus. The warm wing rubbed his back, and it felt good—so good and peaceful that sleep began to overcome his consciousness. A sudden blow to the small of Davide's back woke him, and he saw his thighs had become sinewy straws with black feathers, his feet spindly, scaly phalanges with spikey claws. Something pulled him by the neck and lifted him off the ground. Endovélico changed him into a crow and pulled him through the air on a long, thin leash. Initially terrified, Davide overcame his fear and became accustomed to flying. Together, he and Endovélico flew over the mountain and down into a vast green plain.

They flew a few miles southeast toward Lisbon, which was just waking up. With Davide still leashed, Endovélico coaxed him through a few routines of swooping and stalling, turning and diving until a sense of exhilaration overcame his fears, at which point the leash disappeared.

With Davide in pursuit, Endovélico landed on a substantial hill overlooking Lisbon. A Roman aqueduct transported water down the hill into the city. Endovélico asked Davide if he had ever been to Lisbon. He replied he had not. They flew to another side of the hill, and the Earth Spirit said, "Look down there, where the water meets the land. See the white marble tower jutting into the water? It's more than a league. Can you see it with your keen crow's eyes?"

"I see it."

"That's the Torre de Belém. King Manuel built it fifty years ago to celebrate the great voyages of discovery. We'll begin your voyage of discovery from there, but you will have to fly yourself down. Are you ready?"

"Let me make a few practice flights around the top of this hill, Dom Endovélico."

"We have all the time in the world. We are going back 3,230 years—we can afford another fifteen minutes . . . but don't indulge your fears. We have important things to do!"

Davide practiced flapping his wings and launching himself into a current of wind that came to kiss the hilltop. He flew with it, accelerating, then turning into the wind to gain lift. He circled the hill five times before he heard Endovélico's voice in his head, saying, "enough."

They glided down the hill over rows of beautiful houses and came to rest on the roof of a monastery not far from the river. Looking toward the waters of the Tejo, a forest of masts from hundreds of caravels and naus crowded the harbor. He had never seen so many vessels—only drawings of boats like these. In the middle stood the gleaming white marble Torre de Belém.

They flew to the tower and landed on its flat square roof. Endovélico chased away the other crows and seagulls clustered on the tower's roof to give them privacy before their takeoff into time.

Davide, now proud of his transformation, strutted across the square of the roof as if on promenade. He then jumped onto the arrowhead peak of a parapet. Looking down over the hundreds of ships at the docks, he thought about all the brave souls crewing those ships, discovering new worlds. His little black chest was bursting with Portuguese pride.

Endovélico's patience was at an end. He flew to the parapet where Davide perched and knocked him into the air. Disoriented, Davide found his wings, so to speak, slightly before he would have hit the surface of the Río Tejo. But fly he did, with the wings of the Earth Spirit lifting him up over the waters.

They flew high, higher than ordinary birds, and up above the few clouds that had gathered on the coast of Portugal. They reached an altitude where Davide could see the southwest tip of the country to the place called Sagres, where old Prince Henry the Navigator built his school. But they did not go there. Instead, they flew downhill at high speed, making a beeline across the provinces of Alentejo and Andalusia, heading straight for the Rock of Gibraltar. Davide thought Endovélico would stop there, but he didn't. They flew across the Strait into Africa and over the Portuguese enclave of Ceuta. They perched on the wall of a small fort built at the tip of the Almina peninsula, where Ceuta is located.

"Why are we stopping here?" Davide asked.

"Because I want to see something," Endovélico replied.

As the Earth Spirit spoke, he pointed his wing toward a merchant ship moving through the water under full sail.

As they approached the vessel, Davide read the name of the ship painted on her stern—*Rainha de Alcântara*. He repeated the name. Endovélico's voice said, "Remember that name." Davide wondered why.

If they were on their way to Egypt three thousand years in the past, why does Endovélico want him to remember the name of a Portuguese vessel off the coast of Morocco? The two birds landed on the bowsprit and watched the crew merrily go about their business. The men were a mixture of Portuguese and Moors. A middle-aged woman stood at the wheel with a turbaned man by her side, conferring with her while joking and shouting orders to the crew.

Davide heard Endovélico's voice again. "That's enough. Time to go."

With that, the Earth Spirit lifted off. Davide pursued him toward the sun at an accelerating velocity. They flew so fast, Davide noticed, that they lost their corvine forms and became iridescent beams of light. Halfway to the sun, they turned back toward Earth at an even greater speed. Approaching the blue planet, they circled the globe in a clockwise direction countless times but required little time.

They slowed over the Arabian Peninsula and the Red Sea. Veering north, they flew up the Gulf of Suez, then, decelerating, shifted once more into the shape of crows. Davide could make out the long green Nile in the distance as it snaked across the landscape, its wide delta taking the appearance of the head of a cobra.

Endovélico turned toward Davide and said, "Since we're in Egypt, you must see the Great Pyramid."

They flew to the west bank of the green delta where, across from a city, stood a sparkling white edifice so bright it was like looking at the sun in a mirror.

Endovélico wheeled up in flight, stalling with his broad wings spread, and gazed down upon the colossal structure in awe. "It's the Great Pyramid of Khafre. Follow me," he said to Davide, who was in close pursuit.

The two glided across the cloudless sky and came to rest on the structure's apex. The blocks at the base were the size of oxcarts. There were thousands upon thousands of such blocks, perfectly cut and positioned. All four sides of the pyramid were clad in white limestone and marble sheets, so dazzling Davide could hardly bear to look at them. He thought that no people could have made this without help from somewhere else. Endovélico must have read his thoughts. "I'll show you a project not as perfect but definitely man-made and more useful to the people," he said. "Come, it's less than an hour's flight upriver."

They followed the Nile, bordered on both sides by lush green fields. They then veered southwest, crossing from fertility into a desert of scrub and sand.

Within minutes, they reached their destination and landed on a palm tree. Below, a thousand men were digging a wide canal. "It's nearly finished," Endovélico said.

The canal was a hundred yards wide and eight miles in length, linking a small branch of the Nile with a town called Faiyum clustered around an oasis. West of Faiyum was a significant depression in the sand, which Endovélico said would soon become a lake. He said the last stage of constructing the canal was linking it with the river branch—that event was only days away.

The birds flew to within a few yards of the canal dig. Standing in a horse-drawn chariot, a young man barked orders to a host of surveyors with measuring sticks. The charioteer dressed differently than those he commanded. His head-covering was the same, but in place of a loose white cotton shirt and pleated skirt, he wore a short, striped robe of many colors and designs.

"There's your Joseph," Endovélico said. "He is, in modern parlance, a hydraulic engineer. But come now. There is plenty of time for everything you need to see. Let's bathe in the cool Nile and rest in the shade."

The next day Davide wanted to explore the length of the canal's waterless bed, only yards from connecting with the river. Flying from the river west toward the oasis, Davide was diverted halfway by another sight that genuinely astonished him. Flying high with Endovélico, Davide looked down on a barren high plateau a half-mile from the dry canal. He saw what appeared to be an enormous square nest with thousands of brown-skinned ants scurrying in and out of hundreds of chambers. The two crows zoomed down and perched on a wall of the new construction.

"What is this?" Davide asked Endovélico.

"It's one of the storehouses Joseph is building—the one Herodotus referred to centuries later as 'The Labyrinth.' They've already built the basement and first floor. You're seeing the second-floor rooms without roofs. Herodotus, a friend of mine, was the first historian of modern times. He described the building in about 600 BC when I was flourishing in Lusitania. Are you interested to hear what he wrote a thousand years after it was built?"

"Of course, Dom Endovélico! But where are the books?"

"The books are in a special library—a library for all time. Give me a minute. I will go there and retrieve Herodotus's very words."

"Yes, sir. I am not going anywhere."

Endovélico disappeared. After a moment of silence, he returned to the scene and said, "This is the paragraph I was seeking. Listen: 'I, myself have seen it, and indeed no words can tell its wonders. . . . Though the pyramids were greater than words can tell, and each one of them a match for many great monuments built by the Greeks, this maze surpasses even the pyramids. It has twelve roofed courts, with doors over against each other. Six face north and six face south, in two continuous lines, all within one outer wall. There are double sets of chambers, three thousand altogether, fifteen hundred above, and the same number underground.'"

"That's amazing!" Davide exclaimed. "It must be the largest building ever built."

"Perhaps."

"It must be three hundred yards square. There are cities smaller than that."

"You are impressed," the Earth Spirit asserted. "The labyrinth is one of the three storehouses that Vizier Joseph built. There was one in the delta and one at Thebes in Upper Egypt. This labyrinth will serve the Middle Kingdom of twelve provinces, and it is the largest storehouse. To this day, that canal is known as *Bahr Yussef*—the Waterway of Joseph. Now that you have seen what Joseph did, what more do you want to see?"

"I'd like to see Vizier Joseph planning and negotiating with the pharaoh," said Davide.

"We will have to stay longer. Joseph left today for the capital at Itjtawy to confer with Pharaoh Amenemhat. The capital is twenty leagues downriver near the Great Pyramid. The Nile is rising now, the flood is coming, and the waters are swift. Joseph's boat will arrive at the pharaoh's palace tomorrow morning. We will rest tonight and fly in the morning."

The following morning, the two crows perched on an open windowsill in the pharaoh's meeting chamber. Amenemhat III was informing his vizier that he had just received the report from Semna Gorge, a thousand miles upriver at the Second Cataract of the Nile. The pharaoh told Joseph the river had reached its watermark of fifty-six degrees above low water level ten days ago.

Joseph interrupted him.

"That means two things. First, we will have another splendid flood, reaching new land and draining in time to plant. It also means I must get to the canal immediately and finish it by the time the floodwaters get here within the week. I want the Oasis of Faiyum to become a lake. Your Majesty, I will schedule chariots to take me back to the job site at full gallop if you permit me. We have only thirty cubits more to dig before meeting the river."

"Wait, Joseph. Tell me again, how many more years can we count on these wonderful floods, and what is the status of the Great Storehouse?"

"My Lord, all the signs tell me that we will have good floods for the next twelve or thirteen years."

"And then what?" Amenemhat calmly asked.

"Then, for the same number of years, we will have devastating floods that will cover the fields year-round and prevent planting. Your Majesty, I do believe that between your dreams, my prescience, our observations, and reasoning, we'll be able to cultivate around the new lake formed by the canal. The canal will divert much water away from Middle Egypt and the delta when the terrible floods come. The fields of Upper Egypt may be underwater, but our storehouses will be full. No one will starve, and you will be omnipotent in all of Egypt."

"And the storehouse?"

"We lack only roofs. Roofs over fifteen hundred rooms, Your Majesty. When we finish digging the canal, we'll direct all the laborers to the storehouse to help the thousand workers we have there now. By the next harvest, we'll begin filling the storehouse. We will charge all the cultivators one-fifth of their produce and repay them when the bad times come. The big estates that laugh at us now and refuse to pay will come begging for our grain. We will sell them grain and buy their flood land for a pittance, and you shall own all of Egypt."

Amenemhat III seemed pleased. He dismissed his vizier and encouraged him to get back if he wanted to fish in the desert lake next year.

Vizier Joseph returned to Hawara, the storehouse construction site, in time to witness nature cooperating with the first phase of the Great

Plan he had worked out with the pharaoh. The canal crews were within a few yards of the dead-end branch of the Nile, which curiously paralleled the mighty river on its western side for more than two hundred miles from Upper Egypt to Hawara.

Endovélico explained that for the past two years, Joseph observed the water level of the branch rising dramatically just before the annual flood. The Oasis of Faiyum, a waterhole in a depression in the desert, was only about ten miles west of the end of the river branch. Joseph reasoned that once upon a time, there had been a connection between the branch and the oasis. He thought to restore that connection—turning the oasis into a lake and providing water to irrigate the thousands of acres surrounding it.

In addition, Joseph knew that the current Nile floods were more significant than average and near-perfect, fertilizing far more land and draining in time for fall planting. But if, as he had seen in his visions, the floods should increase beyond "perfect" floods, then the fields would not drain in time for proper planting, and the harvests would be poor.

Joseph was sure his Great Plan was right, and he conveyed his confidence to his friend and sovereign, Amenemhat III. All was going according to plan, but Joseph anticipated a problematic issue that nagged him and would not let him rest. Would he have political problems sustaining faith in the Great Plan, with its storehouses and taxation, for twelve to thirteen years of plenty? He thought it was long to buttress belief and maintain the fear of overwhelming floods. If the canal idea worked, it would produce immediate results and confirm Joseph's long-term plan. He was eager to return to Harawa, where his plan would jump from theory to practice, from dream to reality.

At the urging of his project manager, Joseph arrived at the terminus of the canal dig in time for the first trickle of water to furrow its way across the few yards of dirt separating the swollen branch from the empty canal. Shovelers initially helped the water find its way. Trickles became streams within a few minutes, and streams erupted into torrents. It was all the diggers could do to pull their laughing comrades out of the mud before a wall of water broke through and pushed into the canal bed. Within an hour, the river branch had extended its reach and flow to the oasis, turning it from a pond to a growing lake.

Endovélico explained it to Davide as they perched together on a nearby palm.

"Do you need to see any more of what Joseph did?" asked the Earth Spirit.

"No, sir," Davide replied. "I have seen how Yahweh worked through Joseph. Yahweh, ages ago, must have planned this; creating the river branch and the oasis, and leaving it up to Joseph to connect them."

Endovélico looked at Davide with an enigmatic smile. "If you are ready, then let's fly!"

The shaman took off, obliging Davide to follow. Again, they flew toward the sun. Halfway there, they reversed course and approached the planet at blinding speed. They circled the Earth counterclockwise thousands of times before alighting on the Rock of Endovélico. The Earth Spirit helped Davide into his bed and sang a soft lullaby, putting the dreaming Davide into another state.

Davide awoke at daybreak and wasted no time rousing Ruy. He informed Ruy that the patriarch Joseph was more like an engineer than a saint. He designed canals and vast storehouses.

"Was he as beautiful as they say?" Ruy asked.

"He wasn't ugly, but he wasn't like anyone else in Egypt that I saw."

CHAPTER 9

RUY'S DREAM;
THE DISCOVERY OF PRESTER JOHN

Covilhã, Portugal
Ethiopia
1477-1536

Ruy contemplated what Davide told him about his dream all day. While sitting together atop the rock early that evening, Ruy arrived at a determination.

"I know where I want to go, but I'm having trouble deciding which of my heroes I want to visit. On the one hand, there is my great uncle, Afonso da Paiva. On the other, there is Pero da Covilhã. King John II commissioned both to go together to find the route to India and find the kingdom of Prester John in Africa. My uncle's story is short—he disappeared in Africa, probably took ill, and died alone his first year there. Pero's story is longer, and I remember every tale ever told in town about Pero da Covilhã. To my father's dismay, I swore that I would model my life after him because, you know, he wants me to be a physician like himself. I now think if I choose to visit Pero da Covilhã, I'll also learn about my great uncle's fate. I think that is what I'll do."

Darkness had settled over the mountain, and the moon shone down on Belmonte. Ruy lay down on a bed of fresh straw in his rock-chiseled tomb.

"Relax and get ready for the trip of your life," Davide said.

Ruy stirred with the crow of a rooster. It was dark, but embers from the night's fire were still glowing. He looked over to the coffin beside him, expecting to see Davide, but there was Endovélico. He was supine but had risen on his elbows and was watching Ruy. He was dressed like a Roman centurion with curly white hair and a beard.

"Good morning, Ruy."

"Good morning, sir."

"It is almost dawn. We should be on our way."

"Where to, my Lord?"

"I was eavesdropping on your conversation last night, and I understand you want to investigate the life of Pero da Covilhã. Is that right?"

"Yes, sir."

"What an excellent choice, Ruy Gonçalves, but have you not considered the implications, intimations, and preparations?"

"What do you mean, Lord Endovélico?"

"I mean that Davide's request to visit Joseph was straightforward and without complication. That was 3,230 years in the past. We saw what Joseph did and began to understand his mark on the course of history. We flew back.

Pero da Covilhã died thirty years ago. His mark is too fresh to be understood as history, and even *he* understood his role only late in life. His life was the culmination of centuries of aspiration. It ended with the disappointment of missed opportunity and moral failure—not a failure on the part of Pero—but the culture of which he was the vanguard."

"Dom Endovélico, I don't understand."

"Of course, you don't. That's why you need some education."

"Yes, sir," Ruy replied, watching the Earth Spirit gaze off into a distant time.

"Well, then." Endovélico returned his eyes to Ruy. "First, we must teach you to transform yourself into a bird so we can fly. The truth is that I'm tired of being a crow. If you agree, let's become falcons. Does that suit you?"

"Of course, sir," replied Ruy with strange apprehension.

"Our first destination will be your hometown, Covilhã. Look there." He pointed to the distant southeastern horizon. With our falcon eyes from this rock, we see the morning cookfires in Covilhã. But to get there, we will have to fly halfway to the sun and back in time eighty-eight years to the year 1477. Are you ready?"

"Yes, sir."

"Then stand up. Put this feathered cape over your shoulders and adjust to how it feels."

To Ruy, the cape felt warm and light. There were different colors of brown, yellow, and white. Next, Ruy felt Endovélico standing behind him—directly behind him. He could feel the Spirit's knees, thighs, chest, and even heartbeat. Distracted by the sensations, he had not noticed Endovélico's arms had become wings and were wrapping around him from behind. He felt encapsulated by the warmth of a falcon's essence. Ruy cranked his head around to glimpse Endovélico. He saw a large falcon's head with a sharp black beak and shining black eyes. Just as he turned away, digesting what he had seen, Ruy felt a sharp blow to his back where the falcon's beak hammered him. Endovélico then opened his wings, and Ruy emerged from the warm cocoon of feathers as a falcon himself.

Because falcons are more courageous than crows, it did not take Ruy much time to master the rudiments of flying. Soon they lifted themselves from the rock, bound for the rising sun. With ever-increasing velocity, they flew higher and farther. Soon they were over Greece and Turkey, then beyond the pull of the earth. Halfway to the sun, they reversed course and returned with greater momentum toward the planet to circle the globe as energy beams that slowed over the North Atlantic and headed for the Iberian Peninsula. Approaching land, they passed through a bank of clouds that mirrored the forested coast of Galicia. The long ridge of Serra da Estrela came into view. Midway down the mountain range, they crested the ridge and soared down into the town of Covilhã in the year 1477. They landed on a wall at the old tavern by the Chicken Fountain near the market. It was a cold, blustery winter afternoon. Endovélico suggested they morph into mice and find their way inside the tavern to warm themselves.

"How do I change from a falcon to a mouse?" Ruy asked. But just as his words echoed in Ruy's regal raptor head, Endovélico transformed into an inconspicuous brown mouse.

The shaman responded, "How can you imagine a falcon can speak Portuguese? Don't argue—you can do it if you combine your imagination and your will. Follow me. Be like I am, a little tit-mouse!"

Ruy looked down at the mouse nibbling on his left paw and claw. The sight felt so bizarre that Ruy ceded all reason to his imagination. He thought and willed himself to be a mouse, and he was. The two scurried through a crack in the foundation and found a warm place in a stack of firewood.

Three young men about the age of Ruy entered the tavern and sat at a table near the fireplace. Endovélico's voice whispered in Ruy's head, "João Pero is the one with long black hair and no hat. His friends have just signed on at one of the wool factories in town. But spinning and weaving are not for João Pero. Listen. Ruy, focus! You have the hearing of a falcon—more than that, you can hear João Pero's thoughts as he muses to himself." And as Endovélico said, the man's thoughts came to Ruy.

How can I stay in this place, day after day, when the whole world calls me? Am I not good with languages and strangers? I could run a tavern like this. No—not stuck in one place. A traveling barber? No—too poor. A shepherd? No—done that. Free, but too much solitude. A pick-pocket? No—not around here. Perhaps in Porto or Lisbon, if I am desperate. A drover? Too much hard work and not enough pay. A traveling merchant? *Yes!* That's it! Now, if I only had something to sell. . . .

João began picturing himself as a traveling merchant with a horse and a heaping cart of cloth. Maybe on the road to Lisbon or Santarém or . . . Viseu. He sang an old ditty about walking to the city of Viseu to himself.

Ando eu, ando eu no caminho a Viseu. I am walking, I am walking on the road to Viseu. Yes, that's it, he thought. That's my goal—a cart, a horse, some capital. I must set my mind to that and look for a partner, an investor. Now I am a man with a plan. I feel lucky!

With the last few coins in his pocket, João ordered a round of grog for his friends. His friends, having more coins in their pockets than João, ordered more drinks. They sang songs, and João Pero led them in a sloppy but enthusiastic rendition of *Ando eu a Viseu.*

There was a rumble outside—mules and horses pulling carts across the cobblestones. In the fading light of the winter sunset, the boys walked out to see what the cold had brought to town. A nobleman from Spain directed his two servants with an Andalusian accent. João guessed he was from Sevilla.

Still feeling lucky with nothing to lose, João Pero ambled over to the Spaniard and, in his best Andalusian accent, said, "Welcome to my town of Covilhã, *señor*. May I be of assistance to you? My name is Pero."

Taken by surprise but impressed by the unsolicited offer from the forward youth, the Spaniard replied in jest, "*Pero?* What kind of name is that? In my country, it means 'dog' or 'but.' You're obviously not a dog, so 'Pero,' in Portuguese, must be short for 'Pedro.' What is your family name?"

"*Señor*, my name is Covilhã. I *am* Covilhã—my family founded this town. I am Pero da Covilhã."

Before the nobleman could begin taking him seriously, João Pero's companions burst into laughter. The Spaniard laughed to show that the joke was not on him but that he admired the young man, Pero da Covilhã, for his cheekiness.

"My name *is* Pero da Covilhã, and that is the truth!" The Spaniard laughed again and further engaged Pero's quick wit.

Don Juan de Guzman was looking for young men with quick, agile minds. His brother, the Duke of Medina-Sidonia and ruler of Sevilla, was the most wealthy and powerful noble. Don Juan crossed the border into Portugal to buy roll goods at the famous wool market in Covilhã for re-outfitting the many dependents on his estate. João Pero helped him purchase wool. De Guzman was always looking for young talent to serve in his and his brother's various campaigns. Pero da Covilhã seemed to fit the bill, so Don Juan invited him to serve in his household in Sevilla. Pero accepted. The next day, on a borrowed horse, Pero rode off with Juan de Guzman and his party, eager to press ahead after his fortune in the wider world.

The mice transformed into falcons again. With the Earth Spirit leading, they landed on a high parapet at the Cabral Castle in Belmonte after a few minutes of flight. It was still the winter of 1477. Two strangely familiar boys were standing at the parapet throwing stones at a gaggle of ducks on the ground below. The boys saw the two falcons and took aim. Ruy heard Endovélico laughing as he tugged at Ruy's feathers. The falcons took off and buzzed the boys on the parapet, causing them to take shelter. The falcons then flew west over the ruin of Centum Cellas and toward the mountain range, landing minutes later on the Rock of Endovélico.

"What was that all about?" Ruy asked.

"Didn't you recognize them?"

"I don't think so."

"That was your grandfather, Emanuel, and the Great Navigator, Pedro Álvares Cabral. Remember, it is 1477. They're both ten years old."

"That explains why Davide is not here on the rock."

Endovélico suggested they shift back into human form, so they did.

"Without sounding impertinent, Sr. Endovélico, what was the point of going to Belmonte Castle to see my grandfather and Cabral as boys?" Ruy asked.

"I wanted to give you a point of reference for your history. Your request that I show you the reality of Pero da Covilhã and his partner Afonso da Paiva, your uncle, involves more than you can imagine. In the first place, the life of João Pero, a Gypsy from Covilhã, reflects both the rise and the fall of the Portuguese Empire. It is the best of stories, but even I don't have the time or patience to fly all over creation to show you Pero da Covilhã's reality. You will have to be content with my account of his life from the Akashic Records. That will save a lot of time. If you listen closely, you will *see* what took place with your imagination. At the end of his life, when Dom Pero is on his death bed, we will fly to the kingdom of Prester John and witness his passing."

Ruy agreed with Endovélico's proposal. The Earth-Healer suggested that Ruy retire for the night and resume the story on the following nights.

Ruy lay in his rock-bed and awoke at the break of dawn. He related the wonders he'd experienced to Davide and, during the day, prepared himself for the night to come.

The splendors of Sevilla bedazzled Pero. His assignment was the armory in the palace estate of Don Juan de Guzman, where he oiled and maintained the armor and cloth-mail and kept the blades razor-sharp. Daily lessons with the Master-at-Arms made him an excellent swordsman, thrusting and parrying as if his life depended on it. His newly acquired skills paid off—he accompanied Don Juan on many trade missions, during which swordplay against highwaymen was a common occurrence on the lonely forest trails.

Pero da Covilhã was also a social creature. He used his social skills to acquire helpful knowledge. In his free time, he roamed the great city. In the Jewish Quarter's Alcázar Wall, Pero attracted a young beauty and made friends with her father, an apothecary. From him, Pero learned of the medicinal properties of herbs and the making of magical potions.

Pero befriended a leatherworker from the Moorish neighborhood and brokered some saddle business on his patron's estate in return for Arabic lessons.

On holidays, with his friends from the estate, Pero roamed the parks and taverns frequented by the heirs of Sevilla's elite families. On these occasions, he and his comrades would carry weapons. Armed with daggers and swords, the clan of Dom Juan and his brother, the duke, were ready to meet the clan of Ponce de León, their traditional enemy. In one such encounter in the royal Alcázar gardens, Pero acquired a cheek wound that left an unforgettable hairless scar in his beard. The fight tested the temper of his sword, and he gave better than he received, thus gaining some valuable notoriety in the city.

Perhaps Pero's greatest pleasure in Sevilla was crossing the bridge spanning the Grand Canal into the Gypsy neighborhood of Triana. People treated him as one of their own in Triana, and perhaps he was. To the ever-present guitar and castanets, he learned to dance in the style of the Andalusian Gypsies, seducing the dark beauties with the unrelenting rhythm of his boots.

They acquired a bit of useful knowledge in those taverns. Pero learned that most of the crews for the Spanish voyages of trade and discovery were Andalusian Gypsies from the Triana neighborhood. He learned of Spain's territories and the seas the Spanish fleets sailed from his friends in Triana. Beyond that, the Gypsy seamen knew the extent of the Portuguese outposts, both in the Mediterranean and along the west coast of Africa. They knew because many had sailed on ships owned by the Duke of Medina—vessels whose sole mission was to prey on cargo-filled Portuguese merchant ships as they sailed from colonial outposts. The duke now specialized in attacking Portuguese ships as they left Benin's newly developed gold mines on the African west coast. Those seamen told Pero of more Portuguese holdings than he knew about because the knowledge was secret even in Portugal. They informed him that Don Henry, the Duke of Medina and brother of Don Juan de Guzman, was feared more by the Portuguese than the pirates of the Barbary Coast.

Pero da Covilhã's loyalty, combat ability, and negotiation skill did not go unnoticed by his patron. To further his career, Don Juan suggested Pero join the fleet of his brother, the duke. Pero had prepared himself for almost anything, but he did not want to fight his Lusitanian brothers. Neither was the looting of Portuguese merchant ships on his mind. Pero declined this opportunity, but soon after, the Duke of Medina commissioned his brother to negotiate with King Afonso V in Lisbon about sorting out trade monopolies.

Pero accompanied Don Juan to Portugal. Finding himself in his own country for the first time in six years, he experienced *saudade*—he was homesick, even though he was home. King Afonso V took an immediate liking to him. The king saw in young Pero an audacious Portuguese who spoke Castellano like an Andalusian, Catalan as if from Barcelona, and Arabic like a Moor from Fez. And he used the languages elegantly. The king requested of Don Juan de Guzman that he cede the service of Pero da Covilhã to himself. Don Juan complied.

Thus, Pero da Covilhã became a valet to Afonso V, who, after a short time, promoted him to squire with the privilege to bear arms.

King Afonso V had been preoccupied with winning the kingdoms of Spain by marriage or might for decades. The Portuguese king sent his sister Joan to marry Spanish King Henry IV. But she bore Henry no male heir—only a daughter, Joanna, considered the illegitimate result of her mother's love affair with a nobleman named Beltran.

In 1474, King Henry IV died, leaving no credible contender for the Crown. At this point, King Afonso V of Portugal, whose wife had died twenty years prior, acted on the horrible idea of marrying his own niece, Joanna. He declared himself king of Castile and León and wasted no time raising an army in Portugal to defend the right of his new wife, his queen, and his niece. Most of the people of Castile and León would not accept the rule of an old king of Portugal and his bastard niece.

The people preferred Isabella I of Castile, half-sister of the late King Henry. In addition to this, she had just married Ferdinand II of Aragon, who raised an army to defend her against the Portuguese, who called them the Catholic Monarchs.

A famous battle occurred at Toro in Spain in which both sides had about eight thousand soldiers, but Portugal fielded more horsemen.

Afonso V entered the fray fully confident of victory because he had a secret weapon—his son, Prince John. Known as the "Perfect Prince," Prince John had proved himself a valiant warrior in Morocco in a battle that paved the way to the taking of Tangier. For this, Prince John was knighted.

In the battle of Toro, Prince John attacked the forces of the Catholic Monarchs from the right side of the field and crushed them. However, that was not the case with his father on the left side. Because of indecision, the Spanish troops routed those of Afonso V, who fled from the field of battle. Each side lost about a thousand souls and called it a draw. Although hostilities continued for another three years until the Peace of Alcáçovas, it wasn't a draw because Ferdinand and Isabella effectively took control of Castile and León. The Catholic Monarchs conquered the last remaining Moors in Granada in 1492, unifying all of Spain.

Pero da Covilhã, the teenage valet of the king, fought alongside Afonso V at Toro. Embarrassed and frustrated with the defeat, King Afonso sought help from Louis XI of France but was refused. He returned to Portugal depressed and disillusioned. He was not powerful enough, either in marriage or on the battlefield, to achieve the dream of his ancestors. Beyond that, Afonso had foolishly trusted the French, but no one could dispute his son's vigor. Two years after Toro, in 1477, Afonso V abdicated in favor of his son, who ascended the throne as John II. Afonso retired to a monastery, where he died within a few years. The former king's esteem for Pero da Covilhã did not go unappreciated by his son. In 1479, Pero accompanied John II to negotiations with the Catholic Monarchs. The resulting Treaty of Alcáçovas, among other things, ceded to Portugal the rights to all discoveries in the Atlantic south of the Spanish Canary Islands.

Portugal was becoming flush with gold. The Portuguese fleet defeated the Spanish off the coast of Guinea and carried an enormous cache of treasure back to Lisbon. The Portuguese mined increasingly large amounts of gold in Guinea. The marriage contract between John II's infant son, Afonso, and Isabel, daughter of the Catholic Monarchs, had also yielded a considerable amount of gold as Isabel's dowry.

King John II realized that Portugal would be virtually bankrupt without the newfound gold. Over prior years, his father had exhausted the royal coffers by granting gifts and privileges to keep the peace between

Portuguese noble families. John believed the greed of the noble families and his father's foolish generosity had brought the country to the brink of bankruptcy. Only his victory over the Spanish at sea, his newly producing gold mines, and his negotiating skills had saved Portugal from utter destruction. John II seethed with anger at the thought of his father's squandering of the national wealth to appease the contentious squabbling among nobles.

To rectify matters, John II deprived the noble families of the right to administer justice on their estates and forced them to pay heavy taxes.

The nobles conspired against John II. Many fled to Spain, where John feared an alliance between those noble families and the Spanish Crown.

John needed a loyal subject who could make his way through the morass of Spanish intrigue and uncover the details and personalities involved in any conspiracies against him. He commissioned Dom Pero da Covilhã to be his eyes and ears at the Spanish court in Valladolid. Pero da Covilhã accepted the assignment with enthusiasm, for he too despised the arrogant Portuguese nobility. Pero returned within a year and reported to the king that the king's own cousin and, in fact, his brother-in-law, the Duke of Viseu, was in league with the Spanish court, plotting John's demise. King John summoned his brother-in-law to the palace and stabbed him to death with his own hands. Afterward, the Bishop of Évora was imprisoned and poisoned. Many were executed, murdered, or fled to the Spanish province of Castile. Portugal was now firmly in the grasp of a strong king. When Pero da Covilhã, still in Castile, heard of the murder of the Duke of Viseu, he rejoiced. "We have a man!" he said. "King John acts decisively—not like his father!"

From the coast of Guinea, gold, ivory, pepper, and slaves flowed into Lisbon. Once the kingdom was out of debt, the Portuguese real became the strongest currency in Europe. John was anxious to expand commerce down the entire coast of Africa and around the yet unexplored tip of the continent. His aim was to capture the lucrative spice trade, but each maritime success produced a corresponding problem—piracy from Spain and Morocco. John wanted to eradicate the Spanish pirate fleet. He regarded the Moroccan pirate threat from the Barbary Coast as a nuisance and dangerous distraction and addressed the menace diplomatically. John needed an Ambassador to the Sultan of Morocco in Fez.

In King John's court, he saw the young squire Pero da Covilhã, a man practically his own age, who fought at Toro with his father and helped root out traitors in Valladolid. Pero was perfect—loyal, clever, quick-witted, courteous, and courageous. He could also speak Arabic. Dom Pero was thus sent to the negotiations in Fez to befriend the sultan. He was successful, and Moroccan piracy was reduced. After many months, Pero returned to Lisbon as a successful young ambassador.

While Pero was in Morocco, Dom John II received a curious report from the new fort protecting his gold mines in Benin. Traveling merchants at the mines brought news of a native ruler far to the east. The ruler fit the description of the legendary Prester John, and the report stirred John II into action.

"Why?" Ruy interjected.

"You will soon know. That is the point of this history lesson," Endovélico replied. "Let's get on with the story."

Based on the report from the traveling merchants, John II sent two emissaries from Lisbon to the Middle East to find the kingdom of Prester John. Antônio de Lisboa and Pedro Montarroio traveled by land to Jerusalem but returned, complaining they could go no further because they did not speak Arabic.

Dom John II received this disappointing news, but then he learned Pero da Covilhã had charmed the sultan in Fez precisely *because* he could speak fluent Arabic.

Pero returned to Lisbon as an ambassador and was promoted to a higher position in the royal guard. He immediately became the heartthrob of local maidens. And for Pero, the season was ripe for choosing a wife. His eyes fell upon the graceful Catarina, who commanded a large dowry in addition to beauty. Regardless of the financial endowment, he had fallen in love. They were soon married and expecting a child when the king sent for Pero to visit him in the royal quarters in Santarém.

Standing on the veranda overlooking the Tejo, King John asked Pero if he had heard of the kingdom of Prester John.

"I have heard of it, my Lord, but that is all," Pero replied. "I know nothing about it, and I doubt it exists."

The king continued gazing downriver to the west and seemed to not have heard Dom Pero. "One of my earliest memories was holding my great uncle's hand on the cliff overlooking the Atlantic at Sagres. We watched the caravels of Alvise Cadamosto's armada sail off in the sunset. On that expedition, they discovered the Cabo Verde Islands. I watched as those sails with the Templar Cross sailed directly into the setting sun. From my viewpoint, they turned the sun a glorious red." Transported by memory, the king gazed into the distance for a few more moments. When he snapped out of his reverie, the king said, "My uncle, Prince Henry the Navigator, told me about Prester John." He paused and looked Pero directly in the eye. "Maybe you're the one who can fulfill Prince Henry's dream."

"What dream, my Lord?"

The king looked to the dusky horizon and continued musing as if he had not heard Pero's question. "At the time of the First Crusade, when we formed our budding nation, we knew nothing about India and China and the lands between. For that matter, we still don't, but I am hell-bent on changing that."

Dom John continued, "When our knights returned from the First Crusade, there was talk of a powerful Christian kingdom in the east originally taught by the Apostle Thomas. Once, there was a legend of a Christian king in India named David, but no one knew where India was. Some thought the kingdom of Prester John was the land of the three Magi. Others thought Prester John was Genghis Khan, but he didn't turn out to be Christian. Then there was Africa. Africa *was* in the east. But we didn't know whether Africa was a long slender north-south continent like a snake or huge, running east to west like an elephant. And for all we knew, India was on the east coast of Africa. I asked my historians to do some research. It turns out that two hundred years ago, thirty ambassadors from Ethiopia visited Rome and parts of Europe. They were Christian, and Prester John was the patriarch of their church. Four years ago, as you know, Diogo Cão discovered the mouth of a huge river named Congo, south of Guinea, south of the equator. I sent expeditions upriver in hopes of finding the kingdom of Prester John at its headwaters. But while you were in Morocco, I received more news. At our Benin colony, someone overheard African merchants talking about a kingdom with a powerful ruler in the east."

Pero da Covilhã interrupted, saying, "My king, are you suggesting I lead an expedition to trace the Congo to its source and find that kingdom?"

"No, my friend, you are more valuable than that. I have bigger plans. I want you to travel to Cairo with an associate equally fluent in Arabic. I want you to find the kingdom of Ethiopia on the way to India. Prince Henry's vision for Portugal was the Templar Vision. But the vision does not relate to the First Crusade and the creation of the Templars by the nine knights, some Portuguese. No—the vision traces back to the time of our savior, Jesus Christ, and another form of Christianity not from Rome. It was a purer, original form of Christianity practiced in places like Britannia, France, and here in Portugal *before* the imposition of the Church of Rome twelve hundred years ago." King John continued, "We have reason to believe the Christian kingdom of Prester John comes from and practices that original form of Christianity. The Templars rediscovered it and brought it back to us when our country was founded. Thanks to our Templar backbone, we are strong. With the help of our Templar Knights, we cast out the Moors and defended against the Spanish. One hundred seventy-five years ago, the Pope banned the Order of the Knights of the Temple of Solomon in Portugal. Our King Dinis, who was also Grand Master of the Templars in Portugal, complied with the papal decree and disbanded the Order. Dinis then created the Order of Christ here in Portugal and transferred the Templars' property to the Order of Christ instead of Rome. We are now a strong nation," John continued, "perhaps the most prosperous in Europe, and we have our Templar Vision. I believe the time is right to launch the next stage in Prince Henry's plan."

"What was his plan?" Dom Pero was growing anxious.

The king, wrapped in thought, assumed that Pero knew more about the geopolitics of the Holy Roman Empire than he did.

"Granted, my friend, although we are growing in strength every day… most importantly, the Holy Spirit blesses and guides us. Even with our Templar backbone, we—the Portuguese—are not yet strong enough to challenge the perversion of the Roman Catholic Church with the true faith as rediscovered by the Templars. However, that reality may change if we ally ourselves with the Christian kingdom of Ethiopia and if we find and become allies with the Christian kingdoms of India founded by Saint Thomas. If we can become allies of these natural spiritual partners, we can bring our combined might and resources together to attack and reconquer Jerusalem from the Ottoman Empire, God willing. We could attack the Holy City from the west, the south, and the east with our combined forces. *We* would be victorious in Jerusalem. The Church of Rome tried five times and was defeated five times. After Jerusalem, we will retake Constantinople, then march into Rome for the final victory and restore the true faith in God and the Holy Spirit."

"I want to take part, my Lord! Tell me how I can serve you."

"Complete the double mission of finding the kingdom of Prester John and discovering how to get to India by way of currents, trade winds, and ports of call. You will not be alone; you will take Afonso da Paiva, who speaks Arabic. You may remember him from the Battle of Toro. He fought gallantly by my side, and I rewarded him accordingly."

"I know him. He's from Castelo Branco, down the road from Covilhã. He is a few years older than me and from a very wealthy family. Do you also know that he is a Jew?"

"Of course, I do," the king replied. "And you will appreciate that his Hebrew is as perfect as his Arabic. He is trustworthy and courageous—fluent in all the languages you are. It is good you know Paiva, Dom Pero. I am sending you both to the castle in Tomar for a month of training to ground you in Prince Henry's vision before you depart. My great uncle was our visionary. You may or may not know that Prince Henry the Navigator was Grand Master of *both* the Order of Christ and the Order of Aviz. He was a Templar. After launching our Age of Discovery with the conquest of Ceuta, he built special schools in Sagres, Tomar, and Lisbon to train the sons of noble families to be navigators. Although banned in Europe, these were Templar schools. The sons of Portugal's noble families spent years learning secular and spiritual history, the qualities of noble character, and how to utilize finance, negotiation, and trade—how to command men, fight with the martial arts, and gain the maritime and nautical skills. Because you don't have years at your disposal, at Tomar castle you will learn secrets we've held close from the time when we were Lusitanians. You will learn in one month what Portugal's finest take years to study. Then you will be ready to depart for Cairo." The king continued speaking. "My cousin and brother-in-law, Manuel, is the current Grand Master of the Order of Christ. He will be informed of your progress, and you will meet him before you leave. Friar Sebastian, the Order's Historian, will conduct your course of study. I want you to know, Dom Pero, how vital this mission is to me. If you pass the training, I will vest you with the full power of ambassador. You will be able to make a formal alliance with the king of Ethiopia. I am placing enormous trust in you. The future of Portugal may depend on you along with the future of faith in the True Cross."

Dom Pero da Covilhã knelt and kissed the hand of the king and departed from his presence.

Pero returned home to inform Catarina of the destiny the king had bestowed upon him. He told his wife he would be back within a year. The king had given Pero permission to bring Catarina to Tomar for the month of training. He and Catarina gathered their valuable possessions. She collected hers for a month; he, possibly, for the rest of his life. They chartered a merchant vessel to sail up the Tejo to the island castle of Almourol. From there, they continued with a hired horse and wagon. It was but a day's journey to Tomar.

On the first morning, Friar Sebastian presented the two would-be ambassadors with a piece of parchment with a replica of the official seal of the first king of Portugal, Afonso Henriques.

"Study this seal. Implant it in your memory as I go over a bit of history with you. Before this land was called Portugal, it was the County of Portucale. There was no "g" and no "gral" in the word. This country was predominately Moorish within the domain of the Spanish king of Castile and León. Our first king's father, Count Henry, came from Burgundy, near the city of Troyes in France. Many of the founding Templar Knights also came from Troyes and Burgundy, including St. Bernard of Clairvaux, the protector of the Templars. In fact, St. Bernard, the Templars' patron saint, was our first king Afonso Henriques's uncle. Our fisrt king's father, Count Henry, visited Jerusalem many times during the formation of the Templar brothers. After his last trip to the Holy Land, he helped Afonso IV of Castile and León defend against the encroaching Moorish forces. For his help against the Muslims, the Spanish king awarded Count Henry the County of Portucale. He also gave Henry his illegitimate daughter's hand in marriage—Countess Teresa. Henry changed his name to Henriques, and he and his wife settled in the castle of Guimarães, near Porto. Teresa soon bore him a son whom they named Afonso Henriques. Count Henriques continued to make pilgrimages to newly won Jerusalem and fought the Moors with his Templar comrades. He died in one such battle, leaving his only son still a child. The education of young Afonso Henriques was put in the hands of Egas Moniz, a wise knight and nobleman, a descendent of a king of León and a Muslim sultan.

"When Afonso Henriques was seven, his ambitious mother, Countess Teresa, revolted against her half-sister, the Queen of Castile and León. In her revolt, the powerful Count Traba of Galicia came to her aid and secured Portucale. Countess Teresa and Count Traba became lovers, married, and allied Portucale with Galicia."

Friar Sebastian continued. "The alliance did not sit well with the young boy, Afonso Henriques, or most Portuguese nobility who objected to rulers from León and Galicia. When Afonso Henriques was eleven, the Archbishop of Braga rose in opposition against Countess Teresa and her Galician consort. Afonso Henriques sided with the archbishop, and Teresa ordered both her young son and the archbishop exiled to León. Three years later, while still in exile, the fourteen-year-old Afonso Henriques was knighted in the Cathedral of Zamora.

"The local Bishop came to bestow knighthood, but Afonso Henriques refused to participate in the ritual. To everyone's astonishment, Afonso Henriques administered the oath and vows of knighthood upon himself in an act of defiance and audacity. Anyone who thought this was just rebellious child's-play soon realized they'd been mistaken.

"Not long after making himself a knight, Afonso Henriques left Spain for Portucale and raised an army. He systematically took control of his mother's lands. When he was nineteen, in a surprise attack near Guimarães, Afonso Henriques defeated his mother's and step-father's forces. He exiled his mother to a monastery in Galicia forever and declared himself Prince of Portugal.

"Turning his attention southward, Afonso Henriques began an ongoing campaign against the Moors. He accomplished his goals by forming a natural alliance with companions of his late father; the newly established Knights Templar.

"The Templars were seasoned warriors returning home to Portucale from the victorious First Crusade. They combined forces with homegrown lads newly dedicating themselves to the Order of Soldier-Monks.

"The prince of Portugal, after ten years of fighting both his Christian relatives in the north and east and the Moors in the south, gained a spectacular victory against the combined forces of five Moorish kings in the Battle of Ourique. The night before the battle, the Portuguese soldiers understood the vast number of Muslim warriors arrayed against them. But Afonso Henriques had a vision of the Holy Spirit guiding him to victory. He communicated his vision to his loyal men, and the vision became a reality on the battlefield.

"In the aftermath, the five Moorish kings were beheaded, and Afonso Henriques declared himself the first king of Portugal. It was at this time that the new king began using the seal with the cross pattée and the name, Portu*gral*, which some may read as 'the Door to the Grail.'"

Afonso da Paiva wanted to know the secret to which Afonso Henriques alluded when he connected Portugal to the Grail with his signet ring, whose etching indicated, as Friar Sebastian said, *through you*—meaning Portugal—*the Grail.*

"Good question, Afonso," said Friar Sebastian. The Grail is often pictured as a chalice. Joseph of Arimathea brought a chalice to Britannia. Legend says it had caught drops of blood from Jesus after a Roman soldier pierced him with a spear as he hung on the cross. Therefore, some see the Grail as a vessel containing holy blood. Mary, the mother of Jesus, was pregnant with our Savior—Mary was also a vessel containing holy blood, wouldn't you say?"

"I wouldn't say, Dom Sebastian, because I'm not a Christian," said Afonso da Paiva. "But I understand your point. The man Jesus Christ could be regarded as a Hebrew king, with royal blood."

The friar continued. "And if Jesus, the man, had a daughter, would she not also be considered, so to speak, a grail or vessel containing royal blood?"

"I guess she would," replied da Paiva. "But Jesus had no children."

There was silence.

Friar Sebastian broke the contemplative moment with a revelation. "Wise ones in these parts say that Tomar's original name was Tamarah, named after a daughter, Tamar, born from Mary Magdalene and Jesus."

There was more silence.

The friar looked at them both. "The Church of Rome taught you that Christ was unmarried, died on the cross, and rose again. I suggest you consider that there were other aspects to the life of Jesus Christ as a youth and as a man. Go meditate in the castle chapel, the Charola . . . Afonso Henriques dedicated it to Mary Magdalene."

Pero da Covilhã spoke up: "I believe everything you say about the Grail, Friar Sebastian. I believe the Grail can mean a thing like a cup, a place like Portugal, the womb of someone in the past or present, or even a state of being. But I want to know—how does the Grail relate to our mission to discover the kingdom of Prester John?"

"Good question, Dom Pero. For now, I suggest you bathe in the Nabão River that runs through Tomar. Drink of its water, if you dare. Drink of the spiritual water of Tomar, if you dare. Meditate in the Charola on how the Grail may serve you and how you may serve the Grail. Tomorrow we will discuss the legend of Prester John and the Grail."

Ruy listened to Endovélico's voice and pictured the events as they were taking place. He heard the shaman's voice tell him that was enough history for one night. They would resume on the night to come.

Ruy opened his eyes when he heard the cock's crow. The sun rose over the hilltop village of Belmonte on the plain below.

The following night in the dream world, Endovélico resumed the story of Pero da Covilhã and the kingdom of Prester John.

Friar Sebastian began the session by explaining the many versions of the hunt for the Grail, held in the Grail castle and guarded by the Grail family.

"Many, if not most, of the Grail story's versions originated in Burgundy and the city of Troyes, where the Templars have their roots. The story's main character is a boy named Parzival. He lived with his mother, secluded in a deep forest. Parzival's father, Sir Gornemont, was a foreign king called the White Knight. Sir Gornemont's first marriage was to a Moorish queen named Zaramanc. It was a happy marriage, but for one thing: the queen, fearing for her husband's life, would not allow the White Knight to participate in tournaments. This was too much for him to bear, so Sir Gornemont left his queen and went to Spain, where he learned he had inherited a kingdom in France. At this time, he met and married a childless widow. Soon after that, Parzival was born."

"The White Knight, Sir Gornemont, died in a tournament before he could help raise his son Parzival. Come to think of it, this is much like Afonso Henriques, whose father died when he was a kid. Perhaps this is why the first king of Portugal identified so strongly with the Grail story. But unlike Countess Teresa, Afonso Henriques's mother, Parzival's mother had a twice-broken heart and was jaded by knighthood, chivalry, and the courtly life. She took her young son into the dark forest and raised him far from the influences of men. Parzival also had a mysterious sister, or step-sister, perhaps, Repanse de Schoye. I call her mysterious because Repanse later became a resident of the Grail castle—and the maiden who guards the Grail itself.

"Parzival enjoyed a natural boyhood in the woods, free of all worldly affairs. When he was fifteen, three knights rode through the forest one day and encountered the boy. The knights intrigued Parzival. He thought they were angels and their armor was their skin. He barraged the knights with questions, which to them seemed foolish. The knights departed, and Parzival returned to his mother with news of the encounter. She explained to her son in a most derogatory manner that these were men who called themselves knights.

"Parzival was undaunted. He unequivocally declared that he wanted to become a knight. There was no stopping him. His mother soon relented and sent him on his way to King Arthur's court to claim his inheritance. Parzival arrived at Camelot and made an innocent fool of himself. A kindly knight took pity on the boy and taught him the requirements of honor and combat skills. Because Parzival habitually asked many questions, the knight advised him to restrain his useless questioning.

"While hunting in the woods one day, Parzival encountered one of King Arthur's worst enemies. In a fight, Parzival killed the knight with a hunting spear and seized his red armor and horse. He then won the heart of a noble damsel named Blancaflor and rode off into the forest to tell his mother about his good fortune.

"On his journey into the forest, Parzival encountered the mysterious Grail castle and met the Grail King, also known as the Fisher King. The Grail King was in acute pain because of a wound in his genital area, which crippled him. The Grail King treated Parzival to a feast, and the young man was amazed at the hubbub of opulence and activity around him.

"Suddenly, everything came to a stop. A procession passed through the Great Hall. A beautiful girl in the parade carried a vessel that glowed with a strange light. Unknown to Parzival, the maiden carrying the Grail was his half-sister, Repanse de Schoye. Following Repanse was a young man carrying a white lance. Drops of blood fell from the tip of the lance into the Grail.

"Parzival was presented with the Grail, but he remembered the criticism he'd received for asking so many questions. He kept his mouth shut. In so doing so, he failed to ask the question of the Grail that would prove he was worthy of the Grail's blessing and power. The Grail wanted to hear something from Parzival, like, "Whom does the Grail serve?" But Parzival remained silent. A weariness soon came upon him, and he was shown a bed upon which he could rest. Parzival awoke in the morning to an empty castle.

"Parzival mounted his horse and turned around for one last glance at the Grail castle, but it had disappeared. Riding alone through the dark forest, he encountered an old hag. The old woman told Parzival it was no use continuing the journey to his mother's home because she had died of a broken heart. He had also failed the most critical test of his knighthood—not asking about the Holy Grail. His failure to assert his curiosity caused the Fisher King's wound to worsen, and the land around became even less fertile.

"Parzival's grief could not be described. His belief in himself, his ambitions, and his personality seemed to have vanished because of his stupid negligence. He tried to muster himself but felt only shame and emptiness. He rode through the forest, depressed, without direction. Day after day, he rode onward, sleeping under the stars and moonlight. The forces of the natural world within him urged him to press on. Little by little, his vitality and spirit were restored.

"Parzival concluded that his encounter with the Grail castle was not an apparition. It was real and meaningful. He vowed to find the castle again, even if it would be the last thing he did with the rest of his life. In this sojourn, he traveled for years, experiencing many unique adventures as the legendary Red Knight.

"Late one afternoon, while riding the path through an unknown forest on a mountain called Monsalva, Parzival again came upon the Grail castle. Again, he was honored with a feast. And the feast was again interrupted by the procession of the Grail.

"Parzival looked up at the Fisher King and asked, 'What is the Grail's secret? Whom does it serve?'

"Instantly, the Grail King's wound healed, and there was much rejoicing. Parzival learned the Grail King was his uncle and Repanse de Schoye, the Grail bearer, his step-sister. By passing the test, Parzival pierced the veil between the worlds. He would take his uncle's place as the next Fisher King."

The retelling of the old story entranced Dom Pero and Dom Afonso.

Friar Sebastian reminded Pero of his question: what did the Grail story have to do with the kingdom of Prester John and their assignment to find it?

"Remember that Afonso Henriques's father, Count Henry, was from Burgundy—specifically from the city of Troyes in Champagne. Also living in Troyes at the same time were Hugh de Payne, the founder and first Grand Master of the Templars, and Saint Bernard de Clairvaux, the Templars' patron saint and spiritual guide. Not coincidentally, the first stories of Parzival and the Holy Grail became popular in Burgundy. Later, the poet Chrétien de Troyes, who was of the generation of Afonso Henriques, spread the stories abroad. French was our first king's natural language; he would have first-hand familiarity with the Grail stories coming from Troyes. If our first king's official seal refers to the Grail, then we may safely assume that he took the myth of the Grail seriously, probably more seriously than we know.

"Stop and reflect: Afonso rose against his mother and created a newly independent country—purged of the Moors and Spanish—all in the span of ten years, between his nineteenth and twenty-ninth year. The Templars helped him. It's almost supernatural good fortune, is it not?

"According to Afonso Henriques, the Battle of Ourique, which secured the nation of Portugal, was a spiritual experience.

"As a youth, Afonso Henriques heard all the stories of the Grail out of his father's city, Troyes. When the Templar Knights returned home to Europe victorious after the First Crusade, many were directed to the fledgling Principality of Portucale. Why?

"It was one of St. Bernard's goals. He is the patron saint of the Templar's, whose goal was to establish a new Christian country based on genuine Christian principles. The success of Afonso Henriques, Count Henry's son, indicated that the county of Portucale—now the kingdom of Portugal—was to be the first true Templar country.

"But, Dom Pero, you keep asking about the Grail and Prester John.

"You remember that Parzival's mother sheltered him from the world deep in the forest. It was because she lost two husbands to the fortunes of knighthood. When Parzival became Fisher King and master of the Grail castle, he learned that not only was Repanse de Schoye his step-sister, but he also had a step-brother named Feirefiz—and Feirefiz was a notorious Saracen warrior.

"Parzival dispatched scouts through the Moorish lands to the east, looking for the warrior named Feirefiz. When the scouts found him, Parzival issued an invitation for him to come to Monsalva.

"When Feirefiz arrived at the Grail castle, Parzival welcomed his step-brother with open arms. Feirefiz made himself comfortable and soon fell in love with Repanse de Schoye, the Grail maiden and step-sister of Parzival. Feirefiz converted to Christianity, and he and Repanse de Schoye were married. Feirefiz then took the Grail Maiden back to his lands in the east. They had a son, and they named him Prester John.

"Prester John grew up in the Holy Spirit. He taught Christianity throughout his father's kingdom. When Feirefiz passed away, the realm became known as the kingdom of Prester John.

"Don't you see, Dom Pero? Like many others around him, our first king believed that if Portugal and its king *embodied* the Grail . . . and if Portugal allied with another Grail kingdom—such as that of Prester John—then both Grail kingdoms would prove unstoppable. They would conquer the world for the Holy Spirit. They would rid the world of both Rome and the Muslims. Does that make sense, Dom Pero?"

"Yes, Friar, it all makes sense now," Pero da Covilhã replied.

After some thought, Dom Afonso da Paiva asked, "Does John II still believe in the Grail?"

Dom Pero added, "And where are all the Templars that guarded the Grail and helped Afonso Henriques make Portugal? The Church eradicated the Templars almost two hundred years ago."

The friar replied, "You are right, Dom Pero. The Church did away with the Templars two hundred years ago. But here in Portugal, that was in name only. You should know that. In fact, a clever man like you should be ashamed! How can you sit here in the castle of Tomar and say that?! Don't you realize? Templars surround you. Maybe we call ourselves the Order of Christ and the Order of Aviz now, but we are all Templars—all the same tradition."

"The Templars were not exterminated in Portugal; they simply changed uniforms. Is that what you're saying?"

"Precisely," Dom Pero. "Times have changed, and we change with the times. We may no longer wear the white breast cloth with the red Templar cross on the outside. But on the inside, our Templar's hearts beat true with Templar spirit, and we think with a Templar frame of mind.

"The dream I explained has been passed down to our present sovereign, King John II. You two are here in Tomar because the king selected you to realize this age-old vision. You are here to learn about the vision in detail. Guided and grounded by that vision, the king hopes that you will finally discover the pathway to the Indies and gain us the material power to accomplish this vision through your unrelenting perseverance and courageous endeavors. By that same perseverance, courage, and belief, I might add, you will find the pathway to what Afonso Henriques believed was the Holy Grail. With the help of the Holy Spirit, you will find the way to the kingdom of Prester John and form an alliance. Portugal will then have the necessary spiritual blessing to restore the Holy Spirit to the world."

Dom Pero and Dom Afonso remained in Tomar for a few more weeks. Pero alerted Friar Sebastian that if they were to travel in the disguise of Moroccan merchants, then they must have the means to buy and sell commodities. The friar told him not to worry; he would address the issue before departure.

Two days before leaving for the Spanish border, Cairo-bound, Pero fell to his knees in the Magdalene Chapel of the Templar castle to pray for blessings and guidance from the Holy Spirit. He glanced up at the painting of Melchizedek blessing Abraham at Salem. He wondered whether he would also be blessed like Abraham, but the creaking of the massive door interrupted his thoughts. Hobnailed boot heels clicked across the flagstone floor and stopped short of his pew. The citrusy fragrance of bergamot invaded his nostrils. Dom Pero caught a glimpse of silver on purple silk, then fine boot leather, from the corner of his eye. Pero turned and looked into the eyes he'd dreaded encountering for the past month.

"May I join you for devotions?"

It was Manuel, the Duke of Beja, King John's brother-in-law and the new Grand Master of the Order of Christ. When the king informed Dom Pero he would be trained in Tomar under Dom Manuel's supervision, Pero did not immediately make a personal connection with the nobleman. Only later did his sense of unease develop into the full-blown terror that kept him awake at night.

"Certainly, my Lord."

Pero da Covilhã worked in Valladolid, Spain, as a spy for John II in past years. He had reported to the king that Duke Manuel's older brother, the Duke of Viseu, plotted with the Christian Monarchs to overthrow him. King John summoned the Duke of Viseu to his court and, with his own hand, gutted the duke with a dagger. Pero wondered if the Duke of Beja would seek revenge for his brother's killing.

Pero shifted his position to make room for the king's brother-in-law. He could now practically feel Manuel's dagger about to pierce his left kidney, and there was nothing he could do about it. He made peace with the Father, Son, and Holy Spirit, asking forgiveness for his misdeeds.

Dom Manuel knelt beside him. He crossed himself.

He's begging forgiveness for the act he is about to commit, Pero thought.

The faint whispers of Manual's prayer rung like the bells of the apocalypse in Pero's ears.

So, this must be the end, Pero thought. So premature . . . senseless.

Duke Manuel crossed himself and turned toward Pero with a smile. "Dom Pero da Covilhã, I presume?"

"Yes, my Lord. I am Pero da Covilhã at your service."

"I have something for you."

The duke reached into his great pocket where Pero expected he had concealed his dagger. But there was no dagger. It was a scroll.

"Here is your letter of credit for the Bank of the Holy Spirit in Naples, signed by the king. Once you get to Naples, you and Dom Afonso can use it to purchase all the commodities you may need to support your disguise as Moroccan merchants."

Along with the scroll, Manuel also gave Pero a sack with five hundred ducats, saying, "This will get you across Spain to Barcelona and by ship to Naples. You will sail to Alexandria, then go by camel to Cairo. The man on your right will tell you what to do next."

Startled, Dom Pero recoiled. He looked to his right and saw a small, elderly man with a beard, *yarmulke*, and Orthodox Jewish *payot*, or sidelocks, in front of his ears.

"I am Rabbi Abrahim of Beja. When you both get to Cairo and have learned the city, go to the place known as the Great Citadel. Tall palm trees stand outside the entrance to the Citadel. The tree closest to the gate is where Portuguese spies meet every evening during January, February, and March. You will receive valuable information about proceeding with a caravan on the pilgrimage route to Mecca. The caravan will move south along the old canal banks to the Red Sea and follow along the eastern shore toward Mecca and beyond."

"Beyond? What should I look for beyond Mecca?"

"That's the point of your mission, Dom Pero," Manuel said into his left ear. "Trace the route of the spice traders—the spices come into the port of Jiddah, then to Mecca and Medina. Retrace the route by land and sea to its source in India. When you're done, make your way back to Cairo as fast as possible and pass the information to our spies outside the Citadel. But be aware that while you are in Arabia, Dom Pero, on the opposite side—the west side—of the Red Sea is Egypt, and below Egypt is the land of Kush from the Bible. That, we believe, is the land called Ethiopia. There you should look for the kingdom of Prester John. When you find the route to the Indian spice trade, you will be close to finding the way to Prester John's kingdom. Beyond Mecca, you have to find things by yourselves. That is your mission, to find what we don't know . . . pave the way for the future."

Dom Pero and Dom Afonso spent the next few days under the tutelage of Rabbi Abrahim of Beja. Then it came time to depart on the journey of their lives.

Afonso da Paiva's wife and children arrived from Castelo Branco. Pero's wife, Catarina, was already with him during his month of training, and he regretted that he would not be present for the birth of their first child, due in two months. If they had a son, he and Catarina would name him Afonso after Afonso da Paiva, Afonso Henriques, and King John's twelve-year-old son, Crown Prince Afonso. Pero heard the king doted on his son. Even at the boy's early age, John was instructing him in the affairs of state and New World discoveries. The king anticipated that his son, betrothed to the daughter of the Catholic Monarchs, would someday rule that world.

Nothing could have underscored the importance of Pero and Afonso's mission more than the royal send-off party. Duke Manuel, Friar Sebastian, and the enigmatic Rabbi Abrahim attended. The king had arranged for the support of the men's wives and families during the mission, and Dom Manuel assured the women that their husbands would return home within two years as national heroes. Pero whispered to the tearful Catarina that his absence would be more like one year.

Curled up in his heavy wool blanket, Ruy woke to the sound of wind and raindrops moistening his face. The day had begun, but the sun remained hidden behind a veil of threatening clouds. Ruy roused Davide, and they both descended from the rock by the spiral stone staircase. At its foot, against the rounded surface of the boulder, was the makeshift shack they'd constructed. Davide prepared the breakfast fire while Ruy recounted the lessons in history and myth from the previous night.

That night, they repeated the simple procedure. The weather had cleared, and the stars were in full array. Two hours after dusk, Ruy lay atop the rock on a bed of fresh dry straw and drifted off. Endovélico was there to receive him, and the story of Pero da Covilhã resumed.

The adventurers set out on horseback, heading east toward the Spanish border. Over nine days, they crossed Iberia and arrived at the Mediterranean port of Valencia. They booked passage to Barcelona, then Naples, to conduct their business with the Holy Spirit Bank. The next stop was the island of Rhodes, at that time under the rule of the Knights of Saint John of Jerusalem. In Rhodes, they took lodging in a Portuguese monastery. In the market of Rhodes, they purchased a hundred barrels of honey, a prized commodity in North Africa. They also purchased robes and other accessories to complete their disguises as Moorish merchants.

From Rhodes, they sailed south to Alexandria. Upon reaching this magnificent port, the men fell sick with the Nile fever and nearly died. The sultan's deputy took advantage of their weakened state and, giving them up for dead, confiscated the barrels of honey for himself. Pero and Afonso recovered their health, confronted the deputy, and appealed to the Sultan of Alexandria, who forced the deputy to repay the men in gold for the honey.

Upon reaching Cairo, the city's affluent and cosmopolitan nature astounded Pero and Afonso.

Dom Afonso observed, "People here are from the four corners of the world, and they all understand each other. Although expressed in many dialects, Arabic is the common language."

Dom Pero agreed. "Arabic is for Islam as Latin once was for Christianity." He recalled the Templar Vision King John conveyed to him. "One day," he predicted, "Lisbon will be like this—although the merchants and travelers will be from all over the *Christian* world."

They climbed a hill toward the Great Citadel and, near the entrance, located the palm where the Portuguese spies were to meet during the three winter months of 1491.

For a few weeks, they frequented the teahouses and bazaars of Cairo, smoking hookahs while practicing Moorish Arabic and honing their disguises.

Following the king's plan to trace the spice trade to its origin, they bought three camels and joined a southbound caravan on the eastern side of the Red Sea. They couldn't have known they were tracing the same route Moses tread while leading the Israelites out of the Sea of Reeds, leaving the Egyptian cavalry drowning.

The caravan trekked along the shore of the Red Sea to the town of El Tur, where they'd had planned to embark on a vessel to Aden. However, Pero recalled something Duke Manuel told him: "To trade with those people, you should learn about them. You should intimately know the land and customs of the Muslim people."

Dom Pero learned that upon reaching El Tur, the pilgrim caravan turned inland, east to the city of Medina, where Muhammad had lived, and on to the sacred city of Mecca and the Kaaba, Islam's holiest site. Pero convinced Afonso that, for the sake of their mission, they should not miss this opportunity—they should proceed with the pilgrims. They might be the first Christians to visit the holy sites.

Reaching Medina and Mecca, a wave of pilgrims swept up Pero and Afonso as they marched to the holy shrines. They mimicked the customs of their fellow pilgrims, including penance and prayer to the prophet Muhammad. In Mecca, they joined a throng of humanity in the *tawaf*—circumambulating the Kaaba seven times. With each round, they drew closer to the black-draped cube. Pero whispered in Portuguese, "May God and our Lord Jesus Christ forgive us."

Afonso heard and responded, "Amen."

The two men finally reached the corner of the Kaaba, where the prophet Abraham had inlaid the *al-Ḥajaru al-Aswad*, the sacred black stone. Pero felt compelled to proceed with the custom, like other pilgrims. He leaned forward and pressed his lips to the black stone where millions of other lips had touched. At that moment, he felt not only forgiven by Almighty God but filled with the spirit of the Christ. He knew he would be guided to whatever his destiny would be—Pero felt absolutely no fear for the first time in his life.

After leaving the stone, Pero turned to observe Afonso, who placed his hand on the black stone, then kissed the back of his own hand. He is a Jew, Pero thought—overly concerned with hygiene, not wanting to infect himself with Muslim saliva.

Centrifugal force swept the Portuguese heroes forward. They soon found themselves flung to the fringe of the massive pinwheel of humanity.

They departed Mecca and joined a caravan journeying to the nearby port of Jiddah, where they frequented the company of Arab merchants. The merchants also gave them a sense of the commodities trading—the prices, the originations, and who commanded the markets. In Jiddah, Dom Pero and Dom Afonso boarded a ship for Aden. They were now in the year 1488.

In Aden, a pivotal point in their journey, they made a curious observation regarding their dual mission. They reasoned if they stayed together and helped each other, they would have a better chance of success and return to Portugal together. However, their efforts and Portugal's resources would be better employed if they parted company.

One could seek the route to India, and the other could explore the route to Prester John's kingdom. The probability of at least one returning to Cairo and Portugal would also be higher. They speculated that if they needed to be in Cairo by 1491, it would be best if they split the mission.

Pero had retained a gold St. Christopher's medal so worn that it was indistinguishable from any other piece of gold, yet the two sides of the medal clearly differed as heads and tails. The two men agreed to toss the gold piece to determine which direction each man would go. The flipped medal landed tails-up, sending Pero da Covilhã east toward India and Afonso da Paiva west over the Red Sea strait at Aden to Ethiopia.

The fast friends bade farewell and determined to meet again on one of the first ninety evenings of the year 1491 at the entrance to the Great Citadel in Cairo.

In Aden Pero da Covilhã booked passage on a dhow bound for India. He waited in Aden a month for favorable winds to cross the Indian Ocean. The winds came and he sailed east for three weeks, finally arriving, at the port city of Calicut, India.

Dom Pero was shocked at the city's enormity—its palaces, temples, pools, and gardens. Calicut was a beehive of activity, and he also saw, for the first time, docile elephants transporting goods throughout the town. Pero had never seen such a disparity between wealth and poverty—not in Lisbon, France, Spain, Morocco, or even in Cairo. He surveyed vast neighborhoods of the lowest castes' shacks, wallowing in sewage and pestilence in a constant battle for survival. He also marveled at the royal palace of the Zamorin, surrounded by the opulence of dreams.

Disguised as an emissary from the Sultan of Fez, Dom Pero began his study of the spice trade in Calicut. He befriended a local merchant who told him the Zamorin, although Hindu, surrounded himself with Muslim advisors who dominated the trading industry.

Pero inquired further about the scale of the trade industry, and his new friend boasted that almost all trade with the west had to come through the port of Calicut—and most of it was produced in India.

"What is *not* produced in India?" Pero inquired.

"The spices."

"Where do they come from?"

"Cinnamon from Ceylon, cloves, and nutmeg from Malacca."

"What is Malacca? Never heard of it."

"Malacca is the capital of Malaysia, located at the strait between that country and the island of Java."

Dom Pero made a mental note and nodded with the confidence of someone who was no stranger to the extent of the Muslim world.

"You're telling me cloves and nutmeg come from Malacca?"

"No. The spices must come through the Strait of Malacca, but the natives grow them further east in the Java Sea. The capital of the Spice Islands is Ternate. The spices come from Ternate to Malacca and then to India and Calicut. From here, an Arab ship carries them to Cairo and North Africa. Then from there to Venice and Genoa. Those two cities dominate the trade once it leaves Cairo or Alexandria.

The information elated Pero, but he contained his delight. His good fortune seemed too good to be true, too easily gained. Calicut, the first city where he'd dropped anchor, was a trade hub.

Dom Pero arranged passage on a trading dhow headed south along the Malabar coast to verify what his merchant friend told him. The vessel was scheduled to call at Canonor and Goa. Da Covilhá visited the two ports, and indeed, there was trading activity. Still, it failed to compare to the volume of commodities shipped out of Calicut. Pero remained in India for over a year shuttling between the cities on the Malabar coast.

In December 1489, as the prevailing winds shifted westward, Pero caught a samba bound for Hormuz, the city at the strait separating the Persian Gulf from the Gulf of Oman and the Arabian Sea. Dom Pero saw that Hormuz was strategically located to dominate trade with Persia and across the Indian Ocean. In his report to John II, he wrote, "Most of the spices leave Calicut for Cairo, crossing the Arabian and Red Seas. From Cairo, they go to Venice. If we want to seize this trade for ourselves one day, we must block the Moorish ships' access to the Persian Gulf. We do this by taking Hormuz."

From Hormuz, Dom Pero took a samba bound for the east coast of Africa, where the Moors also had outposts trading cloth and glass for gold and amber.

Reaching Africa, he sailed south along the coast to the city of Malindi, then to Kilwa, and further down to the island of Mozambique. From there, he crossed the channel to the marshy town of Sofala. There, he learned that the Moorish ships did not venture down the coast past this point because of dangerous currents in the channel between mainland Africa and the island of Mozambique. One ship's captain confirmed that information. In Dom Pero's report to John II, he wrote, "If Portuguese navigators rounded the southern tip of Africa, they could easily reach Calicut from Sofala or Malindi, thereby taking possession of the spice trade."

It was still early in the year 1490. Pero da Covilhã had accomplished his mission to find the way to India and more. He was only due in Cairo in January of 1491. He had time on his hands. He traveled by sail up the east coast of Africa to Aden, then north up the Red Sea, stopping in Jiddah, and finally at El Tur on the coast of the Sinai Peninsula. From there he satisfied his curiosity and perhaps increased his own claim to fame by making a pilgrimage to Mount Sinai.

Pero hired a guide with assistants and four camels with a month's provisions and set off east toward what his escort called "Jabal Mousa," the mountain of Moses. After a week in the desert, he wanted to ascend the mountain himself. His traveling companions rebelled at the idea—it would bring terrible luck, they said. They would not wait for him to descend if he climbed it alone. Pero surrendered to this reality, and they returned to El Tur. From there, he sailed up the Gulf of Suez to its northern tip, where he joined another caravan to Cairo, two days away.

It was now January 1491. On the first evening after arriving in Cairo, Dom Pero went to the designated palm tree at the eastern entrance to the old citadel and waited. He heard a Portuguese voice nearby. He turned in joy, hoping to see his best friend, da Paiva, but saw two Jewish men speaking Portuguese. Pero recognized the one dressed as a rabbi as his old teacher from Tomar, Rabbi Abrahim of Beja. They validated themselves with the codeword "Tejo." The second man's name was Joseph, who made his living as an itinerate shoemaker. He had been living in Babylonia, where he learned about Hormuz and its strategic location in the spice trade. When Joseph returned to Lisbon and reported to John II, the king was delighted. He commissioned Joseph and Rabbi Abrahim to meet Dom Pero and Dom Afonso in Cairo. Pero said he had been looking for Afonso da Paiva, whom he left in Aden, bound for Ethiopia two years ago. Rabbi Abrahim regretfully informed Dom Pero that Afonso da Paiva died of a fever somewhere in Ethiopia, with no further information.

The Rabbi gave Pero a few minutes to digest the sad news. He then delivered a letter with the personal seal of John II, addressed to Dom

Pero da Covilhã. The King was enthusiastic about the dual mission of the two comrades from Beira Baixa. Pero instantly accepted his fallen friend's assignment—postponing his return to Portugal to take up Afonso da Paiva's mission to find the kingdom of Prester John. He kept his decision to himself.

As he continued reading the king's letter, Pero saw that John had learned of the strategic importance of Hormuz from Joseph, the shoemaker. "I've been there! I've seen it. He's right!" Pero declared.

The rabbi looked crestfallen—he had taken an oath before the king not to return to Portugal without visiting Hormuz to verify its importance. He thought he would be the first Portuguese to visit the city, but this was not to be. Pero saw the look on his face and replied, "Rabbi Abrahim, I will take you there. I have discovered the way. Afterward, I will complete Afonso da Paiva's mission.

The rabbi was relieved, and they made plans for the trip. Pero entrusted Joseph the shoemaker with his sealed report to the king.

Addressing the two Jews, Dom Pero said, "This information confirms that all we need to do is round the tip of Africa. If engaged at the right time of year, the trade winds will carry us directly to India's city of Calicut, the heart of the spice trade."

Rabbi Abrahim responded, "'All we need to do,' you say. We have already done it. Over a year ago, Bartolomeu Dias sailed back to Lisbon with his fleet. The weather blew them off course west of the tip of Africa, and they found themselves in frigid waters. Lost, they sailed north expecting to see the west of Africa, and to their astonishment, they found the *east* coast! Dias wanted to sail to India, but the crew refused. On the return voyage, clinging to the shoreline, they discovered a passageway they called the Cape of Storms. Our king renamed it the Cape of Good Hope, not to discourage future mariners. You should have seen the hero's welcome Bartolomeu Dias received from the king and the people. He could walk on a bed of flowers for the rest of his life, but he wants to keep sailing on the high seas. He achieved the crowning achievement of the fifty years of work begun by Henry the Navigator.

The Rabbi leaned over and shared a secret he'd overheard from Dom Manuel, the Duke of Beja. Soon after Bartolomeu Dias's return from his successful mission, King John received a visit from Christopher Columbus, a young man that Portuguese trade missions had previously employed. Columbus had been working on a scheme to find a passage to India by sailing west and had come to the court to convince King John to finance the venture. John and his advisors considered Columbus's proposed venture. They found it plausible, but in the end, they declined on the rationale that Portugal did not need a western route to India because it had secretly discovered the eastern way around Africa. Columbus went away empty-handed, declaring that he would seek funding from the Catholic Monarchs of Spain.

Dom Pero found Columbus's scheme interesting, but it did not diminish his enthusiasm and confidence—he was on the verge of turning his tiny Lusitanian nation into an empire. His mind turned to the Templar Vision ingrained in him by Friar Sebastian and King John. Let the Spaniards do what they will, he thought. Pero da Covilhã is part of the spiritual advance guard destined to redeem the world with the Templar Vision.

Pero asked his two new companions about the personal life of King John and his family.

"The king is riding high. Last year Sevilla celebrated the wedding of his eldest son, Prince Afonso, with Princess Isabel, the eldest daughter of the Christian Monarchs. The couple is now living in wedded bliss in Portugal. The Christian Monarch's son and heir to the Spanish throne, Prince Juan, is sickly and probably will not last long enough to be king. Therefore, King John is in good spirits, believing that his son will one day be king of *both* Portugal and Spain.

Pero remembered seeing the young Prince Afonso on his first visit to the royal palace in Lisbon. He was but a child then, and Pero recalled how the king doted on his son, who he created in his own image.

The meeting at the Great Citadel dispersed. Joseph, the shoemaker, departed for Alexandria and was soon back in Portugal with the report from Pero da Covilhã.

Dom Pero and Rabbi Abrahim sailed down the Red Sea to Aden. From there, they sailed to the strait at the entrance to the Persian Gulf and the island city of Hormuz. Pero left Rabbi Abrahim to fend for himself as an Arab trader. The rabbi stepped out of disguise when the opportunity arose and sought solace among the island's small Jewish population.

Dom Pero backtracked to Aden. From there, he boarded a vessel bound for the African port city known as Zeila or Saylac. There he joined a caravan moving west. After three weeks of ascending and descending mountains, he finally reached the realm of Prester John. As he entered the Christian kingdom of Ethiopia, he did not see the land of wealth and prosperity he was expecting. Instead, Pero saw land and people poorer than those in Europe, North Africa, and India. He saw a Christian tribe fighting for survival, fending off attacks from encroaching Muslim neighbors.

Pero da Covilhã soon met the king, a faithful Christian monarch, but he was not the Prester John that Dom Pero was hoping to find. The king's name was Alexander. He gave Dom Pero a warm welcome as a fellow Christian and emissary from the Christian lands of Europe.

Dom Pero insisted on calling the monarch Prester Alexander for poorly explained reasons. The black king was very interested in the Catholic Church in Europe, and Pero was equally fascinated by the practices and customs of the Ethiopian Church and its people.

Dom Pero inquired about the fate of his comrade, Afonso da Paiva, but no one knew of him or his whereabouts. There had been rumors of a person with the appearance of Dom Pero traveling to the north in Sudan a few years ago. He disappeared, and no one knew his fate.

Prester Alexander confirmed the unspoken: Ethiopian Christians could not give King John II of Portugal the aid and help he needed to launch a multi-front campaign to retake Jerusalem. Indeed, Prester Alexander requested that Portugal and other Christian nations come to *his* aid against the Muslim infidels. He suggested that John II use Ethiopia as a base from which to conquer port cities such as Zeila on the Gulf of Aden and proceed from there, perhaps, to Hormuz.

Dom Pero accompanied Alexander around the Ethiopian kingdom for more than a month. He saw that Alexander was a king of the people, and the two of them became fast friends. Pero learned a vast amount of valuable information about Africa and how the people differed from Europeans. He was ready to leave, but Prester Alexander urged him to stay. The king kept him occupied for over a year with increasing responsibilities and journeys throughout the kingdom.

Pero had been traveling for over six years. He was tired, and his *saudade* for Portugal was unyielding. He yearned to get back to his homeland before he forgot Catarina's beautiful face and before she forgot his. He must return to see his own son for the first time, the boy now so aptly named Afonso. He must get back to deliver the encyclopedia of knowledge he had collected about the route to India, Calicut, Malacca, and the Spice Islands. After rounding the tip of Africa, he needed to tell John II how easy it would be to reach these places. He must inform his king that there *is* a kingdom of Prester and that they *will* be an ally against the Muslims. With their help, the Portuguese could conquer such cities as Zeila, Aden, Hormuz, and Calicut, then build alliances with the Christian kingdoms of India. But most importantly—the kingdom of Prester Alexander needed Portuguese help *now*.

As Pero da Covilhã was making his preparations to leave the kingdom, Prester Alexander died unexpectedly. He had no sons to inherit his kingdom—only daughters—so there was a problem.

In that strange land, the kings had many wives and offspring. All potential male heirs to the kingdom—the sons, brothers, and cousins—were prisoners in a particular place, a royal compound on a sacred mountain. Accordingly, the old king's court journeyed to the holy mountain to inform Alexander's oldest brother, Nahu, that he was now the country's ruler.

Nahu came off the mountain to the royal city and met Pero da Covilhã for the first time. He informed Dom Pero that he could not leave the kingdom because of their custom: they would never allow any stranger who visited the realm to leave.

Dom Pero might have answered his obligation to escape at the time, but he was realistic. He could not hire a caravan or guide to take him over three rugged mountain ranges without the king's knowledge. Although Pero always counted on the Holy Spirit's grace, he did not believe the Holy Spirit favored fools. Only a fool would attempt such a journey alone. There was another thing to consider: Afonso da Paiva was not a fool, and he did not survive in Africa.

Pero did what he had done from the day he left Covilhã with Don Juan de Guzman—he adjusted to his new reality, taking full advantage of any opportunities, even in adversity.

In the time he spent traveling with King Alexander, Pero learned as much about the workings of the kingdom as King Nahu had learned in all his years as a prisoner in the mountaintop palace. And he knew more about the Muslim nations surrounding Ethiopia than Prester Nahu could imagine.

Nahu was not stupid, however. He realized Pero da Covilhã's value and capabilities and made the Portuguese man his political advisor. A friendship developed between Nahu and Pero, and the king granted Pero a vast amount of land with many slaves and vassals. In fact, Nahu essentially made Pero da Covilhã into what had eluded him in Europe—a duke.

Dom Pero's new reality was to live the life of a feudal lord. Early on, when *saudade* got the best of him, he argued with Nahu that he must return to Portugal if for no other reason, to bring Portugal to the kingdom's aid.

King Nahu asked, "How can you abandon your lands and people who depend on you for a livelihood?"

Little by little, Dom Pero forced himself to forget about Catarina and his unseen son. In 1495, Dom Pero was forty-five years old. He married a beautiful young Ethiopian of royal descent who bore him many children and led a good life as a noble overlord, land baron, and political advisor to the king. Pero enjoyed this status for another thirteen years.

In 1508, Prester Nahu died, and his young son ascended to the throne. Because of his youth, the son required a regent; thus, the reign over the kingdom passed to his mother, Queen Helen. Dom Pero, now fifty-eight, became the queen's royal advisor.

At this time, two Portuguese monks found their way into the kingdom of Ethiopia. They informed Dom Pero about the fatal horse accident of Prince Afonso, the beloved son of John II. It happened the same year that Dom Pero met with Rabbi Abrahim and Joseph the shoemaker in Cairo. Pero instantly thought that Afonso's death must have ruined John's preliminary plan for capturing the throne of Spain by marriage.

From the monks, Pero learned that four years after the accidental death of his son, the king himself became mysteriously ill and died. The country would not recognize his illegitimate son, Jorge. Before dying, John II conceded to his wife's wishes and appointed her brother, Dom Manuel, Duke of Beja, as his successor.

Hearing the news, Pero exclaimed, "I know Manuel, the Duke of Beja! He oversaw our instruction in Tomar. He's now our king?"

"He's been our king for the past thirteen years, and they've been outstanding years. We nearly forgot he was Duke of Beja because he is known only as Manuel I of Portugal. He has been a great king. Portugal is now the wealthiest country in Europe and maybe the world. We are on the verge of *empire*."

Dom Pero was excited. "Tell me everything you can . . . but first, tell me if King John received the report I sent back from Cairo in 1491 with a spy named Joseph the shoemaker?"

"Yes, the king received your report. You became a national hero that year. Everyone knew your name. Bartolomeu Dias had returned, having rounded the Cape of Storms. Then your message came, confirming that India was within easy reach once around the Cape. Money for ship-building flowed into Lisbon, exciting everyone. But then, our fate suddenly soured. Prince Afonso died in a bizarre riding accident. The king doted on his son and went into a depression resulting in his premature death. He lost interest in everything.

"A year after Prince Afonso's death," the monk continued, "Christopher Columbus appeared in the Lisbon harbor with only one ship. He had just discovered the western route across the Atlantic to what he thought was India. Columbus stopped in the Açores Islands on his return voyage and sought a safe harbor in Lisbon when blown off course. King John was distressed to learn of Columbus's success because, as you know, he'd been Columbus's first choice for funding the voyage. John allowed him to travel to Spain but complained to the Pope, saying the land Columbus found belonged to Portugal by the Treaty of Tordesillas. As you would expect, nothing came of it, but the news of Columbus's discovery spread like wildfire throughout Europe.

"And just about that time, other extraordinary things began happening. In 1492, the year of Columbus's discovery, the Catholic Monarchs finally triumphed over the infidel Moors, defeating them in their last stronghold in Granada and running them out of Iberia. Success was so great they ran the Jews out of Spain while they were at it. Many Jews crossed the border into Portugal. One of them who fled to Lisbon was the famous astronomer and astrologer Abraham Zacuto. He encouraged the king to continue exploring and developing the eastward sea route to the Indies. Dom John II regained his enthusiasm and vision and began making plans for a massive armada to the Indies. And that's when he died."

Pero wondered how that happened. Even though his son and heir had died, Dom John was still young and vigorous.

"Well," the monk said, "he got sick and died at his castle on the Algarve coast. He was forty. He must have known he was ill because Dom John elevated his first cousin, Manuel, Duke of Beja, to be his successor before he passed. When King John passed away, that's how Manuel became king. The queen's brother didn't miss a beat. It was 1495, and the transition from John to Manuel went uncannily smoothly. There were rumors, of course, but no one dared put a name to the suspicion that Manuel may have had something to do with John II's premature departure.

"The voyages of exploration continued. Gold from Africa arrived by the shipload. Manuel suffered the same obsession to capture Spain as all the Portuguese monarchs before him. His first wife passed away twenty years before he became king. One of the first things he did was marry the poor widow of John II's deceased son, Afonso. Princess Isabel was the eldest daughter of the Catholic Monarchs, and without a male heir, she was in line for the Spanish throne. The important thing is this—to secure her hand in marriage, Manuel had to promise to expel the Jews from Portugal, just as Ferdinand and Isabella had done in Spain in 1492.

"Up until that time, Manuel was a friend of the Jews, but the prize was too much—He couldn't pass it up. A year after ascending the throne, he ordered all the Jews in Portugal to convert to Christianity or leave the country without their children. As you can imagine, Dom Pero, most of them became what we call "New Christians." The rest emigrated to Holland, Africa, Italy, Turkey, and Morocco."

"Good riddance, if you ask me," the other monk said.

"No one's asking you," Pero muttered.

"Yes, Dom Pero, but you should have seen Lisbon at Easter two years ago. In 1506, we suffered from the plague, and it had not rained for a year. Some Dominican priests blamed the hard times on the thousands of Spanish Jews who had come to Portugal over the previous decade.

"The massacre started in the center of Lisbon, outside the Convent of São Domingos. During the service, someone swore he saw the face of our Savior, Jesus Christ, illuminated on the altar. Everyone agreed it was a miracle or a portend about the drought and plague. One New Christian in the front row laughed and said it was the reflection of a candle on the gold crucifix.

"The men in the congregation grabbed the New Christian and dragged him out of the church by his hair. They beat him to death and burned his body in the Praça do Rossio. Unfortunately, it didn't stop there. The Dominican friars issued a decree absolving all the sins committed over the previous hundred days to anyone who would kill a heretic Jew.

"The friars drew a large crowd—hundreds—but I must admit, many foreign sailors from the docks had plenty of sins that needed absolving. They went on a rampage through Alfama and the Jewish Quarter, rounding up and killing all the New Christians they could find. The mob burned the *cristãos-novos* at the stake in Rossio Square and the Praça do Comércio by the river. Over five hundred Christ-killers met their maker that first day."

Dom Pero had to excuse himself from their presence. Shaken, he went outside to vomit. When he returned, the monk continued.

"There's more, Dom Pero. The next day more people joined in to absolve their sins. They dragged the New Christians from their homes and churches where they had sought refuge. And not just men—they killed women and children, even dashed babies against the stone walls. Of course, the looting of Jewish houses fomented an air of celebration perfumed with the smell of blood and burning flesh. And not just Jews and New Christians—any prosperous household attracting the neighbors' jealousy was subject to accusations of heresy followed by the judgment of the mob, death, and confiscation of possessions."

"Where was Manuel I?" Pero asked.

"He had gone to Abrantes to escape the plague, then to the castle at Aviz. He was in Aviz when he heard about the massacre. He stayed but sent the royal guard, empowering Dom Diogo Lopes, Baron of Alvito, to execute members of the crowd. By the time royal officials finally arrived in Lisbon, some two thousand souls had lost their lives.

"The two Dominican friars who incited the riot were burned at the stake. They arrested and hanged some Portuguese, but most of the foreign sailors escaped with their loot. The Convent of São Domingos was shut down, and Dom Diogo Lopes expelled all the representatives from the city of Lisbon who served on the king's council.

"When I think of it," said Friar Ricardo, "it was all for nothing." Manuel caused this mess by kicking the Jews out of our country to please his in-laws, the king and queen of Spain. But two years after Manuel married Princess Isabel, she died giving birth to their one and only child, a son named Miguel. Little Miguel died three years later, leaving King Manuel with no further claims to the Spanish kingdom, no Jews, no Moors, no wife, and no son."

"Enough, Friar Ricardo. Don't you have any good news to tell me?"

"Good news?" I've got more good news than you can bear. I'm just getting started. Based on Dias's success around the Cape of Good Hope and your report, the old king was planning an armada when he mysteriously died. Manuel assumed King John's plans with enthusiasm and changed nothing. He sent young Vasco da Gama as captain of a four-ship armada. I remember the hot summer day in 1497 when da Gama left Belém. I was there. The king's astronomer, Abraham Zacuto, was there too. There were thousands of people. Old Zacuto, who was quite a figure, lectured the sailors and gave a blessing in Hebrew. Soon after that, the old man disappeared with the other Jews. Some say he fled to Tunis. Anyway, the voyage was a success. Da Gama rounded the Cape, sailed up the east coast of Africa, crossed the Indian Ocean, and reached Calicut. The venture took over two years, and only a third of the crew returned.

"Although a good navigator, da Gama was not as good a merchant. The spices he brought back were meager, but he still established the route, thanks to you.

"The second armada to the Indies was more ambitious. Young Pedro Álvares Cabral was the captain-major."

Pero interrupted, "Cabral! That goat—I knew him well. We were squires together at the court of Afonso V, and then John II. He is from Belmonte, up the road from Covilhã. Cabral grew up in the castle in Belmonte, and I grew up in my family's castle in Covilhã. Tell me, what happened with Cabral?"

"Cabral set sail from Belém in 1500 with thirteen ships. He lost one mysteriously outside of Cabo Verde. He caught the westerly trade wind but did not immediately turn south with the *volta do mar* current. He kept sailing west until . . . what do you know? He bumped into a whole new continent. Mind you, it is probably the same one Columbus discovered, but much further south. We call it "Brazil" because of the *pau brasil,* or brazilwood trees that grow in abundance and whose hardwood we are harvesting. Since Cabral, we sent two more expeditions to Brazil, but they have yet to find gold or silver. Manuel poured his resources back into the trade route to India you helped discover. And the natives there in Brazil are wild, but we can deal with them. Columbus called the land he discovered "India," but it does not appear to be. This land, Brazil, is much further south than the land Columbus found. Cabral claimed the land for our king and dispatched one of his ships to advise his majesty.

"The remaining eleven ships continued the voyage past the tip of Africa and over the Indian Ocean to Calicut. Pedro Cabral first set up a factory in Calicut, but the Zamorin of Calicut betrayed him. Cabral bombarded the city, then set out for cities further south in Cochin and Cannanore—places you told John II about.

"Cabral finally returned to Lisbon with only three ships. But the ships were *so* full of spices that they paid off the remaining national debt and made the investors, including Pedro Álvares Cabral, very rich.

"But Cabral did not hit it off well with Manuel, so despite his experience, the king did not use him again.

"Just before I left Lisbon, the king made Afonso de Albuquerque, Viceroy of the Indies. He set sail with a huge armada to conquer the island city of Hormuz. I heard he could not take Hormuz, but he established forts along the way, which accomplished the same thing."

Dom Pero was thrilled to hear the news. However, the more he heard, the more he understood he was stuck in a backwater. His countrymen deluded themselves when they referred to Ethiop[ia as "the kingdom of Prester John." The kingdom of Prester John was not going to rise up and invigorate Portugal. Pero da Covilhã was now fifty-eight. He was now an historical figure, and perhaps already consigned to the dustbin of history. His problem was that he still wanted to be part of the action.

As a royal advisor to Queen Regent Helena, Dom Pero convinced the queen to send an ambassador from Ethiopia to Portugal. Queen Helena chose an Armenian named Mateus for the mission. His task was to ask Portugal for assistance in defending Christian Ethiopia against the Ottoman Empire and other Muslim sultanates and sharifates that continually encroached on Ethiopia's borders. Ambassador Mateus and the Portuguese monks went on their way. For over a decade, nothing was heard regarding Queen Helena's request for a formal alliance with Portugal.

During these ten years, David, the grandson of Queen Helena, came of age to rule the kingdom in 1516. Dom Pero went to Prester David and requested permission to return to his homeland. Like his predecessors, the new king denied Dom Pero permission to leave the kingdom. Prester David reminded him that his father, Prester Nahu, had given Dom Pero lands to govern and a lordship to rule and enjoy. Ethiopia was now and forever his homeland. His people and the land he ruled needed him to stay.

In 1517, the young Prester David ambushed and killed his arch-enemy, Emir Mahfouz of the Adal sultanate. In coincidence with Prester David's feat, the Portuguese fleet attacked the Muslim port city of Zeila and burned it to the ground. In the following three years, Prester David enjoyed more victories over his Muslim adversaries and believed the Muslim threat to Ethiopia was over.

In 1520, a diplomatic mission from Portugal finally appeared in Ethiopia. The Ambassador, Dom Rodrigo de Lima, with his associate, Friar Francisco de Álvares, found Pero da Covilhã at home on his estate. Now seventy years old but still robust, Dom Pero had much to say. Dom Pero served as a guide and interpreter for the traveling Portuguese embassy. Rodrigo de Loma had come with a formal Portuguese agreement of alliance and defense.

When the defense treaty was presented to Prester David, the young monarch said he did not need the help of the Portuguese against his Muslim enemies. He was doing well fending them off without help, but perhaps Prester David was suspicious of the motives of the Portuguese. He heard of them burning of the port of Zeila and of the new forts the Portuguese built on the east coast of Africa and on the Indian coast. He told the Portuguese Ambassador it was all a mistake. His grandmother, Queen Helena, although serving as regent, did not have the authority to negotiate such a treaty. However, Prester David told Rodrigo de Lima that he was most interested in the Portuguese training the army and importing firearms and artisans from Portugal.

The Portuguese mission remained in the kingdom for a few years. The friar, Francisco de Álvares, compiled his copious notes into a book entitled *Travel Information about the Lands of Prester.*

As the mission set out on its return journey, Dom Pero and his family accompanied the expedition to the kingdom's borders. There, Pero bade farewell to his twenty-three-year-old son, Rodrigo, traveling with the embassy to receive an education in Portugal. Even this short journey was dangerous. There was war in the air. The Sultan of Adal in eastern Ethiopia was hell-bent on taking over the Christian Kingdom.

In the years that followed, Prester David did not have the same luck that Providence had afforded him as a young leader of his people. The forces of Islam closed in on all sides. Eventually, everything was lost except the remote stronghold on the Mountain of the Princes, where the royal family resided as prisoners. In 1540, the mountain fortress fell, and the attackers slaughtered all the princes and looted the treasury.

Prester David escaped and lived as an outlaw in his own kingdom.

Accepting the wisdom of his late grandmother, Queen Helena, and Pero da Covilhã to reach out to Portugal and Christian Europe for help, Prester David once again requested help from Rodrigo de Lima, who conveyed his request to King Manuel.

Assistance came quickly in the form of four hundred Portuguese soldiers commanded by Christopher da Gama, son of Vasco da Gama. However, when Christopher da Gama and his men reached Ethiopia, they found that Prester David had just died in a battle with the Moorish enemy.. And no sooner had Christopher da Gama entered the kingdom, he suffered the same fate as Prester David.

At this point, Endovélico paused his storytelling. "Forgive me, Ruy," he said. "The history of Pero da Covilhã has gotten ahead of itself. By the time of the demise of Prester David and Christopher da Gama, our hero had been dead for four years. And it was just as well."

"But Sr. Endovélico, I thought you told me we would fly to see Pero da Covilhã at his passing."

"Did I?" the Earth Spirit replied. "Yes, I did, and so we shall. First, let us fly back in time as falcons because you have already done that. When we land at Dom Pero's estate in Ethiopia, we **will** convert ourselves into turtle doves. You will see why."

Having transformed into turtle doves, the two perched on the sill of the large window dominating the bedroom where Dom Pero's family attended to his needs in the final hours of his life. The family treated the two doves as a heavenly sign the end was near.

Dom Pero lay in bed contemplating his life while his wife and servants fanned a breeze. These thoughts ran through his mind: " If I'd only been more forceful bringing up Prester David. If only I'd been able to convince him, as I had his grandmother, of the importance—nay—the necessity of forming a defensive alliance with Portugal. The Templar vision of a global empire united by the Holy Spirit was in my hand.. I was the pivot point of a divine process, and I failed. I failed to realize the vision of Afonso Henriques, of Dom John I and II, of the Great Navigator, and even of King Manuel."

Dom Pero's wife brought him a chalice of water. His trembling hand reached for it, but he knocked it away. It tumbled to the ground spilling the water.

Pero's grizzled head sank into his pillow in despair, and he said, "A symbol of my failure."

He continued muttering as his tearful eyes closed. I will soon know whether Heaven will redeem me or cast me away for my negligence, he thought.

In answer to his fear, the room brightened as the setting sun's red glow peeked through Pero's window from behind a tree. The glow then struck his body and took the form of an angel with two small dove-like shadows, like boots on the angel's feet. His wife and servants later testified to the vision.

But Dom Pero did not see an angel. Instead, he saw a knight in shining armor who looked like himself and, indeed, it was his son Afonso, whom he had never seen. The knight lifted the chalice from the floor. Liquid sunlight filled the cup.

Afonso offered the chalice to his father with these words, *"Meu Pai, Por Tu, O Gral."* My Father, for you, the Grail.

Dom Pero took the cup to his lips and sipped the liquid. The sunlight itself seemed to enter his bloodstream and invigorate every cell. He saw himself again roaming the streets of Sevilla in search of adventure. He passed from this world to the next with a smile on his lips.

Ruy, shaken by witnessing the passing of Pero da Covilhã, did not feel pity or sadness. Instead, anger stirred within him.

Endovélico warned him, "That's too much anger for a little dove. Save it for when we return to Portugal."

The two flew from the window to a nearby forest, where they reverted into falcons and flew in time from 1536 to 1565. Reaching Portugal, they glided up the river Zêzere, past Covilhã and Belmonte, to Centum Cellas. They perched on the highest pediment of the ruin, where Ruy began putting words to his anger.

Facing Endovélico in falcon form, Ruy declared, "Even as a Jew, I wish the Templar Vision would have come to pass. By the grace of God, we Portuguese were given a chance to bring it to fruition. But I am afraid we have diverged too far off the path of justice and our forefathers' dreams, and now we have lost our chance for greatness and eternal glory. Dom Pero may have drunk from the Chalice of Immortality on his deathbed. But I fear we, the Portuguese nation, have dropped the Grail itself and spilled the nectar of our glorious future on the ground. If Manuel I inherited the Templar Vision from his cousin and brother-in-law, John II, he also inherited John II's lust to rule all of Iberia. Manuel, too, wanted this so badly that he gave in to the demands of his future in-laws and expelled the Jews and Muslims from Portugal, just as they had done in Spain.

"Manuel tried to have it both ways, but the initial sin was committed. Thus, Lisbon has forfeited its future as a great metropolis, a world center, like Cairo. No! Since the time of Manuel, our lives as Jews have been hell. Rabbi Jaco, Davide's great-grandfather was burned at the stake, his father, also rabbi, has to disguise himself as a shepherd.

"And Manuel's son John III; he even believed and supported the Inquisition! Did Manuel, Master of the Order of Christ—that hypocrite—even talk to his son about the Portuguese Templar Vision? From what I can see today, I doubt it. And the further we have drifted from Prince Henry the Navigator's vision—and those who went before him—the more things have deteriorated.

"Our colonies are corrupt, filled with black-robed Inquisitors skulking like vultures over a carcass. We have lost ground to the Spanish and the Dutch, and now we lack the power to take it back, let alone conquer Jerusalem and Rome. The Grail is broken. And *we* broke it.

Endovélico consoled the angry teenager in falcon form and said, "Ruy Gonçalves, don't cry over the broken Grail. You can repair it, and it can even be given to you. Be prepared."

Ruy didn't know how to reply. They flew up to the rock before daybreak, and Ruy descended into his sleeping body.

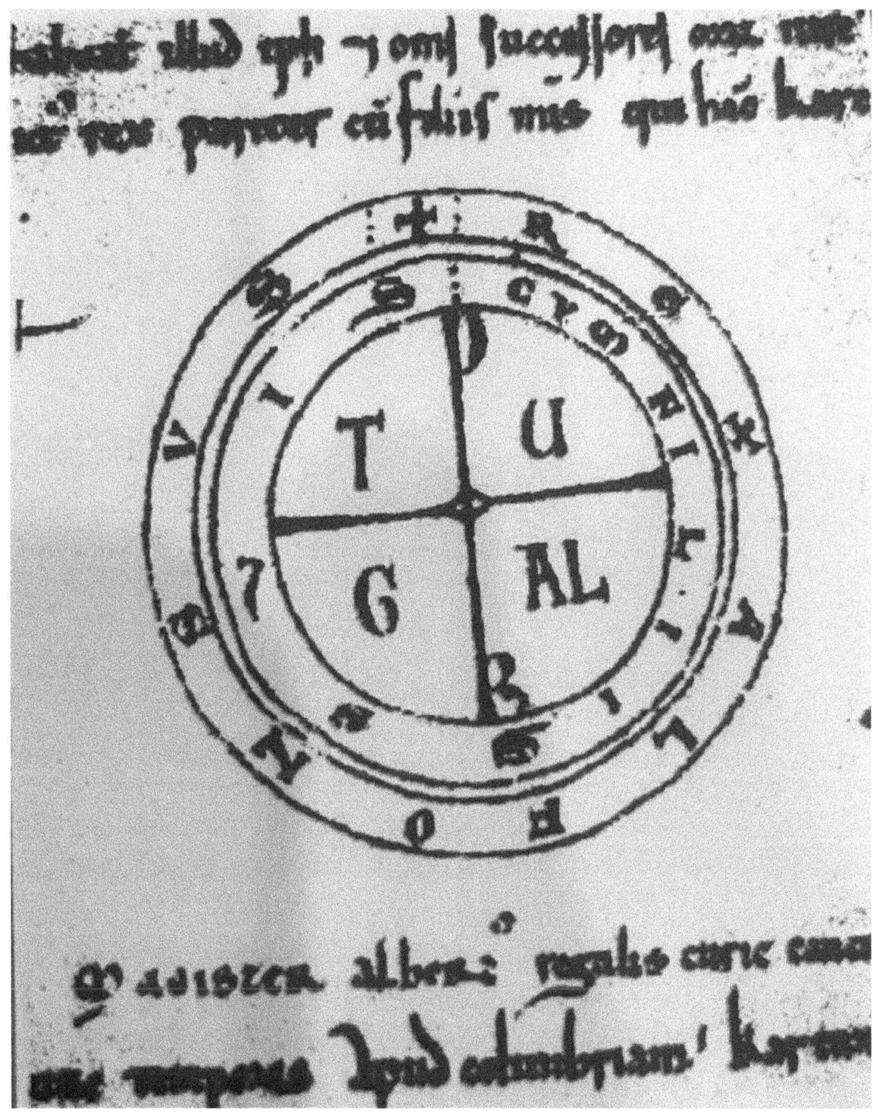

Seal of the 1st King of Portugal, Afonso Henriques.

PoR TU o Gral, Through you the Grail

Statue of Pero da Covilhã in Covilhã, Portugal

CHAPTER 10

COIMBRA

1565-1566

In the summer of 1565, as the boys were tending sheep and dreaming on the Rock of Endovélico, the fathers of Davide, Ruy and Toninho met to discuss their sons' future. Considering the boys were the same age—and good friends growing up together—it was natural to send them off to receive higher education together. Dom Fernão Cabral and Dr.Lorenço Gonçalves, through their contacts, arranged for the boys' acceptance to the University of Coimbra. According to their expressed interest, Antonio was to study arts and agriculture; Davide, medicine and pharmacology; and Ruy, engineering, shipbuilding, navigation, and cosmology. The three fathers would roughly divide the costs according to their means.

A wagoner was hired to carry the young men and their trunks on the four-day journey to Coimbra, along the old Roman road in early autumn. First, they traveled north, up and around the northern termination of the Serra da Estrela range, then southwest along the other side of the mountains, past Oliveira da Hospital and Penacova to Coimbra.

They arranged for the youths to room together at a boarding house near the Alcáçova Palace. The palace housed the old university since it relocated to Coimbra from Lisbon some twenty-five years previous. The university stood high on the hill of the ancient walled Roman city, with the lovely Mondego River flowing at its base. However, the three youths' introduction to the waters of the Mondego was not pleasant.

It was a cold Saturday morning in early November. The university administration ordered all new first-year students to assemble at a specific plaza with their tin cooking utensils, dressed in their new black wool coats and capes. They were led on a meandering course through the old city's cobblestone streets, marching down to the river, creating as much noise as possible. They sang songs recently taught to them by student captains as they banged their pots and cups together. When the parade, which looked like a black snake, reached the bank of the Mondego, it did not stop. Fraternity brothers were there to throw the bright-eyed boys into the frigid current, thus baptizing them in the waters of academic life.

Within a few months, Toninho was invited to join a fraternity, which was, at its core, a drinking society. He moved out of the boarding house and into the fraternity apartments. They treated him like a bond servant between bouts of hazing and drinking. Under these circumstances, Toninho had little time for his studies or childhood comrades. This arrangement was satisfactory to Davide and Ruy because they knew, even at their age, that as Jews or New Christians, they were in a city where the Inquisition was well-established. In a place where the Inquisition had recently burned people of the Torah at the stake, they could not afford the luxury of loose-tongued drunkenness. Besides, it was good to have a friend and confidant lodged among the various young *goyim* 10 of Portugal, future leaders from the country's advantaged and noble families.

Over the winter and through the spring, the boys felt academically challenged for the first time. With virtually no social life, they bore down on their studies to not disappoint their fathers with poor grades. Spring became summer, and although classes did not stop, their yearning for a change of scenery increased. They were eager to venture out from the close confines of the university and old city. They took to fishing from the old Pedro and Inês bridge, then investigated the legendary Monastery of Santa Clara on the south side of the river. Moving on from the monastery, they discovered they were in the Quinta das Lagrimas—the Garden of Tears—a place they had heard of since childhood.

They compared versions of the story of Pedro and Inês and the storytelling went as follows. The year was 1355. In the garden, the Quinta das Lagrimas, henchmen employed by Prince Pedro's father, King Afonso IV, murdered Inês de Castro, the love of Prince Pedro's life and mother of his children.

Years earlier, King Afonso had arranged for his son to marry Constança, a young lady from the Spanish court in Castile. He married her, but the prince fell in love with one of Constança's ladies-in-waiting, Inês. Constança died giving birth to Pedro's first child. Soon after that, Pedro revealed his secret affair with Inês and his plans to marry her. His father would have none of it, banishing Inês to Coimbra. Prince Pedro followed her, and over the next seven years, they had a family with two sons and a daughter.

In early January of 1355, Pedro left Coimbra on a hunting trip. Three cohorts of the king entered the garden where Inês was playing with her children and decapitated her. Legend says the reddish rocks lining the fountain of tears still testify to the crime.

Pedro declared war on his father. There was fighting, but the king died of natural causes during this contentious time. Pedro, now king, tracked down the murderers and killed them with his own hands. He then exhumed the bones of Inês, positioned her on the throne, and made the entire court pay homage to her as Queen Inês of Portugal. The tombs of Pedro and Inês now face each other in the Alcobaça Monastery.

Prowling the forest gardens, trying to absorb the peculiar history of the place, the boys heard young women giggling. They approached the merriment cautiously, and when, in sight of their gay-colored frocks, the boys hid behind a nearby grove of trees. They saw two girls, roughly their own age but more sophisticated, sitting on a bench beside a small pool. In front of them was an elderly man-servant crawling on the ground, clutching the hind leg of a frantic bullfrog. With black flowing hair, the taller girl taunted the servant in good humor for not holding the frog in one place while she sketched the creature on a drawing board with charcoal and colored chalk. The bullfrog broke free and leapt toward the pool.

"Catch him, Baltasar Don't let him get away. He's a special frog."

Baltasar threw his mantle over the frog when it was one leap away from the pool. The nimble beauty jumped up and ran to the cloak. As she bent down to lift the cloth and inspect her captive, a ray of sunlight caught a golden brooch in her raven hair. It reflected through the tree grove, beaming across Ruy's glazed eyes, blinding him for a second.

"Did you see that?" he whispered to the excited Davide, "It's like she's touched by God."

Davide sneered. "You're just love-struck, you fool."

With one hand over the cloth holding the bullfrog tightly, she lifted Baltasar's cloak with her other hand and buried her head inside. Then she made sounds of kissing and moaning. Baltasar was beside himself with consternation and the girl's younger blonde companion was laughing uncontrollably.

The dark one lifted the cloak off the stunned frog.

"Now, let's see this frog turn into Prince Charming and whisk me to his castle," she giggled. "Or better—let this prince gather me up in his arms and take me to his barge, *The Wave of Desire*, moored along the riverbank. We shall flow with the current, follow the sun to the wide Ocean Sea, and be free from the likes of you, Baltasar."

"Then let's see warts on your chin to disgust any potential Prince Charming!" Baltasar retorted.

"Oh, shut up, Baltasar. See what you made him do? He will hop back into the pool before he can transform."

From the trees, Davide pinched Ruy and, with his eyes, urged his friend to take advantage of the situation—make a dramatic appearance as a Prince Charming. Ruy was spellbound by the black-haired beauty. With his fingers, he motioned "no." Perhaps timidity withheld him because he saw himself as an awkward boy from the other side of the mountains. Or maybe it was simply his enjoyment of watching the mirthful enchantress engage in her natural environment without inhibition.

Listening closely, Ruy overheard the blonde girl address her companion. "Let's go now, Ana Sofia. We'll be late for supper." The three got up, leaving the two voyeurs frozen in place behind the trees. The sound of "Ana Sofia" rang inside Ruy's head like church bells calling the faithful to worship. "Ana Sofia" was now an anchor to which he could attach a fresh flood of fantasies.

Nine months had passed since Davide, Ruy, and Toninho had been transplanted from the wool-weaving region of Covilhã and Belmonte to the urban sophistication of Coimbra, one of the oldest centers of learning in Europe.

Toninho had no trouble adjusting to his new surroundings. This was not the case with Davide and Ruy. No matter how gregarious they might be with their new comrades, there was always a distance, a precaution that filtered every perception and interaction with others. The filter between their outer personae and inner reality was their Jewishness. As far as they could tell, their first-year peers at the university would probably not care, even if they were told that they were Jews. If the matter were to come up, Davide and Ruy would project disinterest and assert that their fathers or grandfathers had converted to the Lord of the Gospels. They were all raised as God-fearing Christians.

Davide's courses revolved around medical subjects—anatomy, chemistry, natural remedies, and astrology.

Ruy had never abandoned his aspirations to be a navigator. And why should he? From his point of view, many of the greatest navigators were Jews. Did not João Gonçalves Zarco find and settle Madeira Island? His grandson, Cristóvão Colombo—often known outside Portugal by his surname's Latin form, Columbus—was not Genoan. Instead, rumors said he had Portuguese Jewish blood in his veins.

Why not *me?* I have the temperament of a navigator. I am in Coimbra to acquire the skills to be a master of the seas. If I do well in my years here, I may attract the attention of the admiralty or even John III. They'll send me to Sagres or Tomar for advanced preparation and a high commission.

It had been only a week since Ruy, smitten by a glimpse of love in the Garden of Tears, heard a knock at the door of his dormitory room. A boy announced himself as a messenger from the house of Professor Dom Pedro Nunes. He invited Ruy Gonçalves of Covilhã to spend the following Sunday afternoon at the professor's residence, half a league east of the city walls at the *vila* known as Vale d'Azenha, on the cliffs over the river.

Ruy was dumbstruck. *Pedro Nunes*, he thought—the king's cosmographer, one of the greatest mathematicians—the discoverer of the loxodrome and navigational rhomb lines. Why does he want to talk to *me?* I came here wanting lessons from him, only to discover that he had retired from the Chair of Mathematics two years ago. What could he possibly want with me?

"What? Well, *yes!*" Ruy sputtered. "I accept the invitation. But . . . why? I didn't know Dom Pedro Nunes knew of my existence."

"I can't answer that, *senhor*," said the messenger. "But as you have accepted the invitation, I will return at one o'clock in the afternoon to guide you to the estate. Is that agreeable?"

"Absolutely!"

Ruy dressed in his best outfit, and the boy reappeared as promised. He followed the lad through winding streets to the city's east wall, then along a hill called Areeiro, following a track that led into a forest of chestnut trees. In the shade of these trees was a wrought-iron gate. They passed through the gate and into the sun, where a gleaming white villa perched on the cliff overlooking the river. The front of the house had one story but the rear three, with a veranda surrounding the entire dwelling.

The professor was waiting at the entrance of the *vila*. Ruy's first impression was that he didn't look old enough to be retired. And in fact, Pedro Nunes was hardly fifty years old at the time. He was a short, stocky man with a stoop and thick eyeglasses.

Ruy began introducing himself when the professor interrupted him. Grabbing and holding him at arm's length, he studied Ruy's face. "You look just like your father," he exclaimed.

Dom Pedro held Ruy's hand and led him into the house and into his sizeable study with stuffed bookcases on three walls and various tables with instruments and projects stationed about the room. A south wall of glass doors leading to a terrace over the river and pastoral landscape illuminated the great room. The professor commented on the heat of the day and prompted Ruy onto the terrace, where they sat in two chairs facing each other, bathed in the afternoon sun.

"You seem bewildered about why you are here, young man."

"To be honest, sir, I am."

"Did your father not tell you we were best friends at the university in Salamanca, where we both studied medicine? And later, in Lisbon, we were neighbors in the Chiado neighborhood, on . . . let me remember— yes, Rúa da Flores. Your father and Perpetua were newly married and had the second floor, and Guiomar and I were on the ground floor with our two little boys.

"Your father taught and worked at Todos Santos Hospital on Rossio Square. I taught at the university and tutored the king's younger brothers.

What good times! And exciting times too, if not dangerous. Your father and I were like brothers—we promised to look out for each other in times of need.

"We went off in different directions—your father, back to Covilhã, with his practice, where he has been quite successful. I bounced back and forth between universities and cities—Lisbon, Coimbra, Amsterdam, and Paris.

"Yes," Ruy said. "And you are regarded as one of the greatest minds of our times."

"I wouldn't go that far, filho.," the professor said.

"Dom Pedro, now that you have retired, what will you do with your time?"

"I am doing what I love, and I have earned the right to do so. For the first time in my life, I can devote all my time studying my own interests and writing at my own pace. But I did not invite you here to talk about myself and the old times that used to be. No—I recently received a letter from your *papá*, informing me of your presence here at the university and your intention to explore a curriculum that would lead to a navigator's life at sea. That's a noble intention, and only the most exceptional young men can hope to achieve it. So I have informed your father I will be available to advise you about what courses to concentrate on—and what is a waste of time. We can also discuss how to survive the distractions of university life and if I might add, the perils which lurk in the shadows for someone of our heritage. I'm sure you know what I mean."

Ruy assured the professor he did know, then informed him of his courses. Nunes gave his opinion on which classes were more important, which were less so, and which professors to avoid.

Dom Pedro then called for a servant to bring out some wine. No one came. After a few minutes, he excused himself and went off to the wine cellar to fetch the wine himself, muttering that he would return in a few minutes.

While he sat in silence, Ruy faintly heard someone plucking a soothing melody on a cittern. 9 The music was not far away, but what was its source? He walked to the terrace railing, where the sound was louder, but there was no trace of a human being on the grounds below.

The music came louder and more insistent, sung with a voice deep and expressive. Ruy recognized the refrain from a famous madrigal going around Coimbra.

Yonder goes Inês
in the lonely fields
by the Mondego,
teaching the grass and flowers
the secret name carved in her heart,
with her beautiful eyes
never dry.
What a pity
she had to die to be queen 12

Ruy leaned over the railing and caught sight of a slender, olive-toned foot, tapping the meter of the music. It was not a child's foot, and it seemed to him not quite a woman's foot. He lifted his legs over the balcony railing and positioned himself on the narrow ledge outside to satisfy his curiosity. Crouching and gripping the balustrade with one hand, Ruy leaned out until he could see the whole body of the musician below. His heart leapt—it was Ana Sofia! She was sitting on a divan with her eyes closed, the rays of the afternoon sun warmly flushing her face. Her nimble fingers flew over the strings as she sang.

Ruy leaned over and down to obtain a better view. Ana Sofia opened her dark eyes when Ruy's head and dangling ginger hair blocked the setting sun. Her first reaction was to scream, but she held back. Ruy jerked himself against the railing when he nearly lost his balance, and his head fell lower into Ana Sofia's line of sight. Her fright now conquered, she shrieked with laughter at the ridiculous spectacle. The professor entered Ana Sofia's quarters, ascending the stairs from the wine cellar. "What's so funny, child?" he asked.

"Nothing, *Pai*, a lizard fell off the ceiling and practically fell into the hole of my cittern. I supposed my music attracted him."

Ruy took the time to compose himself, returning to his seat on the terrace just as the professor appeared with a bottle of wine and two glasses.

They sat at a small table facing each other. Dom Pedro poured the wine into two goblets and then spoke.

"Years ago in Lisbon, when we were just getting started, your parents and Guiomar and I were neighbors. We had so much fun. Every day was like finding oysters—if not a pearl, at least a meal. Not that the present days are not exciting, but the shadow that then was just a dark cloud on the horizon has now overcast our nation, and the gold that has washed up on our shores has lost its luster. Times are more dangerous now. You know, I haven't seen Lourenço once since your mother—may she rest in peace—was buried in Santarém. How long has that been? Five years now?"

Ruy could hardly follow the conversation because his attention was elsewhere. It was downstairs with the musical spells of Ana Sofia; anatomically, it was downstairs somewhere between his heart and groin.

"Uh . . . yes, it will be five years in April."

"How is your father doing now? Is he in good health? Keeping busy?"

"Oh, yes, sir. *Pai* still has his practice in Covilhã with patients as far away as Castelo Branco and Guarda. He spends half his time traveling, sometimes to Toledo and Sevilla, but mostly down to Santarém and Lisbon. Did you know he invests in overseas armadas and private ventures?"

"I know. We used to consult about such matters,"

There was silence.

"What a pity she had to die to be Queen."

That lyric interrupted Ruy's attention.

"Of course, I will honor my pledge to your father, and when I am here at home in Coimbra, I will advise you with your studies."

Ruy was relieved to hear this but had trouble focusing on the professor. The cittern playing seemed to be louder. Maybe she's moved closer to the railing to mock me with her music, he thought. If she stops playing, it will be to eavesdrop on our conversation.

"Now, listen closely, young man. You remind me of a student of mine from the old days. He was both a warrior and a scientist. He sailed from the Atlantic to the far east and from Ethiopia up the Red Sea to the

Sinai Peninsula. His observations helped us to understand magnetism and navigational techniques. He died in India eight years ago before he could return home to his beloved Sintra Mountain. He was a true philosopher and truth-seeker. You know him for another reason. You know him as João de Castro, the Fourth Viceroy of India. Of course, he was a talented navigator, but he was also a friend and associate to me. The time I spent as his teacher was paid back many times by the precise records he kept of the things he saw on the seas he sailed. I'm telling you this, Ruy, because you could follow in his footsteps. But you must apply yourself at the university and stay out of trouble. I advise you to study the life and records of João de Castro. Another friend and student of mine you may be familiar with was Martin Afonso de Sousa, the First Viceroy of Brazil. These should be your heroes—you should always emulate men of valor.

"Now, I do believe in doing something for nothing, occasionally, just for sheer goodness, but when you can do something for something in return, I see nothing wrong with that. What I am saying is this: apply yourself here at Coimbra. Follow my advice—stay out of trouble. When you graduate with high marks, I will do what I can to get you an invitation from the king to attend the navigation school in Sagres. After that, you will be on your own. Make the best of it, but don't forget me. On every voyage you take, consult with me. It will be worth your while. I will give you what you need to collect information for me, just as I did with João de Castro. If I can tell you how to make your journey more successful or profitable, you'll have it."

"I don't know what to say, sir. I'm speechless. This is the most blessed day of my life. I will strive with every fiber of my being to not disappoint you—to merit your attention."

"A toast, then," Dom Pedro proposed, raising his glass, "to becoming a navigator and for me to have something new to write about, to increase the world's knowledge."

"A toast, *meu Professor!* I will not let you down."

Dom Pedro Nunes paused and reflected, "You know, Ruy, it's too bad you aren't a few years older. You would have gotten along well with my two boys, Apolónio and Pedro Areas. They're grown now, making their livings in Lisbon and Amsterdam. My two oldest daughters are also married and have been carried off . . . leaving my two youngest daughters here. Ana Sofia, if I am not mistaken, is about your age. Would you like to meet her?"

"I'd be delighted, sir."

"I must warn you—she is a free-spirit and scares most young men, not with her looks, but her tongue."

"Fair warned, sir."

Dom Pedro leaned over the railing and summoned his daughter.

She entered the room wearing the same white cotton shift with sandals on her feet and a wry smile.

"Ana Sofia, this is Ruy Gonçalves, son of one of my oldest friends from my days in Salamanca. He is from Covilhã and is in his first year at the university. He wants to be a navigator."

"A navigator? I think he will do well on the ship's rigging because I saw him hanging upside-down from the balcony watching me!"

Blushing, Ruy stammered, "Yes . . . I heard the cittern and was curious to see where it was coming from . . . when you went for wine, *meu Professor*. I beg your pardon, Ana Sofia, for intruding on your devotions. I was attracted by the poetry and the eloquent voice."

It was now Ana Sofia's turn to blush. To counter his advance and give herself a few minutes to appraise Ruy, she riposted: "the lyrics of the madrigal are from Luís de Camões, who was once a student here. Some say he was born here. Now he's gone to sea, banished to Goa for offending old King John III in a play he wrote. But this man Camões is a poet, and now, maybe he is a navigator on the *Ultramar* like you want to be. The difference is . . . if he's still alive, he is a *man*, which, as I can see, you're not quite there."

Ana Sofia thought to throw him off balance. Let's see how he reacts, she thought. "*Pai* has in his mind that this Ruy is a possible suitor for me. I'm only sixteen, and Ruy can't be much older. *Pai* is thinking of the future. *Pai* knows his father. That means he is probably from a good family, probably intelligent, no doubt Jewish from a *converso* family like me. Ruy doesn't look Jewish, not with that light hair and gray eyes, but he does have a hawk's nose, and some would say he's handsome, at least with a good stout body. I wonder if he can dance or if he's clumsy. I'll find out."

Dom Pedro, sensing that his daughter could handle herself and that he was an obtrusive observer, exited the terrace for his study to let matters play themselves out. He shut the terrace door behind him.

Ana Sofia's eyes transfixed Ruy. He couldn't compose his thoughts. Her left eye is soft and innocently compassionate, he thought. Her right is full of mischief. He was irresistibly drawn in yet remained on guard. She wants to fence, he thought, and her foil is sharp. He was confused but managed a retort. "It is true that, like you, I have not yet fully matured. But I wager I have seen more cities with these two eyes than you have read about in the libraries of Lisbon and Coimbra."

"You seem a *saloio*.[13] Which cities has a backcountry boy from the Serra da Estela seen? Guarda? Castelo Branco?"

"If Princess Ana Sofia were to show any curiosity, I could tell her about Amsterdam's canals and coffee houses or the Tower of London and London Bridge. If you were interested, I could describe the Tejo River to its origin in the walled city of Toledo. Or I could tell you about the ships calling at the port of Sanlúcar da Barrameda and sailing up the Guadalquivir to Sevilla and Córdoba. Or I could tell you about Paris in the spring, or—"

"Stop! You win. I'm sorry I brought it up. I've never been out of Portugal. *Pai* never took us on his trips, and I don't know where Sanlúcar de Barrameda is. I guess you are not the Covilhã *saloio* I thought you were. I'm impressed. It's just that I have seen so many clowns your age at the university since my father arranged for me to attend classes."

Ruy felt a warmth welling up in his chest. He stared at her as thoughts raced through his mind. She sees me and even likes me, he thought, and she is so beautiful. I have not seen anything like her in any of the places father has taken me. No woman like her in Covilhã. She stands graceful, a few inches shorter than me, but at the same time defiant. She is almost a grown woman, yet so petite. Look at her sunburned skin—it's as if she lived outdoors. And a clear complexion, without oil or pimples. Her hair is untamed, with eyes to match—eyes so black, I'm sure she obtains her secrets from the raven. Her mouth is perfect with graceful Lusitanian lips. When she smiles, her perfect teeth gleam as if presaging a glorious sunrise. But beware of her teeth. They are sharp, concealing a sharp tongue controlled by a sharper mind. I am afraid, but my excitement overcomes my fear. I must find a way to draw closer to her.

"Ana Sofia, come closer. You have something on your chin. Have you hurt yourself? Are you bleeding?"

Ana Sofia came closer and looked up into Ruy's face. He wanted to pull her to himself and kiss her, but that was not his plan. He studied her chin from different angles as if he were a physician. She looked up, bewildered, her dark eyebrows furrowed.

"What is it?" she whispered, half with concern, half hoping he might kiss her.

"Ana Sofia, I'm afraid you have a wart on your chin—is it from kissing a frog while looking for your Prince Charming?"

"You son of a—"

Ana Sofia growled as she kicked him on the chin. She shoved him backward, and Ruy fell into his chair, convulsing with laughter. No matter how much she felt the joke was on her, the laughter was contagious. She stood over him with hands on her hips and, with the maximum effort to suppress a smile, proclaimed, "You bastard! You voyeur!"

Ruy rose from the chair just as Dom Pedro opened the door to the study and asked, "Everything all right out there, *minha filha?*"

"Yes, *Pai.* We were telling funny stories. Everything's all right."

Dom Pedro closed the door, and Ana Sofia, pushing Ruy back into the chair, stood over him, demanding an explanation.

Ruy looked up with the apprehension of a penitent hound. "I'm sorry, Ana Sofia, I couldn't resist the temptation. I ran out of things to say, and I didn't want the afternoon to end with a simple goodbye and farewell. I gambled everything, letting you know I'd seen you in the Quinta das Lagrimas with your sister and Baltasar. I saw the prank you played with the frog. I am not a voyeur. I do not go around spying on people. My friend Davide and I were in the garden to retrace the spirits of Inês and Pedro and what happened there so long ago. We heard you and your sister laughing and went over to see what was happening. We didn't want to intrude, so we hid in a grove of trees. I thought you were the most beautiful girl I had ever seen. I heard your sister say your name, and I couldn't get it out of my head for days. It was music to me. Just those five syllables—a-na so-fi-a, repeatedly ringing in my head."

Ana Sofia, who considered herself a young warrior, melted. She knelt in front of him, putting her hands on his as they grasped his knees. She looked up, speechless with moistened eyes.

Ruy continued. "I didn't know who you were in the garden. As far as your father is concerned, I didn't know if he even had children. I knew our parents were friends at one time, and your father was certainly a hero to me. I came here thinking I could take courses from him, but I heard he retired. I didn't know if he was still in Coimbra or Lisbon. My father told me nothing. Even if I'd known of this house's existence, I didn't have the credentials to come knocking on your father's door. I was dumbfounded. But what good fortune! When I leaned over the balcony and saw you, the jolt was too much, and I almost fell. It is now almost too much for me, Ana Sofia. Why do I deserve this good fortune?"

Ruy could say no more. His mouth quivered. He tried to speak, but no words came forth as his heart swelled into his throat. He sobbed uncontrollably, heaving with the same muscles that had convulsed with laughter only minutes before. But his tears were not tears of sadness. They were tears of gratitude to the life force when an unexpected chance defies the limitations of words.

Ana Sofia felt the same flood of mysterious emotions coursing through her body. Also sobbing, she rose up to kiss the salty tears trickling from Ruy's face. She tugged at Ruy's vest, pulling him upward. "Come—let's stand in the corner where *Pai* can't see."

Standing face-to-face, she whispered, "Which afternoons are you free from classes?"

"Wednesday and Friday."

"Good. I'll arrange to have Ida bring us to the garden next Wednesday afternoon, to the same pool where I kissed the frog." She looked up and took his head in her hands. She smiled with one tender and one mischievous eye: "Prince Charming."

They kissed an endless kiss, interrupted only by the sound of a disturbance inside Dom Pedro's study.

"Lovely, Ana Sofia," Ruy said in a louder voice. "Meeting you was splendid. Perhaps we'll occasion to see each other at the university library."

Ana Sofia accompanied Ruy as he exited the terrace and moved through the study, where the professor had been waiting while browsing over tables of unfinished projects. Ruy graciously thanked the professor once again for the favor of his attention. Dom Pedro told him he would send a messenger within the next month when he had time to meet again and asked him to bring his roommate, Davide, along with him.

"I'll show him to the door, *Pai*," Ana Sofia assured her father as she took the liberty of pulling Ruy's shirtsleeve in the direction of the door to the study. As they walked to the door, Ana Sofia turned and slyly winked at her father, who, in turn, flashed her a stern frown.

At the entrance, Ana Sofia opened the door and loudly bade Ruy a formal farewell. Under her breath, she whispered, "next Wednesday," and blew him a kiss.

Reeling with unfamiliar emotions, Ruy practically stumbled down the entrance stairs and set off with confident strides toward the hilltop city. He surveyed the steely-blue Mondego below, meandering west toward the setting sun. We're all going that way, he mused. How fortunate I am.

Ana Sofia returned to her father's study and was met with questions. "What did you think of him? He's not much older than you. You like him, don't you?"

"Oh, he's pleasant enough, *Pai*, if not a little clumsy, being from over the mountains . . . but he has been to many places. What does his father do?"

"I thought I told you. Ruy's father is Dr. Lourenço Gonçalves, an old friend from our days studying medicine in Salamanca and Lisbon. His hometown is Covilhã, where he practices. He has always been a man of many interests.

"I think it started with Ruy's grandfather, Dr. Emanuel Gonçalves, the private physician and long-time friend of Pedro Álvares Cabral. After his famous voyage to Brazil and India, Cabral fell from favor with Manuel I. He couldn't get a commission as a navigator, so he retired as a young man and lived in the family castle in Belmonte. Cabral's voyage left him with two things—wealth and malaria. I imagine boredom in Belmonte killed him faster than malaria, mainly because he had a unique understanding of Brazil, Africa, and the Indies. He knew where the money came from—the investment houses and speculators in Europe.

"Together, Cabral and Emanuel Gonçalves formed an investment partnership with unknown partners to invest in armadas from Lisbon and who knows what other commercial ventures. All this activity would necessitate a good deal of travel, which, I imagine, Dr. Emanuel would have done. Emanuel's son, Lourenço, followed in his father's footsteps, becoming a physician and dealing with the financial centers and investment houses in Europe. Lourenço told me he eventually oversaw all the Cabral-Gonçalves overseas investments.

"After Salamanca, we moved to Lisbon and started our families together, living on two floors of the same building. Those were good times. Even then, Lourenço would spend as much time at the wharves at Ribeira das Naus and Praça do Comércio as he did at Santa Clara University. I imagine he was reporting every tidbit of information to his father."

Dom Pedro shrugged. "Anyway, the adage, 'like father, like son,' only goes so far, and usually not more than two generations. Lourenço took Ruy to all those cities and tried to cultivate an interest in finance and overseas investment. He told me something curious—his son was more interested in being at sea and *sailing* to the cities rather than being in them. Ruy would not allow the captains and crew a respite from his incessant questions. And regarding financial dealings, Ruy showed as little interest in gambling with money as he did in a medical career. He believes the practice of medicine is essential—but not for him. He'd rather *make* discoveries than profit from them. He dreams of riding on the high seas for adventure. His father wants me to help him, and I will, for his father's sake, because I like Ruy. But Ruy Gonçalves has a long way to go to realize his dream.

"That's enough. Ruy has caught your fancy; otherwise, you wouldn't have spent so much time with him alone. But be careful, *menina,* for his sake and yours. These are dangerous times. Times that try men's souls, as they say. None of us is out of danger, even our family. And remember, you are not yet a woman, and he is not yet a man."

"I'll be careful, Father." With that, Ana Sofia retired to her bedroom to contemplate whether her encounter with Prince Charming was reality or illusion.

Ruy arrived at the boarding house and found Davide eagerly awaiting his return. "This is a day for celebration," Ruy declared. "Let's go down to the tavern for some food and drink. I'll tell you about the miracle that has changed my life forever."

Seated across from Davide, Ruy began, "Get ready. Dom Pedro Nunes, the world-famous physician, mathematician, and royal cosmographer, is an old friend of my father, and they have been in correspondence. Can you believe it?"

"Amazing." Davide shrugged, unimpressed. "So what happened?" he said in a monotonous voice.

Ruy wondered what bothered his friend. "The first good news is for you," he said, trying to engage Davide's interest. "Pedro Nunes has agreed to advise not only me but *you*."

"That's wonderful—can't wait to meet him. How does he know about me?"

"My father must have told him."

"He asked me to bring you with him next time he sends a messenger, which should be in about a month. You'll see his *vila* in the woods, overlooking the Mondego. The second piece of news is that if I apply myself, follow his guidance, stay out of trouble, and graduate with satisfactory marks, he will use his influence at court to get me an invitation to the navigation school."

"Well, that *is* extraordinary. What good fortune. It *will* change your life, but it's not quite a miracle, am I right?"

"Yes—that's not the miracle. The miracle is the beautiful *rapariga* 14 we saw kiss the frog in Quinta das Lagrimas—Ana Sofia—she's Dom Pedro's daughter. And I am in love with her. We talked on the terrace, and she kissed my cheek, then we kissed on the lips. I am in love with her, and I'm sure she likes me. She is not only beautiful but brilliant like her father, and she is a gifted musician and a quite spirited young lady. We have arrangements to meet at the Quinta next Wednesday. She will be with her governess, and I will see her there. And she often goes to the library at the university, where she has permission to read."

"Well, that is a miracle! Who would have thought you were a Prince Charming! Here's to you, my friend."

The next day, Ana Sofia found her governess, Ida, picking flowers in the garden.

"Nanna, last week I came to your cottage to visit you, and the door was open. I looked in and saw Fouad kneeling on a prayer rug praying to Allah."

"How do you know he was praying to Allah, *menina?*"

"It was in Arabic, Nanna."

"My child—Fouad, grew up praying in Arabic. He doesn't know how to talk to God in any other language. But I can assure you—even in Arabic, he was praying to God through Jesus Christ or the Virgin Mary. Our parents became Christian when yours did. You know the story. Sometimes, late at night, I have heard your father speaking Hebrew to himself out on the terrace—almost chanting. If he is praying, I am sure it is to our Savior, even if it is in Hebrew. Wasn't Hebrew the language of Jesus?"

"Yes, you are right. You are always right."

"Is there something troubling you?"

"No, I'm all right. I wonder if I could go to Quinta das Lagrimas again, perhaps next Wednesday. But I don't want to go with Baltasar. I'd rather go with you. Francisca doesn't want to go, so it'll be you and me. It's so beautiful there in the summer. Can we?"

"Sure, *menina*. Why Wednesday?"

"I want to attend lectures on Monday and Tuesday, and I have music class with Sr. Freitas here on Thursday."

"Very well—we'll go on Wednesday."

The following Wednesday afternoon, Ana Sofia and Ida proceeded from the Nunes *vila* into Coimbra and down the hill to the footbridge named after Pedro and Inês. Ana Sofia spotted Ruy lounging on the riverbank as they crossed the span. He had pulled his hat over his eyes as if napping in the glorious afternoon sun. Ida led as they crossed to the south bank. Ana Sofia cast a furtive eye at Ruy and smiled. He responded with a gallant tip of his hat, drawing a conspiratorial wink from her.

Ana Sofia and Ida sat on the bench by the pool where the frog lived. Ana Sofia began playing her cittern. Ruy strolled through the trees and into the clearing where the two were sitting.

"What a surprise to find you here," Ruy said. "I was walking by and heard a tune I recognized."

"*Bom dia*, Sr. Ruy Gonçalves. What a surprise! I am often amazed how my cittern attracts the strangest things—frogs, and . . . even you, Ruy. I'd like you to meet our governess, Ida. She has been connected to our family since before I was born."

"It is a pleasure to meet you, Dona Ida."

"Yes, equally. I recognize you. You came to the *vila* to meet with Dom Pedro last Sunday," Ida said, eyeing both as if she suspected a conspiracy.

"My father and Dom Pedro are friends from their university days." Ruy used the present tense, hoping Ida might think Dom Pedro would consider him an appropriate suitor for his daughter. Ruy sensed the possibility of reaching a mutual understanding with Dona Ida. He felt emboldened.

"Shall we all promenade together through the gardens?" he ventured. The governess consented with a nod of her head.

The couple strolled along the paths conversing, through groves, around lily ponds, and over streams. Ida walked a discreet fifteen feet behind the couple, allowing them privacy but remaining close enough to hear anything above a whisper.

Ana Sofia and Ruy exchanged small talk. Beneath their platitudes, Ruy studied Ana Sofia's manner—walking on the balls of her feet with determination, as if anxious to get ahead. She moved with a certain grace and rhythm—her hips shifting under her white linen dress with a cadence that defied worry and threw care to the wind, beckoning him. Come on, her body called. Let's dance to the music.

Ana Sofia saw that Ruy's shoulders were broader than she remembered. He was no longer the upside-down fool hanging from the balcony. His hair was blondish-brown, but his neatly trimmed beard and mustache bore a reddish tint. Thank God, it's not wispy and new, she thought, as an adolescent's soft facial hair. He's a few inches taller—that's good. Most boys find me too tall. His eyes are kind, caring, and inquisitive. I believe they're grey, but I'm not sure. I must get closer. What is he thinking about me? And what is that scent? I want to get closer to him to identify it. It is soft and alluring, and I have never smelled it before. She felt compelled to ask.

What is that lovely scent about you? Is it soap, perfume . . . a kind of herb?"

"Sandalwood oil my father gave me from the Indies, mixed with peppermint oil from Morocco. You like it?"

"It's divine."

"I'll bring a small bottle next time."

"No," Ana Sofia whispered. "I have a better idea."

"Do you?"

"Bring the bottle; I will give it to Ida as a present."

"What are you thinking?"

"To ingratiate her to you, and I know she loves fragrances. She spends all her free time tending her herb and flower beds."

"I'll do it and save some for you."

Ana Sofia looked up at Ruy coquettishly. He interpreted her expression as an affirmation of his affection. And as he continued gazing upon her radiant face, the feeling of confusion and mystery returned. He told himself that her eyebrows might say no, but her eyes said yes. He again felt a surge of joy in his chest, not knowing how it would erupt—in tears, as the last time, or in masculine eloquence. He chose to speak words, but which words? Just be honest, he told himself.

"Ana Sofia, last Sunday was the most wonderful day of my life. Your father offered to advise me in my studies. If I do well, he'll get me an invitation to the navigation school in Sagres."

"That's wonderful, Ruy," she murmured. She glanced up to see the longing in his eyes. As they walked, she edged closer and grasped his hand, hoping her skirt would hide the contact from Ida.

"For the last three days," Ruy said. "I haven't been able to concentrate on anything—not my studies nor even my fortune of meeting your father."

She squeezed his hand.

"I can't get my mind off you—how you look at me, the wisp of hair over your eyebrow, the music of your voice, the dance of your walk, the magnetism of your smile, the vibrant warmth of your lips against mine."

"Stop, Ruy," she whispered. He was becoming too proud of the muse that had loosened his tongue. "You make my heart purr like a kitten. But Ida is not stupid. She will surely know what is happening."

"You make me growl like a lion. And I don't care what Ida knows."

"You *must* care, *meu amor,* for our future depends on Ida."

Ruy paused. '*Meu amor?*' I am her *love.* I'll do what she says. She must be right. Our future depends on Ida.

"I *do* want to keep Ida happy, *meu amor.* Whatever it takes," Ruy replied.

She laughed and swerved close, brushing his hamstring with her slender, linen-covered thigh. She looked at his beaming face and whispered, "Next week—same time, same place?"

He nodded with a smile.

She withdrew her delicate, silken hand from his grasp and danced up the path ahead of him. "Good." She laughed and sang the refrain from a popular ballad about foolish boys.

Ida had been following the pair at a safe distance. She'd likely seen everything. Ruy wondered what she thought. Her expected role in the family was the custodian of virtue against the irresistible allure of young love. He reminded himself she is likely no fool and should not be played as a fool. Ana Sofia was right.

On Wednesday, while Ana Sofia and Ida strolled through the Quinta, there was no pretense of coincidence when Ruy appeared with a vial of sandalwood oil mixed with peppermint. He presented the bottle to Ida. She accepted with a thinly veiled measure of caution, but the inimitable scent enchanted her. She could identify only peppermint, as she had never smelled sandalwood.

The couple wandered off, confident the bribe would have its intended effect. And indeed, Ida gave the couple more latitude. They approached a fountain surrounded by a bed of red flowers with a sharp fragrance. Ruy breather deep the floral perfume and invited her to sit on a bench where water flowed from an opening in a rock wall. Ana Sofia looked at him incredulously.

"Are you joking? Don't you know where you are?"

Ruy shook his head.

"This is the spot where they murdered Inês—those red flowers mark it. Even the water here flows red." She grabbed his hand.

"Come with me, *amor*. Ours is another fountain."

They walked down the path, and within two minutes, Ana Sofia guided him to another gurgling water source with a different ambiance.

"This is the one we will drink from, *meu amor*—the Lovers' Fountain. The other one is the Fountain of Tears. We will never sit there. Let's sit here instead.

The clarity of her mind and her ability to take charge stunned Ruy. He consented immediately, sitting on the bench and pulling her to him.

"You don't know much about Coimbra yet, do you, Ruy?"

"Evidently not, *minha querida*." Ruy ventured a term of affection.

"Have you seen the shield of the city of Coimbra?"

"I don't understand what it means."

"I'll explain. A damsel, princess, or queen is emerging from a chalice. There is a winged dragon on one side trying to drink from the grail and, on the other, a lion also wants to partake of the cup."

Talk of a grail touched a fresh nerve. Ruy considered relating the story of Pero da Covilhã to Ana Sofia but decided against it. He feared she may think he was otherworldly. "The shield is still a mystery," he said. "What does it mean?"

"You know the story of Hercules?"

"I've heard of him, but don't assume I know all of it. You know I'm from the backcountry." Ruy snickered.

"You are in my country now, *saloio,* so I will educate you. Hercules was the illegitimate son of the god Zeus. As a demigod, Hercules had strengths. He lived in Greece and helped the king of Thebes against his enemies. The king gave Hercules his daughter to marry, and they had many children.

"Hera, Zeus's wife, hated Hercules. She caused Hercules to go crazy and kill all his children. Afterward, Hercules became despondent. He went to the Oracle of Delphi to ask what he must do to atone for his sin. The Oracle sent him to ask the king of Argos. Hercules did. The king of Argos told him he could redeem himself by performing ten labors.

"Hercules performed nine of the labors and returned to the king of Argos for further instructions. The king told him that to complete the last labor, Hercules would have to sail to the island of Erytheia, in the middle of the Atlantic Ocean. He had to capture all the cattle owned by the giant, Geryon, and bring them back to Argos.

"Hercules went to the sun god, Helios, to borrow an enormous golden chalice. He used the golden cup to sail across the Mediterranean and up the coast of Portugal. There he stopped to rest and resupply in the realm of the king known as Bebryx. The king welcomed Hercules with lavish hospitality. Hercules fell passionately in love with Pyrene, the king's beautiful virgin daughter. Hercules violated the sacred code of hospitality and seduced Pyrene to satisfy his desire. He then sailed into the Atlantic on his golden cup to capture Geryon's cattle.

"Pyrene soon felt something stir in her womb. It was the growing fruit of her encounter with Hercules. She fled into the forest, ashamed to face her father's wrath. At the end of nine months, Hercules returned to the Portuguese coast with the golden vessel full of cattle. He made his way back to the realm of Bebryx.

"While Hercules was still traveling, Pyrene gave birth in the forest—not to a human, but to a monster with the body of a winged dragon. Pyrene was so distressed at the birth she screamed and cried enough to wake the whole forest. Hercules heard her call for help but came too late. Her screams had awoken the entire forest, and the wild animals tore her asunder.

"Hercules found only Pyrene's head and torso. He became so distraught that he roared her name so loudly it still echoes across the ridges of Serra da Estrela and as far as the Pyrenees, which were named for her.

"Grief overcame Hercules. He could not win for losing: while trying to redeem himself for killing his first family, he had violated the sacred code of hospitality. He was now responsible for the death of his *second* family.

"To make retribution for his sins, he founded the city of Coimbra and conferred nobility upon it. He created the shield with his beloved Pyrene, her face and bust rising out of the grail, a winged dragon on one side, and a lion on the other."

"What happened to the winged dragon Pyrene bore?" Ruy asked.

"I don't know," replied Ana Sofia. "But there is another legend about that."

"Go ahead."

She continued. "There was once an enormous snake that terrorized the people here. The name of the serpent was Colober.

"The king had a daughter who was in love with a young knight. However, the king did not consider the knight noble enough to marry his daughter. The princess proposed to her father that whichever man killed Colober would win her hand in marriage.

"Of all the knights in the kingdom, only one dared to fight Colober, and he was the princess's suitor. The young knight roused Colober from his cave with the smoke of a fire at the entrance. When the snake appeared, the knight struck off his head.

"So, in the end, the handsome knight won the hand of the princess, and they lived happily-ever-after, so they say. The city's name became Columber Briga, later shortened to Coinimbriga, meaning 'Battle of the Serpent.' And now it is shortened to Coimbra."

"That's a good story, Ana Sofia," Ruy responded. "I like it better than imagining Pyrene being torn to pieces, don't you?"

"Yes, but let's not think more about it, *meu amor.*"

But Ruy couldn't control his thoughts. "Pyrene's story is tragic," he said, "but the shield of Coimbra is much better. The chalice—the golden cup of Hercules—*must* be the Grail, and Pyrene is emerging from it, not unlike being reborn. The winged dragon on the left wants to taste the golden cup's elixir, and the lion on the right wants his as well. The dark and light energies are with Pyrene, the embodiment of love, rising between them out of the Grail."

Ana Sofia realized that Ruy tended to let his imagination run wild into some strange and exciting places. Fascinated, she urged him to go on.

"Perhaps Hercules misused the power of the Grail when he seduced the daughter of his host and abandoned her while pregnant. To redeem himself, he created this city. Parzival had to wander many years after finding and losing the Grail castle. They say he also abused a royal maiden and left her abandoned and forlorn. Parzival had many bad experiences before finding the castle again and learning how to ask the pertinent question of the Grail."

"And what is that question, Ruy? I fear I've forgotten—"

"The question the Grail wanted to hear, *minha querida*, was, 'Who does the Grail serve?' Parzival made many mistakes before finally piercing the veil between knowledge and wisdom and finding the Grail again.

"It is as if this story goes round and round over time. Pyrene was the Grail Maiden. Hercules found her and committed an injustice upon her. He found her again and broke down. Then he tried to redeem himself. Or considering the shield of Coimbra, maybe Hercules transformed Pyrene's spirit into the Grail Maiden to make amends for his sin . . . or maybe Hercules. . . ."

"Ruy! Stop. It's just a shield. You're making my head spin. Where did you get your imagination? I've never heard anyone talk like you."

"My imagination? Is there something wrong? I didn't mean to frighten you. I got carried away, I guess."

"Have you always been like this?"

"Yes and no. I recently had a long dream about the Grail, or, at least, I think it was about the Grail. The dream is still fresh. I didn't know about Hercules or Coimbra's connection to the Grail. But I did learn our first king believed there was a connection between the Grail and Portugal and the Templars."

"Did you know that Afonso Henriques was born here in Coimbra?" said Ana Sofia.

"No, I didn't know that. Perhaps that explains Afonso's obsession with the Grail. But I think he saw it as the chalice that caught the blood of Jesus on the cross. Beyond that, the children of Jesus and Mary Magdalene, particularly his daughters and granddaughters, were called the Grail Maidens since they are vessels carrying his bloodline. I didn't know the legend of the Grail went back to the time of Hercules. Whenever that was."

There was silence.

"I guess after that dream, my imagination has been running wild," Ruy said, not daring to tell Ana Sofia about Endovélico.

"Is that all?" she persisted. "Your imagination became active after a single dream? How strange."

"Maybe not," Ruy hedged, becoming acutely aware that Ana Sofia was relentless. He also remembered she was Jewish.

"I'm sure my imagination was spiked going to Toledo and studying the hidden books with Davide and his father, the rabbi."

"What hidden books?" Ana Sofia was beginning to get anxious and feared she had opened Pandora's Box with her questioning.

Ruy responded, "They are twelve books written in Aramaic, a close relative of Hebrew, and translated into Castellano. A group of roaming rabbis wrote the books in the Holy Land in the time of Jesus. The Romans captured and killed them, but their books survived. Rabbi Elias calls the books the *Zohar*. The rabbi kept them hidden in some ruins, but you know what, my love? I don't want to talk about this anymore."

"You can't stop now. You must trust me, or I will never meet you again on Wednesdays."

"All right, *minha querida*, but you must promise me two things."

"What are they?"

"You must swear upon whatever is holiest for you, *beleza*, never to repeat anything I tell you about the hidden books of the *Zohar* or anything else about Belmonte."

"*Juro pela minha vida*," she said, crossing herself. I swear on my life.

"Not good enough. I am serious. What is holiest?"

"Let me think . . . I know. Over there—three hundred *varas* ₁₅ in front of us, by the river. There—at the old Convent of Santa Clara lie the bones of our Saint Queen Isabel in her tomb—she who created this garden in which I found my own true love. Let's get Ida to walk over to the Convent. I'm sure the nuns will let us in, at least me, for a few minutes."

"Aren't you forgetting something?"

"What?"

"The *second* promise."

"What is it?"

Ruy looked down the path toward the governess. Ida was immersed in thought by the Fountain of Tears.

"You must promise to give me, at this instant, a full kiss on the mouth."

"Be careful what you ask for, my love." She slid onto his lap and grabbed his head with both hands.

Ana Sofia's lips were wet and fresh. She pressed them to his with confidence. Her curiosity fascinated and attracted Ruy. Deep inside, an ominous feeling warned Ruy that he shouldn't have revealed anything about the *Zohar*. But the onset of passion now cast that aside.

His grasp was firm and confident, and she was strangely attracted by the secret he withheld. She was surprised by this facet of his personality. But she did not want to venture there too fast, too deep. Let us take it slowly, she thought, but the kitten's purr in her breast had become the roar of a lioness.

From the corner of her eye, through Ruy's bronze-colored locks, Ana Sofia saw Ida getting up from her bench. She pulled away breathless.

"Here comes Ida. Time to go. Whatever Ida may think, it will be good for us to go to the tomb of Santa Isabel, and I mean *right now*."

Ruy and Ana Sofia walked hand in hand toward the river and the Convent of Santa Clara. Ida lagged at a safe distance so as not to hear their conversation. At the entrance to the convent, the nuns permitted Ana Sofia and Ida to proceed. Ruy waited on a bench in the sunbaked courtyard.

Ana Sofia entered the mausoleum with all the sincerity and humility she could muster. She gazed upon the sculpted effigy of the beautiful queen, lying in tranquility. She thought how lucky Isabel was to be so passionately loved by King Dinis. And Ana Sofia fantasized that she was lucky Ruy loved her like Dom Dinis loved Isabel. And more—Ruy was not as headstrong and demanding as Dom Dinis, but perhaps that was only because Ruy is not a king. Shaking herself out of the reverie, Ana Sofia applied herself to the task at hand.

She knelt before Isabel's *gisant*. 16 In a whisper that Dona Ida could not hear, Ana Sofia said, "Before you, Queen Isabel, and all that is holy, I share that I will never reveal or repeat what Ruy has told me—or will tell me—about the hidden books of the *Zohar*. And please, dear queen, convey to the Holy Spirit my request for protection for Ruy and myself against the dark forces surrounding us."

Her task completed, Ana Sofia backed out of the cool, dim sepulchral chamber. She felt a presence suffusing her heart and the core of her being. A rush of love was surrounded by an aura of trepidation. This presence, she concluded, confirmed receipt of her prayerful request. But the sensation was not without an element of excitement and apprehension.

With Ida's arm to support her, Ana Sofia exited the convent proper into the afternoon sunlight of the courtyard. Ruy rushed to her and took her hands in his. "You look like you've seen a ghost," he said.

She whispered in his ear, "I have, and she will protect us."

After the lapse of a month, Ruy and Davide received an invitation by way of messenger to meet with Dom Pedro Nunes at three o'clock the following Sunday. They arrived at the *vila* at the appropriate hour and entered the study of Dom Pedro. The young men thought they were alone with the professor, but Ana Sofia was listening behind a door in the next room.

Ruy introduced Davide and spoke of his aspiration to become a physician. Dom Pedro asked Davide if his father was a physician. Ruy sensed Davide's discomfort.

"No, Dom Pedro. My father is a wise man, and some would say he is a physician of the soul, but he is a simple shepherd with a flock of sheep."

Ruy felt compelled to finish the explanation. "Davide's great grandfather, Rav Jaco, was the chief rabbi of the Belmonte region. They burned him alive sixty years ago in Castelo Branco. Davide's grandfather was also Rabbi of Belmonte but died young. Davide's father elected to become a shepherd, if you know what I mean."

"Yes, I do know what you mean, Ruy."

Davide and Dom Pedro discussed Davide's curriculum and aspirations. Dom Pedro suggested professors whom Davide should seek out and others he should avoid before turning to Ruy. "May we speak in private?"

Davide left the room and went onto the veranda. Alone, Ruy felt a bolt of terror as a sudden apprehension overcame him. Alarm bells went off in his mind. Could Dom Pedro be more than a *converso?* Could he be connected with the Inquisition? Had Ana Sofia broken her oath? Or had Dona Ida told her master of Ruy's love for his daughter?

Ruy and the professor sat facing each other.

"I have written your father; he has sent me some information about you."

"Yes?"

"He has given me the exact time and place of your birth."

"For what purpose?"

"So I can construct your horoscope, which I have done."

"What do you see?"

"You want to be a navigator, and I see by your stars that you will indeed be an explorer, perhaps a man of the sea or of other lands. But that's not what I wanted to discuss. I knew those things already, and they are not my primary concern. I see the natural affection between you and my daughter . . . and I want to protect her from disappointment, from heartbreak. You understand?"

There was a long pause. Ruy didn't know how to respond.

"My suspicion was confirmed. Your sunning is Sagittarius, and your rising sign, at the moment of your birth, is Taurus. This is not bad—it confirms your natural aspirations. The problem is that Ana Sofia's sun sign is Taurus, and her rising sign is Sagittarius. You are minor opposites, but the kind of opposites that attract. To compound matters, she is Venus on the cusp of her first house in trine to Mars, and you have Mars on your rising sign in trine to Venus. There are other curious ties between you two, but I won't go into them now. Suffice it to say—in terms of music—which Ana Sofia understands, if you do not, you are the dominant chord or note in her life scale, and she will be the melodic "fourth" in yours; that is, the melody in your life. I am powerless to do anything about this fateful circumstance. But I warn you—be careful with her. Do not break her heart, or your heart will have no music and remain lifeless forever. You understand?"

Ruy was too stunned to reply with words. He could only nod his head in affirmation.

Ruy and Ana Sofia met on the following Wednesday at the Quinta. Ruy spent his monthly allowance on a beautiful Arraiolos rug, which he gifted to Dona Ida, thinking it was the perfect size for a *sajjāda* 17 for herself or her husband. Ruy reminded himself to visit the Jewish merchant Simão de Pina the next day to draw on the letter of credit his father had established. Ruy waited for Dona Ida and Ana Sofia on the Quinta side of the Pedro and Inês footbridge, where he presented the carpet to Dona Ida. Ana Sofia was pleasantly surprised; she commented on the exquisite design of the rug.

Dona Ida accepted the gift gracefully, "You should not have done this, Sr. Ruy. This is too much—it's beautiful." Ida knew this was another bribe, but her husband's prayer rug was worn, and the new *sajjāda* would make him happy. But this is a bribe! If the relationship between the two lovebirds goes any further, she thought, *I* will be the one called before the master of the house. I should call this to the master's attention, give back the sandalwood oil, and not accept the prayer rug. But she could not.

Ida sat quietly beside the Fountain of Tears. She allowed Ana Sofia and Ruy to stroll the paths in the forest surrounding the two fountains.

Ruy was eager to learn whether Ana Sofia knew what her father had told him about their horoscopes. "Do you believe in horoscopes?" he blurted.

"Of course," she said.

"Did you know your father can make a horoscope?"

"Of course—he taught me. Listen, *meu amor*, I know where you're going. I eavesdropped on your conversation with my father. Late that night, after he went to bed, I even looked at his papers where he had both of our horoscopes. I studied them, and he is right. So, what can we do about it?" she shrugged.

Ruy said nothing more.

They walked along amid the strange, giant trees, trees that were entangled in wonderment. Ruy wondered why Ana Sofia was so casual about the extraordinary coincidence of their horoscopes yet offered no opinion.

Well out of Dona Ida's line of sight, they found an ancient tree whose root structure above ground extended out and around the tree like a hoop dress. They reclined behind the tree in a tangled root mass that formed a natural bed, hiding them from incidental traffic.

Ana Sofia rested her head on Ruy's chest. "We are meant for one another," she whispered. "You for me, me for you. Our story is in the stars." She nestled up and kissed his neck, sensing the warmth of his body.

"I don't have to look anymore," he whispered. "You are all my dreams and more. I love you so much. The mere thought of you excites me. And the litheness of your body in my hands feels so natural . . . I want to explore it."

"Explore my lips, *meu amor*."

With his hands on her waist, Ruy raised her gently to meet his hungry lips. Tongue explored tongue and teeth; he kissed her eyes, her ears, lips, and face. Ana Sofia explored the contours of his neck, opening the buttons of his rough cotton shirt to experience the coarse hair of his chest against the softness of her cheek. Ruy's hands had long since groped their way inside Ana Sofia's garments. One now clutched a firm bare buttock. Another slipped under her embroidered linen chemise, approaching the supple globes of her breasts from below. She felt his swollen organ beating a rhythm next to her sacred parts. It was as if the cadence of his member matched her heartbeat.

Ida's voice called out from a distance. They pushed each other apart as if awakening from a dream. "We must go," Ana Sofia whispered as they straightened their clothes.

The following Monday, Ana Sofia found Ruy where she thought she would—in the cosmology library, near her father's university office. She slid onto the chair beside him and passed him a note, and as quickly as she'd appeared, she was gone. The message read: "Father has been called to the king's court in Lisbon. He may be gone for a month. Tomorrow night will be a full moon. Come to my house at midnight. Wait on the ground beneath the veranda off my father's study.

Ruy followed her instructions to the letter. He waited, resting against a pillar below the veranda, anxiously watching the shimmer of the moon on the river far below. Ana Sofia, treading on cat's paws, crept up behind him. The aroma of peppermint and sandalwood she'd taken from Ida betrayed her, giving Ruy enough notice for him to pivot and catch her before she could surprise him. They muffled their laughter with kisses. Ruy was excited. He looked her up and down, noticing she was dressed for adventure in a simple blouse, loose pants, and sandals.

She grabbed his hand. "Come." Ana Sofia led him down a path that snaked back and forth through the trees and brush and terminated at the riverbank. A rowboat with oars was on the shore.

"There is a small island upstream," Ana Sofia said with mischief in her eyes. It will only take a few minutes to row there. It will be nice, my love. It will be *our* island tonight."

They dragged the boat's stern into the water. Ana Sofia boarded, and Ruy shoved the prow from the bank and climbed aboard. Ruy put the oars in the oarlocks.

"Move over," said Ana Sofia as she maneuvered to sit beside him, grabbing an oar. "We'll get there faster this way, *amor*."

Minutes later, they pulled the boat onto the sandy bank of a small island in the middle of the Mondego. The beach shone like a silver spearhead in the glow of moonlight, with the island's landscape as the spear's green shaft. The moon transformed the quartz grains of the strand into an eerie, magical walkway upon which two dreamlike silhouettes moved in unison.

Ruy removed his boots and found a smooth rock to serve as a pillow for the bed of sand sculpted by Ana Sofia. They rested on the strand, where the night air was calming—it was a time to feel and sense, rather than speak. The call of an owl sounded above the murmur of the river. Its light filtered through whispering pine branches, the full moon poured its silver passion upon the retreating waters. An earthy fragrance mixed with the smell of minerals the Mondego carried down from Star Mountain, complementing the heavenly aromas of sandalwood and peppermint emanating from the warm body beside Ruy. He turned his head to view her profile, and her smile told him that she was as content as he was.

"Do you believe what my father told you about our horoscopes?" she asked.

"Of course, I do, my love."

"Then we might as well be married, don't you agree?"

"Well, yes, when you say it like that, I guess we should consider ourselves married."

"I feel like we were married before the beginning of time before the stars began to move."

"I feel that way too," Ruy confirmed. "We must be legally married when the time is right, but that is a technicality considering our love and mutual commitment."

"Yes, *meu amor,* we are already married. I am yours; you are mine. And now I claim the privilege to what is mine." She raised herself on her elbow and swung her leg over his body, mounting him.

In the gleam of moonlight, Ana Sofia's dark eyes glistened with passion and mischief as they drew close to his own, peering deep into his soul. She planted moist kisses on his eyes and then lingered on his lips. She nimbly unbuttoned his shirt with one hand while his fingers located the hem of her blouse, pulling it over her head. Still straddling him, a cascade of dark hair hid her bare torso from him. He parted the fragrant veil, delighting his eyes. Ruy's hands caressed the two moonlit fruits whose movement in the night gloom teased him, imploring him to taste of their flesh. He sat up, holding her steady at the waist, and savored the dark rosebuds as they hardened between his teeth.

Ana Sofia stood, throwing back her head and allowing the riverine breeze to stroke her long, dark locks, as Lusitanian women warriors must have done in ages past. She kicked off her sandals while untying the drawstring of her trousers. Ruy knelt and slipped the waistband to the ground. He flung his arms around her, embracing her naked body, grasping the cheeks of her buttocks, pulling her to himself. He lavished her belly button with kisses, then roamed his lips to her thighs and groin. He turned her to fondle the firm musculature of her buttocks, then reached up to cup an apple-sized breast to confirm he wasn't dreaming. He spun her around again to venerate her beauty as his hands traced the perfect contours of her backside.

Their eyes met and exchanged the sighs and murmurs of yearning and delight. No time for words. Falling to his knees, he buried his face in the dark, damp foliage between her legs, where the seductive fragrance surpassed sandalwood and peppermint. Ana Sofia moaned and yanked his hair. She tugged him to his feet by his long locks until they faced each other and kissed furiously. She unbuckled his belt, and his pants fell. She reached down and felt his pulsing penis, the first she had ever seen, much less touched. She scrutinized it in her hand. Hot and hard, it seemed to gleam in the silvery moonlight as it pulsed with the rhythm of a racing heart. She didn't know what to do next. With Ruy's manhood still in her hand, she looked up, mesmerizing Ruy with her loving and mysterious eyes as she drew him closer. Ana Sofia pushed Ruy to the bed of sand and lay on him, chest to chest, belly to belly, thigh to thigh. She placed his member between her legs and straddled it. She moved on him rhythmically until the gentle whispering of love words became urgent, then frantic. Ruy instinctually rolled her over as she held onto his neck. He spread her legs with his knee and laid on top. His organ could not find the door to the holy sanctuary without guidance. He tried with his hand, but she rebuked him, reached down, grasped his swollen penis, and glided it along the lips of her vagina. With the passage already well-lubricated, she guided him inside her. Ruy lost his restraint and plunged deep. Ana Sofia let out a muffled scream. "Oh! that hurts! That hurts so much!"

And then, with a humorous sigh, she whispered in his ear, "You have pierced the veil, Parzival."

Ruy was disconcerted and withdrew. Ana Sofia said, "No—go on." He re-entered and began with a slow rhythm, quickening when she responded favorably. They danced as one as they together approached a crescendo. She arched her back and moaned low and deep. Ruy felt his body about to explode with a rush of love. "Take it out!" Ana Sofia said in an urgent stage whisper. Ruy obeyed, and, as he withdrew, he ejaculated on her thigh, blending his seed with her blood and the sand.

Ana Sofia laid back, satisfied. "The last thing we want now, *meu amor*, is a baby," she said. She rose from the sand and gracefully shuffled into the shimmering river. Thigh-deep, she squatted for the cool waters to cleanse her.

They repeated the passionate interlude five times that month. The couple brought dry towels to their midnight forays into sensual paradise and frolicked in the river before and after each episode of love-making, enjoying the act of drying every inch of the other's body.

Ruy matured with an understanding of Dom Pedro's observation that Ana Sofia would be the melody to his chords.

Another full moon reigned over the eve of Dom Pedro Nunes's scheduled return from Lisbon, twenty-seven moons after the night the couple gifted their virginity to each other on the banks of the Mondego. Combined in coition on the strand of their private island, Ruy was late withdrawing from the ecstasy of orgasmic delight. Ana Sofia told him not to worry—that the river would cleanse her. She entered the waters and squatted deep and long against the current, inviting the Mondego to enter her.

Fonte das Lagrimas (Fountain of Tears)
where Inês, the wife of Prince Peter was murdered in 1355.

Tradition says that iron oxide in the stone floor of the Fountain of Tears
signifies Inês's blood from decapitation

Fonte dos Amores (Fountain of the Lovers)

Bench on the path to the Fonte dos Amores

Chapter 11

Goa, India

1520-1566

In 1520, Viceroy Afonso Albuquerque took the port city of Goa from the Bijapur Sultan. He had captured what he regarded as the finest harbor on the Malabar Coast of India. Ferdinand Magellan and his cousin, Francisco Serrão, were among the soldiers participating in the battle for Goa.

At the end of 1521, Dom Manuel I died of the black plague in his palace in Lisbon. It was poorly understood that Dom Manuel's passing signified the demise of the already faint hope for a Templar Christian empire based on the Holy Spirit. John III, King Manuel I's eldest son, succeeded him. Many years before, when Prince John was sixteen, he was betrothed to his twenty-year-old first cousin, Eleanor of Austria. John was keen on the idea, and when he saw his intended, he fell in love with her beauty. Shortly before the marriage ceremony, there was an abrupt change of plans. The young Prince's forty-nine-year-old widowed father, King Manuel, married the twenty-year-old Eleanor instead. The young Prince naturally took offense at his father, robbing him of his fiancée. Some claim this was one of the main reasons he became fervently religious, which gave him the nickname "the Pious One."

Over the next two decades, the Portuguese turned the ancient Hindu-Muslim port of Goa into an international trading center, unique for its time. Portugal monopolized the trade routes from the Indian Ocean to the Spice Islands and turned Goa into an extension of Europe. Goa had become known as "Lisbon of the East." From a religious point of view, there is an argument that it was "Rome of the East," but that reality was still thirty to forty years away. In Portuguese Goa's early days, the domination of trade and commerce was paramount, with evangelization coming as an afterthought. The lure of wealth and adventure trumped proselytizing.

Captain Ferdinand Magellan died on a Philippine beach in 1521—his men would complete his mission without him. The earth was no longer flat—it was now demonstrably round, and there was a new way from Europe to the Orient by sailing west across the Pacific.

As a consequence of Magellan's financial participation in the voyage, Francisco Serraõ's map of the spice islands was shared among certain individuals within the Casa de Contratación, the Fudder Group and the Cabral-Gonçalves group, including one Portuguese Jewish trader and financier named Bartolomeu Pinto.

In 1524, Pinto and his business partner, Gabriel Antunes, sent their two sons from Lisbon to Goa. The young men came armed with a copy of the Spice Islands map and funds from the clandestine investment group their fathers had participated in.. That group, at the time, had branches in Sevilla, Toledo, Covilhã-Belmonte, Lisbon, and Amsterdam. The two sons, Simão Pinto and Rodrigo Antunes, were tasked with setting up a trading enterprise based in Goa, with branches in Kerala and Malacca, and perhaps beyond. The success of the "Antunes e Pinto" enterprise in the Indies was guaranteed by the constant flow of inside information from different critical sources: the Portuguese Crown in Lisbon, the Spanish Casa de Contratación in Sevilla, and Jewish silent-partner investors throughout Europe. With this advantage, the firm of Antunes e Pinto was able to see the cards of all the players around the table. Slyly, with quiet subtlety and requisite anonymity, Antunes e Pinto was able to fund various armadas, whether Spanish, Portuguese, or Dutch—and place side-bets on the outcomes.

In addition to financing national armadas, Antunes e Pinto was to make its fortune from the buying and selling of commodities by responsible captains in command of ships owned or leased by the company. Of course, this necessitated the establishment of expansive warehouses under trustworthy managers near crucial harbors.

The first two years saw the purchase of a substantial warehouse in Goa and the building of two palatial homes for the Pinto and Antunes families. During this time, the two men regularly sailed down the Malabar coast to Kerala and the city of Cochim. Cochim was the first city to welcome Pedro Álvares Cabral a quarter-century before, allowing him to build a fort and a factory.

In Cochim, Simão Pinto and Rodrigo Antunes were welcomed by the Portuguese harbormaster and the Raja of Kochi, with whom the Portuguese had entrusted the management of the city.

The two young men were also treated by a delegation from the sizeable Jewish community, which traced their arrival in Kerala to the fourth century. The Jewish community was an amalgam of newly arrived Jews from the Iberian Peninsula, other traders from Turkey and Arabia, and still other Jewish souls tracing back into the mists of antiquity. The community revolved around the sanctuary known as the Paradesi Synagogue, which had become partially ruined over time.

Simão Pinto's father gave him the name of Baltasar Abravanel as a possible manager of the new Antunes e Pinto operation in Cochim. As it turned out, Abravanel was a rabbi—a short, round, pleasant character from Castelo Branco. He was a confidant of certain members of the trading group. After a brief interview, Baltasar Abravanel accepted the position of manager of the new Antunes e Pinto branch in Cochim.

The years between 1526 and 1531 were spectacular for the growth of the Antunes e Pinto international trading group. Trading in spices and other oriental commodities was relatively undisturbed by Spanish competition, allowing more attention to eradicating local pirates, primarily Berbers, Arabs, and Turks.

The warehouse managers comprised the weak link in the Antunes e Pinto system. Often, these men were *conversos* because, with the passing of Manuel I, there was a growing demand to prohibit practicing Jews from living within the borders of Portugal or Portuguese maritime territories.

Simão Pinto and Rodrigo Antunes were indeed practicing Jews. Therefore, when John III inaugurated the enforcement of his "No Jews in Portugal" policy, Pinto and Antunes sold their newly constructed mansions in Goa. They moved twenty miles east, beyond the official border of Goa, to the town of Ponda, dotted with Hindu temples and Muslim mosques. In Ponda they could practice their faith quietly and conform to Portuguese law while remaining close enough to Goa to conduct business.

In 1529, Spain relinquished all claims to the Spice Islands, giving the territory and its trade exclusively to Portugal. Spain turned its attention to the Philippines, which it colonized.

In 1530, the Portuguese throne declared Goa the capital of the whole of the Portuguese Indies. Lisbon of the East was now a multicultural city, a hub of international trade that would have made old King Manuel I proud.

In 1531, there was an earthquake in Portugal that many blamed on "lapsing *conversos*." Success continued for Antunes e Pinto over the next five years, but mounting tension put a sense of trouble in the air.

In 1536, King John III requested that Pope Paul III establish the Holy Inquisition in Portugal, targeting New Christians suspected of reverting to their old religions and ways. The Pope agreed. He designated the Bishop of Ceuta, the king's personal confessor, as the first Grand Inquisitor in Portugal.

In 1538, Pope Paul III complained to John III about secularization in Goa. He threatened to open all of Asia for trade with Catholic nations if John did not purge Goa of the impiety of lapsed New Christians and Hindus.

In 1540, Dom John III requested the Vatican send missionaries from the newly formed Society of Jesus to the East Indies. The Pope put John III in touch with Ignatius Loyola, whose plan for the new order of Jesuits had been approved that year.

Loyola's first choice for a missionary to Goa and the East Indies refused. His second choice was the thirty-two-year-old Francis Xavier from Navarre, who had been ordained as a priest just three years prior.

As Francis Xavier was about to sail for Goa from the Torre de Belém in Lisbon in 1541, he received a package from the Pope appointing him Apostolic Nuncio to the East Indies. That meant the young Xavier would now represent the Pope and wield all the authority and power of the Papacy in that region.

In 1542, after dropping anchor in Portuguese Mozambique, Francis Xavier arrived in Goa.

After a year in Goa, the restless Francis Xavier left the capital. He sailed down to the southern tip of India and Ceylon in 1543. The remnants of early Christian communities founded by St. Thomas welcomed him in India. It was here that Francis Xavier converted tens of thousands of Hindus to the Catholic faith. He also built nearly forty churches along the south coast of India.

Francis Xavier returned to Goa a celebrity.

In 1545-46, Xavier wrote to John III requesting that the Inquisition be officially established in Goa because "many people are living according to the Jewish law and according to the Muslim sect, without fear or shame in the world." [18] As he informed John III: "I ordered the temples pulled down and all idols were broken everywhere. I know not how to describe in words of joy how I feel before the spectacle of pulling down and destroying the idols." [19]

John III did not respond to Xavier's request for the Holy Inquisition in Goa.

Francis Xavier's temple-burning activities spread to Ponda and its environs. Simão Pinto and Rodrigo Antunes began to think of moving to higher ground. They slowly started shifting assets to Cochim. They visited the southern city with increasing regularity and cultivated good relations with the Raja of Cochim and Rabbi Baltasar, and the congregation at the Paradesi Synagogue. Rodrigo Antunes even participated in a study group based on some books of the *Zohar* that Rabbi Baltasar had brought from Sevilla.

In 1547, Francis Xavier abandoned his hope of spiritualizing the overly secularized Goa and departed from the capital again to pursue his role as a missionary, where his true talent resided. He went to Malacca, then to the Maluku Islands, and finally to the Spice Islands.

He returned to Goa in 1548 and, still restless, made brief visits to Malacca and Chinia.

In 1549, Francis Xavier set sail for Japan. He arrived in the summer. Local rulers treated him well but forbade him from converting Japanese subjects to his faith. He made little progress disseminating Christianity in Japan because he lacked fluency in Japanese, and his "vow of poverty" had no appeal among the Japanese people and rulers. Nevertheless, Francis Xavier stayed in Japan for over two years.

Xavier returned to Goa in 1552, but within a few months he was back again on the high seas, this time bound for China. In August, he disembarked on a Chinese island a short distance off the coast of Canton. He took a Portuguese Jesuit student, an Indian servant, and a Chinese friend with him. After three months of waiting in vain for permission to enter China, the Jesuit student and the servant sailed back to Goa, leaving Xavier with his Chinese friend. Soon after that, while still waiting for permission to enter China, Francis Xavier caught a fever and died on the island.

By 1558, affairs had gone reasonably well for Antunes e Pinto during the recent decade, despite mounting pressures. The partners contributed handsomely to rebuilding the old Paradesi Synagogue in Cochim in gratitude to Yahweh for their prosperity in recent times. The Raja of Cochim even helped rebuild the structure, and this gave the partners added confidence they were making the right moves.

Back in Portugal in 1560, young Ruy Gonçalves and Davide Mendes de Oliveira enjoyed bar mitzvah ceremonies, held in secrecy in the Bet Eliahu Synagogue in Belmonte. In that same year, King John III of Portugal died of internal bleeding. Although the old king had fathered at least nine children, only his three-year-old grandson, Sebastian, was alive at the time of his death to inherit the throne. John III's brother, Cardinal Henry, now served dual roles—regent for the infant King Sebastian and Grand Inquisitor of Portugal. One of the first acts of the Grand Inquisitor was to grant the posthumously canonized Francis Xavier's fervent wish—a formal inquisition in Goa.

During this time, Rodrigo Antunes and Simão Pinto contracted with Hindu artisans to build two regal mansions outside the city limits of Cochim.

The Holy Inquisition was formally installed in Goa in 1561. The Inquisition's offices were located in the old sultan's palace, which came to be known as the "Big House."

The first act of the Inquisition was to focus on the practice of Hinduism within the confines of Portuguese Goa, prohibiting the practice on pain of death.

The Inquisition's second target was the Sephardic Jewish community, which had become *cristãos-novos*. These *conversos* were systematically watched and interrogated to determine if they relapsed into the practice of their old religion. Other punishable interests of the Inquisition ranged from book censorship to divination, witchcraft, sorcery, bigamy, and sexual crimes. The crow-like inquisitors were also looking for vestiges of what they called "the cult of the empire of the Holy Spirit," or in other words, sympathy with the old Templar Vision.

One first-hand account claimed that in the streets around the Big House, people could hear "screams of agony from men, women, and children." In the stillness of the night, others were brutally interrogated, flogged, and slowly dismembered in front of their relatives. Inquisitors sliced off eyelids and carefully amputated extremities, knowing a person could remain conscious even though the only bodily parts were the torso and head.

Despite these horrors, things had gone reasonably well for Antunes and Pinto over the past four years. This may have been due to innumerable bribes on the one hand and the employ of Hindu assassins on the other.

In 1565, Simão Pinto traveled from Goa to the nearby city of Gujarat to notify his friend, the Sultan of Gujarat, that his residence and the palace of his partner, Antunes, were for sale along with their warehouse and inventory at the Goa harbor.

Local spies for the Inquisition surveilled Pinto. They reported to the Big House of recent "suspicious" activities with the Hindus of Gujarat. Now on the trail of Antunes and Pinto, the black friars searched for weak links in the Antunes e Pinto organization. One informer targeted the *converso* wife of the Antunes e Pinto Goa warehouse manager. She seemed to have bought an excessive number of candles on a Friday, presumably for a Shabbat celebration. Under the threat of torture, she admitted she heard rumors that Antunes e Pinto was selling everything in Goa and relocating to Cochim. She added that she and her family did not want her husband to have to move to Cochim.

The warehouse manager was subsequently interrogated, and interrogators confirmed that the trading house was moving to Cochim because of less pressure from the Inquisition in that city. This aroused the Inquisitor's interest. Under pressure, the manager offered additional information—he believed that Srs. Pinto and Antunes had contributed significant sums toward the rebuilding of the synagogue in Cochim in cooperation with the manager of the Cochim warehouse, whose name was Baltasar Abravanel.

The Goa Inquisitor sent a directive to his operatives in Cochim to search the offices and warehouse of Antunes e Pinto, the Paradesi Synagogue, and the residence of Baltasar Abravanel. The search turned up evidence that the Antunes and Pinto families had indeed contributed to the rebuilding of the synagogue, and when in Cochim, the families practiced the forbidden faith. Furthermore, they discovered a secret room in Baltasar Abravanel's basement with benches and chairs appropriate for a gathering. They also found mysterious illuminated pages, as if from a book, written in Hebrew and Castellano.

When this news reached Goa, the Inquisitor immediately ordered the seizure of Baltasar Abravanel and all incriminating evidence. He was transferred to Goa under guard on the first available merchant vessel.

One week later, the trading ship *Faro,* coming up the coast from Cochim, was sighted at sea south of Goa's harbor. That night, authorities seized Rodrigo Antunes and Simão Pinto at their homes in Ponda. They transported them to the Big House to await Baltasar Abravanel.

Inquisitors tortured the three men in separate chambers. Any morsel of information extracted from one prisoner was used to demoralize the other two and make them think they'd been betrayed. The process worked poorly, but the tactic broke the men's spirits over three intensive weeks. The Grand Inquisitor of Goa regarded this as an unexpected and resounding success for several reasons.

First, and most importantly, they had uncovered an extensive Jewish *converso* network stretching from Ceylon to Río de Janeiro, Brazil, including a coded language and a system for the transfer of commercial information and secrets without allegiance to kingdom or church.

A second reason for the Inquisitors' satisfaction was that the evidence collected would justify the immediate seizure of the properties of Antunes and Pinto before they sell to the Sultan of Gujarat or another buyer.

A third reason was that despite extensive torture, the physical bodies of the three prisoners had not been severely mutilated. That meant they would be able to stand at the stake as whole human beings—to be consumed slowly by the flames while fully conscious—experiencing the full consequence and humiliation of their sin. To witnesses of the spectacle, it promised to be an unforgettable testament and warning.

Indeed, the pageant took place amid much pomp and circumstance before a populace torn between spectacle and grief, exuberance, and fear.

The *auto-da-fé* was staged in the commercial plaza of Goa on a sunny Sunday morning early in February 1566. As if not to spoil the festivity of the event, even the wind cooperated by blowing the stench of their burning flesh out to sea.

The Goan Inquisitor's Report would reach Lisbon in five months. Three copies of the report were made and entrusted to three friars who boarded three separate vessels for Portugal. Sending three reports would diminish the possibility of loss by shipwreck. Time was of the essence. Nature ought not to delay the exposure of a crime of this magnitude.

CHAPTER 12

THE SPREADING CATASTROPHE

Belmonte and Coimbra
August 1565

Three ships sailed from the harbor of Goa on the last day of February of 1565, each bearing a copy of the Inquisitorial Report of an exposed network of heresy and espionage throughout Portugal's maritime possessions. One of the ships, *Viriato*, buoyed by favorable winds, tied up at the Fort of Bom Sucesso's pier near the Torre de Belém in Lisbon by late July. Within days, royal messengers carried the news to the Houses of the Inquisition in Lisbon, Coimbra, Evora, Castelo Branco, and across the border to Sevilla and Toledo. No action was taken while the Grand Inquisitors in Lisbon and Sevilla devised a plan and compiled lists of names. The goal was to coordinate a simultaneous mass arrest in various cities across the two countries. A surprise campaign would round up all the known heretics and traitors. The list was headed by Gabriel Antunes, Bartolomeu Pinto of Sevilla, and Dr. Aryeh ben Gavriel of Toledo. Lower came Dr. Lourenço Gonçalves and Elias Mendes de Oliveira. Near the bottom of the lengthy list were the names Ruy Gonçalves and Davide Mendes de Oliveira.

The plan was to be executed during the second week of August, but for reasons unknown, the Spanish preempted by one week. The elder Pinto and Antunes, various investors, and *Zohar* study group members were summoned to the Casa de Inquisición in Sevilla during the first week of August.

News spread quickly, and two days later, near midnight, a rider on the verge of collapse tied his horse to the gate of Dr. Lourenço Gonçalves's *vila* in Covilhã.

Dom Lourenço immediately assembled the necessary provisions to sustain Ruy and Davide on a long journey of escape from Iberia. At midday, the doctor rode his best horse up the road to Belmonte, arriving at Rabbi Elias's shack near Centum Cellas. He found the rabbi sleeping on a bed of hay in the shade of the structure. As Dom Lourenço approached, Gaspár, the sheepdog, barked furiously, waking the rabbi. Confused, Elias rubbed his eyes and looked around as if jerked out of a dream. He felt a wave of urgency when he saw Lourenço.

"What brings you? he asked.

"It's time to save our sons!,"Lourenço responded.

"What's happened?" the rabbi inquired, still groggy.

"The worst has happened. Those connected with Pinto e Antunes have been caught and executed in Goa."

"How did you find out about it?", the rabbi asked.

"Last night, a messenger came from Sevilla. He brought news that the Inquisition apprehended old Bartolomeu Pinto and Gabriel Antunes and most of the members of the study groups there and in Toledo. In Goa, their sons and Rabbi Abravanel have suffered the *auto-da-fé*. We are probably dead men, but we must save our sons."

Rabbi Elias could not believe his ears. He hoped he was still dreaming with the crows. "Lourenço, are you sure—?"

"Of course I am, God damn it!" Gonçalves kicked dirt toward the rabbi, who was still reclined. "Wake up! Did you not hear—?"

"I heard." He shook his head to clear his mind. "I wish I were still dreaming…"

"You're not dreaming and we *are* dead men…but not our sons…"

With terror in his voice, the rabbi realized, "They are coming for us and the books of the Zohar!"

"Yes. Elias. You must take the books with your donkey and the money I have gathered. Go straight to Coimbra. Alert our sons so they can escape. We don't have a day to lose."

"To Coimbra?"

"Yes!", replied Lorenço.

"But I don't know the way.'

"It doesn't matter. I've thought this out, so listen: You won't take the main road around the mountain, but will save a day by going straight over the mountain past Manteigas to the top. There will be few people passing that way. Under moonlight, bury the Zohar at the top of the mountain—above the tree line—at whatever recognizable landmark you can find.

"Then proceed down the mountain till you find the Roman track that follows the Alva River. It will pass the towns of Avô and Côja, down to Arganil. Sell your donkey there. Buy a boat, maybe a dugout, to maneuver through the rocks. Drift down the Alva until it meets the Mondego above Penacova. From Penacova, float downstream with the current. It should take only half a day to reach Coimbra. Don't let the walls of the city intimidate you. While you are on the river, you will see a narrow footbridge crossing the river when the city comes into view. There's only one. On the south bank, the left bank, near the footbridge, you will find the yellow Convent of Santa Clara. The Mother Superior is Maria do Céu Lopes de Portalegre, a relative of mine. Tell her I am seriously ill in Covilhã and need to get an urgent message to my son. She will send a messenger to where Ruy and Davide stay."

"What if—?" Elias interrupted.

"Hopefully, both boys will come. If not, it won't matter. After you talk to Ruy, he'll go for Davide.

"Maybe it is best that Toninho doesn't learn about this until the boys are on their way. I am sure Toninho and his father are not involved, but for his own good, the less he knows, the better.

"Tell Ruy and Davide to gather what things they need for the rest of their lives and meet you outside the Convent. The Convent draws its water from a little canal that leads to a large spring or fountain in a place they call Quinta das Lagrimas. You will have the privacy to tell our boys what they need to know."

"That sounds well-planned, Lourenço, but what is *their plan* after escaping from Coimbra? Why don't you come with me?"

"I can't come with you, my friend. The crows have already landed on my roof. They will see I have escaped and search for me everywhere, including Coimbra. I have many acquaintances in Coimbra, some of whom I can't count on. And don't forget, the Inquisition has a Big House in Coimbra. No, I must go back to Covilhã, face the music, and dance the dance."

"And me—?"

"Elias, my true friend. You have been a widower for how many years now? With Davide gone, you will be alone. What's here for you on this side of the mountain? Your flock? Your secret flock of spiritual lambs? Sacrifice? Let me deal with that! I am already a dead man, but my soul has never been more alive. Trust me! Take this bag of coins. Gather your own money. With the *mezla* [20] of Yahweh, you'll find a way to survive after you get to Coimbra. Don't come back here, and don't go with our boys."

"Why? What's your plan for them?"

"My beloved friend, our sons are young, at the beginning of their destinies. They must go."

"But where, Lourenço? That's what I'm asking! Where can they safely go?"

"*Para o Novo Mundo,* Elias." To the New World.

"But how will they get there?"

"Not an easy question to answer. I must admit I have thought about the possibility of this day since they left for the university. Here, I have drawn a map of southern Portugal for them. It will guide them. Look— you'll see numbers associated with different locations on the map. Here is another piece of paper with numbers one to five and the names of five trustworthy friends who live along the way and may be able to help them in a time of need. They must memorize the five names and numbers, then destroy the paper."

"Let me see." The rabbi reached for the map.

"Okay. The boys, on horseback, will go due south from Coimbra to Tomar. From there, south to Constância on the Tejo. They follow the river by land up to Gavião and by road to Portalegre, then down to Elvas."

"Yes, Rabbi. And at Elvas, if they have any reason to suspect the Portuguese Inquisition is on their trail, they should cross the Spanish border at Badajoz and travel through Spain, cross-country or by road to Sevilla and from there, go down the Guadalquiver River to Sanlucar de Barrameda. That is where most of the Spanish ships for the New World cast off."

"That's good, Lourenço, but if they decide to stay in Portugal, what do they do?"

"At Elvas or Badajoz", he replied, "they sell their horses and buy a boat and make their way down the Rio Guardiana all the way to the

Mediterranean. From there they walk along the beach to Tavira where I have a friend, number four, a captain who owns small trading vessels. He can take them to Sanlúcar or put them on the beach across from the city.".

"Lourenço, I have to ask, why even go to Sanlucar de Barrameda and the Spanish New World? Why can't they go to the Portuguese New World, Brazil, Africa, or the Indies?"

"Too dangerous. In the first place, they would have to sign onto a crew on a ship from Lisbon or Setubal, where they will be watching for them. In the second place, the Portuguese colonies are too spread out. The Portuguese Inquisition is already in Goa, right? What chance would they have in Brazil? And how would they get there? No, in Spain, the Inquisitors will not be looking for them. The Spanish have their own Inquisition to worry about. Besides, all kinds of criminals, outcasts, and Gypsies out of Sevilla and Cordova end up as crewmen for the ships going out of Sanlúcar. And where do they go? They go to a vast continent bigger than Europe, where they have extensive colonies or kingdoms like Mexico and Peru. No, it will be much easier for our sons to make a new life there."

"Very well. You've thought this out, but what happens in the next few days when the town realizes I have just disappeared? The priest will sense something suspicious."

"Right," Lourenço responded. "Suppose we do this: I arrange for our friend Dom Manoel Vaz in Vale Formoso to take your sheep and dogs. I can go there now and be back in a few hours. If he agrees, you can set out tonight with your donkey and sheep and meet him where he pastures his sheep at the foot of the mountain. Leave your flocks with him and go on. He will probably insist on paying—"

"But what about the dogs?" Elias interrupted. "They won't respond to him and will follow me."

"Then you will have to kill them," Lourenço replied.

"My God! I can't do that. Let Dom Manoel tie them for a day."

"Good idea," Lourenço responded.

"That still doesn't explain my disappearance."

"No, it doesn't. But what about this? Tomorrow, I will visit Dom Fernão at Belmonte Castle. I will tell him the whole predicament. I know we can trust him and his son, Toninho. And when we are all dead, at least someone we trust will know the truth."

"What will you tell him?" the rabbi said with growing impatience.

"I will ask Dom Fernão to wait a week, then spread the rumor you drove your sheep up to graze on the high meadows. You fell off a cliff, and days later, another shepherd discovered your remains on the rocks at the bottom. After the wolves got to you, the only things left were bloody clothes and some gnawed bones. Perhaps in payment for your sheep, we could persuade Dom Manoel to have some of his boys leave your bloody clothes and boots at the old synagogue door one night—like Joseph's brothers bringing his bloody coat to his father. Hopefully, the congregation will bury the remains, and you will be officially dead. No one will ever look for you."

"Well, under these circumstances, I guess that is plausible. I must face the reality of our dilemma. And the reality is that we must save our sons at whatever cost. You have a master plan, and I have faith in you. I believe the angels gave you your plan. We have lots of work. Let's get started. I'll fetch some old clothes and sandals to give Dom Manoel while you ride to Vale Formoso and talk to him. I'll get my things ready, some provisions, extra clothes, a bedroll, a shovel, and what's left of my savings. When you return after nightfall, you can help me load the *Zohar* onto the donkey. I'll get the dogs and round up the sheep, and we'll be on our way to Vale Formoso."

Things went according to plan with Dom Manoel and the sheep. He accepted the flock, sacrificed a kid on the spot, and used the blood to stain Rav Elias's clothes and sandals. The dogs were not killed but muzzled and put in a burlap bag for the night, where they whined themselves to sleep.

After a day of plodding up the eastern slope of Serra da Estrela in the August sun, Elias reached Manteigas, a village tucked in a lush gorge just below the tree line. He spent the first night in a pine grove beside a tumbling brook. The next day Elias and Nuvem, his donkey, made their way up the switchback trail in the treeless sunshine. By afternoon they passed a hamlet called Golden Boulders, and after climbing a league or two more, they arrived at the very top of their world. There was nothing higher but the cloudless blue sky. Elias thought about his first critical task—the burial of the *Zohar.* Ahead in the distance, not far off the pathway, a distinctive sarsen jutted from the mountaintop like a defiant fist gesturing at the setting sun. From some distance behind the provocative fist, Elias watched the sun set in the direction of his journey. As the fiery globe dipped below the horizon, the Rav imagined it was shedding its beneficence over the New World on the other side of this round planet.

At that very moment, the location for the burial of the *Zohar* became evident. It was August 12. He first drew a line with the heel of his sandal. The line reflected the line of sight between the fist and the point on the horizon where the sun was setting that day.

Walking the line from the fist toward the sunset, it took twelve paces before he reached earth soft enough to dig. Twelve paces along a line from the stone fist to the sunset on August 12 is where he would bury the treasure.

He unloaded Nuvem and fed him some oats and water from a large leather pouch, then sat among the boulders to feast on his provisions of bread, olives, cheese, and cider. When finished, he took up his spade and began digging. Within two hours in the half-moon light, he had excavated the hardscrabble earth to a sufficient depth and width to accommodate the copper box with the *Zohar*. He lowered the container with Nuvem's rope and shoveled dirt over the treasure. Elias felt like burying his past, but he did not say the prayer for the dead.

At sunrise, he led the donkey down the mountain. With the absence of the hundred-pound load, Nuvem's steps were lighter. The rabbi, too, felt he was being carried toward Coimbra, just like in his afternoon dream in Centum Cellas, but this time, not on a cloud of crows, but on a *real* current, a crest of Life-Love energy that flowed down Serra da Estela from the clenched fist surmounting it. For an older man, his steps were lively and sure.

They made it down the mountain past the villages of Seia and Oliveira do Hospital, arriving at the end of the day at the old Roman town of Bobadela. As night fell, Elias and his equine bedded down in a ruined structure attached to the amphitheater where Elias imagined gladiators once fought. Either gladiators or bulls were caged where they slept—he couldn't be sure. In the morning, he awakened fresh and ready to fight.

After making an inquiry, he was guided to the old Roman road that led to the town of Avô on the Alva River. A heavy morning shower slowed their progress, but the sun returned as they approached Avô, turning the atmosphere into a mist of brilliant humidity. Elias halted atop the old Roman arched bridge spanning the little Alva River. He witnessed, to his surprise, the entire village of Avô taking time to enjoy this warm Sunday afternoon in August—swimming, bathing, and frolicking in a small lake formed by the river.

Also, Rav Elias decided it was a good place to bathe and rest for the next day. He found a quiet spot at the lake's edge, beyond the chatter and laughter of community bathing. He removed his shirt and sandals and led Nuvem into the cool waters with a bar of lye soap in his hand. He lathered her up, rinsed her down, then did the same for himself.

Elias tied Nuvem to a tree and spread his bedroll on the grass beside the water. He lay back and let the full sun dry his body and breeches. The laughter and hubbub drowned his anxieties about the journey. In fact, he was feeling so well that he began feeling guilty and ashamed for wasting time. He looked up at the small gorge the narrow river cut through the town before emptying itself into the swimming hole and sandy beach. On the cliff above the gorge, Elias could see the ruins of an old castle. A rock ledge hung thirty feet above the river on the opposite side of the defile from the castle. Teenage boys assembled in a line to jump off the ledge into a deep pool below—typical youthful fun—but something caught his eye. A black-haired girl of maybe fifteen years, athletic and well-built, with wet cut-off pants and a wet shirt, also stood in line taunting two boys in front of her to jump. Exasperated, she pulled them back and took their turn and went soaring through the air with daring maneuvers before plunging into the water. When she surfaced laughing, she continued to taunt the boys on the ledge.

The girl reminded Elias of the young Esperança Pimentel, gone these twenty years. She was fifteen when he fell in love with her, and she was the only love of his life. In the years before they were married, she challenged him to be more than he thought he could ever be. We tried for so long to have children, Elias thought. Then, finally, Davide came. She was the best mother, friend, and lover until the pestilence took her away to another place where she waits for me.

The brave beauty hurled herself off the cliff with a running jump and, suspended in midair, looked in the rabbi's direction. She laughed as she sliced through the dark waters.

Tears welled up in Elias's eyes—not tears of *saudade* or longing for the past, but rather tears of joy, confidence, and daring, feeling Esperança was with him once more, joining him in a love force flowing down like the river from the mountain above.

Near the Roman bridge stood an inn, Estalagem Dom Egas Moniz. Hoping for a good meal for Nuvem and himself, Elias secured a room and led Nuvem to the stable in the back. The innkeeper, Dona Maria Inês, was a small black-clad feisty widow-woman with an inquisitive temperament and small, piercing eyes. Elias was familiar with this set of characteristics. He was on guard lest more was revealed than needed to be known. Dona Maria Inês wanted to know where he was coming from.

"I raise sheep across the mountains in Belmonte," he said. "And I'm going to Coimbra to settle a dispute about an estate inheritance."

When asked the best way to Coimbra, Dona Maria Inês informed him that the safest way was to continue down the Alva past Côja to Arganil. Stay the night there, then take the south road to the village of Góis on the Ceira River, and from Góis, follow the river to Coimbra.

"Is there a faster way?" Elias asked, remembering Lourenço's instructions about boating down the Alva.

"There is, and you can save a day, but it's not safer. When you get to Arganil, sell your donkey, and buy a rowboat. Take the Alva to the Mondego and then down to Coimbra, if you're still in one piece."

Elias was the only traveler that night to stay at the Egas Moniz inn. The proprietress invited him to dine with her, which he did, fortifying himself with green soup, rabbit stew, bread, cheese, and wine.

"Dona Maria Inês, tell me something," he began the conversation. "How did this village get the name Avô? Is it named for a grandfather?"

"Well, Dom Elias," she said. "It happened a long time ago—maybe five hundred years—when the Moors lived here, and the Christians began to push them south. Old Egas Moniz camped with his army somewhere between here and Coimbra.

"Egas Moniz had his favorite grandson with him, Pedro Afonso, who rode with him at the head of the Christian army. Egas Moniz had set out to capture all the land along the banks of the Alva.

"Pedro Afonso got word from his spies that the Moors had planned a surprise attack. He tried to coax his grandfather into returning to the safety of Coimbra, leaving the leadership to him. The old man refused. It was here they fought a battle with the Moors and won.

"At that time, the grandson was about to wed Urraca, the daughter of Afonso Henriques, our first king. Egas Moniz built that castle on the hill where the newlyweds lived. Soon the Moors returned, and the grandfather and grandson took up the battle again. They were victorious the second time, but the old man was seriously wounded. He survived because of his hardy constitution. The grateful grandson proclaimed that the region would henceforth be called Terras do Avô"

The woman's story fascinated Elias. "Did the knight and the princess live happily ever after, as in the fairy tales?" he asked.

"Legend says they were much in love and used to find secluded places along this river to bathe and frolic in private, protected by their servants," said Dona Maria Inês. "But happily ever after? I don't know. Those were violent times, but they loved deeply and fought hard."

"Tell me something else, Dona Maria. Did Egas Moniz's grandson walk shoeless behind his grandfather to Toledo? How does that story go? I'm sure you know all the details."

"Before Portugal was a country, the Spanish king gave the County of Portucale to Count Henry from Burgundy for helping him fight the Moors. Count Henry died when his first son, Afonso Henriques, was still a child. The count left the education and upbringing to his trusted friend and nobleman, Egas Moniz. Afonso Henriques, still a teenager, formed an army and rebelled against his mother and step-father. He was victorious. In those first years, the power of the Spanish king of Castile and León was at its peak. Compared to him, Afonso Henriques and Portucale were weak. The Spanish king subordinated all other kings as vassals. Egas Moniz advised the young man to proclaim allegiance to the Spanish king. Afonso Henriques agreed but was too proud to do so in person, so he sent Egas Moniz to bow before the Spanish king.

"Years later, Afonso Henriques decisively defeated the combined forces of five Muslim rulers in the Battle of Ourique and believed he had the confirmation of the Holy Spirit. He declared himself the sovereign ruler of Portugal. Consequently, he no longer considered himself subservient to the king of Castile and León but a peer. He refused to pay tribute and renounced his allegiance to the Spanish king.

"This did not sit well with Egas Moniz, our Avô. He didn't care about the sixteen generations of kings in his line that an apparition of Christ had promised Afonso Henriques. This was the here-and-now. The word of honor of Egas Moniz, as well as the new king and Portugal itself, was at stake. In protest, Egas Moniz assembled his wife and children, removed their shoes and his own, tied a rope around his neck and to the members of his family and led them on foot all the way to the Spanish king's court in Toledo. They probably trekked the same path that brought you here, Dom Elias.

"When they arrived in Toledo, Egas Moniz knelt before the king of Castile. He put his life and that of his family at the mercy and disposal of the king as a penalty for breaking the oath of loyalty he'd made on behalf of Afonso Henriques nine years before. Egas Moniz's loyalty so moved the king that he sent the man and his family back in peace to the new country of Portugal. When he returned, the Portuguese received him as a true hero.

"Now, to your question, Dom Elias, whether the grandson, Pedro Afonso, walked behind his Avô to Toledo—I don't know, but I think he had not been born yet."

"What a splendid story, Dona Maria Inês. You tell it so well! Thank you. It's late, I've had a long day, and I'll be up at dawn. Let me settle with you."

"As you wish. I'll be up before you in the morning, and I'll feed you breakfast."

With that, Elias retired.

The rabbi had trouble falling asleep. He thought about Egas Moniz, the grandfather. He thought of his own grandfather, Rav Jaco, who surrendered his life in the ruins of Centum Cellas. He got up and went outside. Through a window, he saw a lamp still burned in the kitchen. Maria Inês was busy at some work. Elias entered and asked her how to get to the castle at the top of the hill. She instructed him to make his way through the maze of alleys between houses stacked together in tiers up the steep hill. He reached the top and circled the ancient stone blocks of the roofless enclosure. He climbed to the highest terrace and sat with his back against a parapet.

Below he could hear the whisper of the flowing Alva amid a chorus of crickets, punctuated with random bursts of nightfall emotion from the populace below. Looking down to his right, he could make out the silver-specked, moonlit river and, above it, the ledge from which the young beauty jumped with all her youthful exuberance. Down to his left, he saw all the aging, sagging tile roofs and the occasional flicker of a candle or dying fire, emitting the faint aroma of burnt wood and roasted meat. A thought crossed his mind: he may never again find such a peaceful place after tonight. He let himself feel the holy magic of the *Zohar* flowing down with the Alva from high on Star Mountain. He felt the presence of his beloved Esperança, or was this the *Shekinah* herself? He felt the presence of the grandfathers, Rav Jaco, Emanuel Gonçalves—even Egas Moniz, who built these massive walls. They would all be with their sons in exile.

The rabbi returned to his quarters at the darkened inn and lay on a straw-filled bedtick. He thought of Egas Moniz, a strange, almost Hebrew-sounding name. He went to sleep with idle speculations softly swirling in his mind until, with sleep, they settled, still unanswered, into his subconsciousness.

Before the light of day, after hot porridge, bread, and tea, the rabbi went to settle his bill. Approaching the innkeeper, Elias could not resist asking a foolish question for which a good answer was unlikely. "Dona Maria Inês, do you think Egas Moniz could have been a Jew?"

"Like you, Dom Elias?"

"*Senhora, por favor!* How can you say that? Because I'm from Belmonte, you think I'm a Jew?"

"Dom Elias, look at me. You think I'm so easily fooled?"

"Dona Maria Inês, you're a good storyteller, and, indeed, you have a keen eye. But my family truly converted with my father when I was a boy, and I am a true follower of the Son of God." He crossed himself.

"Relax, Pastor Elias, and don't cross yourself backward. I'm not going to the priest. Does it look like I care? And to answer your reckless question about Egas Moniz, what difference does it make? Is there a difference between Christian honor and Jewish honor? I have heard that Egas Moniz's father was a Muslim sultan. So how do you deal with that? Think about it. Now be on your way, and I advise you to keep your curiosity at bay and your mouth shut. You won't be so lucky next time.

"Take the river track past Côja to Arganil and down the Alva by boat to the Montego. It will be easier except for the rapids, and you will have to get rid of your donkey. Have a good trip and good luck with your business."

After climbing over Serra da Estrela, Elias thought his trek would flatten out. He had not counted on traversing another range of mountains called Serra do Açor or Hawk Range. The Alva cut through the Hawk Range in a gorge with a rugged path running beside the rushing water.

The rabbi reached Côja by nightfall and spent the night in another inn beside another old Roman bridge. He departed before dawn the next day. He and Nuvem continued following the track beside the river until they came to Arganil in mid-afternoon.

Along the riverbank in Arganil, he found a young fellow fishing from a dugout. He told the man of his intention to buy a boat and go downriver to the Montego and Coimbra. The young man agreed that such a trip was possible. He consented to sell his boat, paddle, and two good bow and stern ropes for a handful of coins, plus Nuvem. They struck a deal. Satisfied with the transaction and perhaps a little guilty, the man offered instructions on guiding the boat through treacherous mountain waters.

"One last word of advice," the fellow said. "If you have anything of value in the form of paper or documents, I advise you to visit the tanner in town and buy a large goatskin bag with a cork-filled mouth and a strong strap. Make sure it has never been used. Roll up your paper and anything else you don't want to get wet and put them in the bag. Keep the bag strapped to you whenever you are on the water."

"You think I'll capsize?"

"Of course, you will, old man. But the river's not deep in most places, and you won't drown, even if you can't swim. But you *will* get wet. There are rapids you will have to negotiate—even falls. You must carry your boat around them. If you are willing to get wet and wear yourself out, you will get to Penacova on the Mondego. From there, just float downriver. Take a nap, and in seven or eight hours, you will be in Coimbra.

"Here—here's some extra rope," he offered. "Wrap up your things, tie them together with this rope, and tie the rope to the boat. When you capsize, you'll only have to worry about saving yourself and the boat. You won't have to worry about your things because they will be with the boat."

Elias thanked him and took his advice.

The following day at dawn, he embarked on his first river ride.

Elias lost count of how many times he capsized the craft. He steered the boat to the edge of falls on two occasions, then found the portage path around the cataracts. Eventually, the landscape flattened, the little river meandered and widened, becoming shallow with sandy banks. He was thankful for his strong bowline and well-made sandals as he pulled the boat over the stony shallows.

Exhausted near the end of the day, Elias glided into the Mondego—a real river, he thought. He paddled for a league or more before the chimney smoke of Penacova came into view. Beaching the canoe on the riverbank, Elias foraged for dry kindling and leaves, grateful it had not rained in a month. He started a fire with his flint and searched for more deadwood and saplings to build a frame to dry his clothes. Elias checked his goatskin bag for the dryness of its contents. By sundown, his clothes and blanket were dry. Elias went to sleep hungry, saving the last of the wine, cheese, and olives that survived the river journey in his bedroll for the morning.

The rabbi woke at dawn and, after breakfast, was off down the river. Relaxing, he felt the strong current under him and the wind and morning sunlight on his back. He paddled around fishermen in small boats and commercial skiffs plying the river. Approaching Penacova, he passed three schoolboys playing on the sandy beach and thought of Davide, Ruy, and Toninho playing on the banks of the Zêzere.

At Penacova, Elias tied the boat and found a neighborhood market where he replenished the provisions of wine, cheese, bread, and olives, but not for himself.

He was soon on the river again, slowly turning from south to west. Toward the end of the day, the rabbi heard the Cathedral of Coimbra's bells in the distance. On the right bank, high on a hill, the old walled city came into view.

Looking for an out-of-the-way place to spend the night, Elias paddled past a long narrow green island, which terminated with the sandy, arrowhead-shaped beach. He pulled the canoe onto the sand and scanned the riverbanks to get his bearings. To his right rose a series of high, forested hills, where the cook fires of a few *vilas* were visible at the top. The city lay further downriver. On the left bank, far in the distance, Elias could make out a substantial yellow building—the Convent, he thought. If he squinted into the setting sun, he could barely see a dark line above the water, which he took for the end of the footbridge. This was the place, he thought, but it was already too late to disturb the nuns and find the boys.

Elias camped on the sandy tip of the island. He gathered some twigs and built a small fire, resting his back against a smooth rock with his legs extending into a sandy bed. He calmed his anxiety by surrendering to the surroundings—the sounds, sights, and smells of nature.

When stars appeared in the dark, moonless firmament, he took advantage of the situation and bathed himself. Naked with soap in hand, he waded into the water up to his neck, dipped his head, and soaped his tired gray hair. Rinsing the soap from his long locks, he plunged his head into the soothing river current. Cleanliness was a strange feeling. He soaped and rinsed the rest of his body, then dried himself with his blanket. Dressed again, he gathered more firewood and rested against his backstop as the heat of the fire dried out the bedroll. No food tonight, he thought. Perhaps a morsel for breakfast, but the rest of the provisions were for the boys.

The distant cathedral bells tolled nine o'clock. Almost without volition, Rabbi Elias began chanting. *"Si'ma Yisrael Adonai Eloheinu Adonai echad…."* He then switched to a prayer in Portuguese. "Blessed are You, Lord our God, and the God of our fathers, God of Abraham, God of Isaac, and God of Jacob, the great, mighty and awesome God, exalted God, who bestows bountiful kindness, who creates all things, who remembers the piety of the Patriarchs, and who, in love, brings a redeemer to their children's children, for the sake of His Name." He then made his personal request to the ancient Holy One, blessed be He, that he, Elias, would be able to alert his son and Ruy Gonçalves in time for them to escape and find passage to the New World; that they would be blessed and guided along their journey into the unknown; that the presence of the Shekinah would not leave them; that they would arrive and find love and raise families in the New World; and that they all would *"benim olam ha-ba"*—become sons of the world to come. He concluded his prayer with a resounding *"ve ha yah!"* And it will come to pass!"

At daybreak the following morning the rabbi was on his way. He beached his watercraft at the Pedro and Inês bridge, gathered his things, and made his way to the nearby convent. At the gate, Elias asked for Mother Superior Maria do Céu Lopes.

"May I tell her the nature of your inquiry?" the attendant asked.

"I bring news of a sick relative."

"Very well. Come in and wait inside." The attendant opened the gate, led Dom Elias across the courtyard, and into the convent's entrance hall. "Wait here."

Soon the Mother Superior appeared and eyed Dom Elias with some suspicion. "You have news of my cousin?"

"Indeed. Dr. Lourenço Gonçalves from Covilhã.

"I'm sorry to hear he's ill. He has done very well for himself, and we appreciate his donations. I hope the illness isn't serious."

"I'm afraid it is, Mother Superior," Elias replied. He may not be in this world much longer. My name is Rufino Peres. I am a servant in his household. Dr. Gonçalves has sent me to fetch Ruy, his son, from the university and bring him to Covilhã as soon as possible. My master has entrusted me with a sizable donation . . . and he was hoping the Mother Superior could sell a horse. No, two horses, with saddles. My horse died on the way and I couldn't carry the saddle. We have to hurry so we can return to Covilhã while the good doctor is still among the living."

Dom Elias handed her a small leather bagful of gold ducats. She accepted it, feeling the weight, opened it, and drew a deep breath.

"Yes, Rufino, I can supply you with two horses with saddles and reins. Is there anything else I can do?"

"Yes, ma'am. My master has requested prayers for him at the tomb of Santa Isabel, and there is another matter as well. I know nothing of Coimbra and fear I would become lost in the city. I ask if the Mother Superior would consider sending a messenger to the dormitory where Ruy Gonçalves rooms. The name of the dormitory is República de Beira Baixa. He shares the quarters with another fellow from Covilhã, Davide Mendes de Oliveira. The message is for Ruy to gather his essential belongings and meet me at the convent gate to ride for Covilhã. I have a sealed letter from his father. The messenger is to give the letter to Ruy or his best friend, Davide, the other boy from Covilhã, if Ruy is not there. Davide should find Ruy and give him the letter."

The Mother Superior accompanied Elias—or "Rufino"—to the stable, where she chose two horses. Mother Maria accepted more than an adequate amount for the equines. She summoned a stable hand, a rough lad of about sixteen, to deliver the message and letter to Ruy Gonçalves and his roommate at the dormitory of República de Beira Baixa.

As the boy mounted the horse, Elias slipped him some coins and told him to gallop, which he did.

Rabbi Elias waited. He remembered what Dom Lourenço told him about a water channel leading from the convent to a spring and how the fountain would make a good meeting place. He found the water channel and asked the convent's gate attendant to direct the two university students to the fountain when they arrived. "I'll wait for them there," he said.

The rock-lined channel ran straight from the back of the convent through fields before entering the shade of ancient trees. Its origin was a spring that gurgled out of worked natural stones at the base of a hill. The fountain splashed into a catch basin. On either side were time-worn stone benches. Elias wondered how ancient this holy spot must be. He dropped to his knees and filled his leather *bota* from the clear water. He noticed the rock slab forming the bottom of the basin changed color below him from algae green to the reddish hue of splashed blood.

On the road from Manteigas, 3 leagues beyond the hamlet of Golden Boulders, on the crest of Serra das Estrelas is found the Clinched Fist

Callejon de la Inquisición en Sevilla.

(Alley-way of the Inquisition in Seville)

Chapter 13

Quinta das Lagrimas

Coimbra
August 1565

The boys arrived to find Elias on a bench to the right of the fountain.

"*Pai!*" Davide exclaimed. "What in the world are you doing here? What's going on?"

"Sit down." Elias motioned to the bench left of the fountain. "I'll explain."

"No, rabbi," said Ruy. "This is not a good place. This is the Fountain of Tears. Let's go into the woods."

"No, *filho*, here is better because there will be tears when I tell you . . . but you are men now. You will have to dry your faces and go forth."

"Go forth?" Davide asked. "Go forth where, *Pai?* I don't understand."

"Listen well." Elias glanced at Ruy. "Your father came to me in Belmonte a week ago. A reliable source informed him that our names—including yours—appeared on a list at the Inquisition palace in Castelo Branco. Our names might as well be on the same list here in Coimbra.

"What is happening here began in Goa six months ago. It is just reaching us now. The Big House in Goa tortured and burned all the principals in the Antunes e Pinto Group. Not only that, they interrogated all the members of the Jewish community on the Malabar coast, and all the members of the *Zohar* study group there have suffered the *auto-da-fé—*"

"Why are we on the list, *Pai?*" Davide interrupted. "What is the Antunes e Pinto Group?"

"We never discussed this because, in my opinion, you were safer not knowing about it. We never wanted this to happen, coming from the other side of the world. But the worst has happened, so now you are informed—

you must take immediate action to save your lives. Perhaps Ruy's father has told him about Antunes e Pinto, but in any case, your fate and Ruy's are the same."

"My father never told me about these people," Ruy said. "But I saw many entries for Antunes e Pinto in his account book."

"I'll try to explain further. As you know, Ruy, since the time of Pedro Álvares Cabral, your grandfather, Emanuel, and my father, Rabbi Simão, and others in Covilhã and Belmonte have been involved in commercial oversees investment with that group. The investors, like ourselves, were Jewish and from other places like Spain, Holland, and France, all sharing knowledge to everyone's advantage. In recent years, the Inquisition has become stronger in the Indies than anywhere else. In Goa and the Malabar coast, getting caught practicing Judaism was a death sentence, not to mention trading commercial secrets between countries. The Inquisition now has a list of names they obtained by torturing people involved with Antunes e Pinto. Our problem is that the list also has names of men in the *Zohar* study groups—not only in the Indies but also here on the continent. Ruy, your father has learned that your name, as well as Davide's and my own, appear on the list. It's because we attended study group sessions in Toledo. Your father thought it was serious enough to ride immediately to Belmonte to send me here and get you two ready to leave. If you stay, it is only a matter of time before the Office of the Inquisition in Coimbra calls you. That would be the last of you, and that day may come sooner than later. We have no time to lose."

"What has happened to my father, Rabbi?" Ruy asked.

"He returned to Covilhã "to face the music," as he phrased it. He thinks he has no place to hide because he is well known. He's informing others who are in jeopardy until they come for him. God bless him."

"*No!*" Ruy moaned.

"Your father came to Belmonte to tell me of these terrible events and run through a plan for both your lives. It's our only hope. Pull yourselves together; I will go over the plan. There is little time. Listen first, then ask questions."

"No, wait, *Pai*. What's going to happen to you?"

"I'm not going back to Belmonte. I will start a new life here or somewhere else with a new identity."

"How?" asked Davide.

"With the help of God. How do we do anything? Don't worry—I am one of the lucky ones. The most important thing now is for both of you to listen carefully. Ask questions if you don't understand everything perfectly. When we finish, you must execute the plan. And I don't mean tomorrow—I mean now. I mean, *right now!* You can't go back to your lodging. I have two horses saddled with supplies for you at the convent. I will give you instructions and all the money you'll need for half a year."

"No, Rabbi Elias! There is something I must do first." Ruy glanced at Davide. "I must tell Ana Sofia I am leaving and why! I can't go without doing this. I am in love with her, and we plan to be married."

"I will do it for you, Ruy," the rabbi asserted.

"No. I refuse to go without doing it myself. Ana Sofia's heart will be broken as it is." And then it occurred to Ruy that today was Wednesday—the day he usually met Ana Sofia in the garden with Ida. But he'd told her he had an examination in cosmology and wouldn't be able to come. She had not indicated that she would go anyway, but he was now hoping she would. If she didn't come to the garden, he would have to find her and tell her. "Rabbi Elias, she may come to the garden this afternoon," Ruy said.

"Be that as it may," the rabbi replied. "God willing, we will work out your problem . . . but now, it is time for you to hear the plan."

The boys sat on the stone bench at the side of the fountain and catch-basin.

"Ruy, your father has worked this out like a surgeon planning an operation. Your destination will be Sanlúcar de Barrameda, the Spanish port on the Mediterranean. There you will join a crew bound for the New World where, God willing, you will make new lives for yourselves—safe from this insanity we live and die with here. The first problem is getting from here to Sanlúcar. This is how you will do it. I have a map in this dry pouch," he said, taking the leather pouch from his neck. He opened it.

"This is a rough map of how your father thinks you can get to the Spanish port most safely. You see here," he pointed. "On the map are circled numbers beside the names of towns and rivers. The numbers correspond to names on another piece of paper." Elias lifted it from the pouch. "These names are friends of your father. You can trust them if you need help in the places circled on the map. You must memorize these five names and the corresponding map numbers."

The young men took time studying and testing themselves until they knew the names, numbers, and places by rote.

"Now, tell me the names," the rabbi demanded when they'd finished. He tore the list into tiny pieces and flittered them into the water channel flowing between them. "You don't want to be caught with a list like that." He handed the map to Ruy. "Take this map. Your father drew it with only the names of the rivers and a few towns. It shows you the shortest way to Sanlúcar and gives an alternate if you think the Portuguese Inquisition is on your trail."

They spread the map on the stone bench where the rabbi sat.

"From here," the rabbi began, "you ride south for two days until you come to Tomar. Use the main road for guidance, but stay off it as much as possible. Ride the fields beside it. From Tomar, ride south following the Nabão River, which flows through Tomar. The Nabão flows into the Zêzere, about half a day's ride before reaching the Tejo River at Constância. The same Zêzere originates in Belmonte. Follow the Tejo northwest for two or three days until you come to the town of Gavião. Leave the river and go south, overland toward Portalegre and Marvão. Take a road if you must, but be discreet. You have a contact in Portalegre if you need him . . . you remember which?"

"Pereira," said Ruy and Davide in unison.

"Good. From Portalegre, continue southeast for two or three days to Elvas, near Badajoz, across the border in Spain. You have a contact in Elvas as well. If you are running from the Portuguese, cross the border at Badajoz. If you choose to go through Spain, then from Badajoz go to Sevilla and then by horse or river to Sanlúcar.

"The shortest way Ruy's father indicates is to float down the Guadiana, which forms a long stretch of the border between Spain and Portugal. If you choose this route, sell the horses in Elvas or Badajoz and buy a flat bottom rowboat. From Elvas, you can drift down the Guadiana all the way to the Mediterranean. It may take a few weeks. When you get to the sea, you will be in the Portuguese town of Vila Real de San Antonio. Don't bother to travel from there along the coast to Sanlúcar because it is all swamp.

"When you reach the Mediterranean, sell the boat and follow the beach west about eight leagues to Tavira. Don't try to row in the sea—you will drown. With a good day of walking, you'll reach Tavira. You have a contact there who owns fishing boats and a commercial vessel that trades along the coast. Pay him—he will take you to Sanlúcar on one of his boats. His name?"

Ruy hesitated. "Santellana," Davide blurted.

"Good. Practice the list," Elias said, opening the pouch. "Here—I have two knives for you. Keep them hidden, but use them if you must, and keep the map inside this dry pouch. When you get to Sanlúcar, go to the taverns. Make friends and make inquiries. Ask which captains are hiring crews and which have good or bad reputations. Find out where the ships are going. Find a ship carrying settlers bound for a new colony—but not in the east. Not in the Philippines or Africa. You should go west to the New World; that is where your future lies; for what purpose—simple trade and commerce, or fighting pirates, Moors,

The boys asked questions for the next half-hour with the map in front of them laid out on the stone bench. Dom Elias made them recite the contacts' names and the entire plan until Davide and Ruy had every important detail correctly.

"What about Toninho?" Ruy asked, stalling, expecting the appearance of Ana Sofia. "Isn't his father on the list? Isn't he in trouble too?"

"No, your father told me Dom Fernão never had indirect dealings with Antunes e Pinto—only through himself. So no one knows his name. He and Toninho are in the clear."

"What if Dom Lourenço is tortured and reveals the Cabrals?" Davide asked.

"That won't happen," Ruy responded. He will poison himself before that."

"When we disappear, who will tell Toninho and our friends at the university what happened to us?" Davide asked.

His father answered. "I will tell Toninho what happened. He is grown. He was never naïve. We must trust him, and his father is not entirely out of danger." Elias opened the pouch again. "Here, son. I scribbled a letter to the university's provost in haste. It says: 'Dear Sir, Ruy Gonçalves and I, Davide Mendes de Oliveira, have been informed by messenger that our fathers were injured when a wheel came off the wagon they were riding in the Serra da Estrela, and the wagon plunged over a cliff. Ruy Gonçalves and I are returning to our homes and our families, and we hope to return to the university as circumstances permit.'"

While Rabbi Elias and the boys discussed these matters, a carriage approached the Pedro and Inês bridge with Ana Sofia and Dona Ida. Ana Sofia had planned to take advantage of Ruy's absence to spend quality time alone with Dona Ida. She needed advice from a mature, married woman. A second month had passed without her period, and Ana Sofia was concerned.

They climbed from the coach on the north side of the bridge and lingered there, as usual. They then walked past the convent toward the Fountain of Tears. As they approached, Ana Sofia recognized the faces of Ruy, Davide, and a stranger, with their heads together over a piece of paper on the stone bench. She approached from behind and startled them. "*Ruy*! My goodness! What are you doing here? You said you had an examination this afternoon. What's going on?"

Ruy's face looked grave when he spoke. "Ana Sofia, this is Dom Elias Mendes de Oliveira, Davide's father. My father is in horrible danger in Covilhã. Dom Elias traveled over the mountain to *warn* us."

"Warn you of . . . *what?*" She barely choked out the words. The sight of Ruy and Davide at the Fountain of Tears with the strange man chilled her. The anxiety on Ruy's face and the sound of his voice filled her with dread. She feared this was not the time to tell him . . . or was it? What's happening?"

Not knowing how to deal with the situation, Ruy said, "What has happened in Covilhã now demands the presence of Davide and myself."

"What happened? Tell me!" she interjected.

Ruy rushed to Ana Sofia and took her by the hands, pulling her to himself. He whispered in her ears. "I just learned about it, *meu amor*. I have much to tell you, but I want to do it privately, even from Davide, his father, and Dona Ida. Please walk with me to the other fountain, and I'll explain."

Ruy and Ana Sofia walked awkwardly hand-in-hand down the path, a stone's throw away, to the Lovers' Fountain, where they sat on a bench beside the spring.

Ruy dropped to one knee before Ana Sofia and firmly grasped her hands. "The Inquisition in Castelo Branco is looking for my father—if they don't already have him. Last week, he rode to Belmonte to tell Dom Elias he is also on their list. Davide's father is a rabbi. I don't know if I already told you that."

She shook her head as tears began trickling from her eyes.

"The Inquisition," Ruy said, "has accused some people of heresy and apostasy—practicing Judaism while pretending to be *conversos*. Others are on their list for espionage, and still others are listed for all three charges."

"Why? What did they do?"

"It started in Goa—"

"Goa?" She groaned. "How does that involve *you?*"

"I will explain, my love. There is a trading and investment company in the Indies called Antunes e Pinto. The investors are mainly Jews and *conversos* who speak many languages from different parts of the world. Their advantage has always been to pool their knowledge to make better trading decisions. My father and grandfather and Davide's father and grandfather have been associated with this group and have made money with them. Many of these men in Portugal and Spain are devoutly religious and formed groups to study the twelve books of the *Zohar* that I told you about."

"Yes?"

Although Ruy did not know the details of what transpired in Goa and the Indies, knowing his own father and something of his accounts, he intuited a reasonably correct history in his explanation to Ana Sofia.

"From what Dom Elias told us, it was something like this—the Inquisition in Goa followed the associates of Antunes e Pinto, including the people who worked in the warehouses. They arrested and tortured them—that's how they developed the list. The crows and vultures learned the principals of Antunes e Pinto knew the intentions of the Portuguese Crown and all the commercial maritime secrets of the Portuguese, as well as the Spanish monarchy, the Dutch, and others. They took it for espionage and notified the governor of Goa. Then it went back to Lisbon.

At the same time, the torturers learned that many of the same people with secrets were also Jews in mystic study groups involving the books I told you about—the *Zohar*. For the Inquisitors in the Big House in Goa, all this represented the ultimate form of apostasy. These men and women stood accused of both heresy and espionage. Many were burned at the stake, and now, the search has begun in Lisbon because the news has just reached Portugal.

"But you were not involved in this, my love—you are not guilty of anything!"

"They don't look at it like that. For them, I am guilty of being my father's son. But more than that, Davide and I went to study sessions in Toledo on two occasions. We also studied the *Zohar* with Rabbi Elias in Belmonte."

There was a pause.

"No . . . no. We did *not* study the *Zohar* in Belmonte. Forget I said that. There was no *Zohar t*o study. You never heard that."

"I never heard that, love. But why?" Ana Sofia cried profusely.

"Dom Elias told us when the news from Goa reaches the Inquisition here in Coimbra in a few weeks, if Davide and I are still here, it will be too late for us."

"No, no, Ruy. How can this happen to us? Maybe my father can help—"

"Absolutely not! Not a word of what I told you to your father. Even he would not be immune."

Ruy stood and sat beside her as she sobbed with her head in his lap. Also crying, he ran his fingers through her raven hair. She thought to keep him from going by telling him of her pregnancy. But she waited.

"My father and Dom Elias have put together a plan. Elias bought two horses from the convent, and they are being saddled. I packed all the things we need."

"Except me," she moaned.

"We will ride from this garden to Tomar, then along the Tejo to Elvas. There we'll get a boat and row down the Guadiana to Tavira. My father has a friend who sails commercial ships in the Mediterranean. We'll sign on with him, see the Mediterranean world, and develop skills as sailors and traders. It could be worse. After a year or two, when the danger subsides, I'll come back for you. We'll find a safe place to live, like Constantinople or Alexandria, or maybe even Tangier, close to home."

Ana Sofia hardly heard him as she weighed things in her mind. This is my last chance, she thought. If I tell him I'm pregnant, maybe he will stay, and Davide and his father will go alone. Then they will find him, arrest, interrogate, torture him, and probably kill him. What have I done! What have *we* done! If I let him go, he may never know his line continues in my womb. But he may come back, as he says. And it sounds like he has a good plan. I believe he will live and be safe.

"Then go, *meu amor.*" Ruy didn't flinch. She turned her head away. She couldn't bear to look at him as she said it again. "*Vai, meu Amor!* "

She stood, reached for his hand, and walked to the stream of water coming out of the rock. She knelt and caught water in her cupped hands. "Here, my love, drink this as an oath of commitment to eternal love and fidelity." He drank from her hands and performed the same service for her. He then wiped the tears from her face with another handful of the precious water.

"It's time," she said. "Let's go back to Davide and his father."

Dom Elias watched Ana Sofia and Ruy walk together to the Lovers' Fountain, glad she had appeared. He thanked God for the intervention. Now Ruy did not have to find her. He might placate her, God willing, and she could let him go without creating additional problems. Time was short. He needed to say his final words to Davide, but the presence of Dona Ida restrained him. He turned to his son. "The horses should be well-fed and watered. Let's go for them."

"Very well, *Pai*," Davide said with a drawn face. He was still in a state of semi-shock, while his father had had days to adjust to their new reality.

As they trudged toward the convent, Dom Elias spoke. "The Spanish are colonizing the New World, calling it 'New Spain,' just like we are colonizing Brazil. The continent is the size of Africa, and the Spanish have the rights to most of it. They have the population to settle in such an enormous landmass, and they are trying to do just that. When you get to Sanlúcar, go to the taverns on the wharf. They'll be full of sailors speaking different languages. A world of information will be valuable to you. Ask about missions to colonize the New World—ships and captains sailing from Sanlúcar bound for New Spain. Sign on as a colonist, laborer, or crew member—whatever makes sense. But whatever you do, don't lose contact with Yahweh. Recite all the prayers you have ever learned every day for your own protection and guidance, so you don't forget them.

"When you find a wife, she may not be a Jew, and we accept that. Observe the laws of the Torah—at least the ones you know and that you can observe. If you cannot do that because of your situation, the Lord should forgive you. Teach the laws to your children. Be an example for them. Teach them the family history you know so well.

"And remember this from the *Zohar*, the Tree of Life has two sides and a trunk. Don't climb too far into the branches of the side of Severity, or the brittle limbs will break from your weight, and you'll tumble down on your head. On the other side of the tree, don't venture too far onto the branches of Love and Mercy, or that uncontrolled goodness will turn and strangle you. Again, you will fall and break your head. Climb up the trunk, son. Teach your daughters and sons to do the same."

They asked the stable boy if the horses were ready when they reached the stables. "Yes, Sr. Peres," he said. "Fed, watered, saddled, and ready."

They each took the reins of a horse and walked back to the Fountain of Tears. Dom Elias had just communicated the essential things to his son. Davide listened in silence, which began to worry Elias. To break the stillness, the rabbi went over the list of important items for the trip: "gold and silver ducats in small leather bags, one for each of you. The map is in the leather pouch. Water bags, a bedroll, soap, razor, and comb for each of you. Hide long knives in the bedrolls. Flint and steel for making fires. A food bag full of bread, cheese, and olives.

I survived well for a week on bread, cheese, and olives, but you should eat meat, fish, fruit, and vegetables. Forget about being kosher."

Elias was filling the terrible silence. Davide was still too stunned to vocalize his last words to his father. They walked into the clearing by the Fountain of Tears and found Dona Ida there alone with her thoughts on one of the benches, left alone to piece together the puzzle. She understood Ana Sofia was heartbroken, but, she reasoned, she would survive, even though this was serious, and Ruy's leaving would affect everyone. It seemed curious that they'd kept the secret from her—if Ruy's father had been hurt in an accident, why did Davide Oliveira have to go also? Something didn't seem right—it smelled of the Inquisition. What would it require to rid the land of that scourge? Ida thought we were safe living in the household of a famous man—a friend of the king—but after all, Dom Pedro is a *converso*, just like Fouad and Ida. They had lived peacefully for many years within the law. Ida now smelled trouble.

Before Elias could converse with Ida, the two lovers arrived at the fountain of sorrows.

Dom Elias took the reins of Davide's horse from his son's hands and held both animals. He turned to Ruy and said in a stern voice, "It's time to mount up, *rapazes*."

The young men climbed onto their horses, with Elias on the ground between them, holding the reins. Elias walked eastward out of the clearing toward the forested path.

"Stop!" Davide shouted. "If we all must die, I'll die with *you, Pai*!"

"And I'm going to die with the woman I love," Ruy declared as he tugged the reins from the rabbi's hands.

Ana Sofia ran to Ruy's horse and grabbed her man's leg, crying, "Remember our oath, my love, and your promise to return. Now go— for your sake and for *our* sake."

Elias held both reins tightly at the halter. He squared himself and looked up. In a voice and tone that no one had ever heard before, he said, "Remember what YHVH said to Abram as he left Ur of the Chaldeans? *Lekh-lekha!* Go forth! You are not to stay among the wicked. *Lekh-lekha!* Go to yourself, to show yourself, to refine yourself. *Lekh-lekha!* Go from your land, from the habitation to which you cling. *Lekh-lekha!* Go forth from your birthplace and from what you believed was your destiny. *Lekh-lekha*—go you forth! To that land, I will show you. I will show you what you could not comprehend and could not know; I will bless you. *Lekh-lekha!* You will be a blessing in that land."

Standing between the boys, he saw their quivering mouths and the tears streaming from their eyes. He handed the reins to them and turned his body to face the path through the woods. In a loud, trembling voice, he shouted once more, "*Lekh-lekha!*" and hit the flanks of both horses with all his might.

The horses, already tense, reared up and galloped down the path. The boys had no time to wallow in despair. It was all they could do to hold on. By the time the horses had slowed to a trot, the past was in the forest behind them. They rode out of the woods and found the trail to Tomar.

That day was the turning point in their lives. And despite the tumult of the day, the sound of its madness resolved into two Hebrew syllables that would reverberate in their heads for the rest of their lives: *Lekh-lekha!*

Rabbi Elias's voice had seemed to come from an ethereal realm, but now he collapsed sobbing to the ground where the horses once stood.

Ana Sofia and Ida knelt beside him, crying. Ana Sofia cried for the loss of her love and the father of the life inside her. Because she realized why Dom Elias could not go with his son. Ida understood that "*Lekh-lekha*" meant sending his son into a new world that he was excluded from." She lamented his heartbreak and that of Ana Sofia.

The three helped themselves up and went over to the stone bench beside the Fountain of Tears. Ida dipped her headscarf into the water and wiped the tears and dust from Elias's face. Elias took the cloth, rinsed it in the gurgling stream, and wiped the tears from Ana Sofia's face. She, in turn, performed the service of ablution for Dona Ida.

Ana Sofia faced Dom Elias and said, "What are you going to do?"

"I don't know. Nor do I care. My job is finished."

"That may be true, but you'd better come home with me," she said.

"How?" Elias protested. "I'm a dead man."

"You're right," Ana Sofia replied, "Rabbi Elias de Oliveira has died and gone to heaven. But here in our presence, you are a new man in a new country, needing a new name. We will figure that out in time. For now, stay with us. My father will not object, and there is more than enough to do around the *vila* helping Fouad, Ida's husband."

"Besides," Ida ventured, "someone may come along who will need *two* grandfathers!"

Dom Elias was puzzled. Ana Sofia looked at Ida in disbelief. "How did you know?"

"I simply *know*, my child, don't ask how."

Dom Elias was still confused. "What do you know?" he asked Ida.

"That I might be pregnant," said Ana Sofia. Ida only smiled.

"You didn't tell Ruy?"

"No," she said, the tears welling up. "Ruy would have stayed."

CHAPTER 14

JUANCINTO TARANTO

Sevilla and Córdoba, Spain
1553-1555

At a little over five feet, wide-shouldered with a jerky bow-legged gait, Juancinto Taranto was not an imposing figure. His black, shoulder-length curls were rarely cut, and his beard was rarely clipped or shaven. As the years progressed, silver streaked his hair. From a distance, Juancinto's appearance was swarthy. At close quarters, however, few paid attention to any features but his eyes, which sparkled with mystery and geniality to match his engaging smile. He was most often judged as a typical Gypsy, a typical seaman, or a typical roustabout trickster. There was a bit of truth to all of this. Juancinto could be a little of everything, hence his childhood nickname, "Cachuro." On the "wrong" side of Sevilla's great canal, in Triana, where Juancinto lived, the name Cachuro had an infinite number of meanings and implications, but the most common were "little bit" and "dog."

Juancinto grew up in the Altozano neighborhood, not far from the Triana market and the Isabel II Bridge over the Alfonso XII Canal. We take up his story at the age of fifteen when he first saw Solea Ballesteros. His mother ordered him to escort his younger sister, Giralda, through the rough neighborhood to a house on Calle Betis beside the canal. There, Giralda would have her first dance lesson at the home of Solea's mother, who was known throughout the city as "La Gitanilla."

La Gitanilla was famous in Triana and notorious in Sevilla as a mistress of Gypsy trades. She told fortunes with Tarot cards, made fertile the barren, potent the weak, and vice versa. She cast curses and healed the sick, but, above all, she was appreciated as a *palos gitanos* [21] dancer and as a teacher in her later years.

Giralda had neither the temperament nor enthusiasm for *palos gitanos* dancing. Still, Juancinto bribed her with sweets and trinkets to continue her lessons, which allowed him to see La Gitanilla's thirteen-year-old daughter, Solea. Although Solea did not initially pay much attention to Juancinto, he was spellbound by her, and she knew it. She moved with grace and danced with controlled fury and determination. And was it mentioned that she was beautiful? Her skin was as olive as Juancinto's, but her eyes were grey-green, and her hair was a chestnut-gold cloud of spirals and curlicues. When she danced, she often created a commotion of whooping and whistling, which attracted other musicians on Betis Street to enter La Gitanilla's courtyard and join the impromptu orchestra. Juancinto knew he had caught Solea's attention, but, although never timid in public, he felt diminished in this crowd because he had nothing musical to offer.

To address the dilemma, Juancinto stole a suckling pig one night from a small farm on the nearby Guadalquivir River. He cut its throat and put the pig in a burlap sack. Before sunrise, he crossed the canal bridge into the heart of Sevilla and found his way to one of the meat markets. With the proceeds from the pig, he purchased an old guitar at a flea market. Juancinto knew enough to tell that the guitar was well-handled and well-loved, not discarded from disuse. His Uncle Paco confirmed that the instrument had good resonance and helped him restring it. Paco agreed to teach Juancinto the various *palos gitanos* styles for the price of one cigar of Cuban tobacco per week. This was a high price for a fifteen-year-old, but Tío Paco was a renowned guitarist in the neighborhood, and Juancinto agreed to pay his fee.

During his initial lessons, Juancinto stole three more suckling pigs from different farms along the Guadalquivir. But his finest plunder was a full-grown peacock from a walled garden in the city. He plucked the dead bird and sold it in the meat market near the wharves on the south side of town for a reasonable price. He also sold the feathers for much more to a merchant who traded in the Philippines. The merchant told Juancinto where he could buy Cuban cigars wholesale downriver in Sanlúcar. He had never been to the port, but stowed away on a barge transporting lemons. He arrived before nightfall. The next day, he purchased a small orange crate of cigars from Cuba, enough to finance his development as a budding musician for five months. Juancinto soon became confident enough to sit behind the accomplished guitarists who played in La Gitanilla's courtyard.

The motivation behind Juancinto's enthusiasm for music was no mystery. The guitarists felt compassion for him and taught him what he was ready to learn.

Initially, Solea observed this phenomenon from a distance, but with each passing week came closer familiarity and more attraction to Juancinto. He spent all his spare time practicing. Within a year, Gitanilla gave Juancinto and Solea permission to cross the bridge and perform in the public places between the cathedral and the walls of the Alcázar. The youngsters became popular, and people tossed coins into the old Gypsy hat that Tío Paco brought from a caravan trip to Portugal for the funeral of a gypsy king.

Things went well until the week before Christmas when Juancinto performed in the park beside the Isabel Bridge. Three fancily-dressed young men not much older than him staggered out of a nearby tavern, drawn by the music and Solea's dancing figure. They hurled lewd remarks at Solea. The larger one asked Juancinto if he was pimping "his Gypsy sister." In an instant, Juancinto whipped out a razor knife and slit the bully's felt vest from cravat to belt buckle, exposing the astonished brute's undergarments tinged with blood. Not wanting to reap the consequences of this act, Solea and Juancinto ran back across the bridge and disappeared into Triana.

They learned the next day that the bloodied boy was the son of Sevilla's chief magistrate. La Gitanilla determined it wasn't safe for her daughter and Juancinto to remain in Sevilla. Because they were hopelessly in love, she organized a solemn Gypsy wedding ceremony. From the proceeds of the wedding, the young couple purchased a quarter horse and a small caravan outfitted with a bed and household goods. They set out northward following the Guadalquivir to Córdoba.

Juancinto and Solea practiced their many talents in Córdoba for more than ten years, returning in their caravan every few years to the Triana neighborhood of Sevilla. Solea followed in her famous mother's footsteps and was gaining renown in Córdoba for *palos gitanos* dancing and singing, accompanied by her devoted husband. Their caravan parked with others outside the city walls. Here they supplemented their revenue with fortunes told to *gitanos* and *españoles* alike, as well as herbal healing potions and verbal spells and curses.

Soon after they arrived in Córdoba, Solea found herself pregnant. In her third month, she stayed in the caravan, telling fortunes for the duration. At the same time, Juancinto went into the city to take up a new trade, hair-cutting. His barbershop consisted of one chair, which he set up in the public market areas of Córdoba. Solea remained in the caravan with her Romany neighbors until little Joaquim—"Quim" for short—could walk.

Wherever the three went, Solea carried her dancing shoes and Tarot deck, while Juancinto carried his guitar and chair with scissors and the long razor blade. By the time Quim was five, he could earn his age in reales by dancing *palos gitanos* style in his own manner. When he was eight, Quim canvassed neighborhoods where his parents worked, advertising music, dance, barbering, and fortune-telling. Life was good for the trio.

History then repeated itself. Quim attracted three thugs to the place where his parents had set up shop near the Calahorra Tower and the bridge of Miraflores. One fellow ordered a shave and haircut and threw a few coins into the hat on the ground. The other two demanded a dance. Solea commenced her dance with an evil eye. She began slowly and menacingly, pounding her cleated heels to the rhythm of Quim's castanets. Juancinto cut oily clumps of hair from his unsavory customer as the man's companions played buffoons and mimicked Solea's movements, approaching her from two sides. One of the rascals laid his hand on Solea's rump. That act presented Juancinto with two options—plunge his scissors into the neck or eye of the customer in the chair or scare Solea's assailants by cutting clothes, as he had done years ago in Sevilla.

He chose the second option. In an instant, the razor was out of his pocket. Jumping up, he grabbed the arm of the lout and swung him around to face him. At the same time, his other hand, gripping the razor, came down on the oaf. Juancinto intended to cut the fellow's garments from chest to penis, as he had done once before. But the man jerked unexpectedly, and the blade sliced through his jugular vein instead of his shirt, spouting a fountain of blood. The man collapsed to the cobblestones in a spreading pool of crimson without a sound. No one came to his aid. His companions fled in fright toward the city center, seeking the peacekeeping militia—the *Santa Hermandad*. Juancinto knew he could run, but soon the *hermandades* appeared, swords drawn, followed by their *comandante*.

Solea felt faint at the sight of the blood and the dead man. She sat on a chair with her son and husband on either side. When he saw the scene, the *comandante* remarked that Juancinto had done the city a favor by eliminating another petty thief while "earning an honest Gypsy living." He understood Juancinto was simply defending his wife, and he believed Juancinto's claim that the death blow was an accident.

Nevertheless, circumstances obliged the *comandante* to incarcerate Juancinto, and in court, the verdict was "guilty of murder." The punishment was death or exile at sea for ten years. Juancinto chose the latter and had one hour to bid farewell to Solea and Quim. The *hermandades* then clapped leg irons on him and transported him with two guards on a riverboat down the Guadalquivir, past Sevilla, to Sanlúcar de Barrameda. From there, Juancinto was enlisted as a bond servant to the captain of the *Concepción*, bound for the distant port of Santiago de Cuba.

Juancinto's first duties were the most disagreeable on the ship—rat-catching in the cargo hold, cleaning vomit and filth from all decks, including sleeping quarters, galley, infirmary.

Rat-catcher was his preferred job, as it presented a certain degree of challenge and cooperation with the ship's cat, Tigra. Once he cornered a rat, Tigra instinctively killed it with a bite to the back of the neck. Juancinto had a better idea. He persuaded the ship's carpenter to devise a curved stick with slots on the end to accept a long strip of rawhide, an instrument much like one might use to ensnare a snake. Juancinto coated the rawhide with coal tar pitch to discourage the rat from biting through it. With a rat cornered, Juancinto would throw down a small pouch of fish heads, distracting Tigra long enough for him to lasso the rat.

Juancinto usually kept two rats, one small, the other large, in a special two-compartment cage the carpenter had made. The shared wall between the cells was a wooden lattice dipped in creosote, with openings large enough for the rats to see each other. Juancinto would feed the smaller rat abundant scraps from the galley and fed the larger rat only enough to keep him alive and angry. When the two rats were the same size, Juancinto would organize a contest—the rats would fight to the death in a sawed-off wine barrel topped with fishnet. The rats were named, and gamblers could distinguish them by their painted tails.

Most of the crew of ninety would place wagers, and Juancinto kept the tally. Juancinto's secret was that he had fed one rat and not the other. Thus the "house" usually bet on the unfed, more aggressive rat. The house won often, but not always.

Juancinto's activity put spare money in his pocket. It earned him the respect, if not admiration, of most crewmen. To make the best of a good thing, Juancinto distinguished among the various crew members those who had qualities serving his long-term interests and those who did not. Those who met with Juancinto's tacit approval were most often the winners of the "rats' death match."

By the time the ship reached the port of Santiago de Cuba, Juancinto was no longer consigned to cleaning deck messes.. Instead, he graduated to entertainment entrepreneur specializing in rat death matches, *palos gitanos* guitar-playing on the deck at sunset, and Gypsy storytelling at night.

Reaching Cuba, Juancinto inquired about his indentured status. He quickly realized his future was not with the crew of the *Concepción.* On the contrary, the whimsical needs of the Casa de Contratación in Sevilla—or their bureaucratic representatives thousands of miles away in the colonies—determined his status.

At the port of Santiago, on the eastern tip of Cuba, Juancinto learned he'd been assigned to an expedition of 650 colonists, soldiers, and merchants bound for the newly created kingdom of Nueva Grenada and its capital, Bogotá. Within weeks, they would sail across the Caribbean Sea to the new port of Santa Marta. From Santa Marta, a trip of four to six weeks by land would put them in Bogotá, where Juancinto's fate as a bond servant would be transferred to the governor.

CHAPTER 15

ATORA OF CHÍA

Chía, Colombia
1555-1560

As the ship approached land just after dawn, Juancinto stood at the upper deck railing. He was seeing the new continent for the first time. And there on the horizon, slowly growing, was a conical, snow-crowned mountain that gleamed in the morning sun. West was the port and town of Santa Marta, named after the peak.

Juancinto was hoping to see the natives of this new land, but at the pier, he determined they looked the same as the people at Santiago de Cuba, who essentially looked like himself. He asked where the Indians lived. He was told Bastidas and his men had wiped out the Indians around Santa Marta thirty years ago, except for those who lived on the spectacular snow-capped mountain to the east.

The long wagon train heading south stretched more than five hundred yards. Juancinto's duties were to assist the cook with firewood and guard the provisions against man and rodent. The caravan traversed an average of twenty-five miles per day. At the end of most days, if he was up to it, Juancinto dragged out his old guitar—bought years ago with stolen pork—and played at one of the campfires. There would always be some colonists from Andalusia who would try to dance *palos gitanos* in a clumsy fashion, replicating what they remembered from the Gypsies in the towns they left behind.

Within a week, the expedition encountered the mighty Magdalena River, flowing from the direction they traveled toward—south. Juancinto wished the river flowed in the other direction so that they could all float to their destination on rafts. But that was not to be. He wondered whether he'd ever have a return trip.

As they followed the trail beside the river, they entered a beautiful wide valley flanked by formidable mountain ranges in the distance on both sides. Compared to Andalusia's arid plains and barren hills, this was paradise—green, well-watered, and fruitful. More than that, Juancinto noticed that the farther they got from Santa Marta, the healthier people looked. These were Indians, busily and happily going about their work in boats full of produce, animals, or goods. Their villages, with round walls and steep thatched roofs, were on the banks of the Magdalena or perched in the hills above. The men generally wore white cloth pants and shirts with straw hats and leather sandals. The women were more colorful, with woven clothes of intricate design and bright dyes. Juancinto reflected on what he saw. Despite the invasion of armored Christian cavaliers with their horses, swords, harquebuses, and smallpox, life went on here, and it did not appear so bad.

They followed the river for three weeks as the wide valley grew narrower, the river swifter as it curled eastward and cut through a mountain range. The expedition trekked up the gorge the Magdalena had created through the mountains until they came to a place called Honda, where the road to Bogotá began. That road stretched eastward, and for three days, they traveled through an endless series of mountain passes before finally reaching the high savannah and its new capital.

Although it was mid-summer, to Juancinto, Bogotá felt like Sevilla in mid-winter. The highland natives were the Muisca. Juancinto bought a wool shirt, sweater, and socks from a Muiscan woman with the money he had accumulated from gambling and haircutting.

After a week in the capital, Juancinto was sent to the *encomienda* [22] of Don Antonio Díaz Venero de Leyva, located outside the old Muiscan city of Chía, some forty miles north of Bogotá. The de Leyva hacienda, or estate, covered thousands of hectares and was maintained by three hundred Muiscan men and women who were virtual slaves.

Juancinto's job was wagoner, transporting corn, avocados, barley, and quinoa from the fields to silos and storage barns. His quarters were adjacent to the barns and within a hundred yards of the Leyva manor house.

His master often tasked Juancinto to drive into Chía for supplies and sundries. Because he was trusted and did not drink alcohol, he was usually permitted free time on market and holy days. On these occasions, he would play his guitar, cut hair, and tell fortunes from the back of his wagon, parked by the central plaza. In this way, he became well-known among all segments of the native population. He lost no opportunity to learn the Muiscan language to a level where he could carry on a rudimentary conversation and translate the revelations of the tarot deck to those who sought his unique talent.

On one religious holiday, Don Antonio gave Juancinto the liberty to take his wagon into Chía. He halted beside the central plaza and began playing guitar for the enjoyment of the gathering public. He played his version of a *palos gitanos* piece from the city of Málaga—softly at first with increasing momentum. Juancinto was a few minutes into the music when he noticed a slow, spinning vortex in the crowd. In the center, a graceful creature danced with her eyes closed—poetry itself in flowing, red-violet robes. Just like the dancers in Triana, her hair was tied in a bun, but the style of her movements was Muiscan. Juancinto wondered whether the dance was her own invention. When she opened her obsidian eyes and gazed at Juancinto, the dance became *their* invention. Her graceful movements triggered his fingers, and her passion inspired his playing. When it ended, there was silence in the multitude. She looked up at Juancinto, still perched on his wagon seat, broadly smiled, then turned and walked away as the cheering crowd parted to let her pass. Juancinto jumped down from the wagon, attempting to follow, but the crowd closed ranks, and she was out of sight.

"What is her name?" Juancinto asked in broken Muiscan.

Someone said, "Atora."

"She is the daughter of the priest of the Moon Temple on Tiguiza Hill," said another. He pointed west to a hill in the distance. "She can be found at her parents' house, but be careful."

Juancinto contemplated driving the wagon toward the hill to find her but remembered she had gone off in a different direction. He needed to get back to the hacienda, but on the way, he could not stop thinking about Atora and playing for her. That night the thoughts continued nagging him, but worse. He now felt guilty: his new passion constituted a betrayal of Solea, his own dancing wife, whom he dearly loved and missed. His sleepless mind vacillated between tender longing for Solea, the safe upbringing of Quim, and fantasies about Atora, who, for him, was living music, calling him to play for her, to perform with her.

The next time Juancinto was sent on an errand to Chía, he took the opportunity to drive his wagon up Tiguiza Hill to find the Temple of the Moon. He drove along the roadway through dense woods, zig-zagging until he reached the top of the long escarpment that overlooked the town of Chía. He came across a topless building of black basalt blocks in a high clearing. He halted the wagon and approached the structure on foot. It was three stories high with a flat roof and a parapet.

No one was about the place. Juancinto announced his presence in a loud voice, but no response came. He saw an open door and ventured inside. Two spiral staircases hugged the tower wall on each side of the open room. The sulfurous smell of spent black powder from a cannon or fireworks filled the room—not unpleasant but strange. The black powder smell mixed with the fragrance of clary sage oil used to fuel the wall sconces on the staircases, which Juancinto guessed were for ascent and descent.

Juancinto proceeded up the stairway on the left, rising clockwise past two doors to reach a third, which opened to the morning sky and a deck-like observatory. In the center of the deck stood a wooden pole, perhaps once the trunk of a great cedar. It towered about thirty feet above the deck. At the top of the pole was a large silver ring with a thirty-foot silver chain. At intervals up the pole were rings of painted wood, like necklaces, each with a cord of the same color. To Juancinto, he seemed to be standing inside one of the drawings produced by the astrologers of Sevilla. He pondered the complexity when a shrill voice in broken Spanish from the doorway behind him startled him.

"What are you doing here? Do you want to die?!"

"No. I don't want to die yet. I am Juancinto Taranto, and I played the guitar for you at the plaza. Don't you remember? They told me your name is Atora. I came looking for you. I don't want to cause harm. I was only curious."

"Being curious can get you killed. You rode past my father's house at the bottom of the hill. I saw you and followed. You are lucky I'm the one who saw you. Only priests and initiates are allowed in this temple—others enter on the pain of death. And you, a Spaniard—they would skin you alive and make you and your horse and wagon disappear. I suggest you leave."

"That sounds like good advice." He said in a light-hearted way, trying to underplay the seriousness of his trespass. He walked to the opposite doorway, assuming it led down in a spiral to the entrance. He turned and looked at her as he opened the door, "But I only came looking for you. Your dancing is in my dreams. I can't play without thinking of you. Would you ride with me to somewhere we can talk?"

"No. I can't be seen with you on Tiguiza Hill. Go to the Valvanera Church at the foot, and I will meet you in the forest behind the church—one hour after the noonday bells. Drive your wagon slowly. If anyone stops you, say you lost your way and ask for the Iglesia La Valvanera." She gave him directions to the church, and he was off.

At the appointed hour, Atora found him stopped at the edge of the forest behind the church and somewhat hidden by it. She was carrying a large basket and was as fresh and beautiful as he remembered from his first encounter. Her black hair was loosely tied back, complementing her dark olive skin and curious, lively eyes. Her complexion contrasted with her dazzling white cotton blouse over blue pants with high leather legging boots.

"Come with me," she said. "Let us gather medicine. That is the excuse I have given my father to be here." He followed her into the woods, walking just behind her, trying to keep up.

She turned and said, "I am told you are a Gypsy, but I don't know what that means. What is a Gypsy?"

She caught Juancinto off guard. He stumbled with his words. "It's a long, difficult story, but I will tell you if you tell me what being dedicated to the moon means. She frowned and handed him her basket, dancing ahead of him on the path. She put her hands to her ears as if listening to the forest sounds and then turned and danced back to him, smiling. "All right—you begin. What is a Gypsy?"

The interlude had given Juancinto time to assemble some thoughts. "Legend says we originally came from India. Do you know where that is?"

"No. Never heard of it. Tell me."

"Did you know that if you leave Chía and walk for many days toward the setting sun, you will come to a vast body of water larger than any lake you can imagine? Have you heard of it?"

"Yes."

"Now, if you had a strong wooden boat half the size of the church, and cloth sails the size of a hundred blankets to catch the wind, and a hundred men and their supplies, you could begin to sail across the water.

We call it an 'ocean.' With a hundred days of favorable winds, you would come to a group of islands we call "The Philippines," which the Spanish conquered from the natives and named after their King Philip. If you sail your boat past the Philippine Islands, you will come to the land of China. Have you ever heard of China?"

"No," she replied in wonderment.

"China is not an island, but part of a whole continent of land with vast mountain ranges, rivers, and deserts, just like where we are now. If you continue sailing your boat south around China on another immense ocean, you meet thousands of islands with different peoples and languages. Sailing west through these islands, you finally come to the land of India. And that is where the Gypsies come from."

Juancinto asked if she understood, and she was wide-eyed with fascination. She had never heard anything like this before.

"Did you know that the Earth, where we are now, is round?"

Atora looked at him in bewilderment. "Round like a ball?" she asked incredulously.

"Yes. We know because the Portuguese navigator Magellan proved it when his crew sailed west from Spain—into the setting sun—and returned two years later from the east.

"We Gypsies have always known. Now the Portuguese and Spanish seafarers and traders know it for certain. Still, they don't talk about it because the priests of the Inquisition will throw them in prison. The priests have always taught the simple people that the Earth is flat. What do you think, Atora?"

"You must be right because, in the sky, all heavenly bodies move in a curve. They appear, disappear, and reappear as if they are moving in a circle. If the Earth is round, then the sun and the non-sparkling stars are not just windows into the other worlds, but balls of different energies circling Earth."

"Yes, but think, Atora, if the Earth is round, perhaps it spins. The Sun is not going around the Earth, but the Earth goes around the Sun. The Earth also spins as it goes so that we are facing the Sun in the daytime and away from the Sun at night. The Sun is not revolving around anything, but quite the opposite, we are spinning, and the sun is stationary. But the Earth does circle the Sun—it's a huge circle that requires a whole year from start to finish."

"And the non-sparkling stars, do they also go around the Sun?"

"Exactly. But more than that, beyond the non-sparkling stars, which we call planets, there are twelve houses or groups of stars in patterns we recognize. They keep the same pattern or order every year. We call this the Zodiac. Do you know about this?"

"Of course. Am I not the daughter of the High Priest of the Moon?"

"I beg your pardon. I should have known and perhaps asked more questions."

"Yes, what about the Moon?" she asked.

"The Moon is a non-sparkling star, to use your words, but it revolves around the Earth every day and gets its light from the Sun. The Moon is more closely attached to the Earth than any other planet and has more influence and power over Earth every day. But both the Earth and the Moon and every other planet get their light from the Sun."

"Oh," Atora said, "that is like our belief—the Moon is like the mother, and the Sun is the father. The Moon takes care of our body, our insides, and the Sun guides our soul—our outsides—and how we comport ourselves in the world. The Moon rules what is hidden in our bodies and in the dream world of our nights. The Sun rules our mind and judgment and the world of our daytime, which we see, hear, smell, taste, and touch."

"And the other, non-sparkling stars?" Juancinto asked. "What do they do?"

"They are special gods with certain qualities we need to live a good life," she said.

"Like what?"

"The red star gives courage to the heart in times of trouble or battle. The morning star is the same as the evening star. She likes to be close to the Sun, and the Sun finds her beautiful. She gives us love. Other stars give us abundance or scarcity. Another god is a trickster—he causes us to be clever, to appreciate or outwit him. At the Moon Temple, we revere him because he shows us how to know the future."

"Atora, your beliefs are much like ours with planets who behave like gods, spinning stories throughout history. For me, it is not farfetched."

"Yes, Juancinto Taranto, but you are strange for me. You make my head dance and spin, and now I'm dizzy. At the observatory, we measure all these straight lines and angles moving in time to know when it is time to plant and harvest. But what is moving are all these balls of different energies. All these gods with stories, dancing around with each other to music which is always new but always repeats itself. What my grandfather told me now makes sense. He said, "The gods dance to music. They dance to a drumbeat, giving rise to space and time."

Their walk through the forest came to a halt. Atora turned to face Juancinto. "I want to dance now. Will you play for me?"

Juancinto took his guitar, which was strapped across his back. He sat at the base of a nearby ceiba tree and began to pick a familiar melody. Atora moved accordingly around the tree, tentative at first, reflecting his notes with subtle gestures and emotion. A rhythm developed, captured in strong, graceful, and repetitive movements.

Juancinto lost his sense of control over his hands. They began playing as they had never played before. He was as if a spectator, watching her and his hands in awe. He stood, and she signaled him to follow. He played as she danced down a path into the dark wood.

Atora turned and stamped her feet to the beat as if La Gitanilla had taught her. She laughed and sang as she led him deeper into the forest. She stopped by a pool of mountain water fed by a small cascade the height of a man bouncing down over the rocks.

In an instant, she had shed her white linen garments. Still dancing, she removed the guitar from Juancinto's hands, placing it on the ground beside the pool. Dancing around Juancinto to the echo of the music, with delicate brown fingers, she unbuttoned his shirt and loosened his belt. His pants fell to his ankles. After pulling off his pants and boots, Atora guided him into the pool, where they sat under the foam of the small waterfall. The frigid water stole his breath, and she laughed uncontrollably at his confusion between sexual arousal and thermal shock. The cold water poured over their heads. She took him in her arms, kissed his blue lips, and tried to warm his shivering body to no avail. She pulled Juancinto from under the cascade and guided him, still quivering, along a short path leading to an enormous, smooth, flat-topped boulder just above the waterfall. The midday sun poured upon the boulder with its broad presence, providing a cleansing in the dense foliage. They lay spread-eagle upon the rock and soaked in the warm paradise of the moment.

Atora asked Juancinto to warm her body with the same hands that played the *palos gitanos* music. Juancinto reached for her and pulled her to him. With magic hands, he played the chords and strings of her body. When his artistry had produced a state of warm delirium in Atora, he asked her to warm his own skin with her slow, dancing figure. With delight, she complied. After love-making, they both lay on their backs on the sunbaked rock and replenished their exhausted bodies with the mixed energies of water, earth, and fire.

Juancinto thought about the last time he made love to Solea and felt a tinge of guilt, longing for her and his old life. He looked up at the green moving canopy above, pierced here and there with beams of sunlight, and thought, where am I, and how did I get to this strange place?

At that moment, Atora rolled over to look at him. "You have not yet answered my question," she said.

Juancinto pulled himself out of his reverie of *saudade,* bewildered. "What question?"

"What is a Gypsy?"

"*I* am a Gypsy. Now you know one."

"Don't play with me, Juancinto. Why do they call you a Gypsy, and what does it mean?"

Juancinto wanted to avoid the subject because he didn't know how to answer. He began developing the geological explanation he started earlier.

"Remember, we just talked about the earth being round and spinning?

She nodded.

"And how long it would take to go from Chia to India?"

"Yes."

"Well, Chia is on the opposite side of the round ball we call earth, which means, when the sun is shining in Chia, it is night-time in India."

"India is where my people came from long, long ago. I don't know why they forced us out of India. Perhaps it was because we were a tribe unto ourselves who refused to be Hindu or Buddhist or Muslim or Catholic. Perhaps everyone hated us, and we had no friends or allies. Did we have to rely on ourselves and our wits for survival? Were we at war with the rest of the world? Our enemies, meaning the whole world, had all the land and the goods. And whenever we traveled to a new land, it was always the same. Our enemies, meaning the whole world, held all the land and goods. To survive, we've always had to outwit the rest of the world—to be smarter and craftier—and yes, sometimes we must steal to survive."

"Did the Gypsies not have any religion or relationship with the gods?"

"We believe in many gods, all ruled by Father of the Sky, Devla. He constantly battles Beng, who rules over the Earth and lives underground. Both Devla and Beng have spirits or angels associated with the planets, the four elements, mountains, valleys, lakes, and rivers. For us, the world is full of spirits, both good and bad, working for and against us. Our ancestor is Rom. He comes directly from Adam and Eve, who we call Damo and Yehwah. We have our own kings and queens and princes and princesses who rule large families. We have our own laws and punishments for breaking the laws. We have our own sorcerers and sorceresses who tell fortunes, cast spells and bring good fortune. We are prohibited from engaging in most trades by law, so we must be smart to survive. I guess you could say we specialize in crafting people's fears and desires. We must stay one step ahead of all the people against us, knowing more about them than they do themselves."

"How did you get from India to here?" Atora asked again.

"Oh, yes—I didn't finish. Why we left India many, many years ago, perhaps thousands, I don't know. We either departed voluntarily, or they pushed us out. But we left as a tribe together. We moved from India to Persia. Then, after a time, some of us moved north to countries like Romania and Turkey; others moved south to Egypt and North Africa. My grandmother told me our people moved to Spain from Africa, from the country called Morocco and a city called Fez."

"Why did the Gypsies move so much? Why did they not settle in a place they liked?"

"I told you. People hated us everywhere we went. If there was a famine or drought, people held the Gypsies or the Jews responsible. They killed us or ran us out of town. We developed the habit of always being ready to move. I guess you could say the Gypsies were a movable nation. We don't have any land or livestock. We don't have an army. The only things we possess are the things we carry with us. We have ourselves and our memories and experience, and our survival skills. We also have our music and dance, which we always carry with us."

"How did a Gypsy from Spain end up here in Chía, the city of the Moon?"

"I killed a man, and this is my punishment. As simple as that."

"How did it happen?"

"It happened a few years ago in a city called Córdoba in Spain. My wife is a dancer. She dances in the Gypsy manner. There are many forms of dance, which we call *palos*. I call the music I play *palos gitanos*—Gypsy forms. Anyway, we made our living in public places in the city. Solea would dance to the music of my guitar. People would gather to listen and throw a little money in the hat. Our son, Quim, who was learning to play the guitar, would circulate in the neighborhoods and bring people to see and hear us. I also cut hair and told fortunes with cards. We had a little house built on a wagon about the size of the one I drive here. We lived with other Gypsies outside of the city. We made a good living together—Quim, Solea, and me."

"And—?"

"One day, a group of drunken ruffians tried to force themselves on Solea while she was dancing. I dropped my guitar and grabbed the razor from my pocket. I tried to scare the man by cutting his cravat, but I sliced his neck, and he bled to death on the street. If the man had not been such a scoundrel, the *comandante* would have executed me for murder, but they were happy to get rid of the guy. They gave me the option of serving my punishment in service in overseas colonies and at sea. So, here I am."

"If you don't mind me asking, when you play your guitar and I dance, do you see your wife, or do you see me?"

"Solea is a trained dancer. She dances in a certain traditional style, and she is the best at it. But you, Atora, you are music itself. Your body and heart move in perfect, graceful harmony with the music you hear, wherever that music may go, or wherever you may take the music. So when I play for you, I see only you."

She laughed at him coquettishly and said, "You are a married man, married to a woman named Solea, daughter of the Sun, and you are now with Atora, daughter of the priest of the Moon. What do you think about that?"

"I don't think anything about that, but I'll gladly take what God or Devla gives me and make the best of it. That's what Gypsies do." He leaned over and kissed her. "But now I must pick up the supplies the *patrón* wants and return to the hacienda by sunset, or he'll whip me without mercy. Will you lead me back to the church?"

They followed the path through the forest they'd taken earlier. When Juancinto and Atora reached the wagon, Juancinto asked, "When can I see you again?"

She frowned and pouted her lips, "Sometimes on market days, my father lets me go into Chía, sometimes not. It depends on how he feels. It is better to the Valvanera church. Ask for Mono, the errand boy, and tell him to fetch me. We can be together again in the forest."

Juancinto mounted his wagon and grabbed his reins, "I should be back within the month."

And before the next new moon, Juancinto was back for an afternoon in the trees at the base of Tiguiza Hill. He met Atora in the same forest, which he now saw more like a sculpted garden than a wild woodland.

"You owe me something, Atora."

"What, you typical Spaniard?" she joked. "You want some gold trinkets?"

"No. What you owe me is what you promised, that is, to tell me about yourself and what it means to be a priestess dedicated to the Moon."

"I will settle my debt, then. I am training to take over from my father someday as Priestess of the Temple of the Moon. What does that mean? On the outside, I study the cycles of the nine gods that circle the land where we live. That determines the appropriate time to plant and harvest, who should be married and when, when to make war, when to make peace. These are things of the Sun, of the outside, visible world. Things of the inside world pertain to the Moon. I am talking about the meaning of dreams, sickness and health, and balancing the forces from the gods. Do you understand?"

"I'm not sure."

"I will try to make it simple. Heat is fire and air. Am I right?"

"Sure."

"And cold is earth and water, by the same reasoning. Cold pertains to the Moon. Does that make sense?"

"Yes."

"You feel the Sun's energy on the outside of your body during the daylight hours. The Moon takes the Sun's energy and makes it its own. The Moon's energy invigorates the interior of all living things. The Moon's energy is inside us, and the Sun's energy is outside. It could not be simpler. Do you understand so far?"

"Yes, I think so," said Juancinto.

"Good," she continued, "The Sun's energy is like gold, but it is fire—it is pure energy, visible from its source. The Moon's energy is more like silver, but more than that, it is like a living mass. We call it 'pulp.' When the outside energy of the Sun mixes with the inside pulp of the Moon, it gives rise to the Creative Force, which manifests in human beings as thought, imagination and procreation. The Sun and Moon are the first two of nine gods that direct and change the Creative Force. You already know what the other seven gods are. Am I right?"

"They are the planets," said Juancinto.

"True. These gods show themselves as wandering stars traversing the night sky without twinkling. We say that these gods dance to the beat of a drum, and this dance and drum beat gives rise to space and time. We are all creatures of the Creative Force. It is what germinates all seeds and brings them to life. To know and dance with the Sun and Moon is to dance with the Creative Force. But we can't all do the dance. Knowing and dancing with the Creative Force is the role of the Priest or Priestess of the Temple of the Moon. Our job is to develop the inner sight, that is to say, the 'Moon Vision,' with which to see the Creative Force in action and direct it or, at least, be in step with it. Do you understand?"

"I only understand because I felt it as I played the music for your dance when I first saw you. My fingers were out of my control."

"That's what I am talking about. You felt it and participated with the Creative Force firsthand. Now, I want to call the Creative Force 'golden energy' because, when you see it in action, the flow of energy radiates a golden color."

Atora then related an experience she once had. "One day, after doing certain exercises, I fell into a trance. I was outside my body, and I saw the golden energy go up my spine."

She was silent for a few moments.

"That's why I say the gold that dangles from my ears is a mere symbol of the golden life force. The material gold itself does not mean anything to me."

She could feel that Juancinto was not convinced. She thought he didn't believe what he was hearing. Nevertheless, she continued. "It is the golden life force that energizes us and opens our awareness that interests me, not these earrings and wrist bracelets on my body. These are just symbols. Here, Juancinto," she took her jewelry off. "You can have them. They don't mean anything to me. I want the *real* thing."

Juancinto was astonished. Not knowing what else to do, he accepted the bracelets and earrings.

Juancinto later buried the trinkets in the ground at the hacienda. He would visit Atora many times over the next three years and discover lots of mutual interests. They often worked on language skills—her Spanish and his Muiscan. He also taught her basic movements in the dances of the *palos gitanos* genre. One day, Atora picked up Juancinto's guitar and felt something knocking around inside its body.

"What's in there, Juancinto?"

Juancinto took the guitar and pulled a small leather pouch from the sound hole. Inside were twenty-two tiny shellacked cards. "My mother-in-law, La Gitanilla, gave these to me four years ago when I left Sevilla."

"What are they?"

"They are Arcana tarot cards."

"What do they mean?" Atora asked.

Juancinto thought for a while. "When I think about it, these cards are something like your Temple, but compressed and carried in a small leather bag. "What I mean is this." He laid out twelve cards and told Atora they represented the twelve signs of the Zodiac or the twelve patterns of stars that move across the night sky in sequence. "They represent the months of the Spanish year."

Atora was fascinated and examined each card closely.

"These seven cards," Juancinto pointed out, "are your non-sparkling stars or what we call planets. But the cards include the Sun and Moon, as well as Jupiter, Saturn, Mars, Venus, and Mercury."

Juancinto laid the last three cards down. "These correspond to Fire, Water, and Air, or the highest world of God's Fiery Will— next, the watery world of the emotions and good and evil, and ,last, the airy world of thinking and dreaming."

Atora looked up at Juancinto, puzzled. "There is no card for the Earth where we live, which is round, as you say?"

"I once asked that too, but La Gitanilla told me there is no card for the Earth because we already know it so well. It is the world in which we live, and all the other cards or forces pour their energies into the earth and cause what happens to us, what *has* happened, or what *will* happen here on the planet. The *gadjos* [23] gives us money to tell them their future with these cards. They think only Gypsies can use the cards, but it is just one of the ways the *gadjos* give us to earn a living. So, of course, we are good at it."

Atora knelt on the ground and examined the cards closely. She was drawn to the card depicting a woman with a crown on her head, holding a book, with a blue robe that turned into water. "That's me!" she exclaimed. "What's the name of this card?"

"You're right, Atora. That *is* you!" Even Juancinto was surprised at the revelatory power of the tiny cards. The name of that card is the High Priestess. She rules over the Moon, like you. Her water is silver, and when she mates with Mercury, the Magician beside her, the liquid turns to gold. She then becomes the pregnant Empress, and the Magician, the Emperor, which is Aries, the first month of the year."

Atora glanced at Juancinto suspiciously and said, "You use these cards to tell the future . . . am I right?"

"Yes. People like my mother-in-law use them, but I am not very good at it. You might say, I just play at it."

"When I first saw you, I caught you in the observatory, where you were forbidden. Now, you are telling me that what we, Muiscans, have constructed in our observatory, you Gypsies have already created in the form of twenty-two cards? And you keep them tied in a pouch and hidden in your guitar."

"No," Juancinto said. "I am not telling you that. I don't even know how to use the cards to tell the future, and I certainly do not understand anything about your observatory."

Atora turned some of the cards over. "What are these symbols on the back?" she asked.

"La Gitanilla told me they were the letters of the Hebrew alphabet. They are the letters Jesus Christ used, but I don't know anything more about them."

"Oh," said Atora, lost in thought.

"Where did La Gitanilla come by these cards?"

"She told me her ancestors brought them from Morocco two hundred years ago. I think she said Fez."

"That doesn't mean anything to me," Atora said. "But these cards. . . ." She caressed them. "I can't take my eyes off them."

"That means they are yours," Juancinto said firmly. "I was just the messenger to bring these cards from La Gitanilla to you. It is my symbol of gold to you."

Atora accepted the cards and said she would treasure and learn from them. Juancinto told her he would show her how La Gitanilla taught him to lay them out, which he did with time.

On another visit to Tiguiza Hill, Juancinto questioned Atora about her ancestors and the history of the Muiscan people.

"I've told you about the Gypsies traveling around Earth to Spain. Now tell me about your people."

"What is there to tell? We've always been here. The original Muiscan people came from Lake Iguaque. The one we call Bachué, the Grandmother, the Mother Goddess, came out of Lake Iguaque surrounded by ancestors. Bachué had a boy in her arms. She stood the boy on the shore, then disappeared back into the lake with the ancestors, who all took the form of snakes. The boy grew into a man and populated the earth. But the people transgressed the divine law given by the Grandmother, so she caused a great flood that wiped out most living things. When the waters receded, the divine Grandmother reappeared and taught agriculture, the arts, and the crafts. The Grandfather taught about the nine gods that energize the earth and all living things. He also taught about the twelve houses in which the sun rises during the year."

"Do the Muiscan people have a leader now?" Juancinto asked.

"Of course," she replied. "We can't be without a leader."

"How do you choose your leaders?"

"That is one of many things my father and I do. When it is time for the Muiscan people to have a new leader, we help the elders decide who the ancestors choose. He will be a young man. We take him to a cave near Lake Iguaque, where he lives until all his senses are quieted into nothingness. Then, when the time is right, he is brought out of the cave into the bright sunlight and moonlight. There are four priests—fire, air, earth, and water—like your tarot cards, but we include earth. The priests prepare the young man to rule. They take him to Lake Iguaque, strip him naked and coat his body with sticky mud. Then they cover him with gold dust."

"Gold dust?" Juancinto repeated, not sure he heard her correctly.

"Yes, powdered gold—he becomes what the Spanish call "El Dorado", the Golden One. The mud symbolizes our origin, and the gold dust is symbolic of the Golden Life Force, which energizes us. The elders have a large raft, a barge made of rushes. They fill the raft with articles of gold and emeralds, and they place the young man, El Dorado, in the middle. Then they paddle the gold-laden barge into the center of the lake. The four elders throw all the treasure into the lake, and then El Dorado dives into the lake and washes off the gold dust and mud. This demonstrates that they do not value the material gold trinkets or dust cast into the lake, rather they value the qualities of the golden Life Force embodied in the young leader, the Golden One. The elders help El Dorado back onto the raft, and they paddle to the shore where a grand celebration marks the start of a new era."

Atora's story of El Dorado enchanted Juancinto. He asked many questions, inevitably the irresistible one: "*Where* is this Lake Iguaque?"

"Not far," Atora replied. "A day to the north by wagon. Why do you ask? Do you want to go there?

"Of course," Juancinto said.

"But *why?*"

"To see the place where all peoples originated and, perhaps, see if any gold ornaments are yet to be found along the shoreline."

"Oh, I see!" mocked Atora. "I'm afraid you're a bit late, my Gypsy friend. Only last year, our ruler in Bogotá, Quesada, with two hundred men, spent three months trying to drain the lake with pumps from ships. The lake is not very big—a man could swim across it. But it is deeper than the Spanish thought, especially in the center. However, they *did* find objects of gold along the shore. But that was last summer. You are late."

"Maybe I am too late, Atora, but I would still like to see this Lake Iguaque since it is so close. If I can convince Don Antonio to give me a few free days, will you show me the way?"

"You ask too much of me, Juancinto."

"Please, Atora, I beg of you. Let's go on this adventure. If I find some gold at the lake, perhaps I can pay off my bondage and start a new life here as a free man."

Atora consented to go with him if he got permission from his *patrón*.

Juancinto returned to the hacienda and, at the first opportunity, informed Don Antonio that he had a Muiscan friend who knew where Lake Iguaque was. He reminded him of the legend of the Golden Boy in the Lake. Juancinto wanted a few days to explore the lake.

Don Antonio was familiar with the legend. He told Juancinto it was only last year that Lazaro Fonte and Herman Perez de Quesada attempted to drain the lake to no avail. Juancinto argued that the expedition did find gold objects along the shore. Juancinto eventually prevailed upon Don Antonio to permit him to take the wagon and treasure-hunt for a few days. Antonio conceded he had nothing to lose, and he was also curious. If the Gypsy found something of value, he would find some way to benefit from it.

Juancinto and Atora rode together in the wagon traveling north by northeast through valleys and rugged mountain passes. At day's end, they arrived at their destination. From high upon a hill, they looked down upon a dead volcano crater that had turned into a green valley. A placid lake in the middle reflected the setting sun.

That night Atora and Juancinto slept in the back of the wagon. They began exploring the lakeshore early the following day. Juancinto walked the whole shoreline in about an hour and found that the water at the shore, for the most part, was deep and over his head. However, a portion of the lake's edge was shallow and marshy.

Juancinto removed his sandals and waded through the mud and marsh grass, searching with his toes for metal objects. Moving systematically through the muddy water, he finally felt something hard and smooth. He reached down with his hand but could not grasp the object, and he could see nothing in the turbid water. He looked further into the lake, where the water was clearer. He thought he saw something gleaming on the bottom, reflecting the mid-morning sun. He moved in the direction of the object and found himself in deeper water than expected. He was, in fact, sinking rapidly into the mud. All attempts to march out of the muck only strengthened its grasp on his body. There was nothing to hold, and the water was now up to his chest. He called out to Atora, who was on the other side of the lake attending to the cook fire. She heard him and saw his predicament. She mounted the wagon and drove it to the shore near Juancinto. He told her to get the rope from under the seat and tie it to the rear axle. She did, wading into the marsh close enough to throw him the rope.

Juancinto tied the rope around his waist and secured it to his leather belt. Atora returned to the wagon. With his head almost submerged, Juancinto screamed, "*pull!*" Atora snapped the reins and dragged Juancinto out of the muck onto firm ground.

"I've seen enough!" Juancinto said. But Atora was not listening. She had turned to study the murky waters from where Juancinto had just come. Her mouth was open, her eyes wide. Circling the hole from which she had just extracted Juancinto was a snake three yards long and with the circumference of a large man's thigh. She uttered a strong command in Muiscan with a ferocity that startled Juancinto.

Neither spoke much that afternoon on the way back to Chía. That night, they camped along the trail. As they were making their bed in the back of the wagon, Atora told Juancinto that the ancestors had tried to drown him, confirmed by the snake she'd witnessed. She commented that she hoped the ancestors would not hold her actions against her.

They arrived in the forest surrounding the Valvanera church by noon the following day. Before departing, Atora reached into her leather satchel, pulled out a gold brooch, and offered it to Juancinto.

"Here, give this to your *patrón* so he will not beat you."

Juancinto arrived at the hacienda before sunset and presented his *patrón* with the gold brooch. Don Antonio had been waiting for his return with the utmost anticipation and curiosity. He received the valuable clip with the Juancinto's explanation that he had found it in the shallows at the edge of the sacred lake. Don Antonio examined it closely, then turned his back on Juancinto and declared he did not believe a single word coming out of Juancinto's lying Gypsy mouth.

"Quesada and Lazaro Fonte and two hundred men nearly drained Lake Iguaque only a year ago. If this brooch had been on the shore of the lake, they would have found it. Therefore, you are lying, Juancinto Taranto!"

Juancinto denied it, but his *patrón* had him tied to the whipping post. After ten lashes, he confessed that his lover, the daughter of the High Priest of the Temple of Chía, had given him the brooch to present to Don Antonio because they had taken so much time to find nothing.

Don Antonio released Juancinto. The following morning, Don Antonio rode into Bogotá to confer with the authorities. He returned in two days and announced that he was sending Juancinto to the governor of the Río de la Plata and the new capital of Asunción to serve the balance of his sentence.

For the next few days, Juancinto rested as the wounds on his back began to scab over. He was prevented from leaving the hacienda and was later shackled to a wagon bound for Bogotá. There, after a week of detention, he was put on a long wagon train carrying commodities to the Pacific port of Buenaventura, two weeks down the Valley of the Cauca River to the city of Cali, and then one week over the high mountain range to Buenaventura.

Each day seemed warmer as the wagon train moved south. Soon Juancinto shed his coat and, the next afternoon, his shirt to let the sun heal his lash wounds. Halfway to Cali, Juancinto noticed black people working in the *encomienda* fields. He had not seen many dark-skinned people since leaving the Caribbean and Santa Maria five years ago. Juancinto told his observations to a fellow traveler and learned the slaves from Africa did not adjust well to the high savannah around Bogotá. They got sick and died or did not work hard enough to satisfy their masters. Around Cali, the Africans were used sparingly to work with indigenous slaves on the *encomiendas*, but on the coast, in Buenaventura, planters used Africans almost exclusively in the hot and sultry sugar cane fields.

"You'll see. You'll think you're in Africa."

The wagon train halted in Santiago de Cali for a few weeks, filling empty wagons with commodities bound for Spain. Here the temperature was never too hot and never too cold, no matter the season or time of day. With the Cauca River running through the valley, Juancinto thought paradise must not be much different.

While still in Cali, a mail rider who recognized Juancinto from Chía stopped at the wagon train's encampment. He gave Juancinto the news that Don Antonio convinced the viceroy in Bogotá and the bishops to destroy the Temple of the Moon and all vestiges of the pagan religion of the Muiscas on the high savannah. The mail rider opined that they were looking for stashes of gold and emeralds, believing the natives had hidden them at the Temple on the hill above Chía.

This news left Juancinto devastated and despondent. Tears had welled in his eyes as the mail rider told of the looting of the Temple of the Moon, which made the rider comment it was the first time he'd seen a Gypsy cry.

For Juancinto, it was the second time in his life that he had brought ruin to a woman who loved him. He resolved to never love again.

The wagon train left Cali with an extra mounted guard. For two days in fine weather, they journeyed up the mountain range bordering Cali to the west. Reaching the summit, the wagon train entered a rainy gloom that matched Juancinto's mood. It persisted for two more days until they reached the Pacific port and island of Buenaventura. Only the sight of a new ocean could distract Juancinto from his melancholy. His first act on arriving in Buenaventura was to bathe himself in the cold waters of the Pacific.

The wagon train arrived in time to meet a galleon from Acapulco full of enslaved Africans destined to work in the local sugar cane fields. Overseers marched nearly a hundred men and boys, all skin and bones, to a holding pen beside the slave market. Juancinto watched as they were sold to local planters. The empty galleon was restocked with commodities from Bogotá and Cali bound for Acapulco on the return trip. From Acapulco, the goods could be shipped west across the Pacific to the Philippines or east across the peninsula to the Atlantic port of Veracruz.

Upon arriving in Acapulco, the ship's captain was to transfer custody of Juancinto to the captain of the next wagon train traveling across southern Mexico to Veracruz. There he boarded a galleon to Havana and another ship sailing south for a month within sight of Portuguese Brazil's coast until reaching Spanish territory and the mouth of the Río de la Plata. From there, they would be river sailing in a northerly direction; first, on the Paraná River for two weeks, then the Paraguay River for a week until finally reaching Asunción, the new capital of the governate of Nueva Andalucía.

Setting sail from Buenaventura, Juancinto lost no time befriending sailors who could tell him how the world had changed during his five years confinement in the New Kingdom of Grenada.

He learned that Spain had poured its treasury into its new major colony of the Philippines. Trade with China and the Orient was enormous. Most of the ships sailing for the Spanish in the Pacific were made in the Philippines or China. Why? Because nobody wanted to sail through the frigid, stormy Straits of Magellan. The trade caravan between Acapulco and the Atlantic port of Veracruz was constant, and there was more money and extravagance in Acapulco than ever seen in Sevilla. The sailors told him of friends who'd died in battles with the Chichimeca Indians around the silver mines of Zacatecas north of the City of México. When Juancinto inquired what lay north of New Spain, the sailors told him of a grand island called California. Still, few people were there, and there was not much interest. Juancinto then decided if he had to run for his life, he would go to California.

Guards shackled Juancinto upon his arrival in Acapulco. Within days, he was put on the wagon train to Veracruz. After five days' travel through unbroken mountains and halfway across the width of southern Mexico, the caravan reached the central market town of Puebla. Juancinto had befriended a few indigenous and Spanish wagon drivers and guards. They described Puebla as a planned city only thirty years old, located at the junction of four indigenous city-states that often warred with each other. Long before the Spanish city of Puebla was created, the valley of Puebla was an important meeting place where "flower wars" were conducted. The guards told Juancinto about fascinating story of flower wars. The Aztec gods of Tenochtitlan, now the City of Mexico, were angry with the people and caused a severe drought. The priests divined that the problem was resolvable only through continuous human sacrifice. Rather than sacrifice their own, the priests devised a way to accomplish many ends with one trick—the flower wars.

Staged battles in the valley of Puebla, the "wars" would begin and end at certain times every year. The battles would be fought against neighboring city-states, with an equal number of warriors on each side. Tenochtitlan had a much larger population than other city-states. In a given year, even if the Aztecs were to lose as many men in a flower war as the opposition, the warrior castes of smaller city-states would be diminished and weakened for years relative to that of the more populous Aztecs. Furthermore, every flower war would provide captives for sacrifice to appease the Aztec gods. Lastly, since the Aztecs exercised their dominance of other territories through warfare, the flower wars kept the young warriors of Tenochtitlan alert, ready, practiced, and belligerent.

Juancinto wondered what the "wars" in his life were doing to him, and at what sacrifice.

Two days out of Puebla, the wagon trained descended out of the mountains onto level plains. Another two days put the travelers in Veracruz, where the port was even more active than Acapulco, glistening with gold and silver and streams of goods shipping in and out on vessels of Spanish wood.

After a day or two of rest, Juancinto embarked on a Spanish galleon with successive southward stops in Havana, San Juan, and Caracas. Juancinto knew that in Caracas he would be transferred to the once-per-quarter ship going to the extreme south, to the Governorate of the Rio de las Plata. In Juancinto's mind, these were the frigid territories poor Magellan explored forty years ago. Going south meant one thing to Juancinto—cold. After living in the high savannah of Bogotá, Juancinto had become more sensitive to the weather. In his mind, he began to fear the frigid temperatures of the deep southern latitudes. He needed a new coat and boots, not sandals.

Juancinto persuaded the quartermaster of his ship to permit him to hunt rats in the cargo hold. After training the ship's cat to trap the vermin, Juancinto collected and trained enough beady-eyed warriors to declare a Rat Gladiator Day.

The success of his gambling adventure augmented meager proceeds from guitar playing. It earned him a new fur coat and fur-lined boots from the Caracas market.

Juancinto was now prepared for a new day on the extended return to Sevilla, Solea, and Quim.

CHAPTER 16

GUITAR AND HARP

Paraguay
Asunción
Lago Ypacaraí
1560-1565

Sailing from Caracas, *La Providencia* followed the northwestern coast of the great continent. Although now out of the range of pirates in the Caribbean, he crew's worries shifted. The challenge now was to remain within sight of the mainland while avoiding coral reefs and rocks below the surface. The final destination was the far-flung outpost of Asunción, located in the upper reaches of a river system the Navigators of discovery still held out hopes would lead to Incan gold or the Pacific Ocean.

Rounding the eastern tip of Brazil, *La Providencia* made port in the new Portuguese settlement of Recife, proofing that traditional enemies—the Spanish and Portuguese—could, by necessity, accommodate each other this far from home, if only in the sense of estranged brothers. Fresh water and supplies were brought aboard. Juancinto was not permitted to disembark.

Sailing south by southeast along the coast, after one week, *La Providencia* briefly moored at the mother port of São Salvador de Bahia. After another week of sailing, she made a final call at Porto Seguro, where the navigator Pedro Álvares Cabral had first landed sixty years before. They re-provisioned *La Providencia*, anticipating another month at sea.

When the ship finally entered the enormous bay of the Río de la Plata, Juancinto had spent two months aboard *La Providencia*. The ship proceeded two days in the bay until the bay funneled into a series of muddy rivers. The ship sailed up the first one on the port side with the name" Rio Paraná. ".

Approaching the tack for the Rio Paraná, the ship sailed past a cluster of roofless structures surrounded by a thick adobe wall. Pointing to the ruins, Juancinto turned to the quartermaster and asked, "What was that?"

The quartermaster, Fernando Cuellar, replied that they were the ruins of the first Spanish settlement on the Río de la Plata. The site was Buenos Aires—abandoned eighteen years ago in favor of the upriver settlement of Asunción. "That's where we are going," the officer said.

Juancinto sensed a connection with Cuellar or at least a propensity to indulge in discussions about history. "The crew says you know a lot about the New World and its history. I must stay here for the next five years, so I'd like to get my bearings. I understand this land is New Andalucía, and I am from *old* Andalucía. I may have grandchildren when I return home, and I want to tell them about *new* Andalucía."

"You are Juancinto, yes?"

"That's my name."

"You're sure you have the patience to learn about this crazy place?"

"What else do I have to do, Sr. Cuellar?"

Cuellar chuckled. "Very well. About thirty years ago, the Italian Sebastian Caboto, son of the famous John Cabot, worked for our king. He was the first European to sail up this river. The king commissioned Caboto to sail to China and Japan with four ships and two hundred men, repeating what Magellan had done. When he anchored off the coast of Brazil, he heard tales of the incredible wealth of the Incan king. Thinking he could find a shortcut to the Incan Empire, Caboto changed the mission plan and sailed upriver, hoping to find a navigable route to Peru.

"He sailed about as far as where Asunción is today. There he found two Guaraní Indians who had gold and silver jewelry. They told him the silver came from a mountain up the river. Caboto thus named the river 'Río de la Plata.'"

"With such a name, do you think he was trying to justify not sailing to China?"

"That's a good point, my friend," said Cuellar. "I don't know, but nothing more came from the expedition. Caboto returned to Spain empty-handed, but the wonderful yet empty name of the river remained."

"A few years later, a wealthy Spaniard from Granada, Pedro de Mendoza, sailed from Spain at his own expense with thirteen ships and two thousand men. The king told him he could rule all of Nueva Andalucía and have as much land as he could conquer. But he had to give most of the treasure to the king, build forts along the way, and create conditions for a thousand new colonists within two years. Those were the king's conditions. That sounds like a good deal, but it didn't go so well.

"Even before entering these waters, Mendoza lost half his fleet in a storm off the coast of Brazil. In 1535, Mendoza sailed upriver and established that ruined town, Buenos Aires.

"The Indians received them well until the *Conquistadores* ran out of food and gifts. Mendoza's men began to take advantage of the Indians, treating them as their servants. The Indians were displeased. They didn't fight, but they moved away, leaving Mendoza and his men helpless. In fact—so I heard—Mendoza spent most of his time in bed with the great pox—you know, Cupid's disease." Cuellar chuckled and crossed himself. "Mendoza sent his men after the Indians but did no good. Without them, they had no agriculture, and the soldiers were not farmers. When conditions reduced them to eating rats and snakes, the Indians mustered their courage, attacked them regularly, and burned their buildings.

"Pedro de Mendoza had enough. He returned to Spain, leaving Juan de Ayolas in charge, appointing him captain-general. His second in command was a Basque named Domingo Martínez de Irala.

"Ayolas and Irala decided that the colony of Buenos Aires had no future. They focused on one of the mission's goals instead—finding a navigable route to the silver mines of Peru and the treasures of the Incan Empire." He shrugged. "Why should they waste time in this God-forsaken place when they could be heroes and conquerors?

"They left a small garrison in Buenos Aires under the command of Juan de Salazar. Ayolas and Irala took the rest of the men and all the ships up the Paraná River to where it joins the Paraguay River. Here they divided the men and ships equally. Irala proceeded east, up the Paraná, and established his group at Puerto Candelaria after three days of sailing. Ayolas sailed north up the Paraguay past where Asunción is located. He created a fort on the river's west bank and named it Fuerte Olimpo. Once built, Ayolas left a small garrison and, with his soldiers, ventured west into the vast, dry wasteland called the Chaco. Eventually, they reached the foothills of the Andes, which was the old border of the Incan Empire.

Ayolas and his men loaded the wagons and saddlebags with booty and started back long journey returning to Fuerte Olimpo. But they encountered the Paraguas Indians, a fierce and tenacious tribe. The relentless attacks wore down Ayolas's little army, weighed down with all that gold. The Paraguas eventually exterminated them.

Juan de Salazar came up-river from Buenos Aires to lead a search for Ayolas, but it was fruitless. Salazar's ship anchored at the place where, years earlier, Sebastian Caboto had found friendly Guaraní Indians with gold and silver. He noticed the site was at the junction of another sizeable river flowing from the west—the Pilcomayo. Moreover, the site had a little bay that could serve as a natural river port for a future city on the cliffs above the river. He christened it Nuestra Señora Santa María de la Asunción.

"Sailing south down the Paraguay from Asunción, he turned left up the other big river called Paraná in search of Domingo Irala. After three days, he found Irala and his men where they had initially pitched camp, at Puerto de la Candelaria. Both Irala and Salazar then sailed down the Paraná to the ruins of Buenos Aires, hoping to find the missing Ayolas and his men. But at the abandoned colony they found nothing and came to the determination that the captain-general was dead.

"Now leaderless, they held an election for a new captain-general, permitted under the terms that Pedro Mendoza established with King Charles V, Domingo Martínez de Irala was elected, and the first order of business was to leave Buenos Aires for good. Everyone and everything moved upriver to the site that Juan de Salazar named Asunción.

"Juancinto, I tell you this because Irala, the Basque nobleman, went on to rule Nueva Andalucía for the next twenty years until his death less than three years ago. Nueva Andalucia, or Paraguay, as we call it now, is largely his creation."

"Why do you say that?" Juancinto asked.

"Irala knew he would have trouble getting colonists from Spain to commit their lives to this wild country—countless leagues up a muddy river. His novel idea was to require all his soldiers—even officers—to marry a Guaraní girl. He persuaded the church to relax its laws against bigamy. The idea wasn't so bad—Paraguayan women are generally good-looking, friendly, and exceptionally intelligent. Irala himself had many wives, concubines and countless children. In twenty years of the practice,

Paraguay became a mixed-race country. The newly arrived nobles from Spain are at the top of society. The pure Guaraní in the jungle are at the bottom. Those in the middle—the *mestizos*—speak a father tongue of Castellano and a mother tongue of Guaraní.

"Irala was pressured by the Crown to find the legendary route to the silver mines in high Peru. His young officers relentlessly called for expeditions west through jungles and deserts to the mountains of the old Incan Empire.

"Twelve years ago, under mounting pressure from the king and officers, Irala launched a major campaign into high Peru. This time he wasn't fooling around. He left Francisco Mendoza as acting governor and assembled an expedition of 350 soldiers, half of them cavalry, and two thousand Guaraní. They were gone a year and a half. After many hardships and battles with the Indians, they finally reached their destination.

Irala and the Paraguayans arrived in Peru just as a civil war ended. Francisco Pizarro had been assassinated, and his brother Gonzalo tried to seize power by rebelling against the colonial government. Simultaneously, the king sent a lawyer-priest with unlimited authority to settle the rebellion. By his wit and charm, the priest, Pedro de la Gasca, persuaded Gonzalo Pizarro's rebellious army to switch sides and support the government. After so doing, Gonzalo Pizarro was promptly executed.

Domingo Irala then appeared with his cavalry and two thousand Guaraní. La Gasca was immediately suspicious, believing Irala might persuade the former rebels to join forces with him. With the king's bestowal of unlimited power, La Gasca officially stripped Domingo Irala of his elected rank of captain-general and governor of Río de la Plata. And what do you think Irala did?" Cuellar asked Juancinto.

Juancinto shrugged his shoulders and said nothing.

"Exactly!" Cuellar replied, chuckling. "Irala said absolutely nothing. He simply shrugged, turned his army around, and returned to Asunción. Nothing ever came of his loss of rank.

"On the way back through the Chaco wilderness, various tribes fiercely attacked Irala's army. After a year and a half in the field, Irala's expedition finally returned to Asunción. They did not come not empty-handed—he marched twelve thousand slaves into the city, primarily the women and children he captured in the Chaco. The enslaved people were distributed to Paraguay's land-owning families with the stipulation that they be freed in one or two generations.

"This kept the peace. The young officers could no longer blame Irala for not taking the Inca's gold. Asunción, located across an expansive ocean and far up a muddy river into the dark heart of the New World, was not the preferred destination for Spanish colonists. What Irala needed more than Incan gold was people. He reasoned that the twelve thousand would have multiplied many times to become free men and women within a couple of generations—a new mixed European and Indian culture loyal to Irala's memory and Paraguay. And thus it is and will come to be.

"In the last year of his life, Irala felt tremendous pressure from the Crown and powerful landed families to submit the Río de la Plata and Paraguay to the *encomienda* system. The old man finally gave in to the pressure against his will. The *encomienda* system grants or sells property to noble families including the rights to all the products from that land and the labor of the Indians who reside on it. The *encomiendas* paid a yearly tribute to the government and Crown."

Juancinto interrupted—he was familiar with the system—after all, he had lived in Bogotá for five years.

"So, you know. The *encomienda* system is practiced all over the New World, but perhaps you didn't know that here in Paraguay, Irala and the Jesuits obliged the hacienda owners to treat the indigenous population humanely, providing for their basic needs, teaching them the Christian faith, and protecting them. But here in Nueva Andalucía, it is evident that, despite the good intentions, the *encomienda* system was abused from the start, turning most of the Guaraní into slaves. Irala died, thank God, before he had to see it with his own eyes.

"The introduction of the *encomienda* system in Paraguay has produced a violent reaction. The proud Guaraní tribes have united on the borders of Paraguay and are fighting the *conquistadores* wherever they find them. Guaraní men, trapped as slaves on the haciendas, are deserting the farms for the jungles to join their comrades in arms. That brings us up to the present," the quartermaster concluded. "So, this strife is what you will experience for the next five years, my friend. I wish you luck."

"Sr. Cuellar, I can hardly express my appreciation for the history you gave me. I now have my bearings. What can I do to repay you?"

"Repay me? Nothing. Just do well and survive. But if you play a *palos gitanos* piece from Sevilla at sundown tonight, I will dream we are sailing on the beautiful Guadalquivir instead of this God-forsaken river."

"I shall do that for you, *señor.*"

When the galleon moored at the pier in Asunción, a young soldier met Juancinto to escort him and his belongings up the hill to the government house, where he waited five hours in the courtyard. An official finally told him there was no work for a murderous Gypsy from Sevilla. The official promised to consign Juancinto to the stockade until a proper job presented itself.

A Franciscan friar who had also been waiting in the courtyard heard the exchange. He approached the official and whispered something to him.

"This is your lucky day," the official said, turning toward Juancinto. "Follow the padre to the site where they're building the cathedral. With Bishop Toro's permission, you might find a job, and I won't have to worry about what to do with you."

The humble holy man introduced himself in an unfamiliar accent as Padre Cairbre O'Carolan. Juancinto followed him through the dusty streets to the construction site. They found Asunción's first bishop shouting orders to plasterers high upon bamboo scaffolding. The padre caught the bishop's attention, and the two men spoke for a few minutes outside Juancinto's earshot. They shook hands, appearing to have reached an agreement.

Padre Cairbre returned to Juancinto and said, "It's official—I must present an annual report to the bishop, and he will handle the papers for the caudillo. You will sleep with us in the stable at the bishop's palace—rise at dawn, home by nightfall."

"If I may be so bold, Padre, where is my new home?"

"Your home will be our tiny hacienda at the southern tip of a beautiful lake called Ypacaraí. The church supports it. You will be our handyman. If you like peace and quiet, you will like the place."

To Juancinto, the arrangement sounded almost too good to be true. He had feared being assigned to an army brigade fighting cannibals in the jungle. This was, indeed, his lucky day, but he was too tired to celebrate or talk. In the stable, where the priest and mule also bedded down, Juancinto laid his head against a straw-filled pillow. Strange visions of him being baptized a Catholic swirled through his head as he drifted into a deep sleep.

The following day, after a biscuit and dried meat, they plodded off toward the rising sun. Padre Cairbre led the mule by the harness strap, and Juancinto followed. The Padre said they were following the old straight pathway that connected Asunción with the Paraná River at the great falls of Iguaçu, six days journey to the east. "But we will get to *our* destination by the end of the day."

Juancinto helped the padre load and strap down the cargo. Now, slogging behind the mule, he speculated about the goods and how they might impact his future. The beast carried three bolts of cotton fabric, a burlap sack of cotton thread on spools, another bag of smaller sacks containing colored powder, a wooden chest of what looked like bars of soap, two jugs of what smelled to be pure alcohol, and finally, a sizeable, flat wooden box that had arrived on the *La Providencia*. If their cargo held clues to the future, Juancinto was stumped. The padre seemed a man of few words, so he hazarded some questions.

"Padre, if I may be so bold, what is in the large crate?"

"What's that you have strapped to your back, Juancinto?"

"It's my guitar, Padre. You can see that."

"Music—that's what's in the crate."

"But—"

"You'll see in due time."

Juancinto looked at him, puzzled. He had more questions. "Where were you born, Padre? I sense Castellano is not your native—"

"I am from Ros Comáin," the priest interrupted, "a damp, gray place in the middle of Ireland."

"I don't know it," Juancinto said, but the padre fell silent, not elaborating on his origins or past. "I was born in Sevilla, but I am a Gypsy," Juancinto ventured. "Strictly speaking, I'm not even Christian."

"I know."

"Why am I here?"

"You are here by the Grace of God. I can only be certain of that. They told me you murdered a man for attacking your wife as she danced, and you received ten years in this good land for your troubles."

"That's right, sir."

"And you have served five of the ten in Nueva Granada."

"Yes, sir."

"You have a son, I am told?"

"I am a family man—I long to return home."

"Good. That may help you adjust to your work."

"What might that be, Padre?"

"You will see soon enough, and so will I."

By mid-afternoon, they'd come to a town the padre called Itauguá. At the village center stood a wattle-and-daub church surrounded by activity—women sitting at make-shift looms. They wove in mid-air like spiders spinning a colorful web. The Padre conferred with certain women who seemed to oversee the enterprise. They exchanged papers full of hand-drawn designs.

An older woman ordered a boy to fetch a bucket of water from the well. They all sat on the ground around a large shady mango tree and invited the padre and Juancinto to join them for mangos. One woman crushed handfuls of green leaves that looked like tea into a gourd and filled the vessel with cold water. The woman inserted a silver straw into the gourd and presented it to Juancinto. He nodded with gratitude and asked his hostess if the gourd was him alone. The women laughed and chatted among themselves in Guaraní. Juancinto repeated his question. Padre Cairbre informed him the women spoke no Spanish and explained that he was to sip the water from the gourd, fill it again, and pass it to the nearest person. The drink was *tereré,* made from the foliage of a shrub called *yerba maté.* After they had passed the gourd around the circle twice, the padre signaled it was time to depart. As Juancinto regained his feet, he felt powerfully invigorated, as if he had awakened after a good night's rest to bathe in a cold stream.

Juancinto glanced at the padre, who winked and said, "Is not *yerba maté* a fine blessing from the Guaraní!"

The two men headed down the trail with the mule between them. Within two hours, they came upon the shore of Lake Ypacaraí, and, as Padre Cairbre had said, it was beautiful indeed. With the warm glow of the setting sun at his back, Juancinto could barely make out the far side of the tranquil waters. A crescent moon appeared over palms and flowering lapacho trees.

This must be paradise, Juancinto thought.

Juancinto watched the moonrise from the lake's edge and heard a man singing in Guaraní. As he approached, Juancinto saw the man wearing a cloth bag over his head with holes for his eyes and mouth and carrying a hoe over his shoulder. The man walked past, greeted the Padre cordially, and resumed chanting the Guaraní melody.

"Why does he wear a bag over his head?" Juancinto asked Padre Cairbre.

"He has leprosy on his face, and he feels more comfortable covering it in public to avoid putting people off. Around here, however, no one cares."

"Why? Is this a leper colony?"

"You guessed it—but you'll have to get used to it. The alternative is an *encomienda* if you're lucky. If not, you could end up a slave for one of the conquistadors at the front with the hostile Guaraní tribes."

"Tell me, Padre, how does a man avoid leprosy? What can I do to protect myself?"

They trudged down the trail toward the hacienda, which was within sight at the southern tip of the lake. Padre O'Carolan explained as they walked.

"I've served these souls for years, and this is what I've observed and learned. It primarily spreads within families, particularly when the members don't live in a clean environment and wash regularly. That is one reason we built our colony on the lake. I believe the disease is transmitted by touch, especially if the leper has clear secretions on his hand. When leprosy goes to the face, there is always sniffling and coughing, which sometimes leads to difficulty breathing and a killing fever. I've seen it transferred between husband and wife, which is unfortunate. But many people, myself included, appear to carry a shield against leprosy. People have touched me with leprous hands and coughed on me hundreds of times, but I have no signs of the disease."

"You're telling me, Padre, that you don't protect yourself against these people?"

"I do not. I regard it a privilege to serve, and I believe I am protected. But make no mistake—it is a disease, not a magical or moral curse. There are a few things you can do to escape it."

"What are those things?"

"First, take advantage of the lake. Bathe several times a day, but especially before retiring. Wash yourself with lye soap, of which I have a good supply. Second, because you will touch and assist our guests frequently, I suggest you ask one of our women to make you several pairs of cotton gloves you can wash daily. Beyond this, if you're with a member of the leper community who coughs, have a cotton or linen kerchief ready. Tie it to cover your nose and mouth. Wash your gloves and kerchiefs whenever you bathe yourself. Are you worried?"

"I'm not worried, Padre, but will I not offend the lepers by protecting myself from their touch and breath?"

"You won't, *mi hijo.*. The natives may speak only Guaraní, but they're not stupid. These people know their condition; they will not judge you by the protective measures you take. They will judge you by your heart—so take heed of that. And don't call them lepers, either in conversation with me or anyone else at this mission. Call them guests, patients, souls, or whatever, but not lepers. Understand?"

"I understand, Padre. What will my duties be?"

"Wherever you fit in, you'll be at my right hand. You'll accompany me on my daily rounds, ensuring our friends lack no food, firewood, or water. You'll carry my medical supplies and perhaps a shovel for the occasional grave."

Continuing the conversation as they entered the hacienda grounds, the padre pointed to a garden beside the chapel, "You will tend the community garden and the pigs and guinea hens. I've heard you play the guitar, so I know you're good with your hands."

"Yes, sir, and I have some carpentry skills."

"Grand. We've got some tools and inherited the wagon in the yard behind the chapel. Perhaps you can replace the broken spokes and rotted floorboards and make it serviceable enough to transport our lace goods to the city."

"Lace goods?"

"Our secret industry. The women call it *ñandutí*—it means spider webbing. Nani oversees that. You haven't met her yet. She'll explain it, as you will be her assistant, too."

Padre O'Carolan shouted out for Nani. A skinny girl came out of a nearby cottage carrying a lantern. She ran to greet and embrace the old man, who turned and presented her with the newcomer.

"Nani, this man is Juancinto Taranto. He has come to help us around the hacienda. He is handy with a lot of experience. You see," he said, nodding toward the leather case on Juancinto's back, "he has brought a guitar."

Juancinto greeted Nani formally. He'd expected a mature woman, not a spindly sprite of a girl. She wasn't beautiful, nor would she ever be, but her expressive eyes were sharp with intelligence..

The padre took the lantern from Nani. "You two get acquainted while I get the tools to uncrate this," he said as he disappeared behind the chapel. In the gathering darkness, Nani asked, "You can play this guitar?"

"Yes. I am from Sevilla. And I play *palos gitanos* style."

"I don't know what that style is. You are a Gypsy?"

"Yes. I am"

"What brings you here?"

"I killed a man to defend my wife, a dancer. For punishment, they sent me to the New World."

"Oh," she said, contemplating the ramifications of his answer to her question.

Sensing her hesitancy, Juancinto took the initiative, "Do you live here with your family?"

Without emotion, she replied, "My family is dead. Padre Cairbre adopted me two years ago. I help him here at the colony."

Juancinto stopped to digest her response, thinking further exploration would be foolishly immature. He found it fascinating that the girl treated him as an equal.

The padre returned with the lantern and handed Juancinto a hammer, pliers, and an iron wedge. "Go ahead—open the box."

Within a few moments, the box opened, and its contents were revealed.

"What is it, Papa? It's so big! So much bigger than your lyre."

"We call it a *cláirseach*, my dear—a harp—and more specifically, an *Irish* harp. Bishop Toro told me it was for sale from the estate of Domingo Irala. I contacted one of his widows, and she sold it to me. Now it's yours."

Nani gasped. "Look, Padre! The strings are not catgut. They look like they're made of gold."

"They're not, my dear. The strings are brass and steel. They're loose now, but we have a tuning fork. Try not to break them. Otherwise, we'll have to substitute them with catgut."

With the harp still in the crate, they carried it into the chapel and placed it across the first two rows of benches. Juancinto lifted the harp out of the box, and the padre retrieved a chair from the chapel's portico. Nani ran to her cottage and returned with a tuning fork. How is it tuned, Papa? Show me the Do string.

"Look here, Nani," the padre indicated, "there are two rows of pins. That row is the diatonic scale; the other is the chromatic scale with the sharps and flats." The priest pointed to what he thought was the high Do string. Nani moved twelve strings down to what she determined was middle Do and tuned that string with the help of the fork.

"Papa, I will tune the harp in the Ionian Mode, like your lyre. Do you think that's right?"

"Go ahead, my dear. It won't hurt the harp."

Nani tuned the other notes in the scale with her voice, confirming high Do with the tuning fork. She adjusted thirty notes in this fashion.

The girl had perfect pitch, and Juancinto marveled at her concentration. She sat back in her chair with the soundbox resting on her shoulder. Her slender fingers barely reached the harp's bass strings. She plucked an unfamiliar melody that vibrated and engaged Juancinto's heart as he stood, barely noticed, in the lantern shadow of the petite girl with the enormous harp. Nani would have been content to play all night, but Padre Cairbre stood and laid his hand across the strings to silence them, suggesting they'd had a long day.

The next morning, Padre Cairbre awakened Juancinto at dawn with a cup of hot *yerba maté* and a plate of fried eggs prepared by Doña Yatytay, Nani's aunt, who lived with her niece in the cottage beside the chapel. Doña Yatytay, in effect, took care of the padre and Nani, preparing their meals and keeping their cabin, the chapel, and the Padre's quarters attached to the chapel, and now, the spare room at the chapel with one more mouth to feed. Doña Yatytay was a pleasant, accommodating woman about the same age as the priest. She spoke no Spanish.

The padre, Nani, and Juancinto began the daily rounds of the community of eighteen dwellings, some with bamboo and wattle walls, dirt floors, and thatched roofs, others with plastered adobe, brick floors, and tile roofs. Padre Cairbre carried his medical supplies, while Nani carried a leather satchel with several notebooks, an assortment of *ñandutí* designs with pens and inks. Juancinto had two goatskin pouches for water and alcohol, a sack for fresh, clean cotton clothes, and an empty bag for collecting dirty clothes from those who could not wash them.

For the first time in his life, Juancinto witnessed the disease he had been taught was a curse. It progressed and assumed diverse forms in different people. Some had feet like clubs; others had hands with stubs instead of fingers. Some limbs were twisted; some faces looked like box turtle shells. Some were prone with no muscles to help them rise. Some had families to help them; others were alone. Pain tormented some; others were numb. Some were pitifully despondent, others joyful, no matter the dreaded circumstances.

Padre O'Carolan treated them all with the impartiality of a physician. In contrast, Nani treated each one as if she were personally related.

The Padre used soap, water, alcohol, aloe, and other plants to treat open lesions.

Nani collected the *ñandutí* web lace from the women and men who had sown it. She distributed colored thread and the web patterns the women of Itauguá had drawn on paper. She also recorded all the transactions between the designing women of Itauguá and the embroiderers on the lake. Before leaving a guest's home, someone would often pull Nani aside for a special request. Although the language was Guaraní, Juancinto, listening closely, often heard the Castellano word *música*. Later, when Juancinto asked her, she told him the patients asked her to return later in the evening with her lyre to soothe their pain with music and help them sleep. Juancinto was curious—he wanted to know more. Nani told him they would talk after finishing their chores and invited him to come with her on her musical visits.

Doña Yatytay had prepared fresh-caught fish and mandioca for lunch and laid a large table in the rear courtyard of the chapel annex. Padre Cairbre would not permit anyone to sit without washing first. But

Juancinto thought the padre meant washing his hands. He started to the washbasin by the well, but the priest wagged his finger, saying, "I mean *bathe*." He pointed toward the lake.

All three wore white cotton shirts and trousers. The padre handed Juancinto and Nani each a bar of lye soap. They all removed their sandals, waded into the lake chest-high, then returned to the shallow water to soap themselves and their clothes. Returning to the deeper water, the padre suggested swimming to rinse the soap off their clothes.

Juancinto had not gone swimming in twenty years, not while crossing the Atlantic, nor even in the sacred lake called Iguaque. Not since swimming on hot summer days in the Guadalquivir River. He looked over at skinny Nani emerging from the water and saw Solea with her wet Gypsy blouse clinging to her fifteen-year-old breasts. He thought Solea was the most beautiful girl he'd ever seen. He still loved her and wondered if she still thought of him.

On the beach, Juancinto took off his wet shirt to feel the hot sun on his back. Nani gasped. "Juancinto!" she cried, "What happened to you? Who beat you like that? Those scars are hardly healed."

"I'll tell you another time, Nani. Let's dress in dry clothes and eat that fish your aunt fried before the flies do."

After lunch, Juancinto anticipated that Nani would ask again about his scars. He would have to tell her about Bogotá, Atora, and the sacred lake. Or lie to her. He was looking forward to a long siesta instead. But Nani turned to Juancinto and declared, "Time to get to work again."

"Work? What work are we doing now?"

"Not *we*. *I* will work on my dyes and tablecloths, and *you*—I thought the padre told you to fix the old wagon in the back."

Juancinto sighed. "He *did* mention it, and he told me where the tools are."

"Get to it. We have no time to waste. I need that wagon, Juancinto. I sold *ñandutí* tablecloths to Asunción; now, I must deliver them and pick up more supplies. It's too much for the old mule to carry, and our ladies in Itauguá need their money."

Juancinto spent the balance of the afternoon in the work shed evaluating what he needed to do to make the wagon roadworthy.

Nani worked behind her aunt's cottage with her cloth, now cut to tablecloth size and soaking in half-barrel tubs of water and primary-color dyes. Doña Yatytay helped her remove the fabric from the vats and hang the sheets on lines strung between trees. As the sheets dried, Doña Yatytay spread them over a large table. She filled an iron with kitchen embers and smoothed the colorful sheets while Nani sat beneath a mango tree, working on her accounts and designs.

Later that afternoon, Nani appeared at the work shed with a gourd filled with a deep layer of *yerba maté* and a pitcher of cool well water. She handed Juancinto the gourd and a silver *bombilla* and said, "Time for a *tereré* break, Master Carpenter."

After draining the gourd, Juancinto's head was again buzzing with energy.

"How do you feel, Juancinto?"

"I feel all right."

"Ready for more work?"

"More work? What do you mean, *chica?* It's almost dark. Let's save some work for tomorrow."

"I mean *God's* work, Juancinto. You can come along if you like. I have to get my lyre. Meet me in front of the chapel if you're coming."

Nani and Juancinto walked the shore of the lake. Juancinto carried her leather satchel with the lyre. They stopped at a dwelling they'd visited that morning. Nani clapped her hands to notify those within that she had arrived. A mother and daughter came out and lovingly embraced her. Nani asked Juancinto to enter the house and help Don Gregorio outside to rest in the moonlight in his hammock. When they emerged, Juancinto helped the man into a hammock strung between two palms. Nani sat in a chair beside him and rummaged through her satchel, looking for the pages of a musical score. To Juancinto's eyes, the pages might as well have been written in Chinese, as he had never seen music written on a piece of paper. Nani asked Juancinto to hold the first page in front of her in the lantern light so she could read it while she played. He asked her, "What is it?"

"It is a sacred hymn written long ago by a saintly woman in a convent. She was a German named Saint Hildegard, who lived five hundred years ago. The hymns were originally chants, but the padre transcribed them for stringed instruments. The hymn I will play is dedicated to Saint Gregory, the patron saint of the man in the hammock. He has requested it for his birthday."

Although Nani spoke of things beyond Juancinto's comprehension, he grunted to acknowledge receipt of the information ."

She began plucking a haunting melody. To Juancinto, it felt like heavenly music. After a moment, Nani whispered to him, "Next page."

Juancinto could see Don Gregorio was perfectly at peace, swinging softly in the hammock with a smile on his lips. Nani proceeded through four pages of written music, but she didn't stop. Instead, she seemed to repeat the hymn from memory, but with flourishes. Instead of choir music in the Cathedral of Sevilla, Juancinto heard birds flying into the sunset, monkeys swinging from the lapacho trees in the truest sunrise, lovers laughing and bathing at the base of a waterfall, warriors returning from a victory elated.

Juancinto detected a glow surrounding Don Gregorio in his hammock and in Nani beside him. A pattern of cool radiance enveloped both. Both of their fields interchanged in a tapestry of color. Don Gregorio had fallen into a deep sleep, but Nani's eyes were wide open and aware as she watched his sleeping body. The music stopped. Nani glanced at Juancinto and asked, "What did you see?"

"I saw a glow of color around you, and I saw a different glow around Don Gregorio. There were currents of energy moving between you like a figure eight." Nani nodded her understanding.

"What do you see?" Juancinto asked.

"Angels," she replied.

"Really? What do they look like?" Juancinto inquired.

"Whatever they want. But they mostly clothe themselves like humans—like you and me—but I think that's only when they're in the presence of people who see."

"Are they still here?" Juancinto asked.

"Yes. Don Gregorio's guardian is sitting on a branch in that mango tree. Saint Gregory is beside the hammock comforting his namesake, and another angel, a woman, massages his body. That is why he feels good, and he has gone to sleep. They are still with him. I believe they are watching his dream. The music seems to attract the angels. I rarely see them without music."

"Would you teach *me* to see angels, Nani?"

"If I could, but I don't know how. Play your guitar. Perhaps you can learn to attract angels with your music."

"By playing hymns the old nun wrote?"

"It would be a start, Juancinto."

"What you played was strange and slow, not like anything I play. To learn your hymns, I would have to hear them many times with my guitar in hand to pick them out and memorize them."

"Oh, Juancinto, there are far too many. There is a hymn for every saint and every day and every condition. You could not possibly remember them all. Are you saying you can't read music?"

"Yes. I can't read music, but music all comes naturally, so I never needed to read it.."

"Not all comes naturally in music. There are secrets to be known about music that do not come naturally. You must be able to read music and understand the laws of harmony to know these secrets."

Juancinto chuffed. "I can't even read Castellano, much less music. I am thirty-seven years old. It's too late for me."

"*I'll* judge that! We're finished here. Let's go to the chapel. Get out your guitar, and let me hear you play."

In the darkened place of worship, sitting on the chapel's wood plank pews, Juancinto played his guitar for Nani. He first played a light *Sevillana* to warm up his fingers, then a *Malagueña* to demonstrate his dexterity. Finally, he sang a *cante* [24] for Solea that he created aboard the ship shortly after leaving Buenaventura. The *cante* moistened Nani's eyes, but Juancinto could not see them in the darkness.

"Juancinto, your music is so different from mine. It is full of life, love— even violence and death—but not much peace. I would say you know more about the music of life than *I* do, and you play with much soul."

"If I play with *alma*, Nani, I take that as a compliment. But there is more to it than *alma*. You and I both know this. When musicians come together and practice their art for the sake of their craft, they can create an atmosphere that the masters in Sevilla call *juerga*." [25]

Juancinto continued, "When we reach the *juerga*, it opens the door for the *duende*. When the *duende* comes, we are no longer playing; instead, we observe this *duende*—this ghost, this angel, or Holy Spirit— as it plays through us. Maybe the Holy Spirit is just having fun with us, a diversion from hard work. But whatever the case, this is what the great ones aspire to, and that is what I saw you do earlier this evening, perhaps without even knowing it."

Nani was transfixed as Juancinto went on. "You call the *duende* so easily and use it to heal people or heal their souls and give them peace. I have never seen anything like it. I want you to show me how to summon the angels. Your music is about peace and harmony. My music is also about love and death, but it swings from ecstasy to agony without finding a middle ground. Occasionally, I feel the *duende*, but if the angels ever come, I can't see them, and my music does not seem to heal anything but my own broken heart."

"What broke your heart, Juancinto?"

"Another time, Nani. Let's get some sleep. Perhaps tomorrow we will have time to play music together."

The next day brought pelting rains. After making the rounds with Padre O'Carolan, bathing, and taking lunch, Nani and Juancinto went into the chapel to make music. Juancinto tuned his guitar to her lyre.

"Juancinto—tell me how you got those scars and your broken heart," she blurted.

"You want to hear about the scars or the heart? They're two different stories. Which do you want to hear? I don't have the stamina to tell both."

"The scars."

"Very well. Since we are together with our music, I will sing my story in *palos gitanos* style.

> I, Juancinto Taranto, Gypsy of Triana,
> Will sing you the *cante*
> Of how my greed and stupidity
> Brought death and destruction
> To the one I love by the name of Atora,
> A heavenly dancer and last trace
> Of the Spirit of her people.

Each phrase bore its own signature, melody, and strum. Nani could see and hear that each note and chord was improvised, but still, each had a reason and was like teardrops squeezed from a broken heart.

> I was a prisoner in a strange land.
> My only friend was my guitar.
> Atora heard my sound

And danced to it.
Her music was not *palos gitanos*
But a soothing sound, flowing and pronounced
Upon the high plateau of *juerga.*

Here Nani could imagine Atora dancing, and her movements were graceful without the drama of *palos gitanos.* In her mind, Atora was dancing to sounds familiar to Nani, and she could replicate them on her lyre. She thought about accompanying Juancinto but limited herself to listening.

She was a beautiful princess
Of the high temple of the silver moon.
She told me of the golden lake
And I made her take me there.
I would have drowned
In the muddy, infested water
Had she not rescued me.

He punished his guitar with such ferocity Nani thought he would break the strings, but he gradually transitioned into sweet musical phrases which told Nani he saw Atora in his imagination.

She asked nothing of reward
But had pity on my shameful soul,
For she gave me a golden charm
To placate my rapacious master.
But the charm only incited Don Antonio
To torture me for the true source of the bangle:
Not the lake, but the Moon Temple
On the hill above Chía.

As Juancinto's fingers slapped his guitar strings, Nani could see Don Antonio's whip drawing blood from Juancinto's back, but for Nani, it seemed more like what her father once told her about Christian monks whipping themselves for their sins.

Don Antonio had me sent to this Guaraní land
While destroying the Temple of the Moon
And Atora, my beloved dancer,
As he rummaged in the ruins for gold bangles.
So, the scars you saw, my dear Nani,
Are tattoos of my greed and stupidity.
I, Juancinto Taranto, Gypsy of Triana,
Am cursed by a God who plays games with me.
He shows me love and takes it away,
As if I am not worthy.
Be just, Oh God, be just.
If I am unworthy, kill only me!
Don't make the ones who love me
die with my touch.

Here Juancinto cried out with his whole being as he hammered his instrument until many of the catgut strings broke. His chest heaved, and he sobbed while wiping his wet face with a handkerchief. Nani was also overcome. She cried. Juancinto blotted her eyes with a dry corner of her scarf. Then he smiled at her. "It's your turn. Time for your story."

She played tenderly as raindrops fell gently on the chapel's roof, developing a rhythm with some heavenly flourishes. She spoke softly:

I, Nani, am the only child
Of the warrior knight, Tibalt Itutburua,
From the country called Basque,
And my mother, Takuapu,
Daughter of Cacique Chavuku,
Of the Jaguar clan of the Paraguarí.

Now Nani played in a proud, regal manor.

This is my story:
My father followed Conquistador Irala
To this land they call Nueva Andalucía
Irala told his soldiers to marry Guaraní women
To populate this land with Iberic seed.

Tibalt, the knight, was alone with no wife.
He was lost on a hunting trip
And entered our sacred valley
With a mound in the center called Cerro Acahay.
My father saw my mother, and they fell in love.
After favors performed by the knight,
My grandfather granted
Tibalt permission to marry Takuapu.
And I was soon born into the paradise
Of Cerro Acahay.
My father taught me the language of Asunción.
Governor Irala, before he died,
Gave in to pressure from the king of Castile
And made *encomiendas* of all Guaraní land.
My father was given Cerro Acahay,
As an *encomienda*.
And so we rejoiced and thrived
Until Irala died.
The new governor made war on all the Guaraní
Still in the jungle.
Vergara ordered Sir Tibalt to fight
The rebellious Guaraní amassing in the jumgle.
My father took me to Asunción,
To Padre Cairbre for safety and education.
My father was killed in battle,
In the fields of Achaia.
Cerro Acahay was given as an *encomienda*
To a noble family who coveted our paradise.

Juancinto could not resist. He conveyed his outrage at the injustice on his guitar.

Padre Cairbre took me to Cerro Acahay
To find my mother,
And to tell the bad news to our people.
But they had already heard.
When we arrived at Cerro Acahay,
There was no one there.

Juancinto did not know how to express his feeling of quiet desolation, but with Nani's lyre, she was able to create the sentiment.

> Within the circle of hills around Cerro Acahay
> There were no humans or animals.
> They had all gone up the Río Paraná
> To the land of falling waters.
> Above the Cerro no eagles flew,
> And beside the flowing streams,
> No birds chirped.
> Angels and good Spirits
> Had deserted this paradise.
> I, Nani, wanted to go up the Paraná
> To find my mother,
> Above the falling waters of Iguaçu,
> But my guardian, the Padre
> Took me to this place,
> To the shore of the beautiful Lake Ypacaraí
> To tend to those with leprosy,
> And console their souls with music,
> Amid scores of Angels and good Spirits.

Juancinto reacted to Nani's lament with amazement. He felt a degree of frustration because he could not capture the delicacy of Nani's *cante* with bold statements from his Spanish guitar. It was the difference between the red cape and sword of the bullfight and the delicate spiderweb lace of *ñandutí*, but, with all the difference, he felt her *duende* present. He wanted to learn to play her heavenly harp music on his guitar and invoke this delicate *duende*.

Nani felt the inevitable release by relating her story in the words of her heart—a heart borne on the wings of her music. Juancinto had shown her how to argue her case before the court of the spirit. And now, even *she* expected a response.

They began meeting at the chapel in the afternoons while the rest of the colony enjoyed their siesta. Juancinto wanted to learn how, with his music, to invoke angels and invite them to bring peace and healing to those who suffered. Nani said she could only impart what knowledge she had if he would first learn to read music written on paper. When he could read music, he could play the hymns of the nun, Saint Hildegard, which the priest had transcribed. Juancinto agreed to learn and, at the same time, to teach Nani to play in the style and compass of *palos gitanos.*

At night, Padre O'Carolan taught Juancinto to read and write in Castellano. Juancinto discovered a whole new world of symbols—symbols for words, notes, chords, and keys—all of which he naturally understood but could now put on paper and discover the laws for their proper use. For the first time in his thirty-nine years, Juancinto felt the possibility of being educated. Education empowered him, and he knew the key to power was the ability to read.

The padre, Nani, and Juancinto made rounds in the colony every morning. In the late afternoon, Nani and Juancinto would visit those guests with a birthday or those who requested what they called a "serenade of the spirits." They played the hymns of Hildegard as well as improvised their own compositions. On occasions, guests requested both Juancinto and Nani to sing their *cantes.* They even encouraged certain colonists to develop *cantes* based on their own stories, accompanied by the Gypsy and the harpist.

The *cantes* from the colonists were all in Guaraní, a language that was becoming increasingly familiar to Juancinto. These events drew the colony closer together. No one left the community entirely cured by the music. Still, it strengthened their spirits and encouraged them to travel to worlds beyond the settlement.

Nani saw angels, and Juancinto saw pulsing auras of energy. With the passing of a few years, Juancinto had made tremendous strides in his education.

Late one afternoon, before washing and bathing in the lake, Nani suggested they take the rowboat to the middle of the lake and make music with the harp and guitar. Juancinto rowed to a point where they could no longer hear the village's clamor.

In pure silence, they began to play, not a hymn or canticle, but melodies called from the heart and a response. It was as if Juancinto strove to make his guitar sing like a melodious lyre while Nani embellished her strings with a flavor of *palos gitanos.*

Juancinto's fingers played with a life of their own. As he watched

Nani, he could not deny that Nani was becoming a woman. If the truth were to be told, she was not "beautiful" in the ordinary sense of the word. Her features, however, while smallish and delicate, were sharp, strong, and formidable, exuding a high quality of spirit. Juancinto was attracted to her soul. He told himself they were spiritually attracted and compatible. That's all it is, he thought.

As they played together on the lake, Juancinto's epiphany of purely spiritual attraction began losing its profundity as he felt uncontrolled energy arise in his groin. He could not deny he was attracted to Nani's innocent, ripening body. He began to stumble with his music. To combat his inappropriate arousal, he recalled the memory-frayed image of Solea waiting on the banks of the Guadalquivir. Then he turned to a fresher image—Atora dancing toward him on the calm surface of Ypacaraí. But Atora sank below the surface. She is dead, thought Juancinto, due to my stupidity and lack of control. A voice told him: your old body is fighting your new spirit. Be careful—you lost the last battle.

Juancinto stopped playing. He prayed for some form of strength and discipline while Nani gracefully finished the duet. A strange thought came to his mind—more like a question—which had barely occurred to him before. But now, it seemed curiously appropriate and would, at least, break his own spell of sexuality.

Juancinto explored the new thought. "Nani, I know you can see angels because I can almost see them myself when I play for the patients. But these angels who flock around you when you play the hymns of Hildegard—they all have familiar names like Michael, Gabriel, Ana, and Isabel. These are all Catholic angels. Are all angels Catholic? I can't believe it. Even we Gypsies have Saint Sarah, and who knows what angels came from India and Egypt. When some of our guests sing their own *cantes* in Guaraní, I know they sing about Guaraní angels and spirits. But you— you are the granddaughter of a Cacique from that place you call Cerro Acahay. Surely your mother, grandmother, or grandfather told you about Guaraní legends, spirits, and angels."

"Yes. I was told stories by my elders and the *curandero*, but these stories are, for the most part, horrible, and I am afraid of those spirits."

"Can you give me an example?" asked Juancinto.

"I can tell you about Porâsý because I have dreamt of her recently. She is a solace to me, but I do not know why she keeps appearing in my sleep."

"Tell me about her."

"First, I must explain some things. In the beginning, there was Tupá, which is our name for God. He is the creator. He is the Sun, and his wife Arasy is the Moon. Together they created the first human beings, giving them both a good and an evil spirit."

"*Two* spirits?" Juancinto mused. "How do you deal with that? They're certainly not equal. Which spirit wins?"

"My grandfather told me the answer to that question depends on which spirit you feed."

Juancinto silent thought about what Nani said.

She continued. "So Tupá created good, and he also created evil. And this evil he called Tau, which, I guess, would be the same being the Catholics call Satan."

Juancinto gestured that he understood.

"As told to me many times, the story goes like this: the first man and woman of the Guaraní tribe had a daughter. Her name was Kerana. When Kerana grew up, the evil god Tau wanted her. He hunted and chased her, and when he caught her, he took her to his hiding place. Arasy, her mother, was so angry that she put a curse on Tau that all his children would be born monsters. And indeed, they were.

"The firstborn was a giant lizard with the head of two dogs. He was slow, earth-bound, and not much danger to anyone.

"The second son was like a snake with a bird's head. He lives in the waters and swamps. I don't want to talk about him now, for I fear he is close.

"The third child was Moñái. He was also like a snake, but his head held two horns like the Catholic Devil.

"The fourth child had the appearance of a human. He had silver hair and blue eyes, ruled over the siesta, and took a particular interest in *yerba maté*. They say he steals children who do not take their siesta.

"The fifth son was the god of virility, and I am embarrassed to talk about him."

"Why, Nani?" Juancinto said. "Don't be embarrassed. What was his problem?"

"His problem was that he had a male organ that was so long he had to wrap it around his waist. And with it, he could impregnate maidens at a distance.

"The sixth son looked like a giant sheep, but he had sharp teeth, and he survived by hunting and eating humans.

"The seventh son was Luisón. He was a hideous cross between a human and a dog. He had a terrible smell, and they say he rules over death.

"This unfortunate Kerana, who bore all these monsters with Tau, had a sister named was Porâsý. She is the one I see in my dreams. So, remember, Porâsý's father and mother were Tupã, the Sun, and Arasy, the Moon. Porâsý was purely good and very beautiful.

"All this was during the earliest times when the seven monsters decimated the Guaraní tribe. Tupã came up with a plan to eliminate the seven monsters and their kin. Tupã gave the plan to Pai Tomé, the *curandero* of the tribe, and he got together with Porâsý and worked out the details.

"Because Porâsy's beauty was irresistible, she would find Moñái, the particularly evil third son of Tau. She would flirt with Moñái until he fell in love with her and asked her to marry him.

"All this happened as planned, and Moñái and Porâsý announced that the celebration of their wedding would take place in the large chamber deep in the cavern that Moñái called home. Moñái invited all his brothers and their people.

"In the meantime, Porâsý arranged for warriors from the Guaraní tribe to build a huge fire at the mouth of the cave as soon as she escaped. This went as planned, but the clever Moñái spied Porâsý trying to escape from the wedding party. He caught her at the entrance to the cave and dragged her back into it. She screamed to the Guaraní to start the fire, which they did, as Moñái pulled her back into the dark recesses of the cave. The Guaraní kept feeding the fire with dry wood for seven days and nights until everything within the cavern was charcoal and ash. The fire had burned the evil out of the spirits of the seven monsters. Porâsý, the sacrificial maiden, transformed into the star that accompanies her father Tupã, the Sun, at the dawning of the day and leaves with him as he bids farewell at dusk."

Nani finished her story as the glorious sun was setting. She looked west and trembled as if seeing a premonition. Juancinto moved to sit beside her at the boat's stern. He put his arm around her to calm her shivers and whispered soothing words in her ear.

That evening they did not bathe in the waters of Ypacaraí but ate and went straight to their quarters.

In the days and months to follow, Nani and Juancinto often rowed the boat out onto the lake to play music together as Venus—which Juancinto now called Porâsý—followed the light into the horizon.

When Juancinto first came to the colony, Nani urged him to spend a few hours each morning in a class with six Guaraní children learning to speak Castellano from Padre Cairbre. Juancinto soon graduated to private lessons with the priest twice a week in the evenings, learning to read and write in his native language. Against the padre's better judgment, they studied the Bible's Old and New Testaments—O'Carolan had been taught it was not appropriate to share the Holy Books directly with lay persons.

Juancinto eventually grew disaffected by the archaic language. The Padre remedied the problem with a book of poems by Garcilaso de la Vega, a poet-soldier from Toledo. Juancinto studied Vega's love sonnets until he understood and could recite every word.

After exhausting Vega's book, Juancinto had the fortune to obtain an old copy of *La Celestina—a Tragicomedy of Calisto and Melibea* by Fernando de Rojas. He purchased a leather-bound copy in a general store in Asunción while delivering *ñandutí* tablecloths and picking up supplies for Nani. She had given him a small allowance from the proceeds of the *ñandutí*, which he used to purchase the book.

For some reason, which he never made clear, Juancinto kept secret his study of the book of poems about the adventures of Calisto. However, Nani observed a remarkable expansion of Juancinto's vocabulary and ability to express himself over three years. She finally confronted him with her observation. He confessed that if there were a secret to his transformation, it was probably his study of the Vega and Rojas books. Intrigued, Nani pressed him on the matter, and Juancinto agreed to share the books with her.

In hindsight, this was probably unwise, but how can one hold a middle-aged, previously illiterate Gypsy at fault for introducing the concept of courtly love and sexuality into Nani's eighteen-year-old sphere of virginal innocence? She devoured the poems of Garcilaso de la Vega— one in particular—which she embroidered with the sound of her harp.

Contigo mano a mano
Busquemos otros prados y otros ríos,
Otros valles floridas y sombrios,
Donde descanse, y siempre puedo verte
Antes los ojos mios,
Sin miedo y sobresalto de perderte.

With you, hand in hand
We discover other meadows and other rivers,
Other valleys full of flowers and shady places,
Where we rest, *and I can* always see you
Before my eyes,
Without fear and fright of losing yourself.

Nani was intrigued by the depth and mystery of the verse. Juancinto accompanied her musical rendition magnificently, but when she tried to engage him on the meaning of the words and more profound concepts of love, he remained strangely silent. She attributed his silence regarding love to his personal experience, his sad *cante,* and was hesitant to explore more.

Juancinto was more inclined to laugh at Calisto's bawdy, tragic, and comedic attempts to woo and win the heart of the beautiful maiden Melibea.

Eventually, Nani became convinced that the romantic love Garcilaso had introduced into her life was as natural as her friendship with Juancinto. At nineteen, she had met the love of her life, and he was, indeed, Juancinto.

Juancinto was aware of the change in Nani. As they played their spiritual serenades, Juancinto no longer saw her as an extraordinary adolescent wrapped in a saintly aura. Instead, he viewed her as a full-fledged woman, radiant and vital, who seemed to be in love with him. His idyllic days at Lake Ypacaraí were ending, and he would soon receive an order from Asunción—sending him back to Spain and his beloved Solea. His thoughts raced. Do I really have a choice in the matter? Even if I stayed in Paraguay, defying the court, they would likely label me an outlaw. Could we find refuge anywhere in Nueva Andalucía? Probably not, unless we both had leprosy. Where would we go? Nani's Cerro Acahay was too close, and now, someone else's *encomienda*. We would probably have to go live with the Guaraní beyond the great falling waters.

Could I do that? At my age? But Solea is waiting for me. And what about Quim? He would now be about eighteen, the same age as Nani. Perhaps Quim is now a father, making me a grandfather. Oh, the stories I will tell my granddaughter! I am twice Nani's age. The Guaraní in the jungle age fast. I would soon be a decrepit burden to Nani just as she reaches her prime. *No!* That's not me. I am *not* in love with her.

Nani herself felt an urgency to resolve the overwhelming feelings she was having. She let Juancinto know of her love for him at their next outing on the lake.

The following afternoon, upon reaching the middle of the lake, Juancinto put down the oars and grabbed his guitar. Nani, hoping to put him into a romantic frame of mind, began to play a rendition of Juancinto's own *cante* on her lyre. She stared at him lovingly from her seat at the boat's bow as she sang his verses.

In response, Juancinto played her *cante* in his own *palos gitanos* fashion, howling some verses and whispering others as if praying.

Nani began to improvise an intricate melody with a call and response character, expecting Juancinto to respond to her call. Juancinto, feeling uncomfortable about where he sensed the music was taking them, put down his guitar and grabbed the oars. While watching Nani intently, he began rowing the boat up the center of the lake.

Eventually, Nani drifted into the composition of the Garcilaso poem that so attracted her. Juancinto continued to row harder now as he felt the chords of his life merge with Nani's. She was singing about finding other valleys full of flowers and shade when she began to miss notes and pluck wrong strings. Juancinto had never seen her do this before. He stopped rowing, reached for his guitar, and began playing in the same key, urging her to continue. She picked up on the same verse, but her playing sounded as if she were playing with a mitten on her hand. She put down the lyre and burst into tears. Juancinto moved to the bow seat beside her. He put his arm around her and tried to comfort Nani with a calm, husky voice, but to no avail. She pleaded with him to row back to the shore.

After that incident, Nani became increasingly disturbed at the quality of her playing. She attributed her physical problem to her growing urge to express her love for Juancinto and the apprehension and fear of his adverse reaction. To her, it was evident that her anxiety was manifesting itself physically, making it impossible to express her true feelings. Not fair! But in all fairness, neither she nor Juancinto could grasp the truth of the situation.

With no way to stop the growing frustration, Nani requested a meeting with the priest. She sat with him for nearly two hours one afternoon. Juancinto was close enough to eavesdrop. He heard her playing her harp inside the padre's room with closed doors. Nani confessed that she was in love with Juancinto. Padre Cairbre informed her that Juancinto had completed his sentence for murder and would soon be called back to Spain. He cautioned her—the love between Juancinto and herself would lead nowhere but into the valley of pain.

The padre made a mental note to proceed at once to Asunción and ask the bishop to expedite the transport of Juancinto back to Spain on the next vessel downriver.

Nani emerged from the padre's room in tears. Juancinto followed her to her quarters and stepped inside the room before she could shut the door. "What is it?" he demanded. She collapsed on the bed and whispered, "Padre Cairbre says the numbness in my fingers is a sure sign of the first stages of leprosy." She buried her head in her pillow and sobbed uncontrollably. Juancinto sat on the bed and tried to console her by rubbing her back and saying soft words, but she would have none of what she perceived as his pity.

Juancinto stood and paced around the room, cursing himself, saying things like, "I told you so, didn't I? Just listen to my *cante*! I bring misfortune upon all the women that I love."

"Do you mean that you love me?"

"I do! You have been my life. You have raised me from the walking dead. You are the most wonderful, amazing person I have ever known. You make me a whole person and a better one than I could have imagined. And beyond that, I love to be with you. I love to touch you and be touched by you. Yes, I love you. But I don't want to harm you. I don't want to call down a curse upon you."

"Curse me? Leprosy is not your fault, Juancinto. You didn't give it to me. You are the best thing in my life. I became a woman in your presence, for you. I love you—everything about you. You make me feel alive. Fulfilled.

But I want to feel fulfilled in a physical sense. If my life on earth is now limited, I want to make the most of it in the time I have left. I want to experience everything—sexual love, childbirth, motherhood before I die."

These words were too much for Juancinto. He sat on the bed, took her in his arms, and smothered her with kisses. With her finger to her lips, she cautioned him to control himself. "Tonight, after midnight, when the moon comes to up, we'll row the boat to the middle of the lake and make love."

They kissed. Juancinto told her he would knock on her door in four hours. He went to his room in the chapel annex and fell on his knees by the bed. I want to stay with her, love her, please her, play with her, make eternal music with her, and heal her. But I have never seen anyone healed of this disease, and where would we live? Here in the colony? And when I am called for Spain and Solea—what then? Juancinto felt the need to pray for a solution, but he had never been given to prayer. Now, at a crossroads in his life, he needed help from beyond. But not from those angels that surrounded Nani. He asked himself where his angels were. Strangely, the image of Solea's mother, La Gitanilla, came to mind.

La Gitanilla was always praying, but to whom? It was Sara la Kali, the black saint. La Gitanilla said she was a Gypsy Princess who walked on water to save the three Marys when their boat foundered off the south coast of France. Juancinto tried to imagine Sara's dark face with a gold crown on her head. He felt her colorful robes swirling around him as if she or they were dancing. When the dancing stopped, the face of Sara la Kali had become the face of Solea. That was his answer.

Juancinto gathered his belongings into an old leather sack and his guitar in a new leather case he had recently sewn. He quietly left the chapel annex without disturbing the padre. He walked in the moonlight along the road he had traversed many times with wagon loads of *ñandutí* cloth. By evening the next day, he had entered Asunción and found his way to the cathedral. He requested an audience with Bishop Toro. A friar led him to the bishop's palace. The bishop saw him; Padre O'Carolan's regular reports had kept him abreast of Juancinto Taranto's status.

Juancinto confessed to the bishop he was running away from the colony to avoid trouble and hardship. He told the holy man he'd fallen in love with the nineteen-year-old helper and adopted daughter of Padre

O'Carolan. Juancinto feared if he stayed any longer, he'd lose control of himself and commit adultery. He was still married to his wife in Sevilla, and now that his sentence was almost complete, he would unite with her soon. The bishop said he understood but wished Juancinto had conferred with Padre O'Carolan before departure. Nevertheless, the bishop permitted Juancinto to sleep in the extra room in the servant's quarters. He agreed Juancinto would have passage on the next voyage for the now, reconstructed settlement at Buenos Aires. The boat would leave in about a week.

The next day, Padre Cairbre appeared at the bishop's palace. After briefly conferring with the bishop, the padre found Juancinto in his room and challenged him.

"What did you do to Nani? She disappeared yesterday and left only this sealed letter addressed to you. Had I not found you, I would have opened it myself."

"What do you mean she disappeared?" Juancinto snatched the letter from the padre's hand.

"Yesterday morning, when we discovered you gone, Nani said she felt sick. She went into the jungle to find a remedy. That was the last we saw of her. We found that letter on her pillow and discovered the open lockbox where she kept her *ñandutí* journal and proceeds. The money was gone, as well as her lyre and clothes. Also, a young man named Pietá, a colonist from the same area of Cerro Acahay, is gone. I presume he went with her."

Juancinto opened the letter and read.

My Dearest Juancinto,

I have gone to find my mother upon the Río Paraná, where the great waters fall. Pietá will help me, so don't worry. If my infirmity allows, I will try to give birth. I know the children of the colony do not inherit the disease. If my condition worsens to the point I can no longer make music, I will ride a canoe over the great falling waters of Iguaçu, there to discover other meadows and rivers. I will see you there. In the world of the undying spirit, you will always live and play in my heart. Please tell Padre Cairbre I am forever grateful to him.

Nani.

Juancinto dropped the letter and fell to his knees.

"May I?" Padre Cairbre motioned to Juancinto for permission to read the letter. When he finished, he sat on the bed and moaned, "I shouldn't have told her . . . it's not certain she has the disease; she's overreacted. May God help her."

Chapter 17

Homecoming

Atlantic Ocean
Sevilla, Cádiz, Spain
April–October 1565

Within days of Juancinto's encounter with the bishop of Asunción and Padre O'Carolan, he found himself on a riverboat bound for the resurrected town of Buenos Aires. He stayed for a few weeks before boarding the four-time-a -year galleon for the Caribbean and Spain.

Hugging the coast of South America before crossing the Atlantic, the trip again took over two months. Juancinto no longer engaged in his commercial enterprise—rat fighting. Juancinto now spent his free time setting the poems of Garcilaso de la Vega to music. He became a favorite of the captain and first mate, and for that matter, most of the crew. In his previous life, Juancinto had been a master of evoking feelings of passion and loss, anger and rage, sadness, injustice, and revenge with his guitar. With her different keys and chord progressions, tempos, and melodic runs, Nani had demonstrated how to convey love and joy, compassion and wholeness, and even healing. Juancinto now applied these lessons for the crew's benefit, particularly at sunrise and sunset. In the infirmary, the ship's doctor encouraged him to play the strange liturgical hymns of Saint Hildegard that he had arranged for the Spanish guitar.

After weighing anchor in San Juan, it took six weeks for the ship to sail into the familiar waters of the Canaries. From there, it was only one day before they sighted African shores. They hugged the Moorish coast until passing Casablanca, now occupied by the Portuguese. Here they left the coast, bearing due north toward Cádiz. Two days later, off the coast of Tangier, they crossed with another Spanish galleon. That night, sleep gave way to nervous anticipation. Juancinto positioned himself in the bowsprit. In the light of a crescent moon, he practiced his renditions of Garcilaso de la Vega's poems, reflecting on how he had changed in the past ten years. I have much to tell Solea, but will she even recognize me after all these years?'

"*¡Tierra a la vista! ¡Dos puntos a estribor!*" the watchman called out in the pre-dawn haze. Land ho! Two points at starboard! Juancinto could just make out the lighthouse of Cádiz ahead in the mist.

In Cádiz, Juancinto spent a day clearing himself at the Casa de Contratación and the houses of government, where he received certification for serving out his sentence. Next came a ride north in the cargo bed of a wagon full of hardwood. After a long day the wagoneeer reached the town of Dos Hermanos, where they stopped for the night. By mid-morning the next day they entered the outskirts of Seville and followed the Grand Canal, past the Alcázar and the Torre del Oro to the pontoon bridge over the canal leading into the Triana neighborhood.

Dismounting from the wagon, Juancinto started across the boat bridge into Triana. Halfway across, he recognized a friend from the neighborhood, the butcher, Don Alfredo, coming from Triana. As the gap between Juancinto and the butcher closed, Juancinto expected Don Alfredo to recognize and greet him. But Don Alfredo walked past, staring at the water below. Have I changed so much? Juancinto wondered. He called out to the butcher. Indeed, he recognized Juancinto Taranto and welcomed him back to the neighborhood, but without raising his eyes to meet Juancinto's.

Crossing the bridge, Juancinto took a shortcut to Calle Betis, expecting to find Solea at her mother's house. Juancinto saw Don Melchor, the tilemaker, two blocks from the Ballesteros house. But Melchor crossed the street, and their eyes did not meet. He came to house number 207, the door of La Gitanilla. He pounded on the door but received no response.

"Solea! Gitanilla!" he yelled.

No answer. The door was unlocked, so he entered and passed through the foyer into the courtyard. All was quiet. Juancinto sat on a bench and waited in perplexed silence until a noise drew his eyes to the second-floor balcony. A door slowly opened, and the hunched figure of La Gitanilla appeared. She was dressed all in black. Without expression on her face, she descended the stairs and approached Juancinto.

He stood, and she grasped both of his arms, and, opening her eyes wide, she asked, "Are you a ghost or are you real? Either way, it doesn't make much difference," she muttered.

"I am as real as you are, Gitanilla. Where is Solea? Where is Quim?"

La Gitanilla whispered, "At the Casa de Contratación. They told us you were lost in a shipwreck off the coast of Brazil. No survivors."

Juancinto let out a small laugh. "Now I understand the unusual welcome. They were wrong, thank God. I'm here in the flesh. Feel me! Tell me where are my wife and son. It's been ten long years."

"Oh, Juancinto," she cried, collapsing to her knees and forcing him to sit on the bench.

"Quim was killed in a knife fight a year ago. He was defending his mother as she danced, just as you did. They waited for you all this time, dancing and singing and playing just as before. We never heard any news about you, but we knew you would return. When Quim died, it almost killed Solea. She was in mourning for the better part of a year, and she was coming out of it when we heard the news from the Casa that you were dead. She went to the boat bridge two nights later and jumped into the canal. They pulled her body out by the ship works, where the canal meets the river. Earlier that day, she found a scribe to write a letter and addressed it to me. She left it on her pillow. It says she saw you in a dream, and you called to her. She said she was going down the river to the ocean sea to be with you again."

Hearing the story, Juancinto's breath left his lungs. He rolled over on the bench and curled up, grasping his knees. He let out a howl heard all over Triana. Everyone in that neighborhood understood the sound without asking.

Gitanilla consoled him to no avail. She said the letter was still on Solea's pillow but added, "I know you can't read it."

Juancinto staggered up the stairs to Solea's room. He opened the letter and read the words, and it was just as Gitanilla had told him. He crumpled the letter in his fist and buried his face in Solea's pillow, smothering himself in her scent. Memories of his beloved flowed over and through him. He was drowning in unfilled aspirations, with nothing left to aspire to. Nothing in this world made sense anymore.

Juancinto remained in Solea's room for nearly six hours. It was almost midnight when he quietly shuffled out of the Ballesteros house and walked along the edge of the Grand Canal to the boat bridge, carrying Solea's pillow. He stopped in the middle of the bridge. Vessels lined each side of the wide canal, and from each side was heard a medley of raucous laughter and quarreling lovers and thieves. Lanterns and candles twinkled in the dark. Strains of *palos gitanos* rose from the right bank as the bells of Sevilla's cathedral, tolling midnight, rang from the left. He had seen enough. Juancinto would not see another day. He climbed over the railing and stood on the edge of the plank deck, gazing down at the reflection of the crescent moon in the dark water between the pontoons. He gazed south, following the current to a few faint lights from the neighborhood of Los Remedios, where they found Solea's body. He held her pillow to his face and filled his lungs with her memory.

"*Tu estas mi remedio, mi amor; a ti me voy.*" You are my remedy, my love. I am coming to you.

He leaned forward on the balls of his feet, releasing the pillow into the water, then following its course with his sad eyes. He slowly let go of his life.

But to his surprise, Juancinto did not plunge into the murky world below, something was suspending him above it. La Gitanilla had grabbed him from behind by the belt. "Don't do it, Juancinto! Wait! Hear me!" She pulled him back into an upright position, and he turned to her as if entranced.

"Solea's spirit visited me tonight and told me to lay out the cards. I laid them out in the long way and studied them until I had visions. I saw you as an older man with a wife you loved and two small girls. Your clothing was different, and I believe you were a soldier. Your children were singing in a strange language. Then I saw your funeral, where you had many friends. They were sad and could not see you as you rose from the dead and started playing your guitar. Then Solea came. She and another woman danced around you. And there was another girl who played the harp as you play the guitar. Can you imagine? You danced with Solea and the other woman. The mourners disappeared, but you continued dancing and making music into the night. What do you think of that?"

Juancinto was dumbfounded. He looked at the black-robed figure of La Gitanilla as if she were a phantom. She helped him over the railing with surprising strength and led him to her house. She sat him in her kitchen, bade him drink a stiff concoction, and tucked him into a bed before his legs gave out. He slept for twelve hours before coming down the steps to the courtyard with his guitar case and leather pouch, ready to travel.

He confronted Gitanilla. "I believe you, *Abuelita*, and I am going back to Cádiz to seek my destiny."

"Good, Juancinto! Your future is glorious, and Solea wants you to find it. It was not to be here in the dark waters of the canal. Go forth! Go with my blessing, *mi hijo*. Go forth to a new land!"

Chapter 18

Lekh Lekha; Davide and Ruy

Southeastern Portugal
Atlantic waters off the coast of Andalucía, Spain
Sanlúcar de Barrameda, Spain
October-April 1566

Even the horses were spooked by Rabbi Elias's thunderous bellow, "*Lekh-lekha!*" and the heavy blow he landed on their rumps. They did not break gallop until they were out of the woods. It was too late for the boys to turn back. They rode in silence over the fields in a southerly direction until they came to the road to Tomar. They followed the road, camping under the stars for two nights before approaching the old Templar city. Following the narrow Nabão River as it wound through the town, they arrived at the town square. They could see the walled Templar castle perched on an imposing hill, defending the surrounding population..

Davide and Ruy had their first disagreement. Davide did not want to stop in Tomar. With plenty of daylight remaining, Davide wanted to make more progress toward their first critical destination, the Tejo River. Ruy wanted to stop and seek out their first contact, Friar Alvaro de Azevedo, custodian of the orchards and fields of the Order of Knights of Christ, headquartered at Tomar.

"Why should we bother him, Ruy? We're not in trouble—at least not yet. We have to get south as fast as we can!"

"You're right," replied Ruy," but he's my father's old friend, and, who knows—he may know something that bears on our circumstances. Don't rule him out because he's a Christian friar. We have only two hours of daylight left. Let's stop here, get a good night's sleep, stock up on provisions, and leave word for my father that we are all right."

264

"Fine, but how do you plan to locate the friar?"

"Don't you remember the notes we had to memorize?" The friar stays in a cottage attached to the outside wall of the castle. It should be easy enough to find."

"All right. Let's go," replied Davide.

In short order, they found the circuitous cobblestone road that led to the castle wall. They reached the friar's cottage halfway up the summit and found him in an adjacent apple orchard. Ruy introduced himself as the son of Dr. Lourenço Gonçalves. The friar nodded in recognition. Ruy told him they were riding south for reasons best left unsaid. He also said his father had hoped the good friar might resupply them with fresh fruit, *presunto* and wine, for which they would be willing to pay.

"Save your money, fellows, although your father had plenty if I remember correctly. I won't eat with the brotherhood tonight, so I invite you to dine in my cottage. We'll have privacy, and you can spend the night."

During a hearty meal at a heavy oak table in the friar's cottage, Davide remarked that Ruy had once made up a story about Pero da Covilhã meeting Manuel I in the castle of Tomar.

"Is that right, Ruy?" the friar asked.

"Yes, I had a dream in which Pero da Covilhã met Duke Manuel in the Magdalene Chapel. It was there that the duke gave Covilhã his last instructions before going to find Prester John."

"How interesting," the friar said. "You dream in detail about someone in your grandfather's generation."

"Well, I *am* from Covilhã," Ruy reminded the friar.

"Have you been to the castle?"

"No, sir, but my father has, and I only imagined it from his description.

"Is that so?" replied the friar. "You are a storyteller, then. You must have a vivid imagination! Would you like to see the Magdalene Chapel for yourself?"

"Is that possible?"

"Yes, it's possible," replied the friar," but we will have to wait until midnight when all the brothers are asleep."

"I'm too tired after a long day," replied Davide, "but you go, Ruy. You'll never get this experience again." With that, Davide spread his bedroll on one of the two straw mats the friar had placed on the stone floor.

In the candlelight, Ruy and the friar kept their voices down as Davide slept in the corner of the room.

After a pause in the conversation, Friar Alvaro made a thoughtful observation: "You know, Ruy, when I think of it, Dom Manuel I and Pero da Covilhã could have met in Tomar sixty years ago. Manuel I was the last of the Templars' great benefactors. And Pero da Covilhã certainly manifested the Templar spirit. If he had returned from Africa, he would have made a great Grand Master."

Claiming to himself the liberty to fib, Ruy remarked, "My father told me much about the Templars. He told me about the great Templar Vision and Portugal's role in carrying that vision to the world and reawakening the Holy Spirit, particularly in Africa and India."

The friar looked at Ruy grimly. "You're talking about serious spiritual matters—complicated matters for a man of your tender years to understand."

Disregarding the caution, Ruy pressed him. "But can you tell me what has happened to the Templar Vision?"

"It is *dead*, or it has succumbed to a deep sleep, brought on by its enemies."

"You mean the Holy Spirit is sleeping, Friar Alvaro?"

"More like in a coma. In Judaic parlance, one might say, the Shekinah has exiled herself from Portugal."

"How did that happen, Friar?"

"You're too wise for your age. I shouldn't have this discussion with you, but since you are your father's son, I will try to explain it.

"The great King Dom Manuel I had too much food on his plate. In his desire for the culinary experience of eating all of Spain himself, he lost his appetite for the modest meat, fish, and potatoes of the Holy Spirit. To marry the daughter of the Catholic Monarchs, Manuel had to capitulate to their demand to drive the Jews out of Portugal. He thought he could have it both ways—have his delicacies and his meat and potatoes too. But it did not work out as he had planned. He lost Spain; he lost his Jews too. The Shekinah left Portugal with the Jews and scattered everywhere. With the sad story of Manuel, after four centuries, the Templar Vision went to sleep." He nodded at Davide. "Just like your companion there, sleeping on the floor. And poor Pero da Covilhã was abandoned in Africa."

The conversation continued until midnight when Friar Alvaro indicated it was time to see the Charola.

In the light of an oil lantern, they made their way uphill to the wall of the great castle, then to a door in the wall near the countess's tower. The friar called the door the *porto do sangre*—the door of blood. They silently trudged in the moonlight across a courtyard to a building where the Brotherhood of the Knights of Christ resided. The friar unlocked a door and entered the castle's kitchens. Ruy followed the friar through the kitchens, the great dining room, and into corridors and stairways beyond. Oil sconces on the cream-colored limestone illuminated the shadowy slate floors. The arched and domed entrances, hallways, and ceilings convinced Ruy the Moors had built the structure, but it was not so. The friar explained that the first Templars, who founded Portugal after their victory in Jerusalem, built it.

The friar and Ruy eventually found their way into a large room with many pews. Ruy sensed he had been in the room before, then realized it was the room Endovélico described to him—where Dom Pero met with Duke Manuel and was afraid for his life. This prayer room adjoined the Charola.

The friar led the way into the Charola. Ruy had seen the cathedrals in Paris and Santiago de Compostela, but nothing ever gave him the sensation he felt entering the magnificent archway separating the prayer hall from the Charola. He experienced not the grandeur of a great cathedral but the intimacy of a personal channel to the higher realm.

The enclosure was round, sixty feet in diameter, with eight grand, arch-crowned pillars rising over a hundred feet into the darkness. Sculpted gold, silver, and Azeitão tile covered the chamber's interior with paintings depicting the history of Portugal and the Holy Spirit. The structure was organic without a single straight line.

Lifting his oil lamp, Ruy made his way to the center of the holy structure, directly under three enormous unlit golden candelabras whose chains reached into the darkness above. He breathed the night air of this sacred place deeply and felt he was standing at the very epicenter of Portugal itself, a race of people in space and time. Below him, he felt the currents of the earth carrying him; from above, he felt the heavens of destiny guiding him; all focused on him and the place where he stood.

Ruy felt compelled to say something, but the wonder left him speechless. It occurred to him to chant the Shema, so he did. He thought of Ana Sofia and how much he wanted to be there with her. He said a prayer for protection for his father and Rabbi Elias.

Sixty-five years in the past, Pero da Covilhã stood in this same spot and asked the Holy Spirit for protection and guidance before commencing his great adventure. Ruy asked for the spirit of his hometown hero to intercede on his behalf and guide him on his way to the New World. He then heard the loud voice of Rabbi Elias again shout, "*Lekh-lekha!*"

At dawn the following day, the two boys left the Tomar.. They followed the Nabão south to its confluence with the Zêzere, which, as the boys noted, had its headwaters hundreds of miles to the north near the Rock of Endovélico. Along the Zêzere, it was only two hours by horseback to the old Roman town of Constância on the Tejo. They ferried across the river and camped along the south bank, again under the stars. Two days of riding west along the Tejo put them at the town of Gavião. There, they left the Tejo and rode cross-country, southwest toward Portalegre. They had hoped to reach Portalegre in one day, but a late-afternoon thundershower changed their minds.

They were about a half-hour past the village of Aldeia da Mata when ominous clouds formed overhead. The first rumbles of thunder warned them to seek refuge. The terrain was flat, with several rock outcroppings breaking the plane of the cattle pasture. The boys hunted for a structure in which to abide the coming storm. In the distance, they saw what appeared to be a small house, but on the approach, they could see it was not a house at all, but a significant *anta* or dolmen from the Neolithic age. The boys had seen many dolmens, but this one was massive.

The structure's walls were comprised of seven large pillars or upright slabs of granite, each about sixteen feet in height, leaning toward each other in the form of a circle. A colossal slab of granite almost two feet thick topped the room the pillars formed. The shelter would suitably protect them from the rain, but they would have to tie the horses outside because of the small entrance. Anticipating spending the night, the young men had time to gather firewood before the rains came. They built a fire inside the dolmen, warmed some food, and made themselves at home.

"I've always been mystified about places like this," Davide remarked. "Who built them so long before the Lusitanians? We call them 'Stone Age,' yet they could miraculously lift and fashion ten-ton boulders as if they were slate shingles."

That night they both slept deeply but fitfully.

As they rode along the track toward Portalegre the next morning, Davide mentioned to Ruy that he had had strange dreams the previous night.

"Go on," Ruy urged.

"I woke and stoked the fire, then laid back and closed my eyes. I could feel these seven stones smelling of moss and fungi and dampness—the smell of autumn. I felt thick darkness—the stars and moon were gone. A cold north wind howled, and it sounded like laughter and crackling. The pillar on the north side shook and came alive, with a silver spiral rising from it. In my imagination, the spiral morphed into a witch with a black robe and hat and a long nose with missing teeth. She laughed; she called me a murderer and said I would probably die at sea or be cut to pieces like Magellan on a foreign beach. She laughed hard, and I did not know what to do, so I recited the Shema that I had forgotten to say earlier. Then my mother appeared, looking like she did when I was seven. She had a machete in her hand and cut off the head of the witch and laughed about it. She told me not to be afraid in another land, that she would always be with me.

"The next thing I knew, I was facing the dolmen pillar opposite the entrance. It started turning green and blue with ascending spirals. Then a beautiful naked girl stepped out of the rock. She had olive skin and looked like Leonor de Calle, the cobbler's daughter who lived at the south end of Belmonte. Her hair was long and black with nothing over her breasts and only an animal pelt over her private parts. She said she had always fancied me and was glad that we were finally alone together. She told me she was cold and pointed to the dying fire.

"She asked if I would warm her body with my hands, and I said 'yes.'

"I got up and went to her, realizing that I was naked and exposed. She joked and pulled me to her. When I began to rub her cold body, it warmed. Then she moved erotically and danced in my arms. She looked into my eyes and said, 'I was frozen like a rock, and you have brought me back to life.'

"I said, 'What is your name? Are you not Leonor de Calle?'

"She looked at me quizzically and said, 'No, I call myself 'Autumn Moon', but you can call me Leonor de Calle if you like.".'

"We danced and tried not to disturb you in your sleep, then we laid down on my bedroll together. That's all I remember. Evidently, we made love because I woke up feeling something cold and sticky on my leg—I am almost ashamed to say."

Ruy listened intently and respectfully to Davide's account of an astral experience that culminated in a wet dream. "That place was like the Rock of Endovélico," he said. "I, too, had a vivid dream last night, but it was sweet and simple. I dreamed Ana Sofia and I were married in the Charola, right in the center, and Friar Alvaro was the priest that married us. Ana Sofia was so beautiful." And that is all he would say.

Trotting along the road in the afternoon sun, they debated whether they should cross the border into Spain at Badajoz or continue in Portugal. They opted to continue since they had had no indication of trouble on this side of the border. They would proceed with the plan to buy a rowboat in Elvas and drift down the Guadiana to the sea.

That night they camped in a forest on the outskirts of Elvas. They rode into town in the morning but found no river. Locals told them to go to Badajoz, where the Guadiana runs through the city. That was the best place to buy a boat.

They rode east toward Spain, about six miles away. They had no trouble crossing the border and entered the old city of Badajoz, with the river flowing through the heart of the town. They lodged at an inn near the bridge over the river.

Before leaving their room for the adjoining tavern, they went over their cover stories. If asked, they were brothers from Viseu who had inherited property along the Guadiana between Elvas and Monsaraz.

Upon entering the tavern, they noticed a poster recently nailed to the wall. It pictured several Spanish ships crossing the great ocean. Beneath the drawing was a solicitation for experienced crewmen and adventuresome colonists for an expedition to explore and settle La Florida. The armada was scheduled to weigh anchor at Sanlúcar de Barrameda on April 19, 1566. All interested parties were instructed to contact Monseñor Emilio de Logroño at the Casa de Contratación in Sevilla by letter or in person, or Captain Juan Pardo at the Casa de Contratación in Sanlúcar.

The boys could hardly contain their excitement. They entered the pub and consumed a hearty meal, celebrating their discovery as an act of Providence. Before leaving, Ruy stood next to the wall with his back to the poster, making sure no one was watching. Davide reached around him, pulled the advertisement off the wall, folded it, and stuffed it in his pocket. This done, in case anyone saw them, they departed in different directions and met at the inn an hour later.

Back at the inn, they resolved that the first thing they would do upon reaching Sanlúcar would be to contact Captain Juan Pardo.

Early the following day, they were on their mounts searching for a boat to purchase. Downriver from the city bridge, they encountered a gathering of elderly men who passed their time fishing and ferrying people across the river. Ruy and Davide struck a deal with a man for a sturdy rowboat with oars and fishing gear. When asked their purpose, they replied with their cover story—two brothers who inherited land along the river near Monsaraz, where the Ribeiro de Lucefécit met the Guadiana. They thought it would be easier to get there by water than by land.

The ferrymen weighed the boys' proposition and observed, "If you don't mind pulling the boat over sandbars and shallows." One man told the boys where they could sell their horses in Badajoz, and on their way, they encountered a Gypsy selling second-hand clothes from a cart. They exchanged their clothes for more rustic outfits, hoping to blend in better on the river and at Sanlúcar. They sold their mounts and saddles at the horse market and bought provisions for the boat trip, which would take over a week.

By noon, Ruy and Davide set off on their river voyage. It was not hard work, but also not what they had hoped. Frequently the river was so shallow that only one could be in the boat while the other walked in the river beside it. On occasion, they both had to drag the boat over sandbars. But they still made progress—about as much as on horseback. There was no danger of becoming lost, being robbed, or arousing the suspicion of black-robed priests.

The first night, they made their camp on the river outside of the village of Señora Ajuga. Rain pelted them, and they sought shelter beneath their rowboat, with one gunwale on a tree stump.

The next day they made progress on the slightly swollen river. By two o'clock, they had reached the Ribeiro de Lucefécit as it flowed in the Guadiana. This was the place where their fictitious property was located. The boys tied the boat to the riverbank, stripped off their clothes, and bathed in the cool waters. Refreshed, they returned to the boat and were surprised by the arrival of a third passenger. A raven had landed on the bow, facing the boys, and squawked at them fearlessly as they shoved off. Speechless, they watched the bird lift off into the wind and circle the boat three times before flying west up the narrow river called Lucefécit.

Both Ruy and Davide instinctively knew the raven was Endovélico, come to visit them the same way they had visited Joseph in Egypt and Pero da Covilhã in Ethiopia. They knew Endovélico would accompany them in spirit and that he had shown up to bestow his blessing. They did not realize that Endovélico had flown as a raven from his ancient sanctuary only twenty miles up the Ribeiro de Lucefécit at Rocha da Mina.

For the balance of the day, they made good progress, and by late afternoon they came within sight of the singular mountain, Monsaraz. On top of the mountain was a busy village hewn out of rock and crowned with a Templar castle. The boys debated climbing the road to the top and passing the night in town, but Ruy remembered the words of Friar Alvaro when he said the Templar Vision was dead. They decided not to test fate and continued downriver for half a league, closer to the mountain, before tying the boat on the riverbank and pitching camp.

Davide cleared an area for their camp and dug a small pit for the fire while Ruy scouted for dry firewood. Not far from the riverbank, he came to a clearing with a stone circle and a ten-foot granite pillar in the center, surrounded by thirty-six waist-high boulders. Ruy had heard about great stone circles near Evora, but he had not seen one before. He rested against the central menhir and gazed toward the setting sun behind Monsaraz. In the distance, he saw a shepherd with his flock and dog moving behind him.

When he came closer, Ruy went to meet the shepherd. He introduced himself. The shepherd was silent but smiling. "What is that stone circle?" he asked.

The shepherd replied that it was the Cromeleque of Xarez.

"Who built it?" asked Ruy.

"Who knows?" replied the shepherd with a twinkle in his eye. "If you think it's strange, you should see something else . . . come on—I'll show you."

Ruy agreed and followed the shepherd past an olive grove into an expansive field dotted with hundreds of chest-high mounds of blackened rocks, ranging from the size of a fist to a loaf of bread.

"What's strange about this? Ruy asked. "Someone did a lot of work trying to clear rocks from this field."

"Take a closer look," the shepherd replied with the same smile.

Ruy approached a rockpile and examined the rocks in the last rays of sunlight. Each stone—and there were thousands of them—seemed to have been purposefully molded or inscribed with symbols. But time and perhaps an intense fire had damaged the etchings, making them look like random scribbles among features that resembled gargoyles. The thought occurred to him—in some distant time, there must have been a remarkable structure here, a wall or a temple covered with meaningful symbols. But what destroyed them? Fire, water, wind, men? The images were unrecognizable and indescribable, but they were not natural formations. Intelligent beings made them.

Ruy returned to the campsite with firewood. He and Davide grilled two fish caught earlier, and as they ate, Ruy described the Cromeleque of Xarez and the field of peculiar stones. He urged his friend to look at the stone circle, but Davide told him he was more tired than curious and hoped for a dreamless night's sleep.

They were up before sunrise and were on the misty river as the world around them welcomed a new day. By afternoon, they had made it to the town of Moura, where they purchased presunto, cheese, and wine and were back on the river until late afternoon. They camped on the riverbank and retired early. Three more days of this routine brought Ruy and Davide the rich smell of the salt sea. Seagulls gradually replaced crows. In their eagerness to see the Atlantic, they allowed the current to carry them past the little Portuguese town of Vila Real de Santo Antonio. When the rowboat met the surf, Ruy remembered the rabbi's caution— not to venture too far out to sea in a rowboat. To the west, the beach stretched as far as they could see. They rowed west, hugging the shore, until they came upon a group of fishermen with their nets spread on the beach. They rowed with the surf, which carried the craft onto the beach.

Ruy approached the fishermen and asked whether they could walk the beach to Tavira, and they replied it would take a day. Ruy announced that the rowboat was for sale.

"How much?" one asked.

"How much do you have?" Ruy responded.

The fishermen went off to speak privately. They emptied their pockets, checked their leather satchels, and came up with the equivalent of two and a half ducats, which they honestly thought was not enough for the boat. They included four freshly caught lobsters in the offer. The boys gladly accepted the deal. They slung their new live possessions, tied together, over their shoulders and began the westward trek on the wet sand, as the lobsters pinched them through their shirts.

Before dark, they made camp on the deserted beach and grilled the meat of all four lobsters. The stuffed themselves, knowing that lobster meat would not last and they had had enough of carrying live critters on their backs. Satisfied with the day, the two slept deeply and arose early the next morning, feeling sand crabs at their feet and the sound of gulls fighting over the nearby lobster shells. After a swim in the ocean and some cheese and wine, the boys again set out across the wet sand. They passed a few fishing villages, and to then their dismay, they found themselves not in Tavira, but at the tip of a long peninsula, with water on three sides. With much shouting, they eventually caught the attention of a fishing boat, which came to their rescue. As luck would have it, the fishermen were well acquainted with their Tavira contact, Captain Diogo de Santellana. One volunteered to ferry them to the captain's dockside residence on the river Gilão, which flowed through Tavira.

Davide and Ruy disembarked at Santellana's rickety river dock. The new friend was paid for his troubles. Captain Diogo was home, having just returned from a trip along the Algarve coast to Lagos and Portimão. Ruy introduced himself and said his father, Dr. Lourenço Gonçalves, gave them the captain's name in hopes he could arrange transport to Sanlúcar de Barrameda.

"Yes, of course," Santellana said. "I know your father. He came here twenty years ago and commissioned me to transport a shipment of Chinese silk and porcelain from Huelva to the port of Lagos. We've exchanged a few more favors since, but I have not heard from him in a few years. How is he?"

Ruy answered. "He's not doing too well now. You may have heard the news that the black crows have disrupted the trading group he was associated with out of Goa. That was about half a year ago. The news arrived in Portugal a month back."

"I hadn't heard, but I've been on the water the past three weeks. Is what happened in Goa the reason you and your friend are here?

Davide spoke up. "We were students in Coimbra last month. My father, who is a rabbi and an associate of Dr. Gonçalves, crossed the mountain from Belmonte to Coimbra to warn us our lives were in danger. My father told us we had to make our way to Sanlúcar to go to the New World."

"My father," Ruy added, "gave the rabbi instructions for us to memorize the names of a few trusted friends who might be able to help us."

"I see," said the captain, considering the possibilities of how he could help. "Is Sanlúcar your last stop?"

"Yes, sir," replied Ruy. "Look at this poster we got in Badajoz." Ruy produced the poster from his knapsack and unfolded it.

"This is a good idea," he said. "They have been assembling an armada to colonize La Florida for the past year, but I see two problems."

"What?" Davide asked.

"First, the Menéndez Expedition is scheduled to leave Sanlúcar on April 19 of next year, is it not?"

"Yes, sir," the boys acknowledged.

It is now October 1565. April 19—which I believe is Easter—is six months away. If you go to Sanlúcar now and sign up for the expedition and they accept you . . . or even if you are not taken, what are you going to do for the next six months? Are you going to work somewhere? Maybe if you are lucky. Are you going to sit around at taverns in Sanlúcar or Cádiz for six months while you spend your father's money? You shouldn't—you will be robbed or kidnapped or reported to the Inquisition. What will you do?"

"We don't know," replied Ruy.

"Right. And the second thing is this: I see two young men . . . how old are you?"

"Eighteen," they both replied.

"Two eighteen-year-old Jewish men who were on track to be doctors or engineers or whatever. Two kids with no skills as sailors or soldiers or even sturdy colonial farmers. Am I right?"

"More or less," responded Davide, shrugging.

"This is what I propose. Sign on as deckhands with me for five months. That's enough time for you to learn sailing jargon and know how to make yourself useful aboard a ship. Change your names and learn to act and talk like landless deckhands instead of Jewish schoolboys. I can't pay you, but I can give you room and board and the experience you will need when signing up for the Menéndez Expedition. How does that sound?"

"Sounds great," replied Ruy. "When should we plan to go to Sanlúcar?"

"Around April 1," Dom Diogo replied.

"How will we know if plans for the armada change if we are sailing all over the Mediterranean and Atlantic with you?"

"We won't be sailing all over the Mediterranean. My markets range from Ceuta and Tangier in the east to Lagos and Faro in the west and all the Spanish and Portuguese towns in between. Which means I am always in and out of Sanlúcar. I am there every two weeks or so. I know everything that is going on there."

Ruy and Davide stepped out of the earshot of the captain and conferred for only a few seconds.

"Good, Captain Santellana," Ruy said. "You've laid out a perfect plan. We will not let you down—we have five months to become sailors.

Courtyard within the walls of the Templar Castle, Tomar, Portugal

The Charola, inner sanctum of the Templar Castle in Tomar

Anta do Tapadao Dolmen,
located a few miles from the village of Aldeia de Mata, Portugal

CHAPTER 19

THE CONVERGENCE

Ruy and Davide
On the *Graça de Tavira* off the south Atlantic coast of Portugal and
Spain.
October 1565 through March 1566

*****

Juancinto and Daniel
Ceuta, Cádiz and Sanlúcar de Barrameda, Spain.
January through March 1566

Ruy and Davide passed the next five and a half months working,
eating, and sleeping on Captain Diogo's boat, the *Graça de Tavira*, a fifty-
ton merchant caravel. They witnessed and participated in maritime
commercial activity, in defiance of all borders, from the southwest tip of
Portugal to the Rock of Gibraltar, with Ceuta and Tangier just across the
Strait from the Rock.

They had been aboard the *Graça de Tavira* for three months prior to
their encounter with Daniel Almeyda, in January of 1566— sailing, in
and out of small ports along the southern Atlantic coasts of Spain and
Portugal with a crew of five others. The crew was composed of Captain
Diogo, his first mate, the cook, and two other deckhands. The crewmen
got along well with Ruy and Davide and taught them basics of
seamanship from a deckhand's point of view. As an added protection, the
two changed their names: Ruy became Raúl Gómez, and Davide was
Dario Olivero.

Their longest voyage, in mid-January, was carrying a full hold of
wine, olive oil, and lumber from the Portuguese port of Lagos to the port

of Tangier. They moored in Tangier on January 16, off-loaded their cargo, and took on new freight of wool, cotton, and dates bound for Cádiz. After two days on the wharf in Tangier, the *Graça de Tavira* was preparing to cast off when a last-minute passenger boarded.

Ruy and Davide watched as the young man climbed aboard. He was about their age, perhaps a little older, good-sized, robust, and he gave off an air of self-assurance. The boys noted he was wearing the clothes of a Moor, but he looked Portuguese, although his demeanor was almost savage. When they overheard him speaking with the captain, they confirmed he was Portuguese.

Once under sail, Ruy and Davide approached the newcomer. "I see you are going to Cádiz," Ruy said. "Are you going to join the Menéndez Expedition to La Florida?"

The young man was almost surly. "I don't know about any armada to La Florida," he said. "I'm going on personal business." The newcomer refused to discuss his affairs further but distracted the boys by observing they were not tending to their duties—the sails needed trimming and the rigging adjusted. "Rig-out that tackle-line there to the brace-block at the end of the yardarm," barked the young fellow.

Davide and Ruy executed his command and approached him with even more curiosity. "You sound like a sailor. Are you from Ceuta?"

"Yes, and I have captained a ship bigger than this to Egypt and back," the stranger bragged.

"Really?" said Ruy in disbelief.

"Really," mocked the newcomer, walking away with a degree of irritation. The boys watched him make his way toward the galley, but their attention was diverted by a large seagull which had been circling the boat. The bird landed on a nearby gunwale and began squawking at them. Ruy was convinced that the bird was Endovélico, attempting to tell the something. Davide agreed and they tried to communicate with the seagull as to the message, but the bird flew away.

Later, on reflection, the boys agreed that Endovélico was trying to alert them concerning the young man who had who had just boarded the ship. They decided not to give up on him.

When the time was right, Ruy asked Captain Santellana about the passenger.

"That's Daniel Almeyda. I have watched him grow up. I knew his parents well. His family ran merchant vessels out of Ceuta, but on a much larger scale than my enterprise."

The captain thought for a few moments, then became more serious. "Daniel says his parents, their ship, and crew recently disappeared at sea. He has good reason to believe the people responsible are in Cádiz. I think he will seek revenge there. And Daniel is technically a Jew through his mother and grandfather, who founded the business. His father is, or was, a practicing Muslim. Be careful with Daniel Almeyda, boys. He is a hothead, and he probably needs to go to La Florida with you."

Later that evening, Davide and Ruy approached Daniel, and Davide ventured, "I hope you don't mind, but we asked the captain about you, and he said we have something in common."

"And what could that be?" Daniel asked.

"We're all Jews," Ruy said. "The captain also told us you were going to Cádiz for revenge. Is that right?" Without waiting for a response, Ruy added, "I only ask because the Inquisition committed crimes against our families, yet we are not seeking revenge. Instead, we are running from the Inquisition. We were students at Coimbra, but now our fathers are forcing us to go to Sanlúcar to sail to the New World. That's why we asked if you were going to join-up with the Menéndez armada to La Florida."

"Listening to Ruy's explanation, Daniel perceived that these boys could be useful if he played his cards right. Daniel became more congenial. "Did the captain actually say 'revenge?'"

"Something like that," Davide replied.

"Well, listen to this." Daniel looked deeply into their eyes. "The same people who are after you just killed my parents and the crew and sold our boat. I have the names of the two captains who did this deed. I have reason to believe they are in Cádiz. So, yes, I am going there to find and kill them. That has been the only thing on my mind. I have not thought about the New World, although I probably should."

Daniel remembered the words of his father's friend, the governor of Ceuta, when he said, "catch a boat going west." Daniel turned to Ruy and said, "Once I do what I must do, then, yes, I will sign onto the armada for La Florida. Maybe we can do that together."

Davide produced the poster from Badajoz and rolled it out for Daniel.

"Look," Davide pointed out. "It shows the armada is leaving on April 19. When we arrived at Tavira at the end of October, Dom Diogo told us we had come too soon. As he put it, 'To keep us out of trouble and teach us something useful,' he offered to take us on as deckhands and bring us to Sanlúcar by April 1."

Daniel assessed the situation from another angle. He spoke his thoughts aloud. "April 19." He hummed, "That leaves me two months to do what I need before teaming up with you in early April and shipping out together."

Ruy and Davide followed the logic of Daniel's thinking and agreed to rendezvous in Sanlúcar in early April. As the sun went down, Daniel retired for the night. Ruy and Davide stood watch for the next twelve hours and kept each other company at the wheel. They further discussed their involvement with Daniel, weighing the pros and cons of collaborating with him. Short of taking another human life, they were on board with Daniel's plan.

They communicated their decision to Daniel in the morning, and he replied, "Good, my brothers. The three of us will sail to the New World together. One for all and all for one—we will keep each other safe."

The *Graça de Tavira* docked in the harbor of Cádiz late that afternoon. Daniel said his goodbyes at the warehouse where the ship's cargo was offloaded. He checked in at a boarding house and then cased-out the waterfront saloons and taverns, hoping to discover something about the two men he was stalking.

******

Juancinto caught a ride in the back of an oxcart full of lemons bound for the port of Cadiz, twenty miles to the south of the port of Sanlucar de Barrameda. He found work playing *gitano* guitar at a sailor's tavern along the harbor's pier, sleeping at night against a palm tree at a nearby plaza. He purchased a comb, scissors, and a straight razor, which he kept in his pocket for protection. He had been playing guitar in the tavern for over a week when he noticed two men—sailors, he thought, frequenting the tavern and watching him more than eating or drinking. Something was vaguely familiar—and it gave him a feeling of unease.

It was about midnight when Juancinto, after playing his music for a solid hour, felt the call of nature. He had to defecate, preferably in private. He left the tavern and walked a block to the pier's edge, where a large wooden enclosure extended over the water. It was a public latrine, a roofless structure provided by the municipality. There was no one outside the toilet, and when Juancinto opened the door, it was empty.

Juancinto discharged his business, and upon leaving, the two men who had been watching him in the tavern confronted him. One stood in front of Juancinto; the other positioned himself behind. The one in the rear grabbed him from behind, preventing him from using his arms. The one in front pulled a long knife and, with a laughing sneer, declared, "Look who we have here—the barber of Córdoba, back from a long trip. We will send you to hell for eternity for murdering our brother." The man began a lunge with a dagger toward Juancinto's chest.. But before the tip could penetrate the Gypsy's shirt, the man dropped to his knees, falling over dead without a sound. A stranger dressed like a Moor pulled a bloodied knife from the dead man's back.

Meanwhile, seeing his brother fall to the ground, the second brother let loose of Juancinto and turned to run. The stranger quickly maneuvered to intercept him and buried his blade in the second brother's side, severing his renal artery. A second stab in the heart quickened his death.

The stranger, speaking Spanish with a Portuguese accent, asked Juancinto, "How large is the shithole in there?"

Juancinto, still in shock, indicated with his stretched-out hands about fourteen inches " It won't be easy, but let's try dump them here. You grab the feet. I'll get the arms and hold the door open." In this way, Juancinto and the stranger carried both dead brothers into the latrine, where they managed to stuff and wrangled them down through the shithole, sliding them head-first into the malodorous waters of Cádiz harbor.

The stranger turned to Juancinto. He announced matter-of-factly, "Get your things. Meet me in one hour in front of the tavern where you were playing. We can't stay here."

Juancinto, realizing he owed this stranger his life, complied with the instructions without question. He soon found himself walking with the stranger along the shore of the inner bay, looking for someone with a boat to row them across the harbor to the road to Sanlúcar. Eventually, they found a fellow coming from a fisherman's tavern drunk and ready to accommodate their wishes in exchange for a bottle of wine. Half an hour later, they had crossed the harbor and were on the well-rutted road to Sanlúcar de Barrameda.

Silently they walked together in the darkness of the starless night.

"I am grateful and much obliged for what you did," Juancinto said.

"You *should* be grateful," the stranger emphasized.

"Why did you do it? Were you following them?"

"I was in the tavern. You were playing your guitar, and I overheard them plotting to kill you. I thought to myself—that old Gypsy seems intelligent and capable. So, I helped you."

"Capable of what?" Juancinto asked.

"Of helping me."

"To do what?"

"What I just did for you."

"Kill a man?"

"*Sí, por supuesto!* You might say I was practicing on those two. I am here for justice—justice for the murder of my parents, and I could use some help."

"I might be capable of helping you, but you don't want *me*."

"Why not?" inquired the stranger.

"I'm bad luck. People drawn to me become cursed."

"Nonsense. Gypsy talk. Your luck turned last night, did it not? From now on, you and I will be lucky. And with me, you will become a tool of justice."

"A tool of justice?"

"Yes—of *righteous* justice. Accept it. Get used to it. The alternative would be far worse for you."

"I accept what you say, young man, because I am not in a position to argue with Fate, but I think you ought to hear my story."

"Very well, Gypsy, tell me your story."

Juancinto began, "The man who was going to run me through with his knife, the one who first called me 'the barber of Córdoba' . . . I'm from Sevilla, but my wife, son, and I worked in Córdoba a little over ten years ago. That's when I accentually killed their brother. He molested my wife as she was dancing. I played for her, and when he approached Solea, he put his hands on her. I jumped up and grabbed the razor from my pocket. I thought to scare him and cut his shirt from collar to belt, but he moved, and I sliced his jugular. He bled to death before anyone could do anything. Because the guy was a rogue, they didn't execute me but sent me as a bond servant to the New World. There, in the New World, I left two women who are probably dead now because they loved me. When I finally returned home to Sevilla last month, I learned my son died in a knife fight protecting his mother, just as I had years ago. Hearing a rumor that I was dead in the New World, his mother, who I lived for, drowned herself in the Alfonzo XIll Canal. This is what I came home to after ten years. Now, I am a walking dead man."

"That's a sad tale. I understand why you feel desolate. But the way I see it, it could have been much worse if those brothers had slit your throat and shoved *you* down the shithole. But it looks like you've lost everything, including your bad luck. Now your fortune is turning. It was my lucky night to find you, and now we have one thing in common which binds us like brothers."

"And what is that?" asked Juancinto.

"What we did," replied the stranger.

"You mean, what *you* did," Juancinto corrected.

"Very well. I saved your hide and protected you from being murdered. You helped me dispose of the bodies. Your guilty Gypsy conscience can turn us in to the *hermandades* . . . or we can act like men and keep the justified murder of those thugs a secret. We could depend on each other like brothers."

"Well then," Juancinto replied, "if you are to be the brother of this old Gypsy, I need to know something about you. You sound Portuguese. What brings you here? Are you a Gypsy too? From the way you manipulated me, I think you may have Gypsy blood, too, right? Is that why you call me brother?"

"My name is Daniel Almeyda. I am Portuguese because I was born and raised in the Portuguese city of Ceuta on the African coast. I am a Jew because my mother was a Jew, and I am a Moor because my father was Muslim. So, I am everything and nothing, and like you, with nothing to lose. My Jewish grandfather founded the trading company years ago. Since then, our family has made a living by trading commodities throughout the

Mediterranean, from Beirut to Tangier. Our wealth and heritage attracted the Inquisition. One month ago, black Dominican vultures from Lisbon with a couple of Spanish pirates descended upon Ceuta and brought that black Catholic plague down on our heads. The priests confiscated my grandfather's warehouses, ships, and camels. They made him a prisoner in his own house.

"My mother and father were on their way back from trading in Alexandria when the two Spanish pirates—and I know their names—hijacked my father's ship off the coast of Morocco. They killed my parents and the crew—threw them into the sea, then sailed the boats to Tangier, telling the harbormaster they had bought the *Rainha de Alcântara* from my father. There is no trace of my parents and the crew, nor were they set ashore. That was three weeks ago. At the port in Tangier, I was told the *Rainha* had set sail for Cádiz, and they gave me the names of the two captains: Alejandro Sánchez and Raúl Estigarriba.

"I have been in Cádiz for the past week hunting for them and the *Rainha*, with no luck until last night. At the tavern where you were playing, I learned that Estigarriba went to Sanlúcar last week after working on the boat at the shipyard in Cádiz. He changed the name of our boat to *El Redimido*. They say there is a lot of activity in Sanlúcar right now because boats from the Guadalquivir are full of soldiers who have signed up to colonize La Florida. They said Estigarriba declared he wanted to participate. There would be seventeen vessels making the voyage, with a few frigates, like *his* boat—*filha da puta!*"

"So now, Juancinto, you understand what our mission is? I will have my revenge. We will kill Estigarriba, and Sánchez, too, if we can find him. I don't care about the boat. I have no title to it, and no one would believe my story anyway. I would prefer to sink it. I intend to set a trap for Estigarriba and bring justice down on his head. That is my mission. Are you with me, my Gypsy brother?"

"I am with you, my Jew-Moor brother!"

Walking on the muddy road to Sanlúcar, they devised their plan as clouds on the eastern horizon gave way to the growing light of a new day.

"Eliminating Estigarriba won't be as easy as sliding him down a latrine hole," Daniel observed. No. We must make his corpse disappear."

"That can be done easily," Juancinto assured Daniel. "Coming from Ceuta, I guess you may not know there is a vast wasteland across the river from Sanlúcar de Barrameda. Endless canals run through swamp and jungle with shifting hills of salt and sand. The region is called the "Doñana." It is the home of wild boars and snakes, not human beings. If a man gets lost, he never comes out. That's where we should take Estigarriba."

"Good idea, brother! That's what we'll do," Daniel concurred. "Now, let's find him. That's the first order of business. Once we find him, then we'll observe his habits. Maybe you can make friends with him. He won't suspect you. We'll learn of his weaknesses and exploit them with a trap which will somehow lead him into the Doñana."

They reached Sanlúcar by nine o'clock and found a room in a boarding house. They strolled along the harbor that afternoon, and Daniel recognized the *Rainha de Alcântara* tucked among a dozen other vessels of the same size.

They surveilled the boat from a distance and observed a portly man, bald with a red beard and bulging stomach, strutting on deck, giving orders. "That must be him," Daniel said to Juancinto. After a while, a Dominican priest boarded the boat, and there was an exchange—the priest passed a bag of money, it seemed, to Estigarriba. A crucifix on a gold chain came from the pocket of the priest's robe. The holy man placed it around Estigarriba's fat neck as if it were a prize.

The next day, Juancinto approached Captain Estigarriba on the newly named *El Redimido,* pretending he was looking for a job. He told the captain he had experience as a sailor on the Ocean Sea, in the Caribbean, and even in the Western Sea, inflating the lie by telling Estigarriba that he had sailed through the Strait of Magellan.

Estigarriba was impressed and signed Juancinto for one hundred *reales*—half due when they reached La Florida and the balance on their return to Sanlúcar.

The captain put Juancinto to work, helping other crew members outfit the vessel to accommodate dozens of soldiers and colonists. The task at hand was to seal the cargo hold with a new coat of black pitch. The captain warned them to keep an eye out for the shipworms that had infested the hull, claiming that the pitch would kill the worms and seal and preserve the hull from further rot. Estigarriba boasted to the crew that, to win the grace of God, he had given the priests half the proceeds from the sale of his cargo. The crew should take some comfort from his act of benevolence, he said, and not complain about the nasty job of spreading hot pitch on the walls of the empty cargo hold.

After a few weeks of Juancinto's hard work and diligence, and after a long day working with boiling coal-tar pitch, Captain Estigarriba invited him to share a pitcher of ale at a nearby tavern. Three pitchers later, the information that Juancinto sought began to flow.

Estigarriba regarded money as the source of all evil. The Jews, he said, with their sinful, ill-gotten gains through usury, were Satan's instruments. He felt he was doing God's will by appropriating their wealth for himself, by whatever method. The captain revealed he had recently purchased a treasure map in Cádiz. It was a map certified to be an authentic copy of the map produced by one of the survivors of Ponce de León's recent quest for the Fountain of Youth. The fountain, it seemed, was a natural well on Bimini, an island off the coast of Florida. Estigarriba was confident he could find the island, fill many barrels with the vital liquid, and sell it in San Juan, Santiago, and Havana.

At the boarding house that night, Daniel and Juancinto marveled at the captain's gullibility. Then they began to think in terms of a treasure map that might lure Captain Estigarriba into the Doñana.

That night, excitement filled Daniel's head and didn't diminish when his head hit the pillow. He tossed and turned with visions of vengeance and finally arose in the wee hours to search for a rowboat he could rent to take them into the Doñana. As dawn broke, he found one and rented it from a fisherman for a week on the pretext of hunting in the marshlands. During the day, he communicated to Juancinto, preparing him to be sick, injured, or whatever necessary to miss work the next day to journey with him into the Doñana.

As the sun rose over Sanlúcar, Daniel and Juancinto headed upstream on the Guadalquivir, rowing hard against the current. Daniel kept a piece of parchment dry in his vest pocket along with a pen and ink he purchased the day before. He kept distance by leagues, as far as one could see, being one league, with a marker on the map he was drawing. By this reckoning, it was about two leagues north and another around the bend to the east before they encountered the first big canal that branched west into the Doñana.

They rowed up the still-water canal for a couple of leagues in a northern direction, then entered a smaller canal and rowed west in a channel barely wide enough for the boat. The landscape on both sides consisted of long hills or small mountains of white shifting sand with green valleys of jungle intersected by more canals and wetlands. Two leagues up this small waterway brought them to their first prominent sight—a small conical green hill with an easily visible, rocky outcrop at the summit. Surrounding the twenty-foot hill was a water-filled trench, like a manmade moat. The ditch joined the nearby canal. Juancinto and Daniel pulled the rowboat onto the channel's bank and looked around.

"This is the place," Daniel proclaimed. It could not be easier to access. No confusion—two left turns in the Doñana and the hill with a rock on top. The place promised to be easy to map, and, above all, it was secluded, with no sign of human activity within five miles.

They debated where to put the site of the buried treasure on the map. Daniel asserted that designating the prize's location by the rock outcrop at the top of the hill made the most sense. It was protected from flooding and easy to see, no matter how much the sand shifted.

"How will you approach Estigarriba on top of the hill without him seeing you?" Juancinto asked. "He'll look up and see you crawling up the hill."

Daniel responded, "If the captain turns around and sees me, then, to be sure, Juancinto, he will not be looking at you at the same time. Hit him on the back of his head with your shovel. If Estigarriba keeps his eyes on you, I'll approach him from his back and lay him out before he realizes what is going on. What I am saying is—whatever takes place on his hill, we will position ourselves on the opposite sides of the captain. One of us will always be at his back with a shovel or a boat oar. I like these odds, and besides, both of us have killed before.

Juancinto agreed, and the plan was set. Daniel sketched the bushy hill with the rock on top and the moat-like ditch. It had taken them six hours to row to the treasure site. They were on-site for about an hour. With the river current, the boat moved faster on the way back, and they arrived in Sanlúcar before sundown. It would be a full-day affair to execute the task from start to finish.

CHAPTER 20

THE CONFLUENCE

Daniel, Davide, Ruy and Juancinto
Sanlúcar de Barrameda, Spain
April 1566.

On the morning of April 1st, Daniel walked along the harbor of Sanlúcar looking for the *Graça de Tavira* and signs of Davide and Ruy. Without seeing anything, he repeated the walk in the late afternoon and with the same result. This was the routine for four more days. On April 5, Daniel spotted the *Graça* anchored in the harbor some two hundred yards from the pier. Three men in a rowboat left the ship, and two deposited their belongings on the dock. Daniel walked toward them, whistled to get their attention, then put his finger to his mouth to signal silence. He motioned for them to follow. They went to a tavern with few customers inside and found a private corner. Daniel ordered breakfast for the three, and they began to whisper in Portuguese.

"What's happening?" Ruy asked.

"Things are going as well," Daniel said. "We've located the *Rainha de Alcântara*. She is being re-pitched and outfitted for the trip across the Atlantic in two weeks, with Raúl Estigarriba as captain. So, that's good news. The other pirate, Alejandro Sánchez, has gone to Toledo, and I don't have time to track him down. We've been working on a plan to kill Estigarriba, and I hope you two can help us."

Davide chimed in, "When you say *we've* got a plan, who else is in on this? Who is this *we.*"

"His name is Juancinto Taranto. You will talk to him tonight. He is staying with me. He's about forty, a Gypsy from Sevilla just returned from ten years of bonded servitude in the New World for killing a man in Córdoba. He is indebted to me because I saved his life, and now we are in a partnership, bound together for life."

"Bound for life, you say?" Ruy asked. "Where is this Gypsy now?"

"He signed up with Estigarriba two months ago after discovering the *Alcântara* here in Sanlúcar. Estigarriba has renamed it *El Redimido* as if he has redeemed the boat from infidels like my mother and father to justify their murder. But you asked about Juancinto; Since working for Estigarriba, he has managed to gain the captain's confidence. Over much drink, he has revealed secrets and weaknesses to Juancinto."

"How so?" asked Ruy.

"For one thing, he is a sucker for buried treasure. And he has a blind hatred for Jews. Knowing this, we are laying a trap for him by luring him into the swampland west of here. We've been out there in a boat, and we are drawing a treasure map to a place where we will kill him. We are working on a good story to go along with the map."

"Maybe we could help," Ruy interjected.

"Good," Daniel replied. "I knew I could count on you. We talked about this on the way here from Tangier. We are running out of time because the armada sails in two weeks. You know that before I can leave, I must settle the score with this pirate, Estigarriba, who wears a crucifix dangling from his neck."

"Count on us," Ruy proclaimed.

"Not so fast," Davide hesitated. "I can't commit murder. It is against a commandment, even the murder of a murderer."

"Oh, my friend, son of a rabbi." Daniel calmed his anger in a manner his mother had taught him. "You've studied the Torah. You know that Moses and Joshua murdered many disobedient Jews. I am simply talking here about an eye for an eye. Or, in this case, two eyes for twenty innocent eyes. Besides, there does not even have to be an actual death. And if there is a death, it will be by *my* hands, not yours."

"Thou shalt not kill is a Commandment. I cannot participate in the breaking of one of Yahweh's Commandments. It would be a bad omen for the commencement of our journey to the New World."

With a killer smile, Daniel countered. "That attitude, my pious friend, will cost you, and the only journey you will be taking will be upriver to the Casa de Inquisición in Sevilla, where you can plead your case to the archbishop."

"What do you mean?" protested Davide.

"I mean," Daniel asserted, " if you don't go along with us, I will have you betrayed to the Inquisition."

"But you will betray yourself."

"No, I won't," said Daniel. "My Gypsy brother, whom you have never seen, will betray you. And when you talk with them about me, I will have disappeared, and they will laugh at you and stretch the rack tighter."

"But your brother?" Davide asked.

"My *brother?* You mean Juancinto, who shares my Fate. He's a Gypsy, not a Jew, you fool. He will do whatever I tell him, and there will be no consequence for him if he goes to the Casa de Inquisición. They may even reward him.

Davide fell silent and looked imploringly at Ruy, who angrily glared at him.

Daniel interceded, "Don't worry, *amigos*. If we plan this well, no one has to commit murder. If necessary, *I* will do it, and it will be *my* responsibility alone. So, with a clear conscience, Davide, please agree to work with us so we can be a band of brothers working for a common cause—our survival."

Davide reluctantly nodded his consent.

They left the tavern and walked silently along the pier, scanning the multitude of vessels of all sizes moored side-by-side, rocking with the incoming tide. They came upon the *El Redimido,* and Daniel stopped. Do you see where they have torn off the original name? That used to be the *Rainha de Alcântara.* It is *my* boat. Do you see the fresh paint—*El Redimido*? I've changed my mind. It is a good name because I will be able to redeem it with your help. Do you see that ugly bald man with the scraggly red beard; the fat-ass strutting around shouting at the deckhands? That is our target. You see that older man carrying a bucket of hot tar behind him?

"Yes," said Ruy.

"That's Juancinto. Do you see what they are doing?

"I can smell the tar from here," Davide answered.

Daniel continued, "They are re-sealing the *Alcântara's* hull, getting her ready to voyage across the Ocean Sea. As you know, the armada leaves in two weeks. Seventeen vessels will depart from here for the New World. Most of them are bigger than the *Alcântara.* They are floating down the Guadalquivir from Sevilla every day. In addition to all the sailors and colonists, there will be fifteen hundred soldiers to keep peace with the natives. There will be a lot of commotion around here; it's a good time to do what we need to do, then jump on one of these boats and go to the New World. Are you with me, my brothers?"

"Of course we are," replied Ruy.

"That is what our fathers wanted," added Davide.

"Come on," Daniel said, walking away from the dock. "Let's spend some time in the town to get its feel as soldiers, sailors and colonists pour in for the armada's launch. Keep your eye out for anything useful— information, gossip, posters, and shovels. Juancinto will probably drink with Estigarriba this afternoon, and we'll see him tonight."

Late that afternoon, they arrived at the boarding house. As soon as Davide and Ruy were settled, Daniel said, "There are certain things we know about Raúl Estigarriba. One, he hates Jews and has worked with the Dominicans to confiscate Jewish property, an activity he enjoys. Two, he likes to gamble. Getting something for nothing intrigues him. Three, he is a sucker for buried treasure maps, and he has already bought one to find the Fountain of Youth on an island near Florida."

"Tell us again what you have done so far," Ruy said.

Daniel showed him the map of the Doñana swampland.

Davide, who was beginning to feel his role in the brotherhood, declared, "I think I can create a story about the treasure map; a story Estigarriba won't be able to resist."

"Explain," Daniel challenged.

"There are certain people who will pay a fortune for ancient Hebrew manuscripts full of illuminations. Even if Estigarriba does not know these people, the priests do. A priest will treat the captain wonderfully and reward him were he to deliver a box full of such manuscripts into their hands."

"Perfect!" Daniel exclaimed.

"Yes," Davide said. "Based on Daniel's map, I will draw a treasure map on a piece of old parchment. It will include a drawing of a copper box that holds the manuscripts. The instructions will be in old

Castellano, and around the edges of the parchment, I will draw some illumination with letters of the Hebrew alphabet."

"Perfect idea," said Daniel. "Tomorrow—"

Daniel had begun speaking, but Juancinto stumbled into the room. Juancinto eyed the two strangers. Daniel kept smiling. Without a word of introduction, Juancinto collapsed on the closest bed and muttered, "My head is spinning. I just drank Captain Estigarriba under the table."

Daniel went to him, shook him, and spoke into his ear, "You drank the captain under the table? What did you learn?"

Juancinto moaned and rolled over. Daniel went to the other side of the bed and continued. "What did he tell you, Juancinto?"

Juancinto opened his eyes and focused on Daniel. Slurring, he said, "Estigarriba has a contract with the Casa to carry thirty soldiers under the command of Captain Juan Pardo. Pardo will have three ships and 250 men. He is lodging in Sanlúcar." With that, Juancinto rolled over again, closed his eyes, and was gone to the rest of the world.

Davide was particularly excited. He rummaged through his sack to find the recruitment advertisement they'd pulled off the wall at the tavern in Badajoz. Davide confirmed from the poster that Captain Juan Pardo was the recruiting officer.

"As far as signing on for the armada," Daniel observed, "I think we are in good shape. The three of us," he said, nodding to Ruy and Davide, "should have no trouble signing on as deckhands, considering your four months on the merchant boat. Juancinto is already a deckhand on the *Redimido*, and he'll put in a good word for us. If they don't need more sailors on the *Redimido*, we'll try the other two ships. The main thing is to stay together. At worst, we'll sign on as soldiers under Juan Pardo or even as colonists. But remember, once we get to La Florida, we're not coming back, which means we will have to become soldiers or colonists because they won't need deckhands.

Returning to what they were talking about when Juancinto made his entrance, Ruy reminded Daniel that Davide was the son of a rabbi. He had a good idea for the treasure map that they'd use to attract Estigarriba. Daniel motioned to Davide to explain it.

"I'll draw the map based on your notes and your sketch of the terrain," Davide said. "And I will draw illuminated Hebrew script around the map; something a Gypsy could not forge."

The other two nodded in agreement.

"To make it more credible, we have to work on a few things. First, one doesn't find a seventy-year-old treasure map just floating around. Someone must *discover* it. And it should be in something like an envelope or a container.. I envision a treasure map rolled up inside a wooden cylinder, buried in a secret room in the basement of some wealthy Jewish family who abandoned their estate in Sevilla or Córdoba or Granada to flee the Inquisition."

Daniel held up his hand. "That sounds good, but for now, let's give Juancinto a chance to sleep off his drunk in peace. In the morning, when he has a clear head, we can include him in the planning. Let's all get some sleep for now."

Early the following day, half-awake, Juancinto became aware there were others in the room besides Daniel and himself. He rose from the bed wide-eyed and looked around. Daniel was awake. He interceded, "Juancinto, we have two new brothers here. They are Portuguese Jews escaping the Inquisition. After we kill Estigarriba, we'll all be in the same boat, fleeing to the New World. I've told them about our plans, and they will help." Turning to Davide, Daniel said, "This is Davide . . . I'm sorry, I don't know your surname, Davide."

"Mendes de Oliveira," Davide replied.

"*Obrigado, amigo.* Davide Mendes de Oliveira is the son of a rabbi. He has a good idea for a treasure map to capture Captain Estigarriba's interest. Please tell us, Davide."

I will create a treasure map that wealthy will pay a fortune for. The map will be lodged in a wooden cylinder with a cap. The map—on old parchment—will have illuminated Hebrew script all around the edges. I will design the map from Daniel's sketch, with directions going into the Doñana in old Castellano that, hopefully, the captain can read.

"If he can't, I can," Juancinto joked, proud of his recently acquired literacy.

Davide asked Juancinto, "Tell me, where and how will you tell the captain about how you got the map?"

"I will tell the captain that last Christmas when I was in Sevilla, I found myself hungry and without resources. I reverted to my old ways and broke into an abandoned, dilapidated house—but a big one. I went to the basement and found a box that contained a map. I'll point out to Captain Estigarriba that the map looks like it's centered in the Doñana marshes. I'll tell him I'd like to recover the treasure before we sail in a few weeks, but I don't think I can find it without help. I'll tell him that if he helps me find this treasure with a rowboat, some shovels, and some time off, I will divide the treasure with him."

"Good idea, Juancinto," Davide said. "To make your tale even more convincing, you could say the house belonged to a rabbi who fled the Inquisition years ago. And in the basement, you found a secret chamber under a hidden door in the floor. Inside the chamber were boxes and cupboards . . . and in one box, you found the map, or better yet, you found a wooden cylinder. You opened the cylinder and found the map."

Daniel elaborated by adding, "Along with the map, you found a letter from the rabbi to his grandchildren. The year was 1493. They were leaving Spain for refuge in Morocco, maybe in Tetouan. Many Spanish Jews escaped to Tetouan before the turn of the century. You know Tetouan? It's south of Ceuta. The rabbi can say he hopes his descendants return to find the treasure."

Ruy contributed to the plan by offering that the rabbi refer to the manuscripts' antiquity and rarity—and their incalculably high value. The treasure map may even refer to the box's contents as the *Zohar*. If the captain is worldly and has traded in such relics, or if he has priest friends, he will recognize the word *Zohar* and be convinced of the map's authenticity.

"All this sounds very good," Juancinto said.

"Today," Ruy concluded, "Davide and I will find the materials to make the treasure map and the old letter, including the wood cylinder. No doubt we will have to find a carpenter's shop to make it for us. We'll carve it up with appropriate Hebrew letters, stain it, oil it, and burn it to make it look seventy years old. We'll do whatever it takes to get the parchment looking just so. Tomorrow is Thursday, right?"

"Yes."

"By Saturday," Ruy said, "we will have the map with the cylinder and the letter. Sunday or Monday, Juancinto can show the map to the captain and convince him to help find the treasure."

"Sounds good," Daniel confirmed. "I will rent a rowboat for a week plus buy ropes, shovels, and knives we will need. Next week, on

Wednesday the thirteenth—no later than Thursday the fourteenth—we will have disposed of Estigarriba. This will give Pardo or Arciniega a week to find a new captain for the *Redimido.* And it will give the three of us time to sign on as crew or soldiers and hopefully be assigned to the *Redimido* with Juancinto. And Juancinto," Daniel continued, "when you talk to Estigarriba next week with the map in hand, carry your razor, in case the captain is so convinced that he tries to kill you to get the treasure map for himself. That would save us some time and trouble, but we would still have to dispose of the body."

Daniel continued laying down the timeline. "if things go well, Estigarriba and Juancinto will row into the Doñana no sooner than Monday the eleventh and no later than Thursday the fourteenth."

Ruy turned to Juancinto. "Do everything to encourage the captain that time is of the essence. Here's the message: you need to find the treasure and sell it to someone who will buy it."

"Right," Juancinto replied. "I will threaten to find the treasure myself if he doesn't go by Wednesday."

"Will Estigarriba use the captain's boat on the ship?" Daniel asked Juancinto.

"I think so," Juancinto replied.

"That would be better," Daniel noted. "But I'll rent two boats, just in case, so one will be available if you need it. Juancinto, you must insist that you leave in the ship's rowboat or a rented one, well before dawn or—even better—toward midnight. You can't be the last person seen with Captain Estigarriba rowing upriver toward the Doñana. You'll have the map in hand. Convince him it may take twelve hours to get to the treasure site, find the box, and row back. And convince him, if he needs convincing, that finding the treasure should be secret. Tell him if the authorities see he's found a treasure, they'll tax him on it."

"It shouldn't be hard to convince him," Juancinto said.

The next day, Friday the eighth, everything went according to plan. First, Ruy and Davide found a carpentry shop that cut, planed, and bore a cylinder and cap from an old four-inch locust fence post. Davide, with his knife and Juancinto's razor, carved Hebrew letters around the cylinder, while Ruy obtained old parchment and a pen with various inks at market. He also purchased a yard of cowhide. They soaked the carved wood cylinder in olive oil and stained it with brown ink. Davide rolled the parchment and placed it inside the cylinder. There was enough parchment for the map and the letter. Then , with the cowhide, Davide made a large leather bag, into which he put the cylinder with the parchment inside.

They left the room and walked to a secluded beach a few miles east, where they dug a pit and started a fire with driftwood and leaves. The cylinder was placed in the leather bag, and the bag was filled with sand. They put the bag into the flames and watched the fire destroy the leather. Before the fire could penetrate the sand to the wooden cylinder, they retrieved it. The results were perfect—the wooden cylinder had discolored and become pockmarked by the hot sand against oil and ink. It truly looked ancient, and the parchment inside the cylinder, still in one piece, looked fragile and time-worn.

That evening, after returning to the boarding house with the cylinder and parchment, Davide busied himself illuminating the borders of the treasure map with Hebrew letters and designs he remembered from the *Zohar* books.

Daniel supplied the map and sketches he had made from his trip into the Doñana. Davide transferred the river and canal routes to the parchment. He included a drawing of the hill with the rock outcropping where a copper box with the Zohar was supposedly buried.

The Portuguese men consulted on the correct verbiage in old Castellano for the map and the letter. In the end, they deferred to the literary judgment of Juancinto, who silently welcomed the opportunity to practice his exposure to Garcilaso de la Vega.

The following day, Saturday the ninth, Juancinto showed up for work at the *Redimido.* He asked the captain if he could have Sunday off.

"What on earth for?" complained Estigarriba. "We sail in a week. I need your scrawny ass here."

"There is something important I have to do before we sail, and time is running out," Juancinto said. "I need to go to Cádiz and get something."

"What's so important?"

"Well, sir, the truth is, it's a secret. But I might as well tell you because of what I need to do. I need help with it. It's something I can't do alone."

"What have you been hiding?" the captain plied him.

"When I came here from Sevilla in January, I buried something in Cádiz, and I need to get it."

"What is it, *hombre?!*" Estigarriba insisted.

"I have an old map to something buried in the Doñana long ago."

"What? What's buried?"

"That's the point, sir. I'm not sure what it is or how valuable it is because I can't read. I have a letter with what looks like a treasure map. But I can't read Castellano, and there is some writing with strange letters."

"Is it coins or jewels?" asked the captain, intrigued.

"That's just it, Captain. If I thought it was coins or jewels, I would go after it myself. But I don't think it is. The drawing on the map suggests that it's just old books buried in a metal box. Maybe it's Jewish. I found the map in a secret room in the basement of an abandoned house in Sevilla owned by a rabbi."

"Really?"

"Yes. So if the treasure is just books, I'm not sure it's worth going after. But since you know a lot about things like the Fountain of Youth and buried treasure, maybe you should see the map and the letter and decide whether it's worth going after or not. If we *do* find something, I'm willing to split it between us."

"Sounds good to me, Juancinto. Go ahead. Don't wait for Sunday; take the rest of today off. And hurry. Take a carriage to Cádiz and back so you will be here by nightfall."

"All right, Captain. I'm on my way."

Juancinto returned to the *Redimido* that evening with the wooden cylinder inside his guitar case. He presented the cylinder to the captain, who examined its Hebrew etchings, removed the cap, and pulled out two rolls of parchment, one with the treasure map, the other with the letter.

Estigarriba read the letter first and hummed. "This looks real. The old rabbi buried a set of books called the *Zohar* in the Doñana before he fled to Morocco. I can turn this into substantial money, but we are running out of time. First, we must find the books. Then, I have to go upriver to Sevilla and find some friends of friends who would pay a fortune for this. But how are we going to do this and set sail in ten days? If we are going to do this, we'd best do it now!"

"Now, sir? It's already dark. We'd lose our way in the Doñana. Best tomorrow. Or better, leave before dawn, so we'll have a full day at the task.

"You're right, Juancinto, but tomorrow is Sunday, and Captain-General Arciniega wants us all at a special mass for the armada. Since we are running out of time, I'll make up some excuse. I will lower the long boat from the ship, and we'll be off before dawn tomorrow."

"*Sí, señor!* For now, I'm tired. If you don't mind, I'm going to my room for a few hours of sleep. I'll be back two hours before dawn. I'll bring some bread and wine. Don't forget to bring a pick and some shovels. And Captain, if you don't mind, I'd like to have the map and the cylinder back for safekeeping, if you know what I mean. You keep the letter."

Estigarriba agreed. Juancinto raced back to the quarters to inform his brothers they would need to set out shortly after midnight.

"Change in plans, men. We are not going into the Doñana Monday or Tuesday. We're going now."

Hearing this, the three Portuguese tumbled out of bed, stunned but ready for action, focused on Juancinto's words.

"The captain wants to do it tonight. I am to meet him two hours before dawn at the *Redimido.* You three have to get the rope and shovels and everything else we need and shove off *now* if you want to get ahead of Estigarriba and me. We are taking the captain's skiff, which means I'll probably be rowing upriver, but we'll have the sail unfurled and the wind at our backs, so we'll make good time." "We don't have a minute to lose. Let's get going!"

The three gathered the goods they would need and rushed to the pier, where the rowboat was moored. Two strained every muscle rowing against the current while the third kept a sharp lookout at the rear for signs of the captain's boat under sail.

They reached the treasure site at the break of day and hid the rowboat in the brush, a reasonable distance up the canal from the hill. After waiting anxiously for a couple of hours, they watched from their hiding place as the captain disembarked from his skiff and mounted the hill.

Daniel assumed the first thing the captain would do at the top of the hill would be to scan the horizon for signs of humanity before digging. This he did, which was the sign for the comrades to begin their approach from three directions. They crept like lynxes, native to this habitat, moving deftly from bush to shrub when Estigarriba's back was turned. Within minutes, they were in the foliage at the base of the hill.

They heard Juancinto's pick strike rock beneath the sand. He muttered something about how hard it was. He dug in a sandier area, throwing up dusty white clouds with the shovel. Daniel, Ruy, and Davide inched up the slope like iguanas with their tongues out, sensing a meal.

Having dug a knee-deep hole in an area the size of a large chessboard, Juancinto said to the captain, "Did you hear that? Metal against metal." Estigarriba dropped to his knees and began scooping out sand with his hands. Juancinto calmly stepped back and, with the shovel, whacked the captain on the back of his head. The man pitched forward and fell unconscious with his head in the sandy pit.

It was all that easy, so it seemed.

The other three comrades scrambled up the hill. "Let's get him off the hill," Daniel ordered, "if someone out there should see us." He grabbed the captain by the boots and motioned for Ruy to take the arms. They dragged the man's limp body down the sandy slope to the marsh grass beside the canal. Estigarriba began regaining his senses but feigned unconsciousness for buying time to evaluate his predicament during the process.

As he lay in the grass, the captain could hear Juancinto's voice and two Portuguese accents, which he presumed belonged to the men who'd dragged him down the hill. One voice said, "Let's strip him, starting with the fine pair of boots." Estigarriba knew his salvation lay with the dagger hidden in the right boot. He moaned and dragged his legs up to his chest into a fetal position with his eyes closed.

Daniel bent and reached for the man's boot, when the captain gave a powerful kick that landed on Daniel's jaw, sending him flying backward. Estigarriba knew he had connected, and in one fluid movement, the portly man slipped the dagger from his boot and pounced on the stunned Daniel. Writhing together on the ground, Estigarriba put Daniel in a headlock with the point of the blade against his neck. He looked around and could see Juancinto and Ruy frozen, afraid to move lest the captain slit their comrade's throat.

"Juancinto! I trusted you, and you set this trap. Why?"

"I'll answer that, you murdering piece of excrement," muttered Daniel, trying to look back at the captain whose arms held his head in a choke-hold. "That's *my* boat, the *Alcântara*, you swine. You killed my parents."

Hearing that, the cunning captain knew he had but one logical course of action. He must kill this man-boy, the avenging witness to his crime. Killing him would increase his odds of survival against the other two—an old Gypsy with a razor and an overgrown teenager with an oar. He could deal with that. Estigarriba pressed the dagger's tip into Daniel's skin below the left earlobe, and blood trickled from the wound. Daniel rocked and twisted like a horse being saddle-broken. The captain tightened his grip on Daniel's throat and began drawing the blade across the back of his neck, expecting to meet the jugular and bathe him in a fountain of blood. Estigarriba hoped the two bystanders would be paralyzed by their comrade's demise. The thought caused the captain to look up at the helpless witnesses. With a menacing smile, he said, "Haven't you boys ever seen a decapitation?"

From behind Estigarriba, the full force of Davide's shovel came down upon his head. The man went limp, dropped the dagger, and released Daniel, who rolled away into the tall grass.

Davide ordered Ruy to apply pressure to the wound on Daniel's neck as he removed the captain's shirt to help stanch the blood flow. Daniel, dizzy from blood loss, still had enough presence to give orders.

"Strip the beast naked and get the rope." Davide tended to Daniel's wound while Juancinto and Ruy stripped and hogtied the captain.

Daniel ordered Juancinto to get the two-foot long iron stake they had acquired from the foundry in Sanlúcar. The stake was made with a hole in the head to accept a rope. Next to the unconscious body of Estigarriba, they hammered the entire stake firmly into the ground with their shovels. Then they tied the naked captain's wrists and ankles together and behind his back, and for good measure, Daniel took his shovel and slammed it full-force onto Estigarriba's hands braking most of his fingers. They then tied the rope binding the captain's extremities to the hole in the iron stake.

With his neck wrapped in bloodied rags, Daniel said, "We're almost done, boys, except for a couple more things." He asked Juancinto to retrieve a small, corked earthenware jar from the boat along with a bucket filled with canal water. When Juancinto returned, Daniel poured the water over Estigarriba's head to rouse him. The pirate, naked but for his gold crucifix, regained his senses with Daniel standing over him.

"This is your Day of Judgment on this earth, Raúl Estigarriba. I will pray for you. First, in the name of my father, Ahmad Almeyda, I pray that a wild boar or a lynx will smell your blood and feast on your guts.

"Then, I will pray in the name of Ahoud, the first mate of the *Alcântara*, that water rats will come up from the canal and nibble on your toes and testicles.

"In memory of my grandfather, Simão Lopes . . . and I hope he is still alive even though now he must wear a dunce cap in public, that before you lose consciousness, I pray that your blood attract snakes to form a crown around your head as they writhe and frolic in and out of the orifices of your head while you are still alive.

" Finally, in memory of the rest of the crew of the *Alcântara* that you cast overboard, I pray that your cries of anguish call forth an army of ants from the soil, and they cover your flesh with a million bites.

" My mother, Bela Almeyda, is probably asking God to have mercy on you and terminate your miserable life quickly. But I say this—let my mother's prayers be ignored, and your mother's prayers ignored also, for the sin of raising such a wretched creature as yourself. I will not kill you outright because one of our party does not want to commit what he thinks is murder. I yield to the possibility you may be saved by some sweet miracle, so, I will leave you alive with a bit of sweetness."

With this, Daniel uncorked the ceramic jar and poured honey over Estigarriba's clinched eyes and down across his nose onto his whimpering mouth and quivering chin. The golden stream trickled into the reddish hair of his chest and around his crucifix, proceeding over his protruding stomach and terminating between his legs. Before the honey jar was empty, flies had already gathered for the fiesta.

The four climbed into the rowboat and skiff. As they slid through the narrow channel, they could hear Raúl Estigarriba howling, begging for forgiveness. They rowed east through the maze of canals in the direction of the big river. When they reached the Guadalquivir, they tied up and waited until well into the evening before proceeding downriver with the current. Shortly before midnight, they saw the lights of Sanlúcar harbor. They set Estigarriba's skiff adrift and let the current carry it out to sea. They rowed to the rowboat to the unattended dock where Daniel had rented the boat.

The following day, Juancinto reported to work as if nothing had happened. He asked for the captain. Villalba, the first mate, told him the captain had not yet arrived, but his boat was missing. Juancinto told

Villalba he wanted to apologize for missing work and the Mass the day before because of illness from spoiled food. The first mate put him to work with the rest of the crew carrying supplies into the hold.

In the afternoon, Villalba left the boat to search the harbor for signs of captain Estigarriba and his craft. A fishing schooner docking at the wharf had the *Redimido's* skiff tied to its stern. Villalba asked the schooner's captain about the boat and was told they had found it adrift at sea with only its oars. The disappearance of Captain Raúl Estigarriba was a mystery.

Villalba went directly to the Casa de Contratación in Sanlúcar, found Captain Juan Pardo, and relayed the news that the captain of the *El Redimido* was missing and presumed dead.

Juan Pardo conferred with Captain-General Arciniega, and they promoted the Portuguese seaman who had been hired as the *Redimido's* pilot to the position of captain.

A messenger was dispatched to the nearby city of Jerez de la Frontera to notify Sra. Estigarriba of her husband's disappearance and that he would be declared dead if he did not return to *El Redimido* by Friday, April 15. Assuming death, a messenger would deliver her husband's full salary, plus a substantial amount as rent for the *El Redimido.*

Captain Juan Pardo boarded the *Redimido* with Nuno de Faria the next morning. He announced that Faria was the new ship's captain. Juancinto followed Villalba, the first mate, as he led Juan Pardo and Nuno de Faria on an inspection of the vessel. Before disembarking, Juancinto caught Juan Pardo's attention and told him he had three friends in their twenties who wanted to sign up for the expedition as soldiers, colonists, or crewmen of the *Redimido.* He added they were all seasoned seamen, and one had medical experience. Captain Pardo told Juancinto to have his friends show up at the Casa de Contratación the following morning.

The three Portuguese young men appeared at the appointed time. Before the meeting, they had discussed how to present themselves and decided they all would claim to be from Galicia, the Spanish province just north of Portugal where Galician, much like Portuguese, was the primary language. They thought to modify their Portuguese enough to pass for Galicians and, as such, not raise suspicions of being Portuguese spies or Jews fleeing the Inquisition.

Davide and Ruy would play the role of medical and navigation students from the university in Santiago de Compostela. They would argue that their families had run into hard times, leaving them no future in Galicia. Daniel claimed to be the son of a fisherman from the port city of Vigo. His father's boat had been lost at sea, and he was now seeking a livelihood with the experience his father had given him.

They made their cases to Juan Pardo and Nuno de Faria, together, in a private room at the Casa de Contratación.

Both Pardo and Faria were skeptical, specifically regarding their origin in Galicia. Juan Pardo's people had immigrated to Spain from the Portuguese fishing village of Aveiro, and Faria was Portuguese, having sailed with hundreds of Galician seamen. Both easily distinguished a Portuguese trying to mimic the dialect of Galicia. In short, they assumed the three young men were Portuguese Jews needing to escape the recent resurgence of the Inquisition in Portugal.

Pardo and Faria were, however, impressed with the boys' characters, believing each to be intelligent and hardy, a cut above most of the other soldiers and seamen. They consented to let the boys make the voyage on the *Redimido,* either filling vacancies in the ranks of the soldiers or serving as crewmen or even as colonists. During the voyage, the various captains would decide how best to deploy them.

Pardo and Faria sympathized with the boys—more so, perhaps, Juan Pardo, as an agnostic, than Faria, an ardent Catholic. However, they did not allow the boys to know of their suspicions, preferring instead to let events play themselves out.

Hearing the captains' verdict, the three young Portuguese and older Spanish Gypsy were overjoyed—the decision affirmed for them the actions they had taken.

The next day they reported to the *Redimido* and learned their assignments. Ruy, Davide, and Daniel then retired to a tavern to celebrate and returned that night with their belongings to spend the night aboard the ship.

Daniel, having been virtually reared on the vessel, strutted on deck as if he owned *El Redimido.* He made a point of being friendly to all the seamen and soldiers and exuded a familiarity with the ship. In this way, he managed to inspect the entire caravela, keeping a sharp eye out for any artifacts from his family. And so it was that he found, near the platform where his parents once slept, covered in wax and lodged in a joint of the floorboard, a small golden earring belonging to his mother. He placed the earring on the gold chain he wore around his neck.

In the evening of the next day, the seventeenth, Captain-General Arciniega funded another public Mass for the fifteen hundred soldiers, sailors, colonists, and townspeople. A priest celebrated the Mass for the large assembly on the plaza and beach beside the Chapel of Carmen de Bajo Guía. Nuestra Señora was paraded before the seventeen ships to receive her blessings.

On the morning of the eighteenth, the activity of embarkation began. Seventeen vessels cast off their moorings and began the process of backing out of their berths. Sailors lowered boats into the river, each carrying a large anchor and a half-dozen oarsmen. They dropped anchor in the middle of the river channel. Another six men on the ship's deck began marching around the capstan, winding the anchor rope and pulling the vessel astern into the channel. Once there, they hoisted anchor, and longboats with more rowers slowly towed the ships from the river harbor into the blue waters of the Atlantic.

On the nineteenth of April, all the ships were on the open sea off of the harbors of Sanlúcar and Cádiz, waiting in formation like horses at the start of a race. It was mid-afternoon when Captain-General Arciniega finally felt a strong, steady wind blowing up from off the Sahara. The signal was given, the bells rung, and the cannons fired.

With a full cargo of soldiers and their provisions, the crew of the El Redimido raised the sails and the vessel began to lurch forward. The masts and timbers shrieked, and the old wooden decks moaned and sighed, as if anticipating a high adventure into the unknown.

Amid the din of boat sounds, laughter and cheers, Davide and Ruy could still hear Elias's shout echoing in the Garden of Tears, five hundred miles away, "*Lekh-lekha!*"

Juancinto felt Solea and her mother, La Gitanilla, whispering words of confidence in his ears. He felt Nani's delicate fingers caress his right hand and heard the sound of her melodic voice, "we discover other meadows and other rivers."

Daniel fingered his mother's earring on the chain beside his heart and thought of the far-off places she always talked about . . . of Khorasan and Iraq and the New World.

Notes

1. The Soul of Rumi. "Sitting Together", page 209. Translated by Coleman Barks. page 3

2. Sanbenito, Sanbenitado. Used during the Inquisition. A penitential garment (hat or dunce cap) worn by a confessed heretic, of yellow for the penitent, of black for the impenitent.

3. Marrano.. A Spanish or Portuguese Jew who was converted to Christianity during the Middle Ages under threat of death or persecution, especially one who continued to adhere to Judaism in secret. Page 20.

4. Genesis 12:1. page 24

5. The Zohar, Volume Two page 5. Pritzer Edition. Translated by Daniel C. Matt. Stanford Univ. Press. Stanford, Ca.

6. The Zohar. Volume Two. page 9

7. The Zohar, Volume Two. page 6

8. The Zohar, Volume Two. page 9

9. The Zohar Volume Two. page 9-10.

10. Goyim. Non-Jewish

11. Cittern. An old musical instrument related to the guitar, having a flat pear-shaped soundbox and wire strings.

12. Poem by Luis de Camões. 16th century Portuguese national epic poet, attended the University in Coimbra and was probably born in Coimbra. page 117

13. Soloio. Redneck, hillbilly, country bumpkin. Page 121

14. Rapariga. Girl, young woman, chick. page 126.

15. Vara= Yard.

16. Gisant. French. Recumbent carved effigy tomb.

17. Sajjãda.. Muslim prayer rug. page 137.

18. Francis Xavier.. Wikipedia page 146.

19. Francis Xavier. Wikipedia. page 146.

20. Mezla. Hebrew. Good-fortune. Life-Force.

21. "Palos Gitanos". "Flamenco" was not a term in use in the 16th century. The phrase "palos gitanos" has been created and substituted for the variety of Gypsy forms of song and dance styles associated with what we understand to be flamenco.Page 179.

22. Encomienda system. Economic system in which grants of property were sold to noble families including rights to all productsfrom the land and the labor of the Indians who reside on the land. The encomiendas paid a yearly tribute to the government and the Crown.

23. Gadjo. In Romani culture, a person (masculine) who has no Gypsy blood.

24. Cante. Song, chant, singing, particularly in Flamenco style.

25. Juerga. With reference to flamenco.Musical, mystical revelry.

26. Duende. Ghost.

Joara

Sequel to Belmonte

The narration of *Joara* differs from that of *Belmonte* in that it is tightly based on the actual chronology of the Juan Pardo's year and a half Expedition into the mid-Atlantic Indigenous heartland. The sequence of action is predicated on official written reports uncovered during the past 50 years in archives in Seville. Of course, the presence in *Joara* of the four main characters from *Belmonte* is purely fictitious, with the possible exception of Juan Martín de Badajoz, alias Juancinto, the "official" sole survivor of the destruction of the five Spanish Forts.

Joara begins as the four main characters cross the Atlantic to America. They arrive in the summer of 1566, at the nascent Spanish colony of Santa Elena, on what is now Parris Island on the South Carolina coast. Juancinto Taranto has changed his name to Juan Martín de Badajoz so as not to be judged as the only Gypsy in the expedition. All four characters are part of the 250-man Expedition led by Capt. Juan Pardo, who is soon ordered to take half of his men and find food from the various Indian tribes in the vast landscape to the west.

In addition, Pardo is to find a short-cut across the Appalachians to the silver mines in Mexico. He is to declare all the land for King Phillip of Spain, and make friends with the Indians, tax them and convert them to Catholicism.

Setting out on the 1ˢᵗ day of December, 1566, the expedition arrives at the Chiefdom of Joara on Christmas Day. Joara is a thriving collection of Catawba villages that Hernando de Soto had written about 27 years previously. Seeing snow on the distant Blue Ridge mountains, Pardo decides not to cross them. He builds a fort , which he names Fort San Juan and suddenly returns to Santa Elena on rumor of an expected French attack.

Pardo leaves 30 men in Joara, including Daniel, Davide, Ruy and Juan Martín de Badajoz, alias Juancinto. Sgt. Hernando Moyano is left in charge of the garrison. Moyano is a treasure seeker and takes 20 soldiers, including Juancinto and Daniel into the mountains and massacres a tribe called Chisca, rumored to have gold. Moyano then proceeds down rivers to a large Creek town called Olamico, located on in island in the French Broad. They build a small fort and wait for the better part of a year, for the appearance of Juan Pardo and the rest of the men.

In Olamico, Daniel courts Immokalee, the daughter of the Chief. She tells Daniel of the myth of La Gran Copala, a fabled city of gold that had obsessed de Soto. Immokalee convinces Daniel that La Gran Copala is only two weeks away down the rivers. With Juancinto, the three steal two canoes and proceed down the Tennessee River to just past Chattanooga. There they have a river accident that becomes a spiritual experience. Walking back to Olamico, they arrive at the time when Capt. Pardo shows up with 125 men.

They all march south from Olamico for a week and then turn around when warned of an ambush by thousands of warriors.

On the way back, a fort is built at the Cherokee river village of Cauchi, near Asheville. Juancinto and Daniel with his wife, Immokalee are garrisoned at this fort.

Pardo then proceeds to Joara, but spends little time there, leaving 40 men at the fort, again, including Ruy and Davide. The two have been in Joara for over a year and have learned to speak Catawban with the help of Vara, the daughter of the medicine man, and her friend, Xequina.

Ruy and Xequina fall in love, which is a problem because she is promised from childhood, to a young war chief named Ayo. Daniel and Ayo become rivals for Xequina's heart and on the "ball field". The rivalry reaches a climax at the Green Corn Ceremony in August of 1567.

By early spring 1568, two Spanish soldiers at Joara have successfully turned homegrown grapes into wine. They lure Ayo's younger sister into a drinking party and she is assaulted. Ayo exacts revenge and then flees to the mountains where he encounters a great amassing party of Creek and Cherokee warriors.

The forts at Olamico and Cauchi have already been burned and the war party is ready to descend upon Fort San Juan in Joara. Ayo is given the chance to lead the assault, but prior to the attack, he manages to warn Xequina.

As Fort San Juan burns, Daniel, Xequina, Davide and Vara escape and establish a new settlement which they call "Fonte Flora" at the confluence of the Catawba and Linville Rivers in present day North Carolina.

Juancinto has unexpectedly found love with the daughter of a medicine man near Cauchi and has gone to live with her prior to the burning of the forts. He has become transformed into a happy Cherokee.

Juancinto is to become the "official" sole survivor of the catastrophic destruction of the five Spanish forts, commissioned by Juan Pardo. Chiefs of the three nations, Cherokee, Creek and Catawba, compel Juancinto and his wife to travel to Santa Elena to inform and, if possible, over-dramatize the catastrophic destruction of the five recently built Spanish forts.

This act, as it turns, is Juancinto's "destiny", conveyed to him by his mother-in-law, La Gitanilla on his return to Seville after 10 years of servitude in Colombia and Paraguay.

Juan Martín de Badajoz and his wife, Teresa and their two daughters live in Santa Elena for the next decade. Juan Martín/Juancinto is still a soldier, again under the command of the infamous Sgt. Moyano. On a patrol to forage food for the starving colony, Moyano intrudes his troupes into the gathering of a local tribal. Moyano foolishly provokes the chief, who, in turn, engineers the massacre of Moyano and all his men, including Juan Martín de Badajoz.

Soon thereafter, the colony of Santa Elena is abandoned and burned. Teresa Martín and her daughters move to Saint Augustine. There, in 1700, Teresa Martín gives official testimony as a first-hand witness to the destruction of Joara.

Dedication

<u>Belmonte. A Tale of the Old World</u>
<u>Is dedicated to</u>
<u>The city of Evora, Portugal</u>
<u>and</u>
<u>Leland Cuellar</u>

www.ingramcontent.com/pod-product-compliance
Lightning Source LLC
Chambersburg PA
CBHW041747310726
48978CB00011BB/342